BRASS VOWS

ANDY MASLEN

D1416336

TYTON PRESS

ALSO BY ANDY MASLEN

Detective Ford

Shallow Ground

Land Rites

Plain Dead

DI Stella Cole

Hit and Run

Hit Back Harder

Hit and Done

Let the Bones Be Charred

Weep, Willow, Weep

A Beautiful Breed of Evil

Death Wears A Golden Cloak

Gabriel Wolfe

Trigger Point

Reversal of Fortune

Blind Impact

Condor

First Casualty

Fury

Rattlesnake

Minefield

No Further

Torpedo

Three Kingdoms

Ivory Nation

Crooked Shadow

Other Fiction

Blood Loss – A Vampire Story

You're Always With Me

Green-Eyed Mobster (coming soon)

For Jo

"Men's vows are women's traitors!"
William Shakespeare.

1

AFGHANISTAN

Reaching for the small brass cylinder saves his life.

The sudden rightwards move means the incoming sniper round doesn't explode his head like a ripe melon.

He plucks the scorching shell casing from the blood-soaked earth on which he lies. Raises it and stares down into its unblinking black eye.

The dark-filled circle grows until it fills his vision.

The payload, a curved lead projectile, scored that it might burst open like a flower, is long gone. Whether it blossomed on impact, or withered in the sand, he has no way of telling.

But he could ensure the last of its brothers will find fertile soil in which to bloom. Take up the pistol. Place it in his mouth. Pull the trigger. All would be simplified. No more pain. No more doubt. No more anger, fear or regret.

No one to mourn him. Not now. No chance of completing the mission.

The heat no longer bothers him. It has sucked the last of the moisture from him so that even the small flies have abandoned his eyes and nostrils, searching elsewhere for a few precious sips of water.

His right ankle is a mess: blood spilling over the top of his boot, shards of bone poking through his shredded trouser leg.

No pain, though: that's good. Adrenaline is the soldier's friend. He knows it won't last, though. Soon, Sister Agony will come a-knocking with her leather roll of instruments: the saws, the pincers, the needles, nippers, pliers and drills. But for now, just a dull ache a thousand miles away.

Ah, Jesus, is this it, then? The end of his career as a fighting man? The end, full stop? After all the war-fighting, the battles, the insertions, the covert ops, the knife fights, fire fights, fist fights. The throat-slittings, neck-breakings, dealing death a thousand different ways; all over in this shit-hole country composed of nothing but pink rock, dead-looking scrub and a million different biting, stinging creatures ready to devour you whole?

No! Not if he can help it, it isn't. He hasn't come this far to die behind a heap of rock. The sun is irradiating the top of his head, burning his skin to an even black. His headdress is long gone, torn off in the sandstorm that choked the life out of his 4x4 and left him stranded fifty clicks from his Forward Operating Base.

He flicks the shell casing away and levers himself up on his elbow, rolls to his right before peering over the low wall of bullet-holed sandstone blocks. The Taliban fighters are two hundred metres out now and closing. He fires a burst over the top, more in hope than expectation.

An answering salvo blows chips off the edge of the stones. One spins up into his eye and slices across the lid. Freshets of blood turn half the world red before blinding him altogether.

He wipes the blood away and squints down at his ruined ankle. Small brown flies have found it and are swarming over the already blackening wound. He kicks at them with his other boot, misses and connects with the side of his shin. Now the pain does arrive: searing hot and driving stiletto blades through the skin, fat, muscle, nerves, blood vessels and bone all the way to his hip joint.

He bites down on the scream that threatens to split his cracked lips apart. Tears squeeze out from between his eyelids and just as quickly evaporate in the bone-dry heat.

The bleeding starts afresh, a steady flow that drains over the side of his boot and runs into the gritty sand.

Bullets whine overhead and the Taliban's assault rifles bark, louder than before. They're close now. He can hear their conversation in between the bursts of gunfire.

He raises a hand to the equipment pouches slung across his body beneath the filthy off-white robe. His scrabbling fingers find a single magazine for the AK. He pulls it free and readies it. Then shuffles up against the stones and raises the rifle's barrel up high enough to empty the rest of the mag.

It is hopeless to shoot like that, but he has no choice. As well as their Kalashnikovs and captured American Colt M4s, the Taliban have a guy with a sniper rifle. Something heavy. Maybe a captured Barrett Light Fifty from the Americans, or a vintage Dragunov from when the Soviets were having a crack at the Afghans.

Every time he's popped his head up, a supersonic round has whined towards him. So far either he's been lucky, or the Taliban sniper has been off his game. No self-respecting British or American sniper would miss from that range. But he knows his luck can't last.

He is down to the thirty rounds in the fresh mag and six left in his sidearm. The Sig Sauer P226 has been with him on half a dozen ops all over the world from Mozambique to Venezuela. It lost its factory shine a long time ago, but it still works every time he pulls the trigger and it never, ever jams. You can't really ask for much more.

Altogether that leaves him with thirty-six rounds. A pathetic number against half a dozen Taliban fighters draped in bandoliers, pockets stuffed with enough spare mags to take out ten operatives.

He drops out the empty mag and tosses it over the makeshift

3

wall he is leaning against. Let them see he is reloading, at least. Maybe they'll stay cautious if they think he isn't out of ammo just yet. In goes the new one, slotted home and pushed into the latch with a quiet click. No palm-slapping heroics that might result in a mislocated catch.

He shuffles sideways on his belly, heading for the far end of the wall. So far, he's been shooting over the top. His plan is to regain a tiny element of surprise and shoot from a different spot. Hopefully their sniper is still focused on the original point he'd popped up from.

The sniper needs to be killed first. Get the accuracy guy and the rest will be easier game. Despite their advantage in numbers, he reckons he can take them out.

Dragging his ankle brings it into contact with the dust, grit and stone chips littering the desert floor. A fresh wave of agony ignites like petrol being trickled onto a smouldering fire. He hisses with the pain of it and continues working his way along to his new firing position.

Shouts go up from the Taliban on the other side of the wall. Christ! They sound so close. It's now or never.

He rolls sideways, onto his back, bringing his rifle over with him. Upside down, his aim is wild, but with the fire selector set to full auto he doesn't believe it will matter. He presses the trigger and sends 7.62 mm rounds spraying out in a fan towards the advancing Taliban.

A head blows apart in a pink mist. No time for even the beginnings of a scream. Fragments of bone and scraps of bearded face spin away into the dust. Another one bites the dust! Ha! He isn't finished yet. *Come on, you bastards! Let's see what you've got.*

He rights himself and squeezes off another burst. Two more of the bearded fighters fall, one with a gaping cavity torn into his side from which viscera spill; hot, wet and red. His comrade staggers on for another step despite missing the top of his head.

That still leaves three fighters advancing, machine guns levelled at him. The answering burst of automatic fire is deafening. Blue gun smoke tints the air and seems to shatter it into

4

its constituent atoms. Every searing breath he draws into his protesting lungs brings with it the acrid smell of burnt propellant and the metallic stink of the red-hot ejected brass casings.

He rolls back into cover and gets ready. The firefight has reached that point they all do in the end. No quarter expected or given. Everyone down to their last reserves of ammunition and adrenaline. But not courage. No. Never courage. He is ready to die here if that is what the mission – and the fates – demand of him. But he is sure as hell not going to go alone.

More sniper rounds smash into the wall. It is thick enough to withstand them, but even so, he feels each kinetic impact thrumming through his body as if he is taking tackles on the rugby field.

The reports are enormous. The sniper is close. Maybe now is the time to put him out of action.

He bunches his muscles and balls himself up, ready to attack. He pats his waist. The long curved dagger in its tooled leather sheath is still there. If he gets the chance, a hand-to-hand exchange with blades will suit him just fine. Last thing, he switches the fire selector to semi-auto.

Chest heaving, he forces himself to take a couple of long, controlled breaths. *Come on, come on, this is it, we've survived worse odds than these. Let's go!*

Pushing off his good foot, he lunges up and onto the top of the wall, finger already curled round the AK's trigger. He spots the sniper at once. A hundred metres distant, standing in the back of a shit-coloured pickup.

He doesn't have time to aim. Not really. He is relying on his training and his instincts. One, two, three, four, five shots ring out as he lines up the AK's iron sights centre-mass on the Taliban sniper. The first four shots miss, but the fifth hits him over the heart. Red blossoms on the front of his camo jacket and he topples sideways into the truck bed.

But as he is killing the sniper, the other Taliban answer with a salvo of their own, catching him in the left arm, chest and right shoulder. He feels the impacts as percussive jolts to his flesh.

Something has switched off his pain receptors. Probably a good thing, given the amount of blood that seems to be spraying out of him, turning the air around him red.

He thinks of *her*. How she looked when he proposed. So happy, her skin glowing, her hair shining in the spring sunshine. It wasn't fair. They barely had six months together before Webster called him in for a briefing.

'Sorry about this, Old Sport, but needs must, eh?' Don said. 'Spot of bother in the mountains northwest of Kandahar. You leave tomorrow, oh-four-thirty. RAF transport from Brize Norton. Nice and simple op, though. You'll be in and out in a day or two. Extraction from this location.'

Don had passed a sheet of paper across his cluttered desk. He'd looked down, noted the contents, then simply left it there amongst the requisition forms, strategy documents, printed-out spreadsheets and personnel files. And he remembered thinking, *From running the regiment to this? Really?* Not much fight left in the old warhorse was there?

His breath is coming in gasps. The mission was compromised before it had even started. Ha! Scrap that. Forget the strategy-speak. The mission was fucked six ways from Sunday.

His time is almost up.

Betrayal. That is the only word for it. Betrayed by the very man who sent him out here. The Department claimed it would look after its operatives until death. But Don Webster had cut him adrift at the first sign of trouble. And as for his partner, he'd never even made the rendezvous. Probably reassessed the threat level and bottled it. Another cowardly betrayer, just like Webster.

He grits his teeth. Well, fuck The Department and fuck Don Webster. He makes a solemn vow, forged in blazing brass and the heat of the merciless Afghan sun. If he ever gets out of this, there will be bills issued and falling due as soon as he gets back to England. Each one stamped in blood-red: OVERDUE.

He doesn't know how long it will take before he is in a position to collect. Months? Years? Decades? It doesn't matter. One day, Don Webster will find out that debts always have to be paid.

The last thing he sees before his eyes close and the world turns red, then black, is an olive-green metal sphere arcing in towards his position. The clarity is amazing. He sees the spoon spiralling away, glinting against the sapphire-blue sky, the way the grenade spins lazily on its axis like a miniature planet, with the firing mechanism at the north pole.

The olive-green sphere hits the ground, bounces twice in lazy slow-motion, and rolls to a stop.

A movement, fast, blurry, catches his eye. His focus shifts to his right boot. A scorpion has mounted the toecap: it stops and faces him. With a jerky little movement it raises its pincered forelegs above its head.

It remains motionless for a few seconds.

'You're fucked, mate,' it says, then scuttles away.

He returns his gaze to the olive-green sphere. Fissures appear in its curving sides. Orange light spills out, dazzling him. It begins to fragment, tectonic plates slipping apart from each other, no longer holding back the molten ocean of pain that awaits.

He hears a great swell of voices, clamouring to be let out: the dead speaking.

The world turns black.

2

LONDON, FIVE YEARS LATER

Gabriel Wolfe looked at his wife, standing beside him in a simply cut dress of turquoise silk, then at the six hardened fighters facing them, foot-long machetes held aloft.

He grinned.

'Ready, darling?'

She nodded, then kissed him.

'Ready.'

With their backs to Chelsea Register Office's impressive classical facade, they linked arms and sauntered under the three arches of paired goloks, as the SAS called the fearsome weapons now glinting in the April sunlight. The bridesmaids – cousins of Eli's from Israel – squealed delightedly as they scattered confetti. With pink, white and blue flakes of rice paper swirling around them, the newly married couple ducked their heads and ran the gauntlet.

The guests mingling on the pavement included men and

women operating at every level of the security services of two countries: Britain, Gabriel's home country, and Israel, Eli's. On the British side, the most senior person there, smiling at the happy couple and picking a piece of confetti from his lower lip was Don Webster. He ran The Department, the shadowy government outfit that employed both bride and groom in a variety of covert roles from counter-terror to targeted assassinations of Britain's deadliest enemies. He'd lost his own wife a month or so earlier to illness.

Although not a direct counterpart, the Israeli contingent included Uri Ziff, the new director of Mossad and Eli's former handler. The guest of honour, however, outranked them both.

Standing a little aside from the main group and protected, reasonably unobtrusively, by a group of young men and women with bulges in their armpits more or less concealed by deftly tailored jackets, was Saul Ben Zacchai, the prime minister of Israel.

Years earlier, Gabriel and Eli had destroyed an Iranian nuclear weapons research facility mere weeks before it would have been able to produce weapons-grade plutonium. Waiting for the fissionable material was a black market ICBM sold by a former Soviet missile base commander to an arms dealer and then on to the Iranians. The missile was aimed at Jerusalem.

Saul's gratitude had extended to help with subsequent missions. Over the years, it had metamorphosed into genuine friendship, albeit mostly at a distance, occasioned both by geography and his job. Arranging security for Saul's team had been Eli's responsibility.

'What?' she'd joked one evening with Gabriel, 'You mean I have to deal with Special Branch, MI6, Mossad and you *still* want me to organise the flowers?'

Gabriel had shrugged as he topped up their glasses.

'I've got to arrange permission from the police for our guard of honour to wave their bloody goloks around on one of London's busiest shopping streets at midday on a Saturday. We can swap jobs if you want.'

She grinned. 'No, it's OK. After all, you're the one with all the contacts at the Met.'

It was true. Over the years, Gabriel had worked alongside senior detectives as he hunted terrorists, murderously corrupt politicians and cops-turned-Serbian warlords. Three of them were among the guests now standing in the spring sunshine, chatting and laughing while the photographer, with the commanding tones of the army officer she was, called for 'friends of the groom', 'the bride and her parents', 'former and serving...er...Regiment members'.

Stella Cole, who'd accepted Eli's request to be her matron of honour, Penny Farrell and Susannah Chambers stood off to one side, holding long-stemmed plastic glasses filled with champagne. Some enterprising soul had walked the three hundred yards down the King's Road to a branch of Marks & Spencer and returned clutching a few bottles.

Gabriel looked over and caught Stella's eye. As always whenever he'd seen her, she was wearing her hair in a ponytail. She smiled back at him and raised her glass, mouthed a single word.

'Congratulations!'

'Thanks!' he mouthed back.

The photographer shouted out a command, phrased as a request.

'Can I have friends of the groom now, please? Friends of the groom.'

The three senior female cops made their way to the top of the flight of steps leading into the register office. They were joined by an elderly man, liver-spotted hands protruding from the cuffs of an unfashionably cut three-piece pinstriped suit: Amos Peled, a deep-cover Mossad agent running a bank in Zurich. One by one, an unusually diverse group assembled, arranging themselves into three tiers with Gabriel at their centre.

Gabriel found himself standing between a female Russian billionaire and the prime minister of Israel. Behind his head, Tatyana Garin introduced herself to Saul.

'An honour, sir.'

'Garin as in Garin Group?' he asked.

It sounded to Gabriel as though he already knew. Then he shook his head. Of course he did! Israeli security had requested a guest list and would no doubt have backgrounded everybody on it.

'Indeed. We have many links with diamond dealers in Tel Aviv. Our saffron is also going to Israel.'

Gabriel tried to relax. He was surrounded by friends and the little family he had remaining to him. He'd searched his heart for any lingering grief that neither of his parents were here to see him married. But there was nothing. A void. It was the same with Michael, dead so long ago that Gabriel could barely remember his face. But his sister Tara had agreed, delightedly, to be his 'Best Woman'.

On the step down from his own, Johnny 'Sparrow' Hawke, now a former SAS member like Gabriel himself, stood chatting about sailing with Jack Webb, an ex-officer with the Royal Hong Kong Police. To their right, the six SAS guys were mock-fighting as to who would be closest to the groom.

Amos Peled was sandwiched between Don Webster and Fariyah Crace, who, with her husband, Simon, had had one of the shorter journeys to Chelsea. Fariyah had treated Gabriel for his PTSD on and off since 2016.

The three cops stood behind Gabriel. As the photographer took her shots, Stella leant forward and whispered in Gabriel's ear.

'I'm so happy for you, Gabe. Truly. You'll make an excellent husband.'

He turned and smiled, earning a sharp reprimand from the snapper.

'Wolfe! Eyes front!'

The crack drew a burst of laughter that she captured in a rapid-fire flurry of shots, her digital camera whirring.

Coming from Stella, the compliment was worth a lot. He knew how her own family had been murdered by a conspiracy within the various branches of the law, up to and including politicians.

Not knowing whether she was still together with Jamie Hooke, a forensic psychiatrist, he'd addressed her invitation as 'Stella + 1'. She'd texted her reply in the singular.

I'd love to come!

Gabriel had concluded they weren't an item anymore. It seemed a shame. On the one occasion when the four of them had got together for a meal in central London, Stella and Jamie had been hardly able to keep their eyes off each other. Now she was living in Sweden, and Jamie had apparently not made the move with her.

The photographer was finished with them. Gabriel descended the steps and headed for a patch of dappled shade under a plane tree, where Eli was standing with her parents. Her dad, Yossi, handed him a full glass of champagne.

'Here, you look like you need a drink.'

Gabriel accepted it gratefully and raised it to his lips. The champagne was still cool though the spring sunshine was already warming it.

'Hey, Dad!' Eli remonstrated. 'What's that supposed to mean? Are you saying my husband is stressed out by the prospect of being married to me?'

Eli's father smiled.

'Not at all, my darling girl. But a man's wedding day changes him. He has new responsibilities. It was the same when I married your mother.'

He looked sideways at Keren Schochat, who smiled indulgently at her husband.

'Of course it was. For a start, he no longer had his mother to do his laundry for him,' she said. 'The first day in our new apartment, I taught him how to use the washing machine. I've never looked back since.'

Gabriel laughed. 'No need to worry on that score. I already know.'

Eli grinned. 'Yes, he does. He puts everything on the same programme and hopes for the best.'

'Not true!' Gabriel said, laughing.

'OK, fine. He knows not to put my bras in there.'

'Exactly. And anything wool I leave in the basket.'

'Yes, because I have a beautiful burnt-orange cashmere sweater that only fits a doll now.'

Gabriel smiled and took a sip of his champagne. His focus shifted from the silly inconsequential banter of a newly married couple. He scanned the traffic moving slowly along the King's Road. No sunglass-wearing goons staring sideways at the crowd outside the register office. No loiterers wearing over-large rucksacks and nervous expressions. Nobody taking too long to light a cigarette or tie a shoelace. A couple of tourists were smiling, taking selfies with their backs to the wedding party. He had no idea why.

Then he ran his eye along the rooflines of the shops opposite. Saw three rifle barrels aimed down at his guests. Saul's security team were in place and well able to deal with any trouble before it *became* trouble.

He sighed. Why couldn't he relax? He'd spent so much time with Fariyah going over his fears for the future. How his anxiety about Eli wasn't irrational, but needn't cripple him, either. Tara had been the same. She'd told him plenty of triad members were married.

'Some even manage to squeeze out a kid or two, BB,' she'd said, elbowing him none-too-gently in the ribs one day as she used her nickname for her big brother.

He scratched at his scalp then ran his finger around the inside of his shirt collar. It suddenly felt too tight and he loosened the top button behind the knot of his fuchsia silk tie Eli had helped him set *just so* that morning.

Eli took his free hand and looked up at him. Once again, he was struck by the way her eyes caught the sun and seemed to flicker from mostly grey to mostly green.

Today her signature scent of lemon and sandalwood had been replaced with something altogether more sophisticated – and sexy: Gabrielle by Chanel. Its smell of jasmine, orange blossom and tuberose coiled up into Gabriel's nostrils and made him smile.

'You OK?' she murmured into his left ear.

'Yeah, I'm fine. I'm happy. Really happy.'

She frowned, just a little, so cute ridges appeared in her forehead, just above the bridge of her nose.

'So why the sigh, soldier? Why the hypervigilance?'

'I wasn't being hypervigilant.'

She arched an eyebrow.

'No? Listen, Gabe, you can't kid a kidder. I know the signs. What's going on?'

'It's nothing. I just tuned out for a second, that's all.'

'You're not still worrying about something happening to us, are you?'

'No,' he said, forcing himself to smile wider. 'It's all good. Just the heat probably. This suit's too hot for the day.'

'Here,' she said, holding out her hand, 'give me your jacket.'

He complied, handing her the jacket, which she folded inside out so its kingfisher-blue lining flashed in the sun like its namesake spearing down off a branch into a chalk stream after a fish.

'Better?' she asked.

He nodded and encircled her waist.

'Much.'

But as he returned her kiss, much to the delight of the SAS boys, who gave a good-natured cheer that had a few passing pedestrians looking round and smiling, Gabriel couldn't shake the feeling of unease.

A clattering from an old diesel engine broke his reverie. He turned to see a 1950s-era single-decker coach pulling up at the pavement. Its green and cream livery, complete with swooping chrome strip demarcating the two colours, bore the patina of age.

The destination sign in the display window above the windscreen announced the venue for the reception.

KEW BRIDGE STEAM MUSEUM

The SAS boys were first on, racing down to the back of the bus where they began singing some extremely unsuitable songs for a man's wedding day. Gabriel shook his head. Maybe he was worried about nothing, after all. He finished his champagne and climbed aboard.

3

ESSEX

In many ways, he reflected, it was a shame the way all the e-retailers had decimated the traditional British High Street. From Amazon to Etsy, eBay to Facebook Marketplace, it sometimes seemed that nobody bought anything in the real world anymore.

He was no less guilty than everyone else, of course. Except that the goods he bought online came, not from retailer websites or auction sites, but the dark web. Untraceable ammunition, medical-grade tranquilisers, firearms, *plastique*: all could be had for a price if you knew where to go.

And he did know exactly where to go. It came with the training.

Arrayed in front of him on his workbench were a cheap button-phone, some electronics components mounted on green printed circuit board, reels of different-coloured wires and a set of electrician's tools including a soldering iron smoking in its coiled steel mount.

Beside his left elbow lay a shallow cardboard box bearing a colourfully printed illustration of a boy of perhaps fourteen, dressed in shorts and a powder-blue V-necked sweater over a white shirt. The boy was smiling with evident satisfaction at a red and green model windmill.

He lifted the lid off, glancing at the manufacturer's slogan.

'"If You Can't Have it, Build It!" Well, you got that right.'

Selecting a long piece of drilled green strip, he reached for a pair of pliers and began bending it into the shape he needed to hold the phone secure.

* * *

A week later, he was sitting in a reasonable facsimile of a police car, a very comfortable Volvo estate resplendent in chequered royal-blue and acid-yellow livery. The car hadn't started out life as a police vehicle. Beneath its peel-off vinyl squares and lettering, it wore the unassuming white paint-job of a family load-lugger.

He'd purchased it from a second-hand car dealer outside Cambridge a week earlier and driven it to a lockup on a largely abandoned industrial estate outside Bury St Edmunds. There, he'd begun the fiddly process of wrapping it in its new law enforcement disguise.

The vinyl was a bastard to apply, though. As evening drew on, he found himself peeling off for the third time a yellow square that just wouldn't sit right over an awkward bit of bodywork. He reached for the cheap black plastic hairdryer he'd bought in a local chemist – *Style Never Looked So Good!* – and played the hot air over the rippling skin of plastic until he could ease out the last of the air bubbles with a thumbnail.

Anyone peering inside the car would have frowned as they wondered where all the *gear* was. The dash-mounted screens, the cameras, the black nylon pouches fastened with Velcro, all the paraphernalia people had grown accustomed to seeing on those tedious true-life cop pursuit shows on the TV.

But then, anyone who got close enough to put their mugs up

against the glass was going to wake up in a weed-choked ditch at the side of the road with a goose-egg on the back of their head and a vague memory of 'a bloke with a beard' who'd lamped them with something hard and painful. (Which, had they seen it, would have turned out to be a six-inch long, hand-sewn, black leather sap, filled with No. 4 buckshot.)

He scratched the ginger beard now. It itched. It *would* do, being made of nylon, but what it lacked in comfort it made up for in its simple but effective role as a disguise.

Facial-recognition software, and those specialists known in the trade as 'super recognisers', paid attention to unalterable aspects of facial topography like eye shape, ear position and bone structure. Amateurs, basically everybody you'd ever meet in the course of your daily life, went for the loudest signals clamouring for attention.

It was why disguises didn't need to be subtle. No need for hours in front of a lightbulb-ringed mirror with a professional theatre makeup kit. Just buy a ginger bowl-cut wig from a party shop or a fake moustache-and-beard and you were set.

Add in plain glasses with heavy 70s-style tortoiseshell frames and you could commit a murder in front of a dozen witnesses in broad daylight, waltz round the corner and take them off, come back again and start taking photos on the old phone and nobody jostling with you for the best position to take a selfie would have any idea it was you they'd just seen offing the victim.

Happy days.

On this particular day, he was parked in a layby a mile to the east of an army base called MOD Rothford, deep in the Essex countryside. Nominally home to a branch of the Royal Logistic Corps, MOD Rothford held a secret deep within its razor-wire perimeter fence.

Take a left after the guard post with its yellow-and-black one-way traffic treadles, and you'd hit the perimeter road – Montgomery Drive. A few minutes later, after passing an assault course and a WWII howitzer mounted on a concrete plinth, you'd arrive at the visitor parking outside the main administration complex.

And there, down a blue-carpeted corridor lined with photographs depicting, among other scenes, a Ford Sierra saloon whose bodywork was bursting outwards like an overripe fruit as a remote-controlled robot detonated the IED beneath it, you would find yourself standing before an office door.

The door bore an aluminium plate on which was painted in gloss back,

D. WEBSTER

That was all. No job title. No hint of rank, function or purpose. None of this information was deemed necessary because, for one thing, the only people who needed to reach the man who worked behind that plain wooden door knew perfectly well who he was. For another thing, it didn't do to advertise that here was the commander of The Department.

The general public had grown used to a new openness from the security services. Websites, recruitment ads in the newspapers, media appearances by the incoming and outgoing heads, even a limited amount of social media. As a result – a result carefully modelled and forecast by planners within those same organisations – that same general public imagined it knew all there was to know about the men and women protecting it, and the organisations where it punched the clock.

Just so.

But while they could reel off the usual suspects, MI5, MI6, Special Branch, maybe even some of the more reticent outfits like 14 Company and F Branch, none knew of The Department. Given that its remit was to kill those of Britain's enemies beyond the reach of the law or the practicalities under which its sister and brother organisations operated, that was just as well.

The man behind the beard, currently sipping from a cup of coffee he'd poured from a spun aluminium flask, knew all about The Department. He should; he'd worked for it for long enough.

He rubbed absently at the place on his left pectoral muscle where a ricocheting Taliban bullet had lodged between two ribs five years earlier.

Like the scars on his left ankle, left arm and right shoulder, it ached in the cold weather. Thankfully, the spring had brought with it a heatwave and his flesh felt warm and pliant through the black uniform.

He unzipped a black nylon pouch on his lap and extracted a hypodermic syringe. The intended recipient of its contents was still a mile out according to the tracker he'd attached to the underside of the truck the previous day.

Two minutes later, the electronic device lying beside him on the passenger seat beeped. He looked up.

The food service company's truck came into view around the sweeping, tree-lined bend to his right. He waited until the gap between them was down to a couple of hundred yards, then pulled out into the road, flicked on the blue lights, and waited.

The truck, decorated with a landscape made entirely from foodstuffs – broccoli trees, cheddar cheese skyscrapers – shuddered to a halt.

He climbed out, adjusted his hi-vis, patted all his pockets as if checking his breathalyser and notebook were all present and correct, then strode towards the cab.

The man cracked his window and leant out.

'What's the problem, officer? Only I've got a delivery for the base.'

'There's a layby ahead. Pull into it please, driver.'

The guy rolled his eyes, but nevertheless drove on until he reached the layby. This one was perfect for the job, being screened from the main road by a thick stand of trees. The type where owners of burger vans would often set up their temporary outdoor cafes.

He rolled the Volvo to a stop behind the van, ran back and strung a line of blue-and-white police tape across the entrance to the layby, then hurried over to stand beneath the driver's window.

'Step outside your vehicle, please. And stop your engine.'

The engine clattered to a halt. The door opened. And the driver climbed out. Stocky, like he might work out. Shaved head, tattoos snaking down his arms from the tight sleeves of his company-branded polo shirt. Probably a decent prospect in a bar brawl or a scrap at a football match.

He came to stand about a yard away, arms akimbo, an open but not totally relaxed expression on his face.

'I wasn't speeding,' he said. 'And I haven't had a drink since Saturday night, if that's what you're worried about.'

'It's nothing like that. Nothing to blow into. But I would like you to look into this.'

He smiled and reached around to the back of his waistband.

The Glock 19 was by no means the largest pistol he'd ever carried, but, let's be honest, point a black handgun at a civilian and ninety nine times out of a hundred you're going to get total compliance.

The guy's hands shot up. His eyes popped wide, so the whites were visible all the way round the deep-brown irises.

'What the fuck, man? Don't shoot. I haven't done anything.'

'I know. Take your shirt off and I need your ID, too.'

'What?'

He raised the Glock higher and extended his arm a fraction.

'Now. Please.'

After accepting the proffered shirt and lanyard, he sent the driver into oblivion with the hypodermic. A minute later, cable-tied at the wrists and ankles, and gagged with a strip of silver duct tape, the driver was lying on his side in the ditch on the far side of the layby, beneath a large rectangle of camouflage-pattern ripstop nylon.

Back inside the Volvo's cabin, using a scalpel and a sheet of self-adhesive transparent plastic, it took him a little under three minutes to substitute his photo for the driver's before reassembling the ID. Three more to get rid of the hi-vis, equipment vest and black police T-shirt and pull the driver's polo shirt over his head.

He climbed up into the cab of the truck, started the engine and manoeuvred it until its tailgate faced the Volvo's rear hatch.

After loading several large items from the car into the truck, he emptied a fuel can in through the driver's window and tossed a lighted match after it.

With the Volvo's upholstery and plastic parts burning merrily, he climbed up and behind the wheel of the catering truck and pulled away, smiling as he headed down the road towards the base.

4

LONDON

The double-tap was loud and percussive in the confined space of the 1950s coach.

A woman screamed.

Gabriel's pulse jerked upwards and he swung round his seat, hand flying to his waist before realising he'd sensibly elected not to wear a sidearm to his own wedding.

The champagne cork Sparrow had fired out of the bottle had ricocheted off the coach's metal ceiling and struck Tara on the top of her head. Some choice Cantonese swear-words followed, then laughter.

Eli touched him gently on the arm.

'Hey,' she said, 'what's up? You're so jumpy. It's like that CIA guy we met down in Mississippi that time. What did he say? "You're as nervous as a long-tailed cat in a room full of rocking chairs."'

'Jumpier. I'm sorry, darling, I don't know why. I can't shake it. I just feel like something bad's going to happen.'

She smiled and leant over to kiss him, then grinned mischievously.

'The only bad thing that's going to happen is Sparrow and those SAS boys are probably going to get you horribly drunk and you'll be unable to satisfy your new bride on her wedding night. And if *that* happens, you'll be in serious trouble!'

He forced himself to smile.

'No chance. Not with you looking the way you do today. I don't know if I mentioned it, but you are so beautiful. I love you.'

'I love you, too, Gabe. Look, we're almost there. Try to relax, OK? We've done the hard part. Now it's party time.'

He nodded, and took a swig of the champagne from the plastic glass. Then another.

Stella came swaying down the aisle, grabbing alternate chrome rails on the seat backs to hold herself steady as the driver negotiated traffic islands and parked cars that narrowed the carriageway.

'Hey, Gabe, how are you? Hi, Eli, you look amazing. That colour really suits you.'

Gabriel smiled up at Stella and offered a reflexive, 'Fine,' as she and Eli started swapping compliments about their outfits.

Stella looked amazing in a soft, floaty dress which reached mid-calf. Bright flowers on a dove-grey background. Gabriel tried to avoid glancing at her cleavage as she leant closer to catch what Eli was saying, but Eli spotted him at once.

'Hey! We've been married, what, half an hour, and you're checking other women out already! Mind you, they are a pair of very cute little puppies, aren't they?'

As Gabriel felt a blush heating his cheeks, Stella looked down, then grinned at Eli as she pressed her hand against the gaping neckline to close it down.

'Sorry. May have had slightly more champagne than's good for me this early in the day.'

'You need to pace yourself,' Eli said. 'There's a lot more at the reception and I told my dad we're not sending any of it back.'

Gabriel looked past Stella's hip at the billboards rushing by as they hit the flyover heading out of central London and towards Kew. Traffic backed up ahead and the coach slowed to a crawl as they drew level with the final board.

This was a huge electronic screen that flashed brilliantly in rainbow colours, rotating ads for holiday destinations, zero-alcohol beers and new family cars. Gabriel was about to look away when the display changed to a stark message in white capital letters on a solid black background. No logo. No image. Just eight chilling words.

ENJOY YOUR DAY, GABRIEL.
I KNOW I WILL.

A burst of anxiety brought sweat to his forehead and the skin inside his shirt felt suddenly hot and clammy.

He turned to Eli and Stella.

'Look at that display!' he said.

'What?' they said in unison, turning to look where his outstretched finger quivered.

But the display had changed. Beneath a sapphire sky, a slim, tanned couple sipped cocktails on sun loungers by an infinity pool.

Bermuda. Come for the Sun. Stay for the People.

'We already planned the honeymoon,' Eli said, frowning. 'You haven't changed your mind about Vietnam, have you?'

Gabriel shook his head, irritated at her. Why was she treating this so lightly? Why couldn't she *see*?

'Before that,' he snapped. 'It was a message for me.'

He repeated the brutally simple text.

'Are you sure?' Eli asked.

'Of course I'm sure! Do you think I'd make something like that up?'

'No, but, darling, you've had some champagne. Maybe the stress of the day is getting to you. Eli entwined his fingers in hers and drew him closer. He kept his eyes fixed on the digital display board. The holidaying couple had been replaced with a green bottle of lager, sweating huge globules of condensation.

None of the alcohol. All of the taste.

Not long now. As long as the coach didn't move too fast, they'd see it. The bottle shimmered and disappeared; a dumpy 4x4 appeared, from which an improbably large family, plus pets, household furnishings and sports equipment spilled like a horn of plenty.

KOMAQ STX. Pack your life!

'Watch. Watch!' Gabriel urged them.

The seconds ticked by. Ahead, after a chorus of airhorns, the blockage freed and the traffic began to move off. The driver put the ancient gearbox into first with a clonk Gabriel felt through the soles of his shoes, and the coach juddered forward.

Gripping Eli's hand, he stared at the screen, willing it to change and reveal the truth. The 4x4 shimmered and began to fade.

The suntanned holidaying couple returned. Still smiling like idiots, still sipping their drinks.

'No!' he cried. 'It was there, I swear it.'

He turned and looked into Eli's eyes. He didn't know which was the more distressing, the fact that someone had made a direct threat against him or the expression of commingled concern and fear in Eli's eyes.

Eli looked up at Stella, then back at Gabriel.

'Are you *sure* it said your name?' Stella asked. 'Maybe it was just one of those clever-clever ads where you have to work it out.'

'Or one of that lot paid for it,' Eli said, pointing down the bus.

'Tanya could afford it. She could probably afford to buy the whole bloody road, couldn't she?'

'Who's Tanya?' Stella asked.

'Billionaire businesswoman. Russian. She and Gabe do favours for each other from time to time.'

'Do I want to know what kind?'

'Probably not.'

'Look, never mind Tanya,' Gabriel interrupted. 'It definitely said my name, OK? It said Gabriel.'

Eli shrugged.

'Like I said. It's someone sending you best wishes. Maybe it was someone who couldn't make it. There were a few, after all.' She threaded her left arm through his right. 'Try to relax. You're just on edge after the ceremony, that's all.'

Gabriel complied. But his feelings of panic had nothing to do with the wedding at all. He felt it. That old tingling sensation that screamed, 'Something's wrong!'

In the Regiment they used to call it the 'spider sense'. Officially, 'situational awareness', though the level the best of them took it to went way beyond anything as mechanistic as noticing 'absence of the normal, presence of the abnormal'.

Master Zhao, his old mentor in Hong Kong, used to talk about seeing the invisible, hearing the inaudible, touching the intangible. They'd venture down from Zhao's three-storey house nestled into the hillside to one of the busiest thoroughfares in Hong Kong, Hennessy Road, maybe, or Yee Wo Street, and stand perfectly still as the crowds swirled around them.

The young Gabriel Wolfe had to let go of the everyday impulse to grab for whatever sensation was loudest or closest and instead let his conscious mind take a back seat to his intuition.

At some point, using *Yinshen fangshi* – The Way of Stealth – Master Zhao would leave his charge and disappear into the crowds. It was Gabriel's job to detect him before he could return and deliver a ringing slap to the back of his head.

Years of practice finally paid off, when Gabriel could whirl round and catch his master's wrist as it arced in towards his head.

But he sat obediently. Anyone trying anything at the reception would be picking a fight with the worst possible group of revellers. Several highly trained Mossad agents on close protection duty for Saul Ben Zacchai, who was himself carrying a concealed weapon under his immaculately tailored Savile Row suit jacket.

Several snipers – from Mossad and SCO19, the Met's specialist firearms command – armed with high-powered rifles.

Seven current and former members of the SAS, one of whom did double-duty as a Department assassin along with his bride.

A clutch of active Mossad agents and IDF members, friends of said bride, including Mossad's current deputy director, Uri Ziff.

A seriously badass detective who, if she'd been honest with him, had offed at least seventeen people.

A former triad bodyguard, who just happened to be the groom's sister.

In fact, now he came to think about it, with the possible exception of Fariyah and Simon, Amos Peled, and Eli's parents, every single guest was trained at the very least to disable an opponent if not kill them outright. He smiled at the thought, caught himself doing so, and began to relax, finally. Maybe it was just a guest having fun. And the message on the poster might only mean what it seemed to mean.

The driver braked suddenly to avoid a car attempting an illegal U-turn and swore, apologising immediately: 'Pardon my French!' Everyone was thrown forwards and they shared their feelings at the driver's manoeuvre with a mixture of good-natured jeering and shouted advice: 'You need to do an advanced driving course, mate!'

Gabriel's head snapped forwards as he put his hands out to stop it hitting the chrome rail in front of him. His gaze fell on the scuffed flooring between his shoes, where the corner of a cream envelope peeked out from beneath his seat. He bent down to retrieve it.

'What's that?' Eli asked.

'It was under my seat.'

'Open it, then! It must be someone's card. Probably fell out of a handbag or something.'

She leant into him as he slit the envelope with his thumbnail and extracted the card. It came out backwards and, as he flipped it over, his heart skipped a beat.

The picture on the front was hand-drawn. A simple sketch done in loose, almost casual strokes of a pen, depicting a solitary male figure in a black suit. With a sense of foreboding like the pit-of-the-stomach feeling in the hours before a big action, he opened the card.

A hand-printed message declared,

> Fate: the wedding guest nobody invites,
> but everybody meets

'Well that's cheery,' Eli said. 'Sounds like another one of Master Zhao's sayings.'

'Someone's going to stage an attack at the reception,' Gabriel said.

'What? Don't be silly. Who? Why?'

'I don't know, El. I'm just saying. The poster, now this card.'

She shook her head.

'Try to relax, Gabe. I'm – I'm sorry, but I think this is all in your head.'

She wasn't going to be persuaded, he could see that. He offered a smile.

'Yeah, OK, you're probably right. I just never thought I'd be here, on a day like this.'

She grinned at him.

'Me neither.'

He looked at the driver. He must have put the card under the seat. Maybe Gabriel would have a quiet word with him once they arrived at the Steam Museum.

5

ESSEX

As he drove the last mile or so to the base, he let his mind travel back to the day he woke up in the Taliban prison.

The grenade hadn't detonated. So instead of being shredded into so much blood, bone and offal, he'd been slung into the back of a pickup.

The cell stank. That was the first thing he noticed. The tiny windowless space, just big enough to lie down in if he kept his knees bent, reeked of shit. The walls were smeared dark brown and black, and a lone fly buzzed in furious figure of eights through the fetid air. The only light entering the cell came from a tiny hole in the ceiling.

He looked down. His boots were gone. He was barefoot, clad only in a filthy loin-cloth. The floor was gritty and sharp rock fragments abraded his skin.

A thick bandage, which looked relatively clean, swaddled his left ankle. He ran his hands over his torso and arms. His questing fingers encountered thick field dressings on his chest, right shoulder and left arm

Experimentally, he flexed the arm. It hurt like a bastard, but he could tell the bullet had been removed. They must have treated him before slinging him into this mediaeval dungeon.

The fly buzzed close to his left ear, making him flinch. He stood, intending to kill it, and banged his head on the ceiling, which had been cunningly placed about six inches lower than the average guy's height. The pain from his crown added its own tenor note to the baritones and basses in the choir of pain tuning up on his body. Even his jaw hurt. Must have banged it at some point.

He sat down again, leaning his back against the wall, which was mercifully cool against his injured flesh.

Why hadn't they finished him off when they had the chance? The depressing answer presented itself immediately. One of two reasons, maybe both. They thought he was valuable and wanted to barter him for some of their own held by the Coalition forces. Or they thought he knew something valuable and wanted to extract it from him.

Well, good luck with that. He steeled himself. They'd all had plenty of training in resistance to interrogation. No, forget the euphemisms. If nothing else, The Department never pulled its punches. Maybe in the Green Army they talked about 'interrogation'. Webster's trainers were clear as mud on the subject. You'll be tortured. You'll break. Everybody does. The real question is, how long can you keep your mouth shut. Every hour buys the rest of your team valuable time.

For this particular op, the quartermaster had given him a suicide pill. Just like the Nazis did, he'd had it fitted into a crown at the back of his mouth. Can't take it anymore? Just bite down hard and say goodnight, Gracie!

He probed for it with the tip of his tongue, which felt like it had swollen to twice its normal size. Trouble was, it made it virtually impossible to locate the dummy tooth with its lethal filling. He raised his right hand to his mouth, wincing at the bolt of pain that lanced down through his arm from the wound in his shoulder.

Using the tip of his little finger, he probed around, then withdrew it and swore. The tip was dark in the pencil-thin beam of light coming down from the little hole in the ceiling. Blood. The bastards had pulled it out. They must have examined him while their medic was patching him up.

The door opened with a scrape over the grit-and-sand floor. A man in Arab dress set a tray down. On the tray were a paper cup of water, a flatbread mounded with some sort of paste, lentils maybe, and a book.

He looked at the pistol on the man's belt and briefly considered making a grab for it. Briefly. The guy caught the look and shook his head. Then he spoke. In English.

'That would be a grave error, my friend. Eat. Drink. Read.'

Then he left, locking the heavy wooden door behind him.

He did as the man had suggested. He was desperately thirsty and downed the mug of cool clear water in a single draught. Tipping the mug upside down, he captured the last couple of drops on his out-thrust tongue and swallowed gratefully.

The flatbread was warm, whether from being left in the sun or having just come out of the oven, he neither knew nor cared. It tasted of garlic and fresh parsley and the bright sparks of flavour brought tears to his eyes. The paste was a lentil daal, smoky and spicy and studded with fragments of charred onions.

Why were they doing this? It made no sense. You could keep a hostage alive for an exchange on a lot less than this. And if you were going to start on him with pliers, lengths of pipe or a car battery, why bother feeding him at all?

Having filled his belly, reserving a corner of the bread to wipe the plate, he turned his attention to the book. The beam of light was barely enough to see by, but by lifting the volume up and moving it left to right, he could make out the title blocked in gold on the black leather cover.

THE GLORIOUS QUR'AN

With English Translation and Commentary

For one brief but exciting moment, he imagined opening it and finding a heavy iron key, or even a sub-compact pistol sitting in a rectangular cut-out. But when he opened it and flipped through the pages, the spark of hope that had ignited in his breast fizzled out. It was just a book.

He flung it into a corner and turned his face to the wall. Whatever mind-games they were playing, he wasn't joining in.

He must have slept at some point. But the slumber was more akin to unconsciousness. He had no recollection of dreaming, but the muzzy feeling in his head told him he must have dropped off. His bowels were griping. And he began to understand why the cell smelled the way it did. Well, he'd hold on as long as he could. Humiliation was a standard part of the warm-up act for torturers. He'd delay their pleasure for as long as he could manage.

They'd been clever, not giving him a metal or china drinking vessel. All too easy to fashion a weapon from them. And the bread had acted as plate and food both, so no joy there. But they'd been careless, hadn't they? Because they'd given him a tray.

He pulled it towards him. It was made of wood. A simple frame supporting a woven rattan-like base. He ripped off the base and discarded it. Then he snapped the rectangular frame at its corners, leaving four circular cross-section rods, two about 30cm long, two about 20cm. After testing the two longer pieces for their rigidity, he picked the stiffer one and broke off a short piece from one end, leaving a sharp point.

He gripped it experimentally and tried a few stabbing thrusts, but the wood was too thin. It would slip through his fist if it encountered anything firmer than custard. He looked down at the loin-cloth. There was plenty of fabric there to fashion a rudimentary grip. Or he could unwind the bandage from his ankle. He settled on the former, not wanting to expose the ragged wound to the dirt.

He bit through the noisome cloth, tearing off a piece 60cm by 10cm, before resecuring it around his waist. This he wrapped around the blunt end of the improvised dagger, stretching it tight as he wound it onto the wood so that it caught on the rough edges.

When he was done, he held in his right hand a serviceable stabbing weapon with a 10cm hilt and an 8cm blade. Now he waited.

Sometime later, he estimated an hour or so, he heard footsteps approaching the door. He swept the debris of the tray into a corner and gripped the dagger in his right hand. Then he levered himself to his feet, favouring his good ankle, and took up a position on the hinge side of the door.

The guard would pull the door back and then step forward into the gloom. He'd naturally look ever so slightly to his left – the non-hinge side. It was human nature: to pay more attention to the place with the clearest view. Human nature, sure, but a strategic error nonetheless. He'd step forward into the gloom and get his carotid opened for his troubles.

Then it would get briefly kinetic. Grab the pistol, drag him inside, slam the door and stab him again and again until he bled out. Change clothes and let the games begin. Exfil and away on his toes, maybe even snagging a 4x4 in the process. Stranger things had happened.

The door swung wide.

He tensed, knuckles whitening on the dagger's cloth-wrapped hilt.

His heart was racing, pulse roaring in his ears, adrenaline sharpening his senses.

A blinding white beam of light turned the cell into a negative image of itself. He flinched involuntarily as the light swept the cell from corner to corner. He could feel it searing his corneas. Left hand held up to his eyes, fingers splayed, he lunged forwards… into empty air.

He stopped. He was outside the cell. The blinding whiteness left his eyes and he cautiously opened them.

The man was back, the same one as before. He was smiling, red lips just visible through the thick black beard. His pistol's mouth looked as wide as a tunnel.

'Perhaps I should take the dagger,' he said in English after what felt like a minute, but was probably only a few seconds. 'It looks quite lethal.'

His accent was all wrong. Educated. Plummy, almost, like one of those African officers who came over from Kenya or Nigeria and were posher than the Brits.

'I know you're considering your options,' he continued. 'Perhaps I'll miss as you attack and you'll get lucky. You might hit me in the eye or the throat then you could seize my sidearm and fight your way out of here. The question is, where, exactly, is "here", hmm?'

The guard – or whatever he was – held out his left hand, palm uppermost. Then he crooked his fingers three times. The universal 'gimme' gesture.

Was there time for a lightning-fast attack, after all? Stab the guard through the palm and drag him forwards and off-balance?

The fingers jerked again.

'Please, we haven't got all day. I don't want to shoot you, but if you force my hand I will, reluctantly, put a bullet in your brain. Which would be a great shame.'

He thought for a moment longer. The clash between the guy's traditional dress, weather-beaten complexion and facial hair, and his upper-class tones was playing havoc with his ability to make rational choices. In the end, curiosity, and a finely tuned sense of self-preservation, won out, and he dropped the pig-sticker into the guard's outstretched hand.

Maybe it was time for a little trade. The Department didn't go by the old name-rank-serial-number business for any operative unfortunate – or careless – enough to get themselves captured. For a start, they didn't have the latter two, and the drill was different in any case. Do, and say, whatever you have to to survive, but protect the mission.

'Where is "here", then?'

The guard smiled. 'Come with me. I'm sure you would like to wash and attend to other bodily needs. Oh, and for the sake of our burgeoning relationship, please don't try to attack me as we walk. I'm sure you are a far better fighter than I, but you are under observation, and a transgression such as that would, I'm afraid, result in your immediate termination.'

He looked up as the guard spoke in those ridiculously flowery phrases and saw red lights winking in the dark curve of the barrel-vaulted corridor. Fine. No attacks. For now. But he was alive, so that was a tick in the 'Pro' column. And if they were intending to torture him, it seemed increasingly likely that it would take its psychological form.

That was not to diminish the threat – after all, many governments, including his own, had long ago figured out which of the two was the more likely to yield reliable product. But at least there would be no physical pain. He'd experienced a great deal of it during his military service and his duties as a Department operative and thought, on the whole, he could live very comfortably without any more.

6

LONDON

The coach pulled into the yard that fronted the Kew Bridge Steam Museum. Raised flower beds made of reclaimed railway sleepers held hundreds of tulips in yellows, pink and white streaked with pale green. Interspersed with the flowers were gaily painted vintage steam engines, static now, but chuffing away as they pulled imaginary loads, drew imaginary water or drove imaginary agricultural machinery.

Gabriel and Eli were first off, standing at the foot of the steps to welcome their guests to the reception. Finally, when the SAS boys had tumbled good-naturedly down, still bantering and, Gabriel suspected, fuelled by stronger stuff than just the champagne, he turned to Eli and kissed her.

'Welcome to our wedding reception, Mrs Wolfe.'

She returned the kiss with interest.

'Thank you, Mr Wolfe.'

'You go inside and make sure the bar's open for business. I just want to tip the driver.'

Once Eli had left him, linking arms with her mother and father and leading them inside, Gabriel climbed back into the coach.

'All, right?' the driver asked.

'Who gave you the wedding card?'

'What card?'

The driver's widened eyes were a classic tell. People who didn't know what someone was talking about frowned. Or looked puzzled. This feigned surprise was overcooked. OK, Gabriel would play it that way.

'I found this,' he retrieved the card from his inside pocket and held it up where the driver could get a good look at it, 'under my seat. And I want to know who asked, told, or paid you to put it there.'

The driver's expression hardened. His biceps bulged inside the tight suit jacket as he flexed his arms on the steering wheel.

'I don't know what you're talking about. I was hired to pick you lot up from Chelsea and drive you here. I did that. Now I'm off back to my depot. If you've got a problem, take it up with management.'

'Oh, I've got a problem, all right. But it's *you* I want answers from. Right now. For the last time, who told you to leave the card under my seat?'

The driver adopted a wheedling tone.

'Look, mate, I honestly haven't the faintest idea what you're on about. Anyway, how do you know the card was meant for you? Anyone could've sat there.'

'No, they couldn't. Because you put reserved signs down, didn't you? Mr Wolfe. Mrs Wolfe. Very cute.'

The driver shook his head, then scratched his throat. He had a scar on the side of his neck. It looked like a crease left by a bullet. Gabriel's pulse had been ticking along at an elevated but steady rate. Now it spiked. If this guy was a regular coach driver, then *he* was a prima ballerina.

'I don't need this aggravation,' the driver said. 'Why don't you just go and enjoy the rest of your day? Have a beer or three. Maybe try it on with one of the bridesmaids?'

He made to start the engine. Gabriel darted out a hand and yanked the keys from the ignition.

'The only one trying anything on is you, my friend.'

'Fuck's your problem?' the driver demanded, twisting in his seat.

The movement caused the left side of his jacket to snag on the seat belt buckle, revealing the butt of a pistol tucked into a shoulder holster.

Gabriel glanced down and saw the weapon. Everything changed. No more time for talking. He lashed out, aiming for a knockout punch to the point of the jaw.

The driver dodged the blow so Gabriel's knuckles only grazed his jaw. Then he was out of his seat and piling into Gabriel, driving heavy punches into his body and winding him. Gabriel snapped an elbow up and back into the driver's throat, but he ducked out of the way of this blow, too, so it connected but only with half-power.

He seized Gabriel's lapels and swung him around in the narrow aisle before shoving him backwards and making for the steps. Gabriel lunged forwards, grabbing him by the back of his collar and dragging him over onto his back.

He chopped down onto the side of the guy's neck, directly over the bullet scar. The driver grunted in pain but returned a flurry of blows of his own, catching Gabriel over the right eye and opening a cut.

Blood streaming into his eye, Gabriel kicked the guy on the side of his chest. It felt like kicking a wall. He heard a snap as a rib went, then the driver was counter-attacking again, aiming lightning-fast punches at Gabriel's eyes and nose.

In the adrenaline-slowed fight-time, Gabriel had time to think that it was odd the driver hadn't gone for his pistol. Maybe there was something to be said for the element of surprise after all.

The driver reared back and now he did pull his pistol free; a

Glock equipped with a stubby silencer. As he was levelling it, Gabriel flipped himself upright and kicked out at the guy's gun arm. It jerked up and the shot pierced the roof of the coach with a sound like a door slamming.

Fear rippled across the driver's face. Then the gun swung round and connected with Gabriel's left temple. As the lights dimmed and black curtains swung closed across his vision, he saw his attacker descending the steps.

7

ESSEX

Deep in his memories, he recalled the guard leading him to a flight of stone steps. He counted eighteen as they ascended the echoing staircase. At the top, they walked down a long corridor until the guard stopped beside a door.

'There's a washroom in there. Showers, everything. Take your time. I'll be waiting here for you.'

The guard produced a packet of chewing gum from a pocket in his robe, unwrapped the foil and popped a single shiny white lozenge into his mouth.

As he stepped inside, he braced himself for the beating he felt sure was waiting for him. It was the simplest of all techniques. Relax and reassure the captive, then disorientate them with brutality out of nowhere before flipping to friendship mode, offering apologies, dressing wounds, providing food and drink.

Instead of a bloodstained room stinking of fear and vomit, he found a pristine bathroom, tiled in ornately patterned ceramic tiles of jade-green, turquoise, gold and white. White porcelain fittings, gleaming chrome taps and a mirror lit by a row of embedded LEDs.

He looked around: no window. That was to be expected. Beside the shower stall, a cork-topped stool bore a couple of thin but clean white towels. He unwound the filthy loin-cloth and the bandage from his ankle, then stepped inside and turned on the water. Miracle of miracles: the freezing cold turned to warm and then hot within a few seconds. A bar of acid-yellow soap sat in a tray attached to the chrome pole supporting the shower head.

He stayed under the water for ten minutes, washing himself thoroughly. The field dressings stayed in place. He hoped his friend outside would offer to have them changed for fresh ones.

Finally, having regained the semblance of a feeling of humanity, he stepped out of the jets and towelled himself dry, careful to avoid his injuries. He crossed to the hand basin and splashed his face with cold water. The man with the red-rimmed eyes staring out at him needed a shave: his beard was almost as big as the Afghan's outside the door. But there were no scissors, no shaving gear of any kind. It would have to wait.

He looked down at the dirty length of cloth he'd discarded before his shower and decided he couldn't bear to put it on again. So he wrapped himself in a dry towel and went outside again.

The guard, still chewing, looked him in the eye and smiled.

'Much better. But forgive me. I should have arranged for some fresh clothes for you. I'm afraid Western garb is rather frowned upon here, but you can wear these for now.' He held out a pile of folded fabric topped with a pair of brown leather slip-on shoes.

A quick trip back inside the washroom, and he emerged, clad now in a long flowing robe much like that worn by the guard.

The men who grabbed his arms and dragged a black cloth hood down over his head said nothing as they manhandled him. Heart beating wildly, he frantically recalibrated his reactions. He stumbled at one point, over a deliberately placed boot, and received a vicious punch to his kidney in return.

The beating didn't begin properly until he was thrust down

into a hard chair and had his wrists cable-tied to the arms. The hood stayed in place as somebody new, slighter than the two goons who'd dragged him down the corridor, began, very methodically, to work him over.

He lost consciousness at one point and when he came round, he was lying in a hospital bed. A white-coated medic peered down at him.

'Ah, you're awake,' he said in Pashto. 'I have redressed your wounds. All bullet fragments are out. They're going to heal up just fine.'

Over the next month, as he healed physically, he was transferred to a cleaner, airier cell, and left alone, with nothing but the English translation of the Qur'an. Once a day a tray bearing the same meal as he'd received earlier slid through a ground-level slot in the door. The food was tasty, but these were short rations. Little by little, he felt his strength deserting him.

And then the music started.

The Arabic cadences weren't unpleasant. Not exactly. Just disorientating. He'd listened to Afghan classical music before and, after a while, as the Western ear adjusted to the unfamiliar scale, it was possible to appreciate its beauty.

Or it was when the whole piece was played from start to finish, at a reasonable volume.

The ceiling-mounted light lay behind reinforced glass. He knew because when it stayed on all night, he tried to smash it with the meal tray. Then the bulb shone brighter. And brighter. He couldn't bear to look at it any longer.

A meal tray slithered under the door. For lack of anything better to do, and to assuage the hunger clawing at his insides like a rat trying to escape, he guzzled the meagre portion of daal and flatbread and washed it down with the cup of water. It tasted metallic. He grimaced.

He flung the tray into a corner and slumped on the thin mattress they'd provided. Singing the national anthem didn't drown out the repetitive phrases of Arabic classical music, but it helped him retain a tiny shred of self-respect.

When the Queen herself appeared in the corner of his cell, he wasn't surprised. After all, it was natural she'd be concerned to check on the welfare of her loyal servant.

He was mildly surprised that she knew Arabic, but he supposed she knew all kinds of languages. He himself could speak nine fluently.

'They are not bad people,' she said. 'Learn from them. And remember, this is their country. Not ours. Not the Americans'. Not the Russians'.'

'But they're torturing me.'

She smiled and shook her head.

'They're educating you.'

He pointed at the water cup, which had toppled onto its side and somehow grown to the size of a dustbin. An evil-looking fluorescent liquid trickled out onto the dusty desert floor. His friend the scorpion, golden carapace glinting in the sunlight, was back, sipping from the puddle's leading edge.

'They poisoned me.'

Her Majesty shook her head.

'Nobody's poisoning you. Look around you. You're free to go. You can leave now and travel anywhere.'

He stood and turned a full circle. Her Majesty was right. The desert stretched to the horizon in every direction. He started to walk. He remembered his manners just in time: you were never supposed to turn your back on the monarch.

'I'm so sorry, Your Majesty. I—'

But she'd disappeared.

The scorpion rose onto its rearmost four legs. They stood face-to-face.

'Come, let's walk together,' it said, holding out a multi-jointed limb tipped with a bifurcated claw. 'This will be a long journey.'

And it was. Almost five years.

The music stopped. Eventually.

The rations became more generous.

He was allowed out of his cell for short walks with his guard.

They discussed the Qur'an. There was little else to talk about, unless you were particularly interested in discussing the weather.

He realised the truth sometime in the third year. To mark the epiphany, he took a new name, one more in keeping with the great tradition that had accepted him into its ancient embrace.

From then on, his friend explained, his education would move into a new, more practical phase. One aimed at setting right a great injustice.

And it began with a man.

A man who had sent him to Afghanistan in the first place.

A man who had sent him into battle and then abandoned him.

8

LONDON

Gabriel opened his eyes.

His head hurt where the driver had smacked him with the pistol and his right eye was sticky with blood. Not fully congealed, so he hadn't been out for more than a minute or two. Plus, nobody had come looking for him. Eli had probably been swept up by her mates from Israel and was even now dancing arm-in-arm with them.

He was alone in the coach. He got to his feet and brushed himself down. The left elbow of his suit jacket was ripped and there was a tear in his left trouser leg just below the knee.

The man who peered back at him from the rear-view mirror did not look pretty. Less a bridegroom on his wedding day, more a bouncer at the wrong end of a tough shift in a low-rent club at the shitty end of a bad street in a crap neighbourhood. He remembered a spot just like it: Johnny Rocketz, in Talinn's red-light district.

He pulled the silk square from his breast pocket and pressed it against the cut over his eye. He scragged violently at his hair with his free hand. What the fuck just happened? And then a jolt of fear crashed through him. Eli!

He ran down the steps, missing his footing on the last one and tumbling to the ground. He sprinted into the reception, meeting Tara on the way in.

'What the hell happened to you, BB? You look like you've been in a fight.'

'I was. But don't tell Eli. Where is she?'

'She's deep in conversation with a bunch of the IDF guys.'

'And she's OK?'

'She's fine. Look, come with me. We need to get you cleaned up.'

She led him through a side door and down a narrow corridor that led to the toilets.

'Men or women?'

'I don't really mind.'

'Good, because I do.'

Tara opened the door to the women's toilets. 'Ladies! I have a wounded man here. We're coming in.'

But the room was empty.

'Sit,' Tara commanded, pointing at an empty stall.

Gabriel gratefully complied while she wetted a bunch of paper towels under the cold tap.

She squatted before him and started dabbing away the blood from his eye.

'The driver had a gun,' he said. 'They must have made a switch.'

'Who's "they"?'

That was refreshing. No panicked questions about the gun or doubting his sanity.

'Not sure. But whoever they are, they trying to put the frighteners on me. There was an electronic billboard on the drive over. Threatening me. Then I found this under my seat.'

He gave her the card and waited for her to read it. She handed it back and resumed ministering to his face.

'What did Eli say?'

He shook his head, causing Tara to jab him in the eye.

'Sorry, BB, but you shouldn't have moved.'

'She thinks I'm imagining things. Told me it was the stress of the day. She thinks it's my PTSD coming back.'

'Did she say that?'

'Not in so many words. But I could see it in her eyes.'

'There,' she said, wadding up the damp pink paper towels. 'You look human again, but you need to get that stitched. Or glued, at least. I saw a shop near the entrance with all these train models. They might have something we could use. I'll look in a minute.'

'Thanks, Sis.'

A cloud flitted across Tara's face.

'Please don't call me that.'

'What, Sis?'

'Mm-hmm.'

'Why?'

'It doesn't matter. Just choose something else.'

'How about LS?'

'For Little Sister? I like it,' she said with a small smile. 'The gun was real?'

'There's a nine-mil hole in the coach's ceiling that'll confirm it.'

She frowned. 'He could have killed you at any point. But he didn't. Why?'

'I don't know. I've been a bit too busy to figure it out.'

'And he's gone now.'

'He ran. I doubt he's coming back.'

'Maybe he never meant to attack you. The gun was a precaution.'

'Maybe.'

'Look, try to enjoy the rest of the afternoon. You and Eli are going away tonight and you're surrounded, literally, by snipers and armed bodyguards. You'll be safe here.'

'We need to figure this out. But I don't want to ruin Eli's day.'

'Agreed. But talk to me later. And talk to her, as well.'

After liberating a tube of superglue from the shop, Tara closed the cut over Gabriel's eye. She looked down at his ripped trousers and the tear in his suit jacket.

'I don't think even Mr Chang on Tsim Sha Tsui could fix those. We might as well try to glue them, too.'

He nodded. He had bigger problems to solve than repairing a handmade suit. 'Go for it.'

A few minutes later, a patched-up, glued-together and smiling Gabriel Wolfe re-joined the guests in the main exhibition hall. Steam engines, from chubby little machines the size of chest freezers to giants towering overhead, puffed and blowed, wheezed and hissed. Gleaming steel pistons thrust back and forth into massive cylinders held together with bolts as thick as a man's wrist.

Sparrow wandered over, arm-in-arm with a very pretty woman: lustrous eyes, full, deep-red lips. Her auburn hair was piled on top of her head, a few loose tendrils spiralling down onto a long neck. He introduced her as, 'Roni Yannai, pride of the IDF.'

He pointed at the piston, gliding back and forth in front of them. Then he turned to Gabriel.

'Makes you think, eh, Wolfie.' And winked at Roni. He focused on Gabriel. 'Jesus! What happened to your face?'

'I slipped coming down the steps of the bus. Caught it on the door frame.'

'Clumsy sod.'

'Shit happens.'

'Get yourself a drink, mate. Best anaesthetic in the world, champagne. Come on, Roni, I want to show you the Hathorn Davey triple expansion engine.'

Leaving Sparrow and Roni to the delights of the steam museum's exhibits, Gabriel made his way through the throng, accepting compliments and worried enquiries in equal measure, before finding Eli.

She looked up and smiled. Then her face fell.

'Your eye. What happened?'

He sat beside her, offering smiles to the trio of Israelis at her table.

'It's nothing, tripped coming down from the bus.'

She touched the glued-up rip on his knee.

'Oh, your lovely suit! It's ruined.'

His reply was forestalled as Don Webster tapped the microphone set up in front of the band's amplifiers and drumkit.

9

He brought the truck to a halt before the red-and-white striped pole.

The gate guard strolled over.

'Where's the usual guy?'

'Stomach bug.'

The gate guard grinned. 'Been trying the stuff you lot send us to eat, has he?'

He smiled back.

'Something like that.'

'Got your ID?'

He held out it for a cursory examination. After following the guard inside to get a temporary pass – an MOD 90 in the jargon – he was back in the cab and being waved through the gate.

At the junction of Montgomery Drive and the less memorably titled Access Road 3, he should have turned left down the latter, towards the kitchens. Instead he carried on around the perimeter road towards the administration buildings.

As he drove closer to the target, he recited his favourite surah from the Qur'an under his breath. It kept him calm.

'And remember when your Lord proclaimed, "If you are grateful, I will certainly give you more. But if you are ungrateful, surely My punishment is severe".'

He parked the van hard up against the main entrance, snapped the ignition key off in the lock and ripped out the wires from under the steering column.

Crouching at each corner of the vehicle, it took him less than a minute to puncture the tyres with the point of a hunting knife. As the truck settled onto its haunches with a chorus of hisses from the rapidly deflating tyres, he walked away across an expanse of grass dotted with cornflowers, field poppies and oxeye daisies, heading for a distant corner of the base where the fence, though still intact, was bowed outwards and rusting. It was also beyond the scope of any of the nineteen security cameras.

Once he'd clipped an exit hole, he pushed through and then, as if he were doing nothing more unexceptional than taking a country walk on a fine spring afternoon, strolled away from the base towards a distant hill.

Breathing easily as he reached the rounded grassy summit, he sat cross-legged and raised a pair of binoculars to his eyes. He had a perfect view of the roof of the admin block.

He pulled a cheap disposable mobile phone from his pocket and dialled a number.

Inside the loadspace of the catering company's delivery truck, buried beneath trays of fresh-baked hamburger buns, several dozen kilos of ground beef, plastic barrels of chopped tomatoes, sacks of onions and potatoes, catering blocks of cheddar the size of house bricks and drums of salad cream, a matching phone's screen lit up with an incoming call.

Over long years of experience, he'd observed small but noticeable differences between IED explosions. The precise colour of the flames, the specific tone of the blast, the exact shape of the

Brass Vows

smoking mushroom cloud that boiled up into the air above the detonation site. But, as a type, they conformed to a basic template.

This one was a classic. The Semtex, bought on the dark web along with the other equipment he'd needed for this op, cracked the heavens with a boom loud enough to shake the ground beneath him. A blinding flash was followed by a fireball the colour of ripe pumpkins, pierced by streaks and flashes of buttercup yellow.

Then it was the turn of the smoke. An evil black mushroom that rolled around itself as it climbed, leaving a lumpy, gnarled stem beneath the blossoming cap. He watched, and waited.

The sirens started up thirty seconds later. He got to his feet.

'Allahu akbar.'

He began the long walk home.

On the way, he phoned Essex Police on the burner. He informed the operator that if she cared to send a patrol car to the location he was about to give her, the officers would find a bound and gagged, but otherwise unharmed, man lying in a ditch.

59

10

LONDON

Smiling out at his audience, Don waited for the hubbub of multiple overlapping conversations to die down. He looked towards Gabriel and Eli, and nodded.

'Ladies and gentlemen, I first met Gabriel Wolfe when he applied to join a certain military unit of which I was the commanding officer.'

Cheers went up from the table the SAS boys had commandeered, along with what looked like a lifetime supply of booze.

'Catering corps!' one of them bellowed.

'Too dangerous. Human resources.'

More laughter. Don waited them out before resuming.

'As I was saying, the young lieutenant who came to see me in my office that day was already a hardened fighting man, with tours of duty as a member of 1 PARA Battle Group under his belt, along with a Military Cross.

'And for many years, he appeared invulnerable, despite the, hmm, mm-hmm, *extraordinary* situations in which he and his fellow members found themselves.

'Our paths crossed a second time, and he once more became a member of my team. But it was when he met Eli,' Don shot her a smile, 'whom I had first recruited from my good friend Uri Ziff, and then assigned to him as a partner during a particularly, ah, *trying* period in his life, that I first saw signs of that tough exterior start to yield, just a little.

'He may not have met his match on the field of Mars, or the pastures and paddocks lying adjacent where he now operates, but in Eli, a woman of great courage, intelligence and beauty, I think it's fair to say that he has truly found her.'

The spontaneous applause and cheering forced Don to pause for ten or twenty seconds, before he patted the air for silence.

'My old CO once gave me a valuable piece of advice about speechmaking. "Webster," he said to me over brandies in Nicosia one night, "speeches are like campaigns. The shorter the better." It's advice I have always followed. So, please, join me in raising a glass to the happy couple, Gabriel and Eli!'

Gabriel looked around, smiling, glass to his lips, as all the people most dear to him in the world turned towards him and Eli and raised their own glasses.

As Gabriel was setting his glass down on the table, he saw Don frown and reach into his jacket pocket. He pulled out his phone and raised it to his ear.

'No!' he gasped, then glanced guiltily at the mic, which was still on, and switched it off.

'Something's wrong,' Gabriel said to Eli.

'What?'

'Look at Don. He looks like Bush did when they told him about 9/11.'

Don's face had turned pale. His right hand flapped ineffectually by his side as if trying to flee the scene on its own. He nodded sharply, and pocketed the phone. Then he headed straight towards Gabriel and Eli's table, his lips set in a grim line.

'A word, please. Outside.'

They followed him out into the yard and over to a corner behind a still-chuffing static steam engine painted bright blue with white trim.

'What is it, boss?' Gabriel asked, feeling that the bright sunlight was inappropriate for whatever he was about to learn.

'Someone just detonated a truck bomb at Rothford. Right outside the admin block.'

'Oh, no!' Eli said. 'Casualties?'

'Five dead, seventeen wounded, nine seriously. Luckily most people were at a conference at the MOD, but it's a bloodbath. Whole place is in flames.'

'What do we do?' Gabriel asked.

'You two, nothing. It's your wedding day. But I have to get back there. I'm sorry.'

'Of course,' Eli said, laying a hand on Don's shoulder. 'And don't worry about Jerusalem. We'll miss you at the blessing, but we understand.'

Don shook his head violently. 'No. I promised you I'd be there for the blessing. And I will. But it might have to be a briefer visit than I'd hoped for.'

And with that, he walked away from them, phone to his ear, already summoning his driver.

Gabriel and Eli left the reception at six, just as they'd originally planned. The white open-topped Jaguar Mark V swept them out of the car park and onto Kew Bridge and their hotel in Richmond. Somehow they'd managed to retain their composure during the rest of the afternoon after Don's devastating news. But neither had drunk much and both were now utterly sober.

With the raucous cheers of their friends and family echoing in their ears, they waved over their shoulders before settling back against the Jaguar's worn red leather upholstery.

'Are you OK?' Eli asked.

'No. Are you?'

'Of course not! Do you think they were targeting Don?'

Gabriel shook his head. 'I don't know. They clearly knew exactly where they were heading. Rothford's not high profile, is it? I mean, that was the whole point of siting HQ there.'

'So the messages were a warning?'

'You believe me now?'

She nodded. 'I'm sorry for doubting you before. I thought…'

'You thought it was my PTSD.'

'Yes. Stress is a trigger, that's what Fariyah told you. You explained it to me, remember, when we were having our full disclosure evening?'

He nodded. A few days after they'd got engaged, Gabriel had cooked dinner and then, after clearing the dishes away, poured more wine. He'd taken Eli's hands in both of his and fixed her with a direct stare.

She'd grinned. 'What is this? You about to tell me you're already married?'

He'd smiled back at her. The woman he loved. The woman he knew, at that precise moment, he would spend the rest of his life with.

'No. But I think we should know everything about each other before we go any further.'

She'd frowned then, though her lips quirked into a lopsided grin.

'Everything? I'm not sure you're ready to hear about my dark past.'

'I'm serious, El.'

She sat straighter in her chair and took a sip from her wine glass.

'Serious. Yes. I'm ready. What did you want to tell me?'

'My PTSD. It's—'

'I know about that. How could I not? I don't know if you've noticed, but it's me that talks you down when you've had one of your nightmares.'

'That's not it. Just…just listen. It's not gone away. Not

64

completely. It's a lot better since I've been working with Fariyah. And I've learned so much more about what triggered it.'

'You mean Michael?'

'Michael, and Tara. All that stuff with Ponting. It defined my whole life. I'd never have met Master Zhao if not for him,' he said. 'Never gone into the army. Nor the Regiment. I wouldn't have met Britta or joined The Department. Sasha Beck would never have come after me and I'd never have met you.'

Eli took his hand in hers and squeezed gently.

'So something good came out of it.'

'Something fantastic came out of it,' he said smiling, then leant across to kiss her. He tasted wine and the chilli and ginger he'd cooked the fish in. 'But I don't think I'll ever be totally free of it and you need to know what you're signing up for if we get married.'

Eli jerked forwards, eyes blazing, 'If? Now listen here, soldier, there's no "if" about it. Why do you think I proposed? Do you think I'm some weak little girl who'll faint at the sight of blood, or a man crying, or screaming at 3:00 a.m.? Is that it? Do you think I need *protecting*? Because let me tell you, Gabe, I've been in love with you since the first day we met.'

He smiled. Remembered the way she'd come on to him. The sight of her in pale-grey underwear, exercising in his spare room when he brought her a morning cup of coffee; trying to avoid staring at her breasts, outlined by the thin fabric of her vest. The look she'd bestowed on him would have ignited soggy det cord.

'So, that's a "yes", then?'

She slapped him on the shoulder.

'Don't you want to hear about my sordid secrets, then?'

He refilled their glasses.

'Of course. Tell me all about it? Were you screwing the president of Jordan for Mossad? Posing as a lesbian in Vienna to infiltrate a neo-Nazi group?'

'You wish! Hold on, I need to think.'

'Really? You need to *think*? How deeply buried *are* these secrets?'

She nodded decisively. Two sharp bobs of her head.

'Are you ready? It's pretty heavy.'

'Hit me. I can take it.'

She looked up at the ceiling and closed her eyes.

'It was 2003. My parents sent me to live on a kibbutz for a year. I was on a work detail with this boy called Avram,' she said in a faraway voice. 'He was fifteen. He had such lovely eyes: deep brown, and long lashes like a cow's. We were picking olives. It was a boiling hot day, no cloud, not a breath of wind. He said I was pretty and did I want to go into the olive store with him to cool off. So I said yes, only it wasn't to cool off. I gave him my virginity.'

She opened her eyes and looked back at Gabriel, who was doing some rudimentary maths.

'In 2003, you would have been...'

'Thirteen. Are you shocked?'

'It's kind of young.'

'Life was different on the kibbutz. Freer. I was a curious young woman,' she said, smiling. 'And, anyway, it was almost my fourteenth birthday.'

'And that's your big secret.'

'I've never told anyone before. Not the details, anyway. Not even my girlfriends. So you see, you've got PTSD and I was a teenage nympho!'

He'd laughed then, and rounded the table to kneel in front of her and hug her.

'How do my eyes compare to the lovely Avram's?' he'd murmured into her ear, inhaling her scent of lemons and sandalwood.

'Come upstairs and I'll tell you.'

* * *

The driver pulled up in the hotel courtyard. This time Gabriel did give a tip, rather than a hammer-strike to the face.

Upstairs in the honeymoon suite, they sat on the edge of the bed and swivelled round to face each other.

'Don'll be fine,' Eli said as she loosened Gabriel's tie. 'And it's not the first time someone's attacked a security service HQ, is it?'

Gabriel knew what she was referring to. The Real IRA had fired a Russian RPG-22 anti-tank rocket at the MI6 building on the south bank of the Thames twenty-odd years earlier.

'No, but we've always kept a lower profile than them. Nobody outside The Department and Privy Council knows where we're based.'

Eli waggled her head. 'Plus some high-ups at Five and Six. And Sam Flack, the quartermaster. And—'

'Fine! I get the picture,' he said, trying to navigate a path through the emotions warring inside him. 'Sorry. Just on edge.'

Eli got to her knees and bounced her way behind him on the springy mattress.

'I'm going to relax you. Don't say anything. Just let me do my magic.'

He twisted round. 'If you're going to relax me, maybe I should help you get more comfortable.'

She lowered her eyelashes.

'Why, Mr Wolfe, whatever do you mean?'

He reached round to the back of her neck and undid the hook and eye fastening the neck of her dress. Slowly, he undid the silk-covered buttons that ran down her spine.

Eli slid off the bed and came to stand in front of him. When she was able, she shimmied out of the dress.

'Well?'

Gabriel took his time, letting his eyes rove over her body from head to toe. He'd always thought the idea of traditional bridal underwear to be something of a cliché. Now, he experienced a rapid reversal in opinion.

'Wow,' he managed.

'Is the right answer.' Eli looked down. 'Now, if you can manage to contain yourself for a few more minutes, I'm going to do what I said I would.'

He lifted his chin as she unbuttoned his shirt collar, then

worked her way down over his chest, popping one shirt button after another. Huffing with frustration, she undid his cufflinks: eighteen-carat gold ovals engraved with an entwined G & E over a wavy guilloche enamel finish.

Once she'd freed him from his shirt, she returned to kneel up on the bed behind him, and began massaging his shoulders, working her fingers into the muscles each side of his neck.

'You *are* tight, Gabe,' she crooned, as she smoothed her palms over his shoulder blades before returning to his neck.

'Getting looser, though. It's been a hell of a day.'

'You don't regret getting married, do you?'

'Of course not!' he said, half-turning until she took his head in her palms and returned him to eyes front. 'It's fantastic. I just wish it could have gone off without some terrorist trying to blow up the office.'

She leant closer so he could feel her breasts pressing into his back.

'Hey, it's a Department wedding,' she murmured into his ear. 'Terrorists come as standard along with the bride's bouquet and a seating plan.'

The sensation of her lace-trimmed corset gently scratching against his back suddenly became too much to bear.

'Right. I'm relaxed,' he said, standing and turning to face her. 'No more Department talk until tomorrow morning. It's time for pillow talk.'

Eli smiled at him as he loosened his belt. 'Well, it's about time.'

* * *

Forty-six miles northeast of Gabriel and Eli's hotel, the man who'd detonated the truck bomb opened a laptop and found an airline's website.

He typed in his destination.

Jerusalem

11

_____

Gabriel lay awake for an hour after Eli had dropped off.

Listening to her breathing, he tried to reconcile his joy at having married her to his anxiety about Rothford and the ominous messages someone had arranged for him to see earlier in the day. Then there was their flight to Israel in the morning. After much discussion, in which Eli's Jewish faith and his total lack of religious feeling figured, they'd elected to get married at Chelsea Register Office then travel to Jerusalem for a Jewish blessing. The Israeli state wouldn't recognise the ceremony as having any legal force, but it didn't matter – they'd be legally married in the UK.

And what about the honeymoon in Vietnam after that? Would he really be able to focus on enjoying himself with the horror of the bomb still fresh in his mind?

Just when he thought he should get up and go for a walk, sleep claimed him, reaching up from the depths and wrapping long, sinewy arms around him and drawing him down so fast he barely had time to register that he was falling...

...to find himself back at Chelsea Register Office.

Blackened with mould and marred by slimy patches that glistened in the candlelight, the wallpaper was peeling away from the walls in long, skin-like strips, revealing weeping pink plaster beneath.

He wrinkled his nose at the smell: burnt meat mixed with the plasticky aroma of C4. The registrar looked up at him from the paperwork she was completing at her table. The right side of her face was burnt away, right down to the bone. It gave her a grotesque quality, like a Mexican Day of the Dead mask, white teeth grinning obscenely on one side of her face while blood-red lips curved upwards into a hideous smile on the other.

'Ready to start?' she asked in a fire-roughened voice.

He turned to his right, but Eli wasn't there. He shook his head.

'Where's Eli? I can't do this without her.'

A voice, male, gravelly, seeming to carry an echo of somewhere dank, dark, and worm-filled, came from his left.

'This is something you have to do on your own.'

He tried to turn and identify the speaker but his neck was locked.

The short hairs on the back of Gabriel's neck erected and he felt a fierce thrill of pure, ice-cold terror swarm over him like freezing spiders, their legs pattering disgustingly across his skin.

With a grunt, he managed to propel himself out of his chair and turn to face the speaker.

The man was composed entirely of soot-black lines, seemingly scribbled into being on the surface of reality. He got to his feet, the lines shifting, separating, re-joining in new configurations, before settling into a rough sketch of a man again. The quivering pair of lines that formed its lips pulled apart.

'The old man thinks of you as a son, you know. But he'd sacrifice you in a moment, like Abraham sacrificed Isaac.'

'Who are you?' Gabriel whispered.

The sketch man raised a loose-boned arm and placed five wriggling lines in a fan over his heart.

'Me? I am you. Or what you could be, if he tires of you.'

Gabriel shook his head. He pointed at the sketch man's face and was dismayed to see that his own arm was losing solidity. In place of fingers and thumb, hand, wrist, forearm, charcoal-dark

70

lines were assembling themselves into a child's attempt to depict a human limb.

'You're not me. But I know you, don't I?'

Sketch man's lined lips erased themselves and redrew into a grin that stretched out sideways until its ends overran both cheeks.

'Maybe you do. But you have to find me before I find you, don't you?'

Then the sketch man lunged towards him and grabbed his other hand, the one still comprising flesh, blood and bone, and jerked him forwards.

He leered into Gabriel's face, his eyes angry black spirals spinning in towards their centres like malevolent whirlpools.

'But you'd better hurry, Gabriel, before I really FUCK YOU UP!'

Sketch man screamed the last three words from an ink-black hole below the two crude dots of his nostrils.

Gabriel awoke, heart thumping madly in his chest as though he'd just finished a sprint up a Welsh mountain. He was drenched in sweat and for a few terrifying moments, the sketch man was quivering just on the edge of his vision, before the loose collection of black lines resolved into the pattern of the hotel bedroom's wallpaper.

He rolled out of bed and staggered into the bathroom. Splashing cold water on his face, he leant towards his reflection, taking in the red eyes and haunted expression. What the hell was that all about?

He returned to the bedroom, to find Eli sitting up in bed, rubbing her eyes.

'Hey. You OK?' she mumbled.

'I'm fine, just need a drink of water. Go back to sleep. Big day tomorrow.'

''kay.'

She patted him on the back, then sat bolt upright.

'You're all clammy, Gabe. What happened?' Now there was no bleariness in her voice. She was all business. 'You had a nightmare, didn't you?'

71

She cupped his face in her hands and stared into his eyes. It must have been nearly dawn because the dim light filtering in past the curtains was enough for him to discern the worried expression on her face.

For a moment, he debated whether to fob her off and stick to his glass of water story. But that would hardly be a great start to their married life together, would it? Lying to her on their wedding night?

'It was horrible. There was a man, like a crude sketch. Pencil lines, you know?'

'What did he say?'

Eli knew him well enough, had held him in the middle of the night often enough, to know that the bad ones always featured messages from Gabriel's guilt-ridden past. They were the ones that had him screaming, or crying, or racing to the bathroom and retching. The horrific characters who peopled his nightmares, maimed by machetes or riddled with bullets, always had something to tell him. They were avatars of his subconscious: parts of him trying to alert the waking man to dangers only the unwaking man had so far perceived.

'It's fading. But he said Don would sacrifice me.'

'What does that even mean? Don loves you like a son.'

'I know. That's what the sketch man said to me.'

'This sketch man is you, right? That's what Fariyah would tell you.'

'Yes. He's my subconscious.'

'So, you're anxious because you're pulling away from him and towards me. Maybe you're afraid he'll love you less because you don't need him so much.'

'I don't know, El,' he said, ruffling his hair, which was still damp with sweat. 'I think it's more to do with those messages yesterday.'

Eli yawned, covering her mouth with her hand.

'Look, we can't do anything now, but we've got a five-hour flight coming tomorrow – or do I mean later today? Let's talk about it some more then.'

She drew him down and held her arm out wide until he settled himself close against her. He'd thought he wouldn't sleep, but the next thing he felt was a thin sliver of sunlight across his face like a blade warmed in hot water. He checked his watch. It was just before 8:00 a.m. Six hours before their flight to Jerusalem.

12

JERUSALEM

From the cafe table, he had a commanding view of the landmarks of the Old City.

The tower, which the Jews called the Tower of David, and he called *al-Qala'a*, or the Citadel, would make an excellent sniper nest. He pictured the long barrel of a rifle poking out of one of the slit windows in the golden stone, glowing now in the morning sunshine. Or perhaps he'd be lying on his belly on the parapet, protected by the iron railing.

As he sipped the strong, unsweetened coffee from the tiny china cup, he let his eye rove along from the phallic shape of the tower to the more feminine shape of the Dome of the Rock. Glinting in the sun, the dome itself resembled a vast gold breast, encircled by multicoloured glazed tiles in blue and green. He chided himself for such inappropriate and impure thoughts. He knew he had much work to do before his newfound faith was embedded within him.

The prayers of the Jews leaning against the Western Wall reached his ears as a murmur. They wept for the destruction of the Temple. Soon, others would be weeping for much more immediate destruction.

He finished his coffee, left a shiny, bi-coloured ten-shekel coin in the saucer, and rose from the lightweight aluminium chair in a fluid movement in which his centre of gravity was always directly over his feet. He had years of training to thank for his physical poise.

The narrow streets of the Old City's Armenian Quarter thrummed with foreign voices, speaking dozens of different languages. He isolated phrases here and there and saw the translations floating in the air around him...

A gawky Danish girl, blonde plaits held in place by a tie-dyed headscarf, huge green rucksack dwarfing her: '...*you know, Herod's brother committed suicide in captivity...*'

A fat German toting a state-of-the-art DSLR camera, his belly straining the front of a Hawaiian shirt depicting green-and-yellow macaws: '...*so much history here...*'

A goateed Italian hipster, red beard and twirled moustachios glistening with fragrant oil as he posed for a selfie beside his girlfriend: '...*great on my Insta...*'

Such fools! Their minds so dazzled by the surface of things that they wandered through their own lives like tourists. Not a mission, not a purpose among them beyond securing yet more photographic proof that they had been *here*, eaten *there* or posed in front of *this*.

He was different. He *had* a purpose. And in a day or so, it would be fulfilled. Isaac would turn on Abraham.

On the way back to his hotel, he stopped to buy some falafel from a wizened old man grinning toothlessly at him from behind a stainless-steel food cart. The snacks were hot in their brown paper bag and he had to roll the fragrant mouthful of fried chickpea dough from side to side in his mouth to avoid burning his tongue.

On these streets, jostling with the brightly dressed tourists, he blended in. His beard was not as extravagantly oiled as the Italian boy's and might otherwise have marked him out as different. But in his Western garb – beige cargo pants and faded chambray shirt – he was unremarkable.

For the mission, he would cut an altogether different figure, but for now, he was content to roam unnoticed between the street vendors with their tacky souvenirs of beaten brass, and the thronging tourists, each clutching a smartphone as if it secured a supply of oxygen in an otherwise alien environment.

He brushed past a terracotta pot planted with geraniums, releasing from their hairy leaves a lemon fragrance. During his reconnaissance phase, he'd got close enough to her on more than one occasion to catch her distinctive fragrance of lemon and sandalwood. She would look good in black. Austere, elegant, yet with that underlying vulnerability all grieving women radiated, whether they knew it or not.

Back at the safe house, he nodded to the middle-aged woman in the dark-green headscarf who was on duty outside. Her kohl-rimmed eyes drooped, just a little, by way of acknowledgement. He entered the cool, dimly lit space within. He found the man he had come to see in the inner courtyard beside a potted olive tree, sipping mint tea from a tall glass in a silver cage.

'As-salamu alaykum.' *Peace be upon you.*

'Wa'alaykumu s-salām.' *And peace be upon you, too.*

He still thought it odd that a religion in whose name such a great deal of violence was committed should be so keen on peace. But then, most religions had been pressed into service at one time or another as a justification for industrial-scale violence.

He himself had no such need. His violence had an entirely secular rationale. Abraham had betrayed Isaac. Left him to die. To be tortured.

Now it was time for revenge. On the patriarch and on his new favourite. For while there could only be one Abraham, Isaac could always be replaced with a new favourite son. As he had been. Wolfe could enjoy his moment in the full heat of the patriarch's loving gaze until it was switched off like a floodlight on a night-time airstrip.

He approached his contact and sat down opposite him, waved away the offer of mint tea for himself. He had met plenty of arms dealers over the years. On both sides of the line dividing legal from illegal. Which in certain jurisdictions was thinner than the brass used to make shell casings.

Some carried themselves with all the bravado and swagger of a movie star, waltzing into nightclubs pulsating with overloud electronic dance music, flanked by muscle-bound heavies and girls wearing a couple of ounces of gold lamé apiece. Russians, usually, drunk on easy money and six-hundred-quid-a-bottle champagne.

Others, the kind with whom he preferred to do business, were discreet to the point of anonymity. Chainstore suits. Imitation-leather briefcases. He thought of them as *dazzlingly ordinary*.

The armourer sitting at the mosaic-topped table fell squarely in the latter category. His wares had been used to conduct terrorist outrages in shopping centres, editorial offices, music venues and places of worship across the globe. Yet from his pleasant, if run-of-the-mill features and quiet demeanour, his simple two-piece grey suit and polished black shoes, you would be forgiven for thinking he might be in the machine tools business, or perhaps commercial insurance.

His name was Ahmed. Allegedly. He had no idea whether that was his real name. He was married to a young and very attractive girl from Jordan. He carried photos of their two children, a toddler in whose brilliant smile he could see the boy's father. And a baby, a girl, still too young to be smiling at all.

'You have what I asked for?' he asked him now.

'It was not difficult. These are standard pieces of inventory.'

'May I see them?'

Ahmed nodded and smiled. 'Of course.'

He looked towards a corner of the courtyard shaded by a fig tree whose upper branches reached the ironwork balcony that encircled the enclosed space.

A boy of perhaps twelve or thirteen appeared from the shadows carrying a sand-coloured canvas holdall. He set it down at Ahmed's feet and melted away again, as if he had never really been there.

Ahmed motioned towards the bag. Giving him permission. The heavy-duty brass zip rasped as he opened it.

A whiff of gun oil drifted up and into his nostrils, exciting somewhere deep in his brain a kaleidoscope of images, sounds and smells. Blood, gunfire, mortars, mines, IEDs, shit, vomit, fear-sweat, screams, battle cries, the whine of incoming supersonic rounds, soldiers crying for their mothers.

He lifted the M4 assault rifle free. It was in relatively good condition. The metal parts were largely undented, and bore few scratches or signs of misuse. Not that it mattered. If not quite at the level of the Kalashnikov's indestructibility, the US-made carbine was a combat-tested weapon that would be more than up to the task he had in mind.

Ahmed smiled at him.

'A nice weapon, no? The Americans were kind enough to furnish the Afghan Army with many thousands over the years. Once they departed, the Afghans decided military service wasn't all it was cracked up to be and left them to the secondary market, as you might say. They have proved popular, and not just among the Taliban.'

'It's fine. Thank you.'

He pulled back on the charging lever and let it go with a satisfying snap. The fire select lever worked as it should, clicking into each position cleanly.

With the M4 lying on the ground, he reached into the bag for the pistol.

'Beretta M9,' Ahmed supplied helpfully. 'Threaded for a silencer. More bounty from our American friends. You know, I could have got you anything. A Humvee, fifty-cal heavy machinegun. Anything.'

'These are fine for my needs,' he said, as he field-stripped the pistol then reassembled it and screwed on the silencer Ahmed had placed on the table. 'Ammunition.'

Ali nodded. 'A full magazine plus a spare for each weapon in the bag, as requested. I would ask,' he said, holding a hand palm-outwards, 'that you refrain from loading them until I have left. Not a trust issue, you understand. I just prefer to let my customers explore their purchases in peace.'

He looked the gun dealer in the eye.

Of *course* it was a trust issue. Normally a man like Ahmed would have tooled-up muscle standing in the wings ready to unload on anyone foolish or coked up enough to try and shoot their way out of a deal. Isaac's links to the Taliban had ensured a one-on-one meeting.

'Whatever you say. Let's talk money.'

Ahmed smiled, inclining his head.

'Of course. The Beretta is two thousand, five hundred dollars. The M4, five thousand. The ammunition another five hundred. But as you are a new customer, I would like to offer you a package deal,' he said, his smile widening. 'Call it an introductory discount. Seven thousand dollars for everything and I will throw in another hundred rounds of ammunition for the M4.'

He regarded the dealer calmly. He was being greedy. Probably thought he was onto a good thing compared to negotiating with the Taliban.

'I doubt you paid more than twelve hundred for the Beretta,' he said. 'As for the M4, I think three thousand would be a better reflection of its market value. Let's agree on five thousand and you include another fifty rounds for the pistol as well.'

Ahmed's smile faltered for a second, then returned to full power.

'If your budget is limited, my friend, I could always let you have a Kalashnikov or two. I have a great many at my warehouse. It will only take a few days to bring them to you. I can let you have them for nine hundred apiece. What do you Brits say? "Cheap as chips"!'

He shook his head.

'I have no use for a Kalashnikov. And I don't have three days, either.'

Ahmed's mouth turned down as though someone had just told him his favourite restaurant had closed for good.

'That is too bad. I think I can go to six and a half. But I am cutting my own throat. My margins are not nearly as wide as you seem to imagine. I have overheads, expenses, running costs.'

'All of which are the same thing, but no matter.'

He knocked his teaspoon onto the floor and bent over to retrieve it. When he straightened it was with a magazine for the M4 in his right hand.

Lightning-fast, he slid it home into the underside of the rifle then levelled the weapon at Ahmed.

'Or I could just take them,' he said.

Two loud metallic scrapes caught his attention. The woman with the kohl-rimmed eyes had drawn a pistol and was pointing it at his head. The young boy who'd brought the guns to the table was propping an AK-47 on top of the huge pot holding the fig tree and squinting down the barrel at him.

Ahmed looked disappointed.

'Well, of course, you *could* do that. Or try to, at least. But I think it would not end well for either of us. Let us stop this silly haggling, which demeans both and profits neither. Tell me your walk-away figure.'

'Six thousand and you can forget the extra ammunition. I won't need it.'

Ahmed pulled his lips into a tight line as if his guts were griping.

'Six-two-fifty. But this is daylight robbery.'

He held out his hand, nonetheless.

After a three-second pause, more for form's sake than any true indecision, he took Ahmed's hand and shook it.

'Deal.'

Back on the street again, he flagged down a taxi and gave the name of his hotel.

While the driver honked and hustled his way through the traffic, he thought back to the men who'd tried to break him. What they'd done to him didn't matter. Not anymore. What mattered was that they believed him. That they believed in his conversion to their cause. He was as much an instrument to them as he was to Abraham. Nothing more, nothing less. So let them go on believing. They would see the destruction they wished, and could attached whatever significance to it they desired.

But the truth was both more complex and more simple than they could imagine. Their torture had hurt him – hurt him a great deal. And for a while afterwards, when their conditioning had filled his every waking hour, seeping into his pores like a poison gas, he had wondered whether he was starting to lose himself.

But little by little, first at night, during the brief periods when they left him alone, and then, increasingly, during the day, he had regained himself. Found his motivation to retain his personality and cling to the one idea that would keep him sane.

He'd sold them the mission as the chance to strike a deadly blow at the heart of Britain's security apparatus. They'd been eager buyers, not even troubling to haggle over the price. Furnished him with the cash and the contacts to set it all up.

And in less than twenty-four hours, the deal would bear fruit. All bills would fall due.

13

JUDAEAN HILLS, ISRAEL

Had Gabriel and Eli decided to hold their blessing in the city, the operation would have been more complicated.

Not that it would have mattered. He'd had plenty of time to plan it. But the open-air setting, and especially the vast expanse of rocky scrub and impossible-to-cordon hillside, made their selection a perfect kill zone.

He knew there would be extensive and tight security on the day and that Saul Ben Zacchai's team would have been sweeping the site regularly in the days leading up to the blessing. But they hadn't had the training he had.

He'd made an earlier recon trip and buried the M4 in a dust-and-waterproof carrier almost a week beforehand. Now, he could pose as a tourist, strolling through the magnificent scenery of the hills with his backpack and walking pole.

His disguise was perfect, too. Beards signified a great many things on both sides of the religious divide that had scarred Israel since its foundation. Now, with his dark suit and broad-brimmed black hat, he was just another pious Orthodox Jew, visiting one of Judaism's holy sites.

On his way up, still half a mile from the place he'd cached the assault rifle, he'd been stopped by two plain clothes police who flashed their IDs as the woman brought him to a halt with an upheld palm.

'*Shalom!*' he said effusively, laying on his English accent with a trowel. 'What a beautiful day!'

'Good morning, sir,' the female cop replied in English. 'What's the purpose of your trip today?'

He beamed at her, then held his arm wide and swept it in a half-circle that encompassed the vista of Jerusalem and the blue-green hills that descended on all sides.

'I have returned home,' he said. 'I hope that doesn't sound too melodramatic. But Edgware – that's in London,' he added for their benefit, 'is a long way from here. I have achieved my life's ambition. You are so lucky to live here. You do know that, right?'

She favoured him with the smallest of smiles.

'There's a private function half a mile in that direction,' she said, pointing at a narrow rocky path that led over a small rise, 'and for today only, the general public are not allowed to get closer than this. I'm afraid you'll have to continue your journey by a different route.'

He pushed the brim of his hat up and wiped the sweat from his forehead with a white cotton handkerchief.

'Private function? What, like a party you mean?'

It was risky, but he couldn't help himself.

'Please move on, sir,' she said, resting her right hand on the pistol at her hip.

He looked down. It was a pretty aggressive move considering he was just an over-enthusiastic British tourist, but he played his part in the little drama.

'Oh, right, of course.' He looked over his shoulder. 'So, if I were to head that way and explore over there, that would be OK?'

'Explore where you like, sir. We don't want to spoil your trip. Just keep to that side of the hill and you'll be fine.'

'Right you are!' he said, injecting the earlier bounce back into his voice.

'One last thing, sir.' It was the male cop who'd spoken.

'Yes, officer?'

'Would you mind showing us what's inside your backpack?'

'Is that really necessary?'

'I'm afraid so, sir. Just a precaution. And if you're just up here sightseeing, I'm sure you wouldn't have any objection. Would you?'

Behind him, the female cop had moved to her left by a yard or so. She'd flipped her jacket back and now her hand wasn't just resting on the pistol, it was curled around the grip.

He favoured each of them with a glance and a tight little nervous smile. Oh dear. They'd been doing so well, too.

'No, course not. No objection at all. Here, hold this.' He held out the walking pole and the cop took it reflexively. 'Thank you. Now, let me just…get…' he made great play of struggling to free himself from the backpack's straps and plastic buckles, 'this thing off my back. Gosh it's hot up here, isn't it?'

He released the plastic catch closing the flap and spread the top wide. Before the cop could peer inside, he grabbed the Beretta and pulled it out in the move he'd practised over a hundred times in his room, to ensure the silencer wouldn't snag on the way out.

With the end of the silencer jammed into the cop's belly, the already quiet report was muffled to the point it was covered by his cough. The cop's eyes widened as he realised he was dying.

The female hadn't picked up that anything was wrong. As her colleague collapsed into the dirt she swore and drew her pistol, but he was already pointing the M9 at her. Three shots tore through her chest wall and burst her heart. She died on her feet, scarlet blood surging out of her mouth and down over her white shirt.

As she was falling, he turned back to the male cop and finished him with a double-tap to his head.

He replaced the Beretta in the backpack and dragged the cops off the path and behind some bushes. The blood was already soaking into the bone-dry earth and he kicked more dust over both patches until the discoloration was obscured.

Beyond the bushes, the ground fell away steeply. He peered over the rocky cliff. Two hundred feet below, a thick wooded area entirely enclosed by rockfalls beckoned.

Grunting with the effort, he dragged the female's body by the ankles and finally rolled it over the cliff edge. Without waiting to see where it landed, an amateur's move, he returned to the male cop's corpse and manhandled it – a harder task, since it was heavier – to the edge, then sent it tumbling and crashing off the cliff-face and into the trees.

His suit was dusty now, but he'd kept clear of the blood. After brushing himself down, he returned to the path. If anyone asked, he tell them the truth. He'd encountered a tricky obstacle.

Twenty minutes later, sweating freely, he reached the place where he'd hidden the M4. He took the entrenching tool from his backpack and spent ten minutes digging down until the top of the bag was visible. He pulled it clear and unzipped it.

Inside, the M4, stripped down and wrapped in thick polythene secured with duct tape, looked as fresh as the day it had been sitting on Ahmed's mosaic-topped table. He slit the polythene and transferred the components to his backpack.

It was time to drop the disguise. Anyone he encountered from now on was going to die before they realised they were in his sights. He spun the hat away into a patch of scrub and donned a sand-coloured baseball cap instead. Sunglasses cut the worst of the glare. With the Beretta held loosely at his side, he made his way to the cave he'd pinpointed during his reconnaissance.

He donned a pair of tactical gloves before hauling the spiny branches away from the entrance. The bike waited for him, fuel tank full, checked over by a mechanic in town and shod with the knobbliest tyres he'd been able to find in Jerusalem. Beside it, another holdall held his tactical outfit: grey-and-brown mountain camouflage and sand-coloured combat boots.

Five minutes later, he was ready.

'See you shortly,' he whispered with a smile, and patted the bike's angular tank.

14

———————

The wooden platform on which Gabriel and Eli stood with the rabbi was cantilevered out over the hillside so it was hanging in mid-air. The traditional wedding canopy known as a *chuppah* was fashioned from four beams of sun-bleached wood and festooned with white-flowering vines.

Standing in front of friends, family and former comrades-in-arms, Gabriel felt he was on the brink of something perfect.

He turned to his left and looked at Eli. She was grinning at her girlfriends, who'd secured front-row seats. He thought she'd never looked so beautiful. Her dress was a simple white cotton sheath, just skimming the ground. From beneath the scalloped hem, her toes, resplendent in brick-red nail polish, peeped out in their gold sandals. Even in the few days that they'd been in Israel, her skin had taken on a golden tan.

She returned his gaze.

'Happy?' she whispered.

'Very. You?'

'Mm-hmm. For one reason, in particular.'

'What's that?'

Saying nothing, she took his left hand, bent his wrist back a little so that his palm was outwards, and placed it on her belly. Gabriel frowned. Had his wife got stomach ache? And why would that make her—

As the light of understanding dawned in his brain, he felt it, an overwhelming sense that he was standing on the brink of something immense; something that would close so many open circles in his life; something that, against all the odds, all his expectations – all his fears – would complete him.

'You're—'

'Yup.' She grinned.

The rabbi, whose name was Anna, held up her arms and called for silence. The joyful singing from the Israeli contingent faded and people sat in the rows of folding chairs or stood at the back, leaning against the gnarled trunks of ancient olive trees.

In her emerald-green dress, intricately woven prayer shawl and *kippah* – skullcap – sitting on a mass of corkscrewed auburn curls, she was about as far from Gabriel's idea of a rabbi as it was possible to get.

'We're liberals,' Eli had said back when they were planning the wedding. 'They treat women as equals, and they'll let us have a mixed-faith blessing.'

Anna cleared her throat.

'Welcome, everybody. Gabriel and Eli chose to marry in London. So they arrived in Israel, Eli's homeland, as husband and wife. Gabriel is not religious, but the couple wanted to have a blessing here to recognise the importance to Eli of her Jewish faith and the couple's commitment to building a life together.'

Gabriel squeezed Eli's arm, completely unable to stop grinning, then, as the rabbi began her address, looked up into the sapphire-blue sky over Jerusalem, streaked here and there by white clouds and criss-crossed by high-altitude vapour trails. A large bird of prey was hanging motionless above the *chuppah*.

Over the years, Gabriel had become fascinated by raptors, convinced they appeared at particularly significant moments in his life. He'd started researching them in his off-time and immediately identified the large eagle overhead. The Bateleur's white wings were tipped with outspread primary feathers like the fingers of a hand, almost pure white underneath except for a black trailing edge.

He took the bird's appearance overhead as a good omen, since the website he'd used to research it described it as an incredibly rare visitor to Israel. He himself was an infrequent visitor. Once in the aftermath of the mission he and Eli had conducted to destroy the Iranian nuclear missile, and now here, today, to receive a blessing for their wedding, and, though only Eli and he knew it, for the new life growing inside her as well.

As the rabbi spoke about the meaning of love and the Jewish faith, Gabriel looked out at the smiling faces arrayed before him and Eli. Most of the people from the London ceremony were here. Don was seated towards the back, beside Uri Ziff. The SAS boys had taken a whole row and had obviously bonded with Eli's former comrades in the IDF.

The sun was blazing down, and the heat was tremendous, despite its only being late April. He was grateful Eli had persuaded him to dress in linen for the blessing. His white suit was doing a heroic job of repelling the worst of the sun's power, although he could still feel the sweat rolling down the sides of his ribcage under his shirt.

The air over the hills was a misty blue, scented with rosemary and a smell he knew intimately but could only describe to himself as hot rock. He shook his head, still trying to process Eli's news, so eloquently expressed in that simple, unobtrusive gesture.

Anna paused in her address, then swept the congregation with her high-intensity smile.

'It is traditional in Jewish weddings for the bride and groom to have seven blessings said for them. Gabriel and Eli have asked seven people dearest to them to each give a blessing. The blessings will cover the seven things most important to every newly married couple: love; a loving home; humour and play; wisdom; health; art, beauty and creativity; and community. I'd like to ask Keren Schochat, Eli's mother, to come up and give the first blessing.'

Gabriel smiled at the woman who was now his mother-in-law

as she made her way between the seats and came to stand with them and Anna. She looked at him and in her wise eyes and generous smile, he saw the woman his wife would one day become.

Keren waited for a moment, then looked down at the card she held in her right hand.

'May you be blessed with love. Though your lives may take unpredictable turns, may your love for each other be always as predictable as the dawn. May the love you feel for each other grow and deepen as the roots of the olive tree, sustaining you and uniting you in peace.'

After she read the blessing, it was the turn of Tara. Then Uri Ziff, Johnny Hawke, Eli's Dad Yossi, and Don Webster. Finally, after Don had taken his seat, the rabbi nodded towards the back of the rows of seats.

'And finally, may I ask our special guest, Saul Ben Zacchai, to come up and give the final blessing.'

Observed by his security detail and, no doubt, other Mossad agents in less obvious locations, the prime minister of Israel came to stand between Gabriel and Eli. He looked at them in turn, a hint of a smile playing on his lips. Then he reached out and took a hand each in his.

'May you be blessed with community. May you be blessed with the knowledge that you are part of a worldwide circle of friends and family. May they sustain you, now and in the future, with trust, with support, with laughter and, most important of all, with love.'

After Saul had returned to his seat, Anna took Gabriel and Eli's hands in hers.

'Gabriel and Eli will now make a series of promises to each other. They have chosen to do so before you, their family and friends, so you may act as witnesses to their love, devotion and faithfulness.'

Still smiling, she turned to Eli.

'Eli, do you promise always to love Gabriel, to be with him

and to fight for him, in sickness and in health, in good times and bad, to cherish him until the end of your days?'

Eli looked across at Gabriel. Tears glinted in the corners of her eyes.

'I do.'

'Well done,' the rabbi whispered, making Eli smile. 'Now, please repeat after me, I am for my beloved, and my beloved is for me. I love him as my soul.'

Eli swallowed. 'I am for my beloved, and my beloved is for me. I love him as my soul.'

The rabbi turned to Gabriel.

'Gabriel, do you promise always to love Eli, to be with her and to fight for her, in sickness and in health, in good times and bad, to cherish her until the end of your days?'

He looked into her eyes, sending her a message of enduring love.

'I do.'

'Please repeat after me, I am for my beloved, and my beloved is for me. I love her as my soul.'

In a strong, clear voice he was pleased to hear wasn't wobbling as much as his insides were, he spoke aloud the vow.

'I am for my beloved, and my beloved is for me. I love her as my soul.'

The rabbi nodded.

'Thank you, both,' she said.

* * *

From his vantage point between two huge rocks, under the thick leaves of a tree growing straight out of a crevice, he looked down on the cantilevered wooden deck that hung above the thickly wooded hillside below. He gave the organisers credit: they'd done an amazing job. The swags of flowering vines created a *chuppah* that combined traditional and contemporary aesthetics into a single, elegant structure.

The rabbi was explaining, presumably for the benefit of the

Brits, how the *chuppah* symbolised the home Gabriel and Eli were going to build together. Her melodious voice floated up the hillside.

'Abraham the patriarch's tent was open on all sides as a sign of his hospitality,' she said. 'So the chuppah's sides are open to represent the welcome and openness Gabriel and Eli offer their friends and family who will come to visit them.' She raised her right hand and gestured at the flowering vines. 'The covering represents God's presence over the covenant of their marriage.'

He sneered. He'd hear no sermons on Abraham's hospitality or any other of his supposed virtues. He hadn't even needed a commandment from God; he'd willingly sacrificed Isaac, leaving him to be shot, mutilated, tortured and brainwashed. No, in this version of the story, it was Isaac who'd wield the knife, and Abraham who'd scream as his lifeblood drained into the dry, dusty soil.

Abraham was standing off to one side, talking to the Mossad director, Ziff. He had no quarrel with Ziff, but unless he gave him a clear shot there was a real risk of his going down as collateral damage. He wanted to avoid that at all costs, if possible. Having British intelligence and security on his tail was going to be bad enough. But adding Mossad into the mix would tilt the odds too far in the wrong direction. Ziff must live.

The chatter of a low-flying helicopter made him look up. Military. They couldn't see him and he doubted they'd even have bothered with thermal imaging. Not at this time of day. The sun-drenched rocks would white-out the display with reflected heat. It banked to starboard, beginning another sweep of the hills. Time to move.

He slithered down between the rocks, keeping to the deep shadows. The spot he'd picked was barely thirty yards from the two men. Holding the M4 in his right hand, he used his left to help guide him down, digging his gloved fingers into cracks to slow his descent when it threatened to turn into an uncontrolled slide.

Finally, he reached the bottom, and the last, perilous few yards of open ground before he reached his destination. He needn't have worried. The prime minister's bodyguards were all on the far side of the space, keeping watch on the paths and more obvious approach routes.

* * *

Anna signalled a waiter, who brought up a wine glass, which she ceremoniously wrapped in a white napkin.

'In traditional Jewish weddings, the groom breaks a glass to symbolise the destruction of the Temple,' Anna said. 'We're a bit more modern than that, so both Eli and Gabriel will perform the final part of today's ceremony. In the liberal tradition, the broken glass can stand for many things, from the frailty of all human relationships to themes from the couple's lives. Gabriel and Eli have told me they see this gesture as symbolising their shared purpose in trying to right wrongs that still exist in a world which, though so splendid for them today, is still broken in many places.'

She bent and placed the wrapped wine glass on the floor equidistant between Gabriel and Eli.

He looked into her eyes.

'One...'

'Two...'

'Three!' they shouted, and stamped down on the glass, which shattered with a satisfying crunch.

'*Mazel tov!*' Anna cried. Then, raising her voice, so it carried right to the back of the gathering. 'That concludes the formal part of the day. Thank you all for bearing witness during the blessing of Gabriel and Eli's marriage. Now,' she paused for a count of three, 'it's time for the party!'

At this a cheer went up from the Israelis, although Gabriel noticed that the SAS boys were making their voices heard, too, egged on by their new friends from the IDF.

Eli and he walked down through the centre of the rows of seats, stopping to accept kisses, hugs and congratulations on all sides.

Gabriel looked up. The Bateleur still described lazy circles in the sky above them, rising on a thermal that swept up off the sun-bleached sides of the hills. But now a crow was swooping down on it from above, cawing as it launched a flurry of attacks that unsettled the larger raptor without ever making contact.

* * *

Heart pounding, the man who thought of himself as Isaac raced for the spot of cover he'd picked and raised the M4 to his shoulder.

Ziff was laughing at something Webster had said. Probably a joke about how operatives were ten-a-penny but you couldn't get a decent brandy for less than a hundred quid a bottle. Bastard.

All he needed now was a little luck. Then he shook his head. Luck had never played a part in any operation he'd run. Nor would it now. He bent and picked up a pebble the size of a plum and hurled it high over the heads of the two men. It landed on the far side of the open space, clanging off an aluminium table set up with drinks and snacks.

At the clang, Ziff turned, leant closer to Webster, then moved away to investigate.

He nodded.

You made your own luck in this business.

He aimed at Webster. Then he called out. Just loud enough for him to hear.

'Abraham! Remember me? You should have sacrificed a ram instead.'

He stepped out from behind the tree, waiting for Webster's face to betray first surprise, then recognition.

* * *

Gabriel looked around, trying to find his boss. Don was off to one side at the back, chatting to Uri Ziff and Amos Peled. Gabriel wanted to thank him for coming, given that he had a full-blown terrorist attack to deal with back in England.

A loud voice startled him. 'Wolfie! You're in handcuffs now, mate, good and proper!'

It was Sparrow, drink in hand, grinning as he approached, hand outstretched. The two former comrades shook hands.

And it was then that the gunfire started.

15

Even as he was diving for cover, Gabriel was performing a lightning-fast combat appreciation. One shooter, armed with a fully automatic weapon. From the sound, an assault rifle. Not a Kalashnikov. Something more modern. A German Heckler & Koch, or an M4, most likely.

A woman screamed. Gabriel looked up from behind the rock where he'd thrown himself. One of Eli's cousins lay in the dirt, clutching a bleeding wound in her upper arm.

Even as they hustled their charge away from the scene and back to his armoured 4x4, Saul Ben Zacchai's bodyguards were returning fire. But they were only equipped with pistols. Over the loud reports of their Jericho 941 pistols, he heard the rough-edged bark as the shooter fired another burst.

A fat-bellied terracotta pot filled with dark-red geraniums burst apart like a grenade, spitting razor-sharp pottery fragments in all directions. More screams. More blood dripping onto the parched earth and gritty stone pathways among the olive trees.

The bodyguards were shouting, coordinating their counter-attack. Saul had been hustled away, but something told Gabriel he wasn't the target. Not in Israel, where however violently his political opponents and detractors might disagree with his policies, none would try to assassinate him. And no Palestinian would get within a mile of him.

He had time to notice Uri, crouching behind a thick stone wall and talking to two men and a woman in dark glasses. The woman ran off towards the car park, while the men emptied the magazines of their pistols in the shooter's direction to give her cover. Gabriel prayed she was rushing to fetch something more potent than a handgun.

The shooter loosed off another short burst of automatic fire, keeping everybody pinned down. The bodyguards were returning fire as best as they were able, but the setting, while perfect for a blessing, was a tactical disaster.

Suddenly, Gabriel realised he didn't know where Eli was. He cursed himself. He'd only spoken his vows a few minutes earlier and already he'd lost sight of her. He risked a look over the top of the rock and saw her rushing towards her wounded cousin. The shooter started up again.

He screamed involuntarily.

'Eli! No!'

She was caught completely in the open, yards from any kind of cover.

Then Don broke cover and rushed towards her, arms outstretched.

'This way!' he yelled, dragging her away from her cousin and towards the thick-trunked olive tree he had been using as shelter.

At the last moment, he shoved her behind the tree and out of danger.

More automatic fire.

Don spun round and fell backwards. His lips were stretched tight in a grimace of agony as bullets ripped into his unprotected flesh. He clutched his left arm, then staggered as red blossomed on his shirt.

Blood spurted from his back as the bullet tore its way through him and exited high on his right side. He toppled to the ground, screaming as he fell.

From the direction of the car park, a blast of automatic fire drowned out Don's cries of pain. The female Mossad agent was back, firing an IWI ACE assault rifle from the hip in the shooter's direction.

'Cover me!' Gabriel yelled at her. Then he broke cover and raced in a crouching run to where Don lay in the dirt, blood spreading from beneath him, shining in the sun briefly before soaking away into the bone-dry dirt.

The Mossad woman fired short bursts in quick succession, three shots at a time. Making the most of the rounds in her weapon before she'd have to reload.

Gabriel reached Don and scooped his hands under the older man's armpits before dragging him away to safety behind a huge boulder chiselled with a prayer.

The trio of Mossad agents were keeping the shooter pinned down, the men using their pistols to give their female colleague time to switch out the empty mag and slot in a fresh one.

Don's lips were moving, but the gunfire made it impossible to hear him. Gabriel leant forward and twisted his head to bring his ear closer to Don's mouth.

'He caught me in the open. I ran. It's my fault, Old Sport. Should have let him take me before he started spraying lead around, hurting people. So glad I lived to see you,' he rasped out a breath and inhaled raggedly. Gabriel didn't like the bubbly sound the old man's breath made. 'To see you and Eli get hitched,' he groaned.

The bullet must have missed Don's heart because he was still breathing, even as his eyes closed. Gabriel lifted him as gently as he could and checked the exit wound. It was horrific. A bloody crater as big as a half-grapefruit, in which shards of splintered rib mixed with pulpy flesh. He took off his jacket, wadded it into a ball and pushed it hard against the wound while cradling Don in his arms.

Gabriel looked round frantically and screamed for help. Caught a dazzling flash of sunlight full in the face. He shook his head. He heard voices from all directions. Shouts. Screams. Some

English, some African. The sun was too bright. He screwed his eyes tight shut against the glare searing his retinas.

No. This couldn't be happening. The boss couldn't be hit. It was troopers like Wolfie and Smudge who were supposed to take the flak.

'Medic!' he screamed. 'Medic! Man down here. Medic!'

The gunfire stopped. As the smoke cleared, Gabriel looked down at the man who lay, barely breathing, in his arms. Oh, Christ! The insurgents had got the boss.

Someone rushed up to him.

'Here, let me take him. I've got this. Let him go. Gently.'

Gabriel surrendered his charge to the green-uniformed paramedic.

'Look after him,' he ordered her. 'He's the boss. I have to go.'

Then he was up on his feet and moving fast in the direction he'd last seen the insurgent gunman.

The roar of a motorbike engine from his right had him swerving and racing through a stand of olive trees. The female Mossad agent caught up with him. He held his hand out for her rifle.

'Give it to me.'

She shook her head. 'Get out of my way.'

She levelled the rifle and started firing methodically. Deafeningly loud single shots as she tried to hit the gunman or his bike.

Gabriel looked around, saw Eli crouching beside the paramedic holding Don's hand. Part of him wanted to join her but another, shouting louder, called him to arms.

A cop had just arrived on a dirt bike, its knobbly tyres throwing up dust and grit as he slewed it round to a sliding halt. Gabriel waited for him to join the prime minister's protection team then swung his leg over the tall saddle and kicked it back into life. By the time the cop had sprinted back to see who had boosted his ride, it was too late.

16

Away from the carefully tended area where they'd held the blessing, the hills reverted to a more primitive landscape that had stood unchanged since Biblical times.

In the heat haze as the sun beat its fists against the hillside, the eucalyptus, olives, cypresses and white-flowered vines took on a spectral, blue-green cast. Gabriel opened up the bike's throttle and sped down a rocky path in pursuit of the gunman.

He scanned the landscape to each side, straining to catch even a glimpse of the man who'd put the boss down. Because he had to pay. Gabriel would *make* him pay.

The bike hit an inclined sheet of flat rock and was airborne for a few seconds. Freed from the drag of rubber on rock, the rear wheel spun up and the engine screamed as the revs built.

With a crash that bottomed out the telescopic front forks and almost sent Gabriel over the handlebars, it landed, veered left, then right, before he could get it back under control.

Now Gabriel heard it. A second engine note, faint at first but growing louder as he gained ground on the gunman. He twisted the throttle grip wide open and changed up as the engine protested.

Spiny bushes whipped past, sending sharp thorns raking along his arms and legs. He felt nothing. All he could sense was the evidence of his eyes, as he kept the gunman in view.

The path widened, then disappeared altogether as the ground levelled out into a broad expanse of gritty dirt studded with thorn bushes, olive trees and boulders. Ahead, he saw the gunman's bike leaning over as he took it round a curve in the hillside, left foot extended like a motocross rider, momentarily disappearing from view. Gabriel stuck his own foot out, sliding the sole of his shoe along the ground as he leant his own bike into the bend.

The gunman must have heard Gabriel's bike. He glanced over his shoulder. Gabriel saw a bushy black beard and wild white eyes. An Islamist? Was that it? But how had he got wind of the wedding? Security had been so tight, one of Eli's friends had almost been arrested after turning up without his invitation.

All that would have to wait.

Gabriel saw the man's left arm disappear then come out again holding a pistol. Without turning, he swung it out behind him and fired twice. The bullets went wide, though Gabriel flinched all the same. Two more shots. Two more misses.

Gabriel swung the bike left and right in looping swerves and gunned the throttle harder. He was gaining. The guy's antics with the pistol were slowing him down.

Wishing he had a weapon of his own, Gabriel closed the gap between them to twenty yards. The pistol swung round again, and now the guy did risk a quick look. He squeezed off more shots. One passed so close to Gabriel's head he heard the whine as the bullet blew past his ear

Ahead he saw a path leading down at a steeper angle. He had an idea. As the gunman sped past the fork, Gabriel leant his bike over and took the lower route. In seconds the gunman was out of sight. Gabriel stood up on the foot pegs as he urged the bike through narrow gaps, dried-out streambeds and patches of scrub that tore more holes in his trousers and ripped one shirt sleeve away entirely.

He looked to his left. Above him, he caught sight of the

gunman. This was going to work. He put on a burst of speed, narrowly avoiding a fallen tree trunk, then dropped down a steep gully that had the bike bouncing from front to back wheel and back again like a bucking bronco in a rodeo.

Beyond the next stand of olive trees, he saw the place where the two paths joined up again. Just beyond it, the hill was thickly wooded. He sped up to the junction and, leaning forwards and over the handlebars to keep his weight over the front wheel, muscled the bike up the slope before executing a sliding half-circle in a small clearing and bringing it back down to a spot three metres above the path.

The gunman was maybe fifty yards back, leaning low over the handlebars. Gabriel judged his speed, calculated the distances, then stomped the gear selector into first and goosed the throttle.

With a scream from the engine, the bike leapt forwards. Gabriel aimed the front wheel at a spot where the ground rose slightly, and became airborne again.

The flight seemed to take minutes, during which he had time to register the gunman's bright-blue eyes, wide above his black beard. Odd for an Arab. There was something about that icy gaze that spooked him.

Then his front wheel hit the guy's handlebars with a metallic screech that pierced even the combined roar of the two over-stressed engines, and the bikes crashed to the ground, spilling their riders into the dirt.

As he tumbled and bounced over the rocky terrain, Gabriel saw his bike rotating, back wheel over front, engine over saddle, fuel tank over gearbox. It was following him down the rocky path as if possessed by a malevolent desire to smash him under its steel frame. Maybe it would crush his skull against a boulder for good measure. Each time a metal part hit a rock, orange sparks flew.

Finally he slid to a stop, hard against the fat, twisted trunk of an olive tree. He lay there, stunned for a few seconds, trying to clear his vision, which had doubled. He saw two gunmen lying in a tangle of man and machine, thirty feet away.

As the men and their bikes resolved into a single figure,

Gabriel staggered to his feet. Lying in the dirt under an olive tree, was a pistol. He ran for it and snatched it up. But the slide was locked back – out of ammo.

The gunman was on his feet now. The collision had opened an ugly gash on his cheekbone and blood was streaming into his beard, staining the dust-whitened black a greasy maroon. Maybe Gabriel couldn't shoot him, but he could knock him out then find a way to tie him up. *Then* he'd start with the interrogation.

He rushed the gunman and swung the pistol at the side of his head … which was no longer in the path of the incoming Beretta. The gunman seemed to slide out of range before adopting a fighting stance, legs apart, knees bent, fists up.

Gabriel flung the useless sidearm into the bushes and attacked, chopping a bladed hand at the guy's throat. The gunman blocked his strike and hit back, his counter-strike landing off-centre on Gabriel's jaw and spinning his head around.

Gabriel dodged the follow-up blow, a vicious, clawing move aimed at his eyes that would have blinded him. This was no amateur, useless without a weapon in his hands. The man was a professional. Yes, plenty of terrorists could fight with knives or even their bare hands if the situation demanded it, but there was something about the guy's moves that rang alarm bells for Gabriel.

He swept a foot round, intending to trip his man before putting his lights out with a kick to the temple. The kick connected, but the guy turned his fall into a roll, scything his own right boot around in a mirror move that caught Gabriel just above his right ankle.

As he fell, he straight-armed his opponent in the face, connecting with his nose and bursting the delicate blood vessels inside.

But the guy wriggled out of range and then, before Gabriel knew it, he was trapped under the guy's knees, the breath being squeezed out of his lungs.

In came the guy's arms, his hands curling into steel pincers that locked around Gabriel's throat and started squeezing. He felt the blood pressure ramp up instantly in his eyeballs as though they'd burst if he couldn't release the man's grip. Above him, that ice-blue stare was curiously impassive. No glare, no bared teeth. He was just doing what needed to be done. *A professional,* the insistent voice in Gabriel's head repeated. *He's a pro.*

What did it matter? Gabriel's vision was clouding, even as he struggled to break the man's grip around his throat. He abandoned the struggle. No way was he going to free himself this way. His opponent was too strong, and his position gave him too much leverage.

Instead, Gabriel swept both hands around on the gritty ground above his head. His scrabbling fingers closed on something hard, and with what remained of his strength, he swung it up and over his head. The rock, about the size of an orange, hit the guy's head with a crunch that vibrated all the way up Gabriel's arm.

The gunman grunted and fell backwards. Gabriel struggled to tip him off and levered himself to his feet. He threw a one-two combination of punches at the guy's midriff, hoping to drive his wind from him and render him vulnerable to a knockout blow. Either he missed the solar plexus, which would have been game over, or his opponent had seen the move coming and tensed his abdominal muscles into natural body armour.

Swaying, he got to his feet. Warily, the two men circled each other. Fists up. Neither willing to risk another attack without fully understanding his enemy.

'Who are you?' Gabriel hissed out between gritted teeth.

'Isaac. As are you.'

Then he darted forward and aimed a strike at Gabriel's eyes. Gabriel danced away from the blow and countered with a kick aimed at the guy's left knee. On target it was a devastating blow that would shear ligaments and put his man on the ground, screaming in agony.

Instead, the guy caught Gabriel's incoming foot and jerked it upwards. Before his leg straightened completely, leaving him at the gunman's mercy, Gabriel tensed, curled, and flipped over in a somersault from a standing start, using the guy's own strength and energy against him.

The move freed his foot and as he landed he chopped down on the side of the guy's neck. He received a rapid flurry of jabs to his face in return that had him reeling back.

The gunman's eyes suddenly flashbulbed as he looked past Gabriel's shoulder.

'Kill him!' he shouted.

Gabriel spun round, already tensing against the expected knife thrust or close-range shot. But there was nobody there. *Shit! The oldest trick in the—*

A sick pain exploded behind his eyes, and dark curtains swung closed across his vision, obscuring the view of the city far below through the heat haze. As the world lurched sideways and his knees gave way, he saw the gunman righting the cop's dirt bike, swinging his leg over the saddle and kicking it into life.

The engine roared and Gabriel Wolfe collapsed, imagining as he hit the hot, hard ground that he was back in Mozambique, with Smudge and the others, fleeing Abel N'Tolo's People's Army for the Liberation of Mozambique militiamen with their long-bladed machetes and their teeth filed to sharp points.

17

A militiaman was shaking Gabriel. No, not shaking, cradling him. He opened dust-crusted eyes to find he was staring up at Eli.

'Are you OK, darling? I just found you. You were out cold.'

He struggled up onto his elbows. His head was pounding but other than that he felt fine. Fine enough to re-join the hunt for Don's attacker, anyway.

'I let him get away, El. He pulled the oldest trick in the book and I fell for it like a rookie.'

She shook her head.

'He won't get far. They're locking down the airports, trains, ports, everything. They'll catch him.' She hauled him to his feet. 'Come on. We need to get you checked out. I'll take you to the hospital where they took Don.'

On the drive to Sheba Tel Hashomer Hospital, Gabriel squeezed Eli's hands in his.

'My God, El, he shot Don. What's going on?'

She shook her head. 'I don't know. What did you see of the gunman?'

'Not much. My memory's patchy. He had a black beard. I

thought he was an Arab at first, come for Saul. But no, because he could have, couldn't he?'

'Killed him, you mean?'

'Yes. But he didn't. Don was definitely the target. I mean, he was talking to Uri, and the gunman could easily have taken them both out.'

'The gunman, Gabe?'

'Beard, and these really piercing blue eyes. I felt like,' he rubbed a hand over his face, 'I don't know, El, I felt like I'd seen him before.'

'Seen him where? Combat?'

'Maybe, though I don't think so. It won't come. I'm too strung-out.'

'The doctors can give you something to take the edge off. Especially if we tell them about your PTSD.'

He shook his head.

'No, it's fading. I need to be sharp.'

* * *

Three hours later, having had his wounds – 'superficial', according to the Israeli doctor who'd examined him – checked over, Gabriel found himself in a featureless corridor sitting beside Eli on hard plastic chairs.

With its pervasive smell of disinfectant, bright-white corridors and bustling medics in scrubs of varying hues, Sheba Tel Hashomer hospital was no different to the many other medical facilities Gabriel had seen during his long career. General hospitals, military hospitals, field clinics, impromptu operating theatres in jungles and deserts, on ships, at military bases.

He'd even done some trauma surgery of his own, in a farmhouse kitchen, after a would-be dictator had been shot by a Hell's Angel he'd cheated.

But he'd never felt so helpless as he did now.

A woman in a white coat, long dark hair tied back,

stethoscope dangling at her chest, hurried past them, clogs clopping on the tiled floor.

Gabriel got to his feet.

'Excuse me, doctor? Our friend, what's happening?'

She stopped and turned to face him. Dark circles under her eyes accentuated her pallor in the blue-white light of the fluorescent tubes.

'He's lost a lot of blood. They're still working on him. It's – ' she ran a hand over her mouth, ' – it's not looking good, I'm afraid. I have to go, I'm sorry.'

With the sound of her clogs diminishing as she hurried down the corridor away from them, Gabriel crossed the narrow space and slapped a flat palm against the opposite wall.

'This can't be happening!'

He felt it deep in his chest, a weightiness as if someone was reaching up from beneath the ground and pulling him down to join them. Don had been like a father to him and now he was lying mortally wounded on an operating table with God knew what being cut out of him or pumped into him to keep him alive.

Eli laid a hand on the back of his neck. 'I have an idea. Come with me.'

'Where? They won't let us anywhere near the theatre.'

'That's not where we're going.' She smiled and took his hand. 'Come on. Trust me.'

She led him to a prayer room furnished simply with rows of plastic chairs and a table at the front on which lay a copy of the Torah on a white cotton sheet with embroidered blue edges. Behind it, a curving vinyl screen bore a projected image of an olive grove at dawn, the sun casting slanting beams across the trees, turning the earth between their trunks the colour of old gold.

Eli pointed to a chair on the end of the second row.

'Sit.'

He complied, feeling empty inside, content to let Eli lead him. If she wanted to pray, let her. He didn't think it would do any good.

'Close your eyes,' she said. 'Then you can just be silent.'

Gabriel bent his head and let his eyelids droop. In truth, he'd been battling fatigue since arriving at the hospital, residual adrenaline and caffeine fighting against his body's hormones trying to switch his brain off so he could recover from his ordeal.

Speaking in a low, soft voice, Eli recited a prayer that sounded to Gabriel's ears as though people had been reciting it for millennia.

'May He who blessed our fathers, Abraham, Isaac and Jacob, Moses and Aaron, David and Solomon, heal Don Webster, because Eli Wolfe pledged charity, without a vow, for his sake.'

As she spoke, Gabriel tried to focus on her words, but his mind was striving to form connections between the attack in the hills and that on MOD Rothford. They had to be connected, and to the driver at their wedding in Chelsea, the poster and the wedding card under his seat.

The gunman had shot Don. Nobody else. Even though he had a great many targets, including senior figures from Mossad, not to mention a dozen or more members of British and Israeli Special Forces. But why?

'Amen,' he found himself saying as Eli finished the prayer.

'Come on,' she said. 'Let's go for a walk. Get some fresh air. Don's in the best possible place and they said they'd call us as soon as he was out of surgery.'

* * *

Outside, the sun was blindingly bright as it reflected off the white polished stone of the hospital's walls. They walked, arms linked, away from the main entrance, then took a right turn at a signboard pointing the way to the various departments.

They found themselves outside a modernist block of eight or nine storeys – a philanthropic gift from one of the hospital's many sponsors. Incongruously, three giant purple crocodiles were crawling up its vertical front wall, a whimsical notion of the architect's, or maybe the donor's own caprice. *'You get your congenital heart centre, but I want massive plastic crocs.'*

He smiled despite himself.

'What?' Eli asked, catching his expression.

He jerked his chin towards the bizarrely oversized reptiles. 'Any thoughts?'

She looked and smiled.

'No idea. Maybe it's supposed to cheer up sick children.'

'Yeah, or give them nightmares, more like.' Trying to ignore the insistent little voice inside his head telling him that, one day, he might be in need of a place like that, he turned to her. 'El, what the hell are we supposed to do?'

'We wait, like I said. The doctors will tell us what's going on.'

'I mean, *after* that. How can we go on our honeymoon after someone just tried to murder Don and succeeded in blowing up his HQ?'

'Do you want to cancel it?'

'No! Of course I don't.'

'Listen, while Don's convalescing, there'll be some kind of interim management in place at The Department,' she said. 'They'll have to put together a plan to deal with the fallout from this and find the gunman and the bomber, if it's a different person. We'll get our orders, I'm sure.'

'And in the meantime, we just carry on as normal.'

'As much as we can, yes.'

'And if we get recalled from Vietnam?'

'Then we get recalled. We do what we're told and we join the hunt. But until then, I would very much like to at least try and spend some quality alone time with my new husband.'

When they arrived back at the waiting room set aside for friends and relatives, it was to find Uri pacing up and down, fiddling with a pack of cigarettes. He looked up as they arrived.

'Damn it, I could really use a smoke. Can we go outside?'

'Any news?' Gabriel asked.

'Yes, come on, I'll tell you when we find somewhere private.'

Outside, Uri led them to a gravelled garden dotted with

tough-looking plants whose pink and green striped leaves resembled swords. In a secluded corner he opened the cigarettes and shook one free. He offered them to Eli and Gabriel, who both shook their heads.

'Good for you, it's a filthy habit. My wife says it'll kill me. You know what I say?'

'What?' Eli asked.

'We all have to die of something and, in my job, the chances that it will be a cigarette are actually pretty low.' He paused. 'For some reason, Rebecca doesn't find that funny.'

'Uri, the news,' Eli prompted.

Gabriel was grateful for her intervention; he felt like shaking Uri and screaming in his face that Don was lying in an operating theatre while he cracked lame jokes about dying of cancer.

'Sorry, sorry. It's such a shock. Don's a good friend. I got a call from a contact in London,' he said, inhaling smoke deep into his lungs then letting it out as he spoke. 'He told me you've got a new acting head.'

'That was quick. Who is it?' Gabriel asked, mentally running through a list of possible candidates.

'Nobody I've heard of. Margot McDonnell. Does that ring any bells with you?'

Gabriel frowned. The name meant nothing to him.

'Probably a high up at Five or Six. But I've not heard the name before.'

'Like I said, me neither.' He ran a hand over his head, dislodging his *kippah* and then resettling it. 'It's what I would have expected. We'd move fast, too, if my boss was hit.'

'Did your contact say anything else?'

No. But I'd be expecting a call if I were you.'

Gabriel and Eli glanced at each other. The honeymoon was looking ever more precarious.

They went back inside, stopped to buy more coffees from the vending machine, then made their way back to the waiting room. Another two hours passed.

Gabriel had just got up, paced a circle and sat down again for the hundredth time when the doors opened and a short, dark-haired man in green scrubs came in. Gabriel and Eli rushed over. Gabriel's pulse was racing and he felt a sick feeling in his gut.

The man wasn't smiling. That had to be bad news. He steeled himself to hear the worst. Doctors smiled when the patient had survived the operation. Didn't they?

18

Gabriel experienced a weird vision. A kind of flash-forward. He saw himself in a black suit, Eli beside him, black dress, veiled. A graveside. Black umbrellas like crows' wings. A vicar intoning the funeral rites over an open grave. Rain. A cold wind disturbing the foliage of the trees.

He clenched his jaw and the scene melted away.

The doctor's lips were moving. He tuned back in.

'…am Dr Edelman, the anaesthetist. Your friend is out of surgery. He is stable but unconscious. We have transferred him to the post-operative intensive care facility here.'

'Why is he unconscious? Why can't you wake him up? Was it the bullet wounds? Is it blood loss?' Gabriel asked, hearing the anxious questions leaving his lips like machinegun fire but unable to slow himself down.

'I'm sorry. I wish I could give you a precise answer. He lost a great deal of blood. We gave him thirty units. It may be shock; a way for his body to shut down while he recovers.'

'But you're an anaesthetist. Surely if anyone should know, it's you?'

Eli placed a hand on Gabriel's arm. 'They're doing their best, Gabe, I'm sure they are.'

He looked at her, registered her concerned expression, then looked back at the doctor.

'I'm sorry. When can we see him?'

'If you wear PPE, you can see him now. Would you like to come with me? We'll get you gowned up.'

* * *

Despite the air conditioning, Gabriel felt overwarm in the surgical scrubs, cap, mask and gloves. Beside him at Don's bedside, Eli leant over the prostrate form of their boss and friend. He could see the way her eyes were tight with anxiety: it triggered a cold wave of fear in him. Don couldn't die. Mustn't!

'Boss,' he whispered. His voice cracked, even on this one, short syllable. He tried again. 'Boss.'

Don lay unresponsive, eyes closed. Gabriel could see his eyes moving beneath the lids. Flickering movements as if he were following a bird's progress in the air. That was a good sign, at least.

He was intubated, the crinkled white breathing tube stuck down his throat and into his lungs. Wires led from monitors on his cranium and torso, along with a clip on the index finger of his left hand. Two digits over, his wedding ring glinted in the cold light of the fluorescent panel directly over the bed.

Gabriel stretched out a gloved hand and gently touched the tip of his finger to the simple gold band. Don had lost Christine, his wife of fifty-three years, just a month before he and Eli had got married. She'd been walking with friends in the Brecon Beacons and had collapsed in the car park after scaling Pen y Fan.

She was dead before she reached the ground, the doctors said. A massive coronary had snapped her from this life to the next between two beats of her heart. She'd felt no pain, they said: she'd not had time to. Had not, in all likelihood, even had time to register what was happening to her.

Don had said he was grateful for that small mercy at least. Not having to see her suffer was a relief. But Gabriel had seen the effort it cost the old man to maintain his composure. He felt the unfamiliar bump on his own ring finger inside the nitrile glove the doctor had given him.

Would he be so stoic if Eli died? Especially now? Taken from him by a bullet, or an insidious attack from within her own body? He doubted it.

He reached for her hand and took it, squeezed, and received an answering pressure. Maybe she felt the same thing he did: the preciousness, the fragility, the precariousness of life. Of happiness. Of that basic human need to be with someone. He felt tears pricking behind his eyes.

If Eli's prayer meant anything, then he hoped he'd be able to talk to Don again. To share a drink. To reminisce. Please, God, let him live.

Beside him, the ventilator hissed cool, sterile air into Don's lungs. The ECG bleeped about once a second. Beyond the door, he could hear running footsteps. A shout. Then silence again.

He looked down at the man who'd been a father figure to him. Who'd always been so much more than just 'brass'. And he made a vow.

He would find the man responsible. And he would make him pay.

19

After stopping briefly at the hillside cave where he'd been camping, the man Gabriel had sworn to locate rode into a dusty, sun-bleached suburb of Jerusalem at the eastern foot of the hills. There, he parked his bike up a back alley, leaving the keys in the ignition.

The stripped-down M4 lay half a mile west in a restaurant dumpster, shoved down deep beneath empty cans of cooking oil and cabbage stalks.

No doubt the British had liaised with the Israelis and set up some kind of joint operation to find him. He intended to be gone long before they found so much of a trace of his presence. In the event that wasn't possible, he was prepared to fight his way out.

There weren't many orthodox men about so far from the centre, but still enough that, back in his suit, he blended in. His first stop was a pharmacy, where he bought some dressings. He applied to them to his wounds in a back alley.

Earlier, he'd reconnoitred the spot he headed for now; a tiny barber's shop in a back street unwatched by CCTV either within or without. Had he been staying in a hotel, he would have attended to this particular step in the privacy of his own room.

But his current accommodation had neither mirror nor running water.

He pushed through the door, setting a little brass bell jingling on its coil of blued steel.

The owner, fiftyish, white shirt straining over his belly, was sitting in one of the shop's two chairs reading the sports section of the *Jerusalem Post*. He folded it and placed it on the counter before levering himself out of the chair's embrace.

'*Tzaharayim Tovim!*' he said. Good afternoon.

The man offered his own greeting in Hebrew and took the proffered chair, placing his backpack at his feet. The mirror gave him a view of the plate-glass window and the street beyond.

Sticking to Hebrew, even though the man's accent was clearly not local, the barber asked the age-old question, used by barbers from Jerusalem to Jacksonville.

'What are we doing today?'

'Take it all off.'

'The hair?'

'And the beard.'

The barber hesitated. 'Are you sure?'

'I'm not Orthodox, if that's what's worrying you.'

The barber shrugged. 'It takes all sorts to make a world. All off, it is.'

As the barber picked up his clippers, the man kept one eye on the street beyond the window.

'Did you see the match?' the barber asked, catching his eye in the mirror above the countertop.

'Which match was that?'

'Against Maccabi Tel Aviv. We thrashed those guys.'

The man shrugged.

'I don't really follow football. Sorry.'

'You don't?' Oh, well, OK then.'

Apparently stunned into silence by this admission, the barber worked deftly for half an hour, speaking only once, to comment on the lump that had formed on the side of his client's head.

Finally he whisked the black nylon cape from around the man's shoulders and held up a mirror at the back of his head.

Having pronounced himself satisfied, he tipped the barber generously, picked up his backpack and asked, 'Could I use your bathroom, please?'

'Sure. In back,' he said, pointing at a door covered in old boxing posters.

A few minutes later he emerged dressed in a plain grey T-shirt, beige cargo shorts and sneakers. The suit was balled up into the daysack and destined for the first trash can he came to.

He paused at the door and turned back to the barber, who was resettling himself into the chair and opening the *Post* again.

'Shalom,' he said.

'Shalom. Shmor al atzmeha.' *Goodbye. Take care.*

He nodded. He intended to.

His skin still stung a little from the moisturiser the guy had applied. He checked his appearance one last time in the barber's shop window and nodded. Totally unrecognisable. The sun was hot on his newly shaved skull. He stopped at the first general store and purchased a straw trilby with a snazzy leopard-print band.

He joined a queue at a bus stop and, fifteen minutes later, was dismounting in Ben Sira Street.

He headed for his favourite cafe, selected a table on the edge of its allotted square of outdoor space and signalled a waitress. She came straight over, pulled a pencil from the twisted knot of hair and smiled down at him.

'Can I get a latte, please? And do you have any rugelach?'

'Sure,' she said with a pretty smile. 'Almond or chocolate?'

'You know what? I'm hungry. Bring me one of each. Please,' he added.

Once she'd returned with his coffee and pastries, he launched a browser on his phone and brought up a tourism website he'd bookmarked.

He was too young to have fought there, but still, the country's place names excited him with their associations of bloody, prolonged fighting. Da Nang. An Lao. Hue. Khe Sanh. Dien Bien Phu.

Ironic that it was now such a popular holiday destination. Ah, well. Times changed, didn't they? For everyone.

He flipped to a travel website and booked a seat on a one-way flight from David Ben Gurion airport to Noi Bai International in Hanoi.

20

HA LONG BAY, VIETNAM

Where the tourists traversing the Judaean Hills had to contend with dusty, sun-baked ground and scrubby evergreen vegetation, those luxuriating in Ha Long Bay's tropical embrace were cosseted by turquoise waters and an encirclement of mountains so thickly forested they resembled, from a distance, moss-covered rocks.

Watercraft of every size, from small fishing vessels to multi-decked pleasure cruisers, plied their trade among the mountainous islands that studded the bay like the knobby spines of submerged sea creatures, wreathed in lush greenery and vivid, hot-coloured blooms.

Floating on his back in the cool water, finally feeling the steel bands around his chest begin to loosen, Gabriel watched Eli as she strolled down the sand from their bungalow.

Her lemon-yellow bikini accentuated the deep tan that had bloomed on her skin almost as soon as they'd touched down in

Jerusalem. On her left wrist, a bracelet of coral and white shell beads glinted in the sun. He'd been lucky enough to date some beautiful women, but none brought out in him such feelings of amazement as she did.

He found himself staring at her navel, marvelling that somewhere beneath that taut belly, a new life was growing. Everything would have to change, but somehow he knew they'd find a way to make it work. She waved and broke into a run, sprinting the last dozen or so yards before executing a splashy dive into the shallows and swimming out to his position.

'Why didn't you wake me?' she asked, after kissing him long enough that they both dipped beneath the surface.

'You were asleep. And snoring. I had to get some peace and quiet.'

Her mouth dropped open.

'I was not snoring! I never snore!'

He grinned. 'Oh no, of course not. Must have been a tourist motorboat going past.'

She slapped water into his face.

'If this is how you treat me now we're married, I might have to get a quickie divorce.'

He pointed to the nearest island, about two hundred yards out into the bay.

'Reach that before me and I'll let you.'

Her eyes flashed. 'Right.'

She struck out immediately in a smooth powerful crawl stroke. Gabriel gave her a three-second start then followed, confident he'd overtake her at least by the halfway mark.

Close to the summit of a nearby islet known locally as Fighting Cock, the man observed the racing swimmers through a high-powered spotting scope. The jungle vegetation was alive with aggressive insects, but he ignored those who penetrated the miasma of repellent he'd applied. Compared to the insults his body had suffered during his years in captivity, insect stings had lost their power to surprise.

He knew exactly how the next few weeks would play out. The

powers-that-be would stand everybody down while they decided on the best course of action. The wild card was Gabriel Wolfe, the new Isaac. He'd buck against the restraints and eventually take matters into his own hands.

He had no doubt Wolfe would find him. After all, were their roles reversed he would track down Wolfe. Therefore, the smart move was to initiate a pre-emptive strike.

Owing to a hitch with one of his Russian contacts, his final, irreversible disappearance was still a month distant.

Going off-grid could be achieved in one of two ways. The first, beloved by survivalists, the more radical types of US militias, and enthusiasts of a certain strand of streamed TV drama would result in evasion of the civil authorities, possibly for ever. But pursued by the *uncivil* authorities, the authorities who had invented most of the techniques in the first place, these hopefuls would be in chains within weeks.

He had no intention of dying in a shootout or giving up his secrets to stone-faced interrogators in some black site drenched in blood and screams.

That meant he was going to pursue the second route to anonymity. The expensive, illegal and time-consuming route.

Stage one, currently in progress, was a process known on the dark web as a digital deep-clean. Although his years as a guest of the Taliban had left him disconnected from the internet, there was still a great deal of his digital footprint still remaining. The Department had always been good at keeping its people off the more obvious social media sites but there were still places where they could be found. By their paymasters, if nobody else.

Stage two was the physical transformation. Plastic surgery, of course, but not the routine tweaks advertised on TV and even the backs of buses snorting their way through the fume-laden Jerusalem traffic jams.

You could fool basic facial-recognition software with a lift, or even more radical procedures these days. But the AIs used by the security services either already could, or would soon be able to, look deeper than the surface.

Certain ratios between ear height and facial features, the distance between inner eye corners, bone structure: these were harder to alter and therefore easier to use when tracking suspects.

The procedures he'd paid half up front for to the Russian crew he was using would radically transform him in ways far beyond the capabilities of AI to detect.

His facial bones would be broken and pieces would be removed. Bone shims would be added from his pelvis. His ears would be sliced off, remodelled and reattached, but not before the auditory opening on each side of his skull had been sealed with a titanium implant and reopened lower down with a drill.

Once the bony architecture was healed, giving him a new jawline, cheekbones, eyebrow ridge and nose shape, the cosmetic changes would be tackled. They would resculpt his eyes, nose and lips; injecting filler here, removing fat there, nipping, tucking, plumping, narrowing, stretching, cinching, lifting, until the only thing that remained of the old face was the colour of his eyes.

And his teeth.

Never a fan of visits to the dentist, he'd had to steel himself even to discuss this aspect of the process with the Russian orthodontist. The Russian had explained, with the help of a graphic PowerPoint presentation, exactly what would happen inside of the man's mouth.

'First we take out all teeth.'

'Even the healthy ones?'

'All. Then we insert implants and screw in healing abutments.'

'Healing—'

'Abutments. Temporary plugs with titanium caps. Six months to heal over and for bone to grow into and around implants.'

'And then?'

'Shiny new teeth! Well, colour of old ones. Four screws on bottom, four on top. Hey presto! Old dental records now no good.'

'Will it hurt?'

'Not at time. We use best dental anaesthetics money can buy.

Afterwards, fuck yes! But don't worry. We have world-class analgesics, too.'

In an ideal world, he'd have added a couple of inches to his height, or shaved a couple off. But that level of work was still five years off and, in any case, beyond both his budget and tolerance for prolonged and possibly permanent pain. Instead, he'd settled for work with a physio team including a ballet instructor formerly of the Bolshoi until certain unsavoury activities with the younger dancers had ended his career. With his gait altered and specially designed orthotics in every pair of shoes to maintain it, this most fundamental aspect of his physical identity would also be gone for ever.

But it would all take time.

And until that time had elapsed, he had to find a way of keeping Wolfe off his tail.

He followed Eli's progress through the spotter scope, impressed with the lead she was steadily building over her husband.

He thought he'd found the point of leverage that would work.

21

After a lunch of barbecued fish and a sharp, herby salad with lots of red onion, garlic, chilli and coriander, Gabriel and Eli slept for an hour then took out the little boat they'd hired, first loading in the snorkelling gear they'd bought earlier.

They motored to a quiet spot, far away from the raucous crowd of twentysomethings who'd arrived on a tour boat while they were sleeping and were now seemingly engaged in a water-based drinking competition.

Gabriel pulled on the flippers, spat into and rinsed his mask and slipped the rubber flange of his snorkel into place over his gums. He grimaced at the plasticky taste of the silicon mouthpiece – a harsh, artificial flavour after the fresh, herby tang of the fish they'd eaten earlier.

He nodded at Eli, who dipped her own head in acknowledgement, then they climbed over the side. He turned turtle and kicked out, sliding down into the cooler layers of water, which was so clear he could see every detail on the seabed, even though it must have been at least twenty feet below him.

Once he'd got his bearings, and turned to check Eli's position, he swam down, looking left and right. Down here, once the metallic gurgles as the bubbles they'd created getting in dissipated, it was blissfully quiet.

A school of tiny iridescent silver fish flickered past, flashing electric blue and then a vivid emerald green as they changed direction seemingly as a single organism.

As his eyes adjusted, the water around him seemed suddenly to fill up with fish, although they must always have been there. Orange and white clown fish hugged the waving tentacles of sea anemones on the corals below him while larger bright blue and yellow fish swam around him in the open water. They seemed not so much frightened as curious, nosing up to his mask and even tapping the plastic lenses.

A dark shadow on the seabed made him look up. Close to the surface, and rendered a black silhouette by the bright sunlight hitting the water, a three-foot shark cruised along, its tail flicking lazily from side to side. Too small to be a threat, there was nevertheless something about its streamlined shape that excited a tingle of fear deep in his gut.

He looked around for Eli and saw her flippers undulating as she swam down behind an outcrop of rock festooned in multicoloured branching coral. It felt good, he could finally admit to himself, to be off duty. He knew that within a week or two, but hopefully not sooner, he and Eli would be briefed on their part in catching the terrorist or terrorists who'd attacked The Department and its boss. But she'd convinced him to wait. To let the brass figure out the strategy before sending the hard men and women into action.

For now, they could relax. Don was, if not well, then at least being looked after. Every operative had been placed on high alert and told to maintain a low profile. He and Eli were off the radar out here in Vietnam. Nobody knew where they were, not even her family.

The Department was a secretive organisation, even by the standards of the UK's elite military and law enforcement units. It was extremely rare for an operative to know the identity of another. Virtually all operations were solo affairs. That he and Eli had worked together was, as Don had told him more than once, 'off the books, even for us, Old Sport, mm, mm-hmm, which is saying something'.

He swam up to the surface, blew out the water from his snorkel and took a few breaths. He scanned the seabed for Eli but there was no sign of her. A flicker of anxiety rippled through him. He forced it down. She'd just swum off to investigate further along the reef. As she'd proved that morning, when she'd comfortably beaten him in the race to the islet and immediately demanded he cook lunch as his forfeit – 'unless you'd rather I find a Vietnamese divorce lawyer?' – she was a strong and fast swimmer.

The man was used to operating at depth. Before joining The Department, he'd been a member of the Special Boat Squadron. They'd always joked that everyone was frightened of the SAS, but the SAS were frightened of them.

Unlike Wolfe and his wife, he was equipped with military-spec diving equipment. The LAR V Dräeger rebreather was the same piece of kit he'd used in service. Strapped to his front, and considerably more compact than conventional scuba tanks, it emitted no bubbles and was virtually silent, allowing him greater leeway in shadowing his target.

Discovering their intentions had been child's play. He'd followed them into the dive shop and, when he saw what they were buying, planned his move accordingly.

He'd thought long and hard about weapons, before realising that he had no need of anything but his hands. Anything bladed or pointed would be good for threatening her, but, unless he wanted to kill her, none would do the job he required. Confident in this part of the operation, he had entered the water from the beach on the far side of the bay from their bungalow and simply waited for her to appear.

As she flipped her way around and over the mounds of vermillion, magenta and turquoise coral, holding out a hand for the little reef-swelling fish to investigate, he allowed himself a little time to admire her body. He felt a pang of envy. She was lithe but muscular, with the subtle curves he liked. Her hair streamed out behind her in the water, waving softly like fine seaweed.

Keeping Wolfe in sight, too, he urged her to swim further in his direction and away from her husband. He had a speargun looped over his shoulder, and he would use it on Wolfe, if he had to, but that wasn't part of the plan. Or not right now, at any rate.

As if sensing his unspoken desires, she rose to the surface, took a breath and dived down, kicking strongly with arms flat against her sides so that silver bubbles streamed upwards over her belly.

She executed a graceful turn in the water, almost like a shark, before slipping into a narrow ravine between two tall columns of coral-covered limestone. When she emerged, it was into a hollow formed by towering walls of coral.

The phrase 'kill zone' bubbled up in his mind. Inexact, as he planned no killing today. But the site was ambush-perfect.

The geography of the corals meant he could swim up behind her, to a distance of less than ten feet, while remaining invisible to her. Every now and again, a bubble would escape from her snorkel and wobble up from behind the corals, giving him a fix on her position.

He readied himself, then kicked hard, closing the distance between them to eight feet, six, four, two—

He reached out and grabbed the snorkel, tearing it, and the mask, off her face. Panicked, she whirled around, eyes wide. A stream of bubbles burst forth from her open mouth. He closed with her. This was the crucial part of the snatch. He got behind her and enfolded her in his arms, holding her wrists tight against her belly.

She thrashed in his grip, trying to kick behind her, but even without the flippers, the drag from the water would have rendered her attempt to hurt him useless.

Her lungs would be burning and the panic would be using up the oxygen they contained faster. That was all to the good, though he regretted the fact she'd think he was drowning her. Of all the ways to die, he'd always thought this one ranked among the top three.

He wished he could tell her that it was going to be all right. That she wasn't going to die. Strictly speaking, that was a lie. Both because in the end, like everybody, she *would* die; and because there was a slight but unavoidable risk that she would, actually, drown here and now. But he would have preferred to reassure her, nonetheless.

As these thoughts chased each other around in his head like the fish sporting among the corals, seagrasses and brittle stars, her struggles grew less. The moment was approaching. And when it arrived, he would have to act fast.

He clutched her tighter, waiting. There. She went limp in his arms. She'd passed out. Within a second or two she'd draw the breath that would flood her lungs with water; he didn't want that to happen.

Clamping his left hand over her mouth and pinching her nose with his right thumb and forefinger, he swam for the surface. Swimming on his back with Eli lying on his front in the textbook rescue pose, he took her all the way back to shore where he revived her with a modified version of CPR and mouth-to-mouth developed by the SBS and personally experienced by all its members.

Trying to be as gentle as he could, he gagged her as soon as he was sure she was able to breathe unaided.

* * *

Gabriel returned to the surface and executed a full turn, paddling himself round with his hands. Of Eli, there was no sign. Try as he might, he couldn't shake the fear that had loomed up from the depths of his mind and was now circling him like a shark with the scent of blood in its nostrils. Where the hell was she?

He struck out towards the shore, flicking his gaze left and right, then upended himself and dived down beneath the water, scanning the seabed. Nothing. He turned and flippered his way over to the last spot where he could remember seeing her. Nothing there, either. Further out into the bay two tall, coral-encrusted columns of rock stood like sentries guarding the sights further out on the reef.

She might have become trapped, or hurt herself somehow. Maybe even now she was struggling to free her foot from a flipper that had jammed in a crevice. His mind flashed on an image from an old movie: a scuba-diver thrashing around in panic, her foot held fast by the zig-zagging shell of a giant clam. Even though he felt sure that was just Hollywood artistic licence, it did nothing to calm his free-revving nerves.

Fish scattered before him as he swam between the coral sentinels. The additional adrenaline coursing through his system was using up oxygen too quickly and he had to stroke up to the surface to refill his lungs before diving back down again.

But there was nothing to see. No discarded flipper or facemask. No speargun lying where she'd wrenched it away from a would-be assassin. Nothing. Just a blood-orange-coloured octopus coiling its tentacles around something on the seabed. As it flicked out another sucker-encrusted limb, Gabriel caught a glimpse of its plaything, and his heart stopped. He kicked out, propelling himself all the way down to the rippled sand where the octopus sported with its toy.

He stretched out his hand and tried to brush the octopus out of the way. It responded by squirting out a jet of brownish-black ink that turned the water into liquid smoke. He cursed himself. Desperate to retrieve the object but feeling his lungs burning as he ran out of oxygen again, he let himself float upwards to take another breath before returning to the sea floor. At no point did he take his eyes off the ink-cloud.

Waving his hand back and forth through the murk, he managed to disperse it enough to reach down and pick up the thing that had so fascinated the octopus. Even though its thin twine had snapped near the knot, the bracelet still held most of the alternating coral and shell beads that had caught Eli's eye in the dive shop.

22

Gabriel surfaced with Eli's bracelet clutched in his right hand. He swam back to the boat and was dragging it onto the beach a few minutes later.

He ran back to the bungalow and closed the door before slumping into a bamboo-framed armchair.

His pulse was racing and there was nothing he could do to slow it down. Because it was clear what had happened. This was the latest action in the campaign of terror against The Department. First had been the messages on the bus, confirmed as hostile by the driver's sidearm and professional level of unarmed combat skills. Second, the bomb attack on MOD Rothford. Third, the attempted murder of Don Webster. And now, Eli had been kidnapped.

But it didn't make any sense! Why Eli? If the terrorists were going after The Department, OK, blow up its headquarters and assassinate its boss, but Eli was just an operative. And not even one of the longest serving.

Why hadn't *he* been targeted? He was closer to Don. Christ, the old man had even intimated that one day Gabriel might want to think about taking a command role. He'd repelled that as if it was an incoming grenade and he was armed with a cricket bat, but still, it signified, didn't it?

Suddenly convinced Eli would be striding up the beach, a scowl on her face, demanding to know what had possessed him to leave her out there, he jumped out of the chair and crossed to the door.

With his nose pressed to the glass and his right hand shading his eyes, he strained to catch a glimpse of that lemon-yellow bikini. But apart from an elderly couple strolling hand-in-hand near the water's edge, bending occasionally to pick up a seashell, there was nobody on their patch of beach.

He turned away from the window. She was gone. Just vanished out of the water. The situation felt so unreal, like a bad dream. Maybe that's what it was. Maybe his PTSD had been triggered by all the stress of the last few days. Eli could be right here, in their bungalow? Yes! He'd panicked over nothing. She was hiding. He laughed aloud and shook his head. Bit childish playing that kind of game but, hey, newlyweds were supposed to be giddy with love, weren't they?

'Eli?' he called out, his stomach jumping. 'El! You can come out now!'

She stayed in her hiding place. He could just imagine her face, fingers clamped across her mouth to prevent herself laughing out loud and giving her position away.

He decided to approach the search methodically. Army fashion. So, where exactly was the intruder? The bedroom seemed a good bet. He raced in and ripped the bedclothes aside. Nothing. Not even a hump of pillows artfully positioned to suggest a sleeping form.

He dropped to his belly and looked underneath. Nothing. No Eli, no wife of just a few days. Nobody. Not even a dust bunny he could rescue and take care of. What did dust bunnies even eat, anyway? Dust carrots, obviously. He chuckled at the thought. Eli'd crack up when he told her.

'Come on out, Mrs Wolfe,' he called as he flung the louvred wardrobe doors wide. But apart from a few outfits and a handful of wooden hangers that clicked against each other, the wardrobe was empty.

This was a dumb way to find her. Why not just call her? In fact, if he used her own phone, she'd be sure to hear it, wouldn't she? Hear it, pick up and come straight back to him. A pedantic inner voice told him that was impossible, but he was too panicked to listen.

They'd not been taking their phones to the beach. It had been part of their 'honeymoon contract'. His was on the dressing table, lined up with his keys and wallet. Eli's should have been right next to it, keeping it company. Or if not there, which it wasn't, on her nightstand. He checked, opening the drawers too when the surface yielded nothing but a paperback book and a half-empty glass of water.

It wasn't in the drawers, either. The bathroom, then. Maybe she'd been checking the internet while she brushed her teeth. Nope. As he exited the pebble-floored walk-in shower, he realised it must be in the living room after all. Stupid man! Who showered with their phone?

It took him a while to thoroughly search the living area. He flung the sofa cushions away, spinning them into opposite corners of the room, then shoved his fingers deep into the guts of the couch, feeling sure that he'd encounter the phone at any second. He shook his head. It was buzzing, as if a swarm of insects had taken up residence. He batted his open palm against his right ear. Hard to think straight with a bloody beehive between your ears.

He straightened and looked over to where one of the thick, rectangular sofa cushions had collided with a standard lamp. If *he'd* wanted to conceal a phone, he knew *exactly* where he'd put it.

The kitchenette, though small, was well equipped. He yanked a fileting knife from the slotted block of teak and returned to the living area. Three efficient slashes to the thick cotton cushion covers opened them up for inspection. Nothing. He needed to go deeper. He stabbed the tip of the blade into the cushion and pulled it towards him, spilling its fluffy grey guts all over the place. Dropping the knife, he scrabbled through the debris, searching for the phone, the *damn* phone! Where *was* it? It had to be somewhere.

Seconds later, the other two sofa cushions had been eviscerated and he was ankle-deep in the stuffing.

With a yell of frustration, he flung the fileting knife away from him. It bounced off the wall with a clang, whickering back towards him so fast he had to duck before it took his right eye out.

Something cracked inside him then. He looked at his hands, turning them over and over. They were shaking. Stars were sparking around the edge of his vision.

He went into the bedroom and sat heavily in an armchair. He had to think clearly if panic wasn't to overwhelm him. He closed his eyes and drew in a deep breath, held it for a couple of seconds, then let it out in a hiss. He knew many different breathing routines but suddenly hated even the thought of trying. What the hell use was all the bullshit yoga practice and Eastern voodoo when the only person he cared about had just vanished from right under his nose?

He flung the door wide and raced down to the boat, dragging it out onto the water and yanking the engine's starter cord. It wouldn't catch. Ignoring the surprised stares of the strolling couple, he uttered a stream of invective as he repeatedly tore the cord out from the spring-loaded spool.

On the seventh tug, the motor caught and he opened the throttle wide, powering back to the spot where he thought he'd last seen Eli. Over the next hour, he quartered their section of the bay, diving repeatedly over the reef, searching for her.

Finally, exhausted, retching salt water after leaving it too long to surface and grab a fresh lungful of air, he lay on his back in the gently bobbing boat and stared up at the sky, where gulls were scrapping over a fish one bird had plucked from the water.

The physical tiredness did what his earlier breathing exercise had failed to. It calmed him enough to start thinking. What had happened? And what did it mean?

If the terrorists had wanted Eli dead, they would have killed her there and then. It wouldn't have been hard given she was unarmed and underwater. They hadn't scrupled to spray automatic fire around at the blessing, so clearly they weren't into game-playing or subtle messaging. That could only mean one thing: they wanted her alive.

That led to two unpleasant conclusions. Either they wanted to interrogate her because they believed she had information they needed. Or they wanted her as a hostage, to extract concessions from The Department.

Another unpleasant thought broke through into his consciousness. Maybe the leverage they had was intended to work not on The Department, but on him. First he had to discount the other theory. They wanted Eli for what she knew.

Because what information did Eli have? Really. What did *any* of them have? Sure, they knew about past operations, and how they had been carried out. But none of them knew much about the intelligence-gathering that went on before they were deployed. Nor about the target selection criteria. The catch-all phrase, 'enemies of the state' pretty well described the way they saw their targets.

No. That didn't fit with what he knew. Fine. Then he could move onto his second hypothesis. That person or persons unknown had snatched Eli out of the crystal-clear waters of Ha Long Bay in order to exert pressure, either on The Department or on him. But pressure to do what?

They never took prisoners, so a hostage-swap was out of the question. If the kidnappers had got close enough to do what they'd done so far, they would surely know that. Abort an operation? Christ! What did that imply? That they already had details of who was being targeted? That would throw a blinding spotlight onto one of about three people, Don included. No, Gabriel shook his head violently, that wasn't it. It couldn't be.

From their actions so far, the logical conclusion was that they were trying to shut The Department down altogether. His mind circled back to the one theory he hoped desperately wasn't true. That they were going after not just the organisation, but its people, too. But then, why Eli and not Gabriel?

Still furiously turning the different possibilities over in his mind, he motored back to the beach and dragged the boat out onto the sand.

Back inside the bungalow, he opened a bottle of vodka and poured a huge glass, draining half in a single pull. As the spirit burnt its way down his throat, he clung to the edge of the polished wooden work surface as if it were the only thing stopping him from sliding off the edge of the world. He emptied the glass down his throat and poured another, forcing himself to stop long enough to add a fistful of ice cubes and two wedges of lime from the fridge.

The alcohol didn't so much relax him as numb him. The anxiety was still there, only now it felt that it was happening to another person, a person close to Gabriel but separated by a thick, insulating blanket. He pushed through the French doors at the front of the bungalow and slumped in one of the wicker armchairs.

Down the beach, a young family had set up camp. Dad, mum, four kids – three boys and a girl – all with tanned skins and white-blonde hair. Had to be rich, staying out here. He wondered briefly about them. What sort of jobs the adults did that they could afford flights and accommodation out here for six.

He'd begun to wonder about him and Eli, after they'd got engaged. What would *their* married life look like? Back then, they hadn't discussed having children. Not exactly. But on one visit to his psychiatrist, Fariyah had suggested that there was no reason why they shouldn't. It would just require a change in their lifestyle.

'What?' he'd scoffed. 'You mean Mummy and Daddy both being government assassins might be hard to integrate with the school run?'

Fariyah had inclined her head and smiled. 'It might,' she conceded. 'But we both know that's not what I meant.'

Now, in a way he hadn't before, Gabriel did know. There would come a time, not too far off, when one or both of them would have to choose between their profession and the sort of life other people took for granted. Then he looked at his own early life. Because that had worked out well, hadn't it?

His parents had had two of the dullest jobs you could imagine, an English tutor and a diplomat. And their cosy Mum-Dad-and-three-kids family had been torn to shreds just as effectively as if they'd been in a Land Rover going over an IED.

From deep in the recesses of his vodka-addled brain, a quote from an old English lesson with Master Zhao bubbled up to the surface. *To lose one parent, Mr Worthing, may be regarded as a misfortune; to lose both looks like carelessness.* Did the same go for children? Gabriel laughed aloud, then clapped a hand to his mouth, flushing with shame. He scanned left and right, but nobody was close enough to have heard him.

There was nothing careless about what had happened to Tara. He'd killed the man responsible for his sister's disappearance, and all the subsequent grief that had infected the family like a black plague.

How many people had he killed in total, including Steve Ponting? He tried to count them up but stopped when the total rolled past fifty like the needle on a speedometer.

But had his life to date, all that training, all that war-fighting, all those hits, those kills, those deaths, been leading, inexorably, to this moment? Half out of his mind with worry, drowning his fear in vodka, thousands of miles from home, the woman he'd thought he'd be spending the rest of his life with vanished?

A wave of emotion surged out of nowhere and threatened to engulf him. Anger, fear, shame, guilt: why? He'd been under orders for most of them and the rest were justified acts of retribution and vengeance.

His mind tripped on that final word in the thought-train crashing about in his head. Was that what this was all about? Vengeance?

23

Eli opened her eyes, then immediately wished she hadn't. Pain shuttled from one side of her skull to the other, using her eyeballs as a shortcut. She closed the lids, but retained the image of what she'd seen in that brief instant.

The room was clean, light, airy even, with narrow windows set high in the walls. Wood predominated. That was good. Cells didn't have wooden walls. This was not a prison. Nor a US black site operated by the Pakistanis or the Saudis or the Syrians in return for weapons, expertise or cold, hard cash.

Wood could be scratched at, picked at, splintered, pried apart and broken through. Burnt, if necessary.

Why, though? Why kidnap someone and then facilitate their escape? It didn't make any sense.

Was she bound? She'd forgotten to check. Experimentally, she flexed her feet. Drew her ankles apart. They moved. As did her wrists. And she clearly hadn't been blindfolded.

A dagger of fear struck at her insides. Kidnappers who didn't mind being seen by their captives were confident that being identified didn't matter. Either because they were one hundred percent sure of not being caught...

...or because they had no intention of letting their victim walk free.

Cautiously, she opened her eyes a second time, bracing for the pain. It came, as severe as before, but this time she was ready. Hissing between clenched teeth, she breathed into it, using a simple routine Gabriel had taught her. In for five, hold for three, out for six, hold for two.

Little by little, the pain dissipated. She knew what it was, had experienced it before. The psych team and the medics had told them all about the scientific names, but everyone at Kidon who carried a gun in the field simply called them Gaza martinis. No real reason, since Hamas and the rest didn't bother with knockout drops. If they caught you, they tortured you then shot you, dumping your bullet-riddled corpse over the wire for your comrades to find.

She'd been on the recovery team that had finally found Mili Yaron. They'd wept as they carried her mangled body back to the truck. Her sightless eye sockets had haunted Eli's dreams for months, leading to several visits to the unit psychiatrist. The terrorists had hung a cardboard sign round Mili's neck. It just covered what was left of her breasts. Painted in crude but legible black characters, both Arabic and Hebrew, it read, 'Send us another Jew bitch. Our knives are sharp.'

There'd been no Gaza martinis that day, although they'd sunk plenty of the real thing as they wept for Mili all through the night. Their reprisals had been swift, focused and extremely violent. They hadn't stopped the nightmares, though, in which Mili, blind, naked and bleeding, had wandered after Eli through the dusty streets of East Jerusalem, pointing at the horrific wounds on her chest wall and pleading with her to 'Avenge me, Sister'.

Still breathing evenly, Eli pushed herself up onto her elbows. She was lying on a simple military-style cot, just wide enough for a soldier to turn over on without falling out of bed.

Something was wrong. She corrected herself. Something else. She looked down. The yellow bikini was gone. Now, she was clad in grey sweat pants and a baggy white T-shirt. She pulled the neck out and peered inside. No bra; though, when she checked, she was still wearing knickers. An ugly flush of fear pulsed through her.

She ran her hands over her entire body, starting with the back of her head and working her way over her breasts, belly and groin to her thighs, knees, shins and feet, before reversing the process. Nothing hurt and there was no soreness between her legs. A huge relief, but also interesting. They hadn't beaten her while she was out, nor had they raped her. Neither eventuality would have surprised her: their absence was a greater puzzle. In fact, they'd got her out of her bikini and into fresh clothes.

Without getting up, she scanned the room. A lidded blue plastic bucket sat in a corner. In another lay a dented aluminium canteen in canvas webbing, its metal lid attached on a short chain. Water? She freed her tongue from the roof of her mouth with an audible click and gently, oh so gently, rolled off the cot and onto the floor.

With her head still throbbing, although the pain had definitely lessened, she crawled on hands and knees across the floor to the canteen. She unscrewed the lid and sniffed the contents warily.

Figuring there was little point holding back since they clearly had other ways of drugging her, she tipped her head back and drank down half the water inside. It was cold and tasted of nothing. No metallic aftertaste that might indicate the presence of drugs. Maybe a faint hint of chlorine, but that was it.

Did the chlorine mean it had been sterilised with a tablet? That would imply they either had no running water here or the water wasn't potable. Did that give her any clues about where she was being held?

The first hypothesis suggested she was out in the boonies somewhere. The second that the country was too underdeveloped to have effective sanitation infrastructure for drinking water. She filed the thoughts away. Right now, she had more urgent concerns, like trying to remember what had happened to her.

She lay back down on the cot and closed her eyes. Pictured the lagoon in Ha Long Bay and the journey down into the reef from the little motorboat they'd hired.

At the first thought of Gabriel her heart seized. Oh, God, what would he be going through? When she hadn't surfaced, he'd have come looking for her. First in the water, just swimming around the reef. Then, when he couldn't find her, he'd have got back into the boat and quartered the lagoon looking for her.

He'd have cycled through every possibility, from a shark attack to her getting trapped in an underwater cave. And, yes, kidnapping. There'd been no blood in the water, and no caves she'd seen, so he would have arrived at the correct answer pretty quickly.

Would he have gone to the cops? It took her under a second to dismiss the idea. No. She wouldn't have if the roles had been reversed. He'd have looked at the way it had happened and made the correct call: enemy action. And therefore something way beyond the capabilities of local law enforcement.

She wished she could let him know she was OK. Unmolested, unhurt and being looked after, albeit in the most rudimentary of ways. But alive nonetheless: they clearly had other things in mind besides killing her.

The windows seemed to offer the best chance of escape, but even without approaching them, she could see they were too narrow to squeeze through. Either her head or her hips would get stuck. They might provide a weak point in the walls, however. But the more she looked at the way the walls were constructed, the greater grew her doubts that this room would be easy to leave any way except by the door.

Because it would have been stupid not to, she went over to the door and tried the handle. It didn't move. She shrugged. What would Gabriel have said? 'Nothing ventured...'

She went back to the cot and tried once more to recall the events leading up to the point where she'd been taken. Gradually it came back. She'd been swimming over that little area of plain sand, like an underwater lagoon, enclosed by the curling arms of the reef. She'd sensed something in the water close by, something big, and had begun to turn, imagining a shark. Then he'd ripped her mask off and her snorkel along with it, and clamped his arms around her.

She could remember the feeling of panic as she thrashed around, trying to extricate herself. He'd been too strong, and, with the element of surprise, he'd been able to trap her in an unbreakable hold.

Her last memory was a thought, just four words: 'I'm going to drown'.

But she hadn't. Her attacker must have got her up to the surface while blocking her airways so water didn't enter her lungs. While she was unconscious, he'd administered the Gaza martini to keep her out and then…what?

She had no idea. There was nothing left that she could access. She had no idea what day it was or how long she'd been out for. She checked the bucket. It was empty. Could mean anything. That she'd hardly been in the room long enough to need it, or she'd been there plenty long enough but her captor had been emptying it. She sniffed it. Caught the sharp whiff of bleach but that was it.

She went over to the wall with the high, narrow windows and tried to jump high enough to get a look outside. It proved impossible, although she did manage to set off a ferocious banging in her head that had her whimpering and retreating to the comfort of the cot.

She slept.

On wakening, Eli raised her head experimentally off the mattress. No pain. Good. She swung her legs over and got to her feet. Still no pain. But she did need to pee. After squatting over the bucket and replacing the lid, she grabbed the canteen, finished off the water then walked to the door.

Hammering on the wood with the base of the canteen, she called out, 'Hey! Get in here! Whoever you are, I want to see you. Why am I here? What do you want? Hey! I want answers. Get your ass in here before I break my way out and come find you.'

Panting, she stood on the hinge side of the door where it would obscure her as it opened, and waited, chest heaving. The effort had winded her. She guessed it was some residual effects of the Gaza martini.

From the other side of the door, she heard footsteps. She readied herself, gripping the canteen tighter. Even empty, it would make a decent weapon. A good hard smack in the face would disorientate her captor long enough for her to grab his gun and make her escape.

A voice, a man's voice, came through the wood.

'The door opens outwards so don't bother trying to hide behind it. I want you to cross to the other side of the room and start banging on the wall with the canteen.'

Shit! Was there a hidden camera? She scanned the ceiling then reprimanded herself. Of course there wasn't! But she'd made enough noise whacking the canteen against the door for him to tell it wasn't her fist or the bucket.

He spoke again and she profiled him from his voice. English native speaker. South of England. Educated. Not young but not old either. Say, thirty to forty-five. And was there something military in his clipped diction and precise phrasing?

'I'm not hearing anything. Bang once a second and keep it up. If you stop, I'll leave you for a few more hours and then we'll try again. You've got three seconds to comply.'

Eli thought it was a smart move. She crossed the room and started hitting the wall with the canteen, keeping the beat nice and steady. *Too slow for dancing*, Els, she thought. *Not for fighting*.

She heard a key in the lock, then the handle descended and the door swung open. She got her first look at her captor.

24

Gabriel wracked his brain for any insight, however insignificant or crazy, that might explain or even just illuminate the terrorist's motives.

Could Don have committed some act of violence or betrayal extreme enough for his attacker to take the ultimate revenge? Gabriel supposed it was possible. After all, in killing Sir Toby Maitland, he had unleashed Lizzie Maitland's fury, which had almost cost him everything. And Don hadn't always been 'the old warhorse' as he liked to refer to himself. At some point he must have been a young warhorse. He'd served in the infantry before being badged in to the SAS, Gabriel knew that. But Don? He was the absolute definition of an honourable soldier, an honourable *man*. Gabriel made a mental note to look up Don's service record when he got back to England.

Gabriel shook his head. The trouble with all of this theorising was that it depended on a condition being met that stretched credulity to breaking point. Whether Eli's kidnappers wanted vengeance on Don or on him, they had to know, not only of The Department's existence, but also the identity of its operatives.

He went back inside and poured more vodka, skipping the ice and lime.

'So you know about us,' he slurred to the empty room. 'How come? Are you a journalist? No. No chance. Anyway,' he took a slug of the spirit, 'journos don't go around shitting up army bases with truck bombs and shooting M4s in the Judaean Hills, do they?' He shook his head, then staggered sideways, knocking a carved wooden table lamp off the coffee table. 'Shit! Broken. Oh, well. You have to pay for damage caused.'

He slumped into the soft embrace of the sofa cushions and drained his vodka, then reached forward to put the glass on a pile of art books stacked on the coffee table. It fell off and smashed on the tiled floor. He leant over and tried to brush the shards into a pile, but succeeded only in cutting his fingers. As the blood flowed, he leant back, closed his eyes and began to cry.

* * *

When he awoke, it was dark outside. His head was pounding and his mouth was dry. He stood up and felt the sharp pain as a piece of the broken vodka glass pierced the sole of his foot.

'Fuck!' he shouted. 'Fuck it all!'

Ignoring the pain, which felt like a stiletto trying to exit his skull through his right eyeball, he found a dustpan and brush and cleared up the broken glass. The vodka had evaporated. He righted the table lamp he'd knocked over, switched it on, then straightened the art books.

He put the half-empty vodka bottle back in the fridge and switched on the kettle. He'd had enough of the self-pity. He needed a clear head for what was to come. Coffee would be a good start.

While he waited for the kettle to boil, he pieced together the thoughts that had rolled through his drunken mind hours earlier. He found a notebook and a pen and wrote down anything he could remember that seemed useful.

Right at the top was the simple conclusion that had eluded him earlier.

Eli's kidnapper wants to get to me.

Because what other purpose would it serve to take her? Don was already in the hospital, clinging to life. Just. Thanks to the Israeli doctors and a lot of very expensive medical technology. He had to have been the target. But get to Gabriel how? The answer presented itself at once. Because they knew he'd come after them. They wanted to stop that from happening. And they knew the only way they could put him out of action, short of killing him, was to use Eli as a bargaining chip.

He stopped writing. *Short of killing him.* Because they hadn't, had they? They hadn't killed him, and they hadn't, he was sure, killed Eli. This was about containment. The target had been eliminated, as far as they knew. Now they were trying to exfiltrate and get themselves extracted without being killed in return.

They. They. *Theytheytheythey*...who the hell were *they*?

Two voices spoke in unison from a dark corner of the living room.

'You know who they are.'

His pulse catapulted into the hundreds and he dropped the pen onto the tabletop. As he whirled around, his hand went to his hip – a reflex action that secured nothing but the realisation he was unarmed. Of course he was, because who carried on their honeymoon? Two figures stood silently in the darkness. A black man and a pale-skinned woman with flame-red hair.

'Smudge, is that you? Britta?'

But the shadows were silent. He went closer, heart jittering in his chest.

'You know who they are,' they said again.

His feet refused to move any closer to the two figures. Why weren't they getting any clearer in the light of the table lamp? It was as if they pulled all the light in and reflected none of it back.

'This isn't real. *You* aren't real. You stopped appearing. You're both dead.'

The redhead raised her right hand. Gabriel saw skeletal fingers wrapped around a pistol butt. He couldn't identify the weapon. Which was wrong. He could correctly name any weapon ever manufactured: NATO, Soviet Bloc, East Asian knockoffs, he knew them all.

Her index finger tightened on the trigger.

'They are you, Gabriel. They are *you!*'

'No!' he screamed.

The gun fired with a loud click, then there was nothing. Just a roaring noise that faded to a low-pitched rumble and then silence.

Gabriel clutched his hands to his belly. Looking down, he expected to see blood welling out between his knuckles but there was nothing. He looked up again. The figures were gone. In their place the skeletal form of a standard lamp like an oversized Anglepoise, and a black paddleboard.

He looked around him. The room was empty. The click had been the kettle switching off; the roaring, the boiling water calming down inside.

That was a bad one. He'd been fighting off the idea that his flashbacks and hallucinations had returned for a while now. So far he'd been able to persuade himself that he was just seeing red-haired women in crowds and thinking they were Britta. But Smudge hadn't come to him for years now.

And what did Britta mean: 'they are you'?

He made a pot of strong coffee, poured a cup immediately then took the whole lot outside and sat on the veranda, listening to the gentle shushing of the surf as it lapped the sand.

A terrorist who knew about The Department. Its location, its boss and the identities of at least two of its operatives.

They are you.

A terrorist who felt, or believed that Don had injured them grievously.

They are you.

A terrorist who wanted to prevent Gabriel from exacting payback.

They are you.

'But it's not me, is it?' he said to the moon, full and low in the sky, casting a glittering line of scattered reflections onto the water.

He gasped. No. It wasn't him. It was someone *like* him. An insider. An operative. It had to be!

Now he knew what he had to do. Where he had to be. And it wasn't Vietnam. He could contact the local police and eat up days hanging around while they inched their way through the same tortuous processes the British cops would use if a Vietnamese tourist reported their spouse missing.

When did you last see her? Could she have wandered off? Gone to stay on another island? Can we take your statement? Your fingerprints? Your DNA? What do you do for a living? Did you have an argument? Have you ever hit her before?

The local cops had zero chance of finding Eli and bringing her captor to justice. Less than zero, since Gabriel wasn't even going to involve them.

He scrubbed a hand over his face, then held the beaded bracelet up to the light. Eli couldn't be dead. She *had* to be alive. He *would* find her, and he would kill the person who'd taken her.

25

Her captor looked disturbingly…normal.

In his grey marl T-shirt over stone cargo shorts and dark-brown boat shoes, he could have been any of the well-heeled foreign tourists they'd seen since arriving in Hanoi. His shaved head threw extra emphasis onto his eyes, large, slightly hooded and shaded by thick, curving brows.

He looked so relaxed. It bothered Eli.

She'd been trained to assess an enemy's threat potential based on over twenty-five separate physical and behavioural characteristics. Assailants with a pallor, for example, were more likely to attack than those with flushed faces. The former indicated the body was in full fight-or-flight mode, with blood diverted from the skin to vital organs and muscles. The latter were merely anger displays, low-cost strategies to avoid physical contact.

The only aspect of his laid-back body language that jarred was the pistol gripped in his right hand.

How could anybody be this effective and conceal any sign of stress? He was highly trained, that much was obvious. She had him down as a spook of some kind.

Physically, he was unremarkable. She could see that he was

lean; no hint of a burgeoning paunch beneath the shirt. No softening of his jawline. His arms and legs were toned, but she wasn't looking at a gym-rat, hitting free weights every day and chugging protein shakes to build muscle mass. In fact, he looked a lot like Gabriel.

His shaved head revealed little sign of male-patten baldness. Coupled with his unlined face, it put him, in her estimation, anywhere from thirty-five to forty-five. Given a good diet and regular exercise, both of which he looked like he followed, maybe even a little older.

The only thing that struck her as anything *but* normal was the look in his eyes. Correction, *behind* his eyes. This man had seen things, done things, that other men had not.

She'd seen the same combination of wariness and a sort of moral fatigue in the eyes of law enforcement and military professionals. Not the thousand-yard stare of the recently traumatised. No, this was more of an appraising glance, as if its owner was weighing up the world every second of the day and finding it wanting.

The pistol barrel wagged in the direction of the bed.

'Please, sit,' he said, with a brief smile as if he'd invited her to his home for the first time and was eager to reassure her.

'I'm good where I am, thanks,' she replied, spreading her weight evenly between her feet.

He raised his eyebrows.

'Really? I'd have thought you might be suffering from the mother of all hangovers. That little fentanyl and diazepam cocktail I gave you is a little vicious on re-entry, I'm afraid. Why don't you take the weight off?'

She folded her arms across her chest.

'Why I am here?'

He fired a round into the wall just to the right of her head. In the enclosed space, the noise was deafening. Eli ducked away reflexively before straightening to discover that the workman who'd been pushing his pneumatic drill through her skull had returned from his tea-break. The pain, and the sudden stink of gun smoke, sent a wave of nausea through her.

'Eli, I don't want to hurt you, but you have to understand one thing,' her captor said. 'I prefer to phrase what I want as requests, polite requests, even. But they're really orders,' he added in a stage whisper, before motioning at the bed with the pistol barrel for a second time.

The pain in her head meant further resistance was futile. If she didn't sit down, she'd fall down. She stumbled across the floor and lowered herself onto the cot.

'Who are you?' she murmured, anxious not to intensify the throbbing behind her eyeballs.

He walked into the centre of the room and sat cross-legged on the floor, a movement so sinuous he appeared to flow from standing to sitting without any effort whatsoever.

'I'm just a seeker after justice, Eli. Happily, my journey is almost at an end,' he said, offering that relaxed smile again.

A high-pitched tremor of fear vibrated through her like a guitar string. Eli had heard that sort of language, delivered in that sort of tone, before. Serene, fit-looking young men, calmly explaining why the threat of injury, mutilation or death held no fears for them. Why should it when they were about to obliterate themselves and as many innocent people as they could manage?

'What journey? What justice?'

He scratched the tip of his nose with the muzzle of the pistol.

'Good question. As you may already have concluded, it was I who blew up MOD Rothford. It was I who sent Gabriel those messages on your wedding day, which I hope you enjoyed, by the way. And it was I who terminated Don Webster,' he said. 'You're an intelligent woman. Why don't you work it out and tell me?'

Eli said nothing. Partly because another wave of pain had just surged from her left temple to her right and partly because she needed not to comply immediately with his requests, however benignly phrased. It was also interesting that he didn't know Don was still alive.

'Eli?' he prompted, lifting the pistol from his lap. 'I'm waiting.'

She wanted to ask him how he knew about her and Gabriel. But she sensed that would earn another just-wide-of-the-mark shot and she wasn't sure she could cope with the added pain.

'You think Don betrayed you in some way. Did you serve under him in the Regiment?'

For the first time since he'd entered the room, his face betrayed a hint of emotion, and it wasn't pretty. His lips drew back from his teeth in a snarl that was more animal than human. Then it was gone, so fast she could have missed it while blinking.

'I don't *think* anything,' he said, back to that unnervingly calm voice. 'I *know* he betrayed me. We are talking about historical *fact*. Much more *recent* history than the SAS.'

As the meaning of his last sentence became clear, Eli experienced a profound sense of shock.

'Why?' Eli asked, reeling from the revelation that her captor, and Don's attacker was also a former Department operative.

He sighed. 'It's a long story.'

'Guess what. I don't have any plans right now.'

He inclined his head, another surprisingly graceful movement, as if he'd trained as a dancer before switching careers to that of a government assassin.

'I was married to a fellow operative, just like you and Gabriel. Her name was Alix. We were a great team. Six years ago, we were tasked with eliminating an Afghan politician who was working with the Iranians to funnel cash and weapons to the Taliban.

'Our cover was blown just three days into the mission. And they threw us under the bus, Eli, can you believe that? They disavowed us, left us out there to take our chances. Abr— Webster washed his hands of us, sacrificed us on the altar of secrecy. Our extraction got mysteriously cancelled when the third member of our team never showed up at the rendezvous.

'Alix died when her 4x4 hit a mine. Well, you know what that's like. Nothing much to bury, is there? Not unless you can put pink mist in a coffin. Definitely outside my skillset, that one, I'm afraid.

'So that left me, pinned down behind a pile of rocks by a bunch of Taliban. Heavier than I had been that morning by the weight of three 7.62mm bullets. Then they tossed a grenade over. I thought that was it, but God was smiling on me that day. It was a dud. Maybe the Yanks had mixed up a training batch along with the real thing.'

Eli had been listening intently as he recounted his tale. The details were too specific to be fantasy. And she knew that Don's reaction was entirely within the bounds of their standard operating procedures. The Department would do everything it could to extract its operatives, but not if it meant compromising either operational goals or the unit's broader remit. They all understood it, even if it became the subject of black humour between them.

Something he'd said in the middle of his story was nagging at her. He'd started to call Don by a different name, then corrected himself. *Abr—*. The only name she could think of was Abraham.

26

LONDON

If he was to stand any chance of freeing Eli, Gabriel knew one thing. He had to keep his emotions out of it. The almost day-long Singapore Airlines flight from Hanoi to Heathrow had given him plenty of time to work on suppressing the fear, the anxiety, the hatred and the uncertainty. He'd even managed to parcel off his anxiety about her pregnancy, deciding he'd be more effective if he could just forget that until after it was all over.

By the time the Boeing 787's wheels screeched on the tarmac under a grey London sky, he had succeeded. All that was left was a grim determination to do whatever was necessary to get her back. It wasn't healthy, he knew that. Fariyah would probably give him a lecture about the danger of shutting one's emotions down. How they were 'an important psychological safety valve'.

Maybe. But they were also a hindrance to operational success. And anyway, as he had no intention of going near her, she wouldn't find out, would she? If he ended up damaged somehow

– correction, more damaged – well, he could always book a couple of appointments so she could straighten him out.

He reached the car park. The slice of sky visible at the end of the low-ceilinged parking deck had turned a bruised purplish-grey. He could hear the rain hammering down, a droning drumbeat that accentuated his mood. His car hunkered down between two metallic-grey executive saloons. Both German. Both with blacked-out privacy glass.

After considerable research, involving many hours of enjoyable test driving on the winding roads and stretches of fast dual carriageway in Suffolk, he'd found a suitable replacement for the Camaro. The all-black muscle car, a gift from the widow of a friend, was simply too big for English roads. After having it rebuilt following a nasty accident, Gabriel had put it into storage.

Its successor was about half its size: a Jaguar F-Type R two-seat coupe in British Racing Green with a bespoke cream interior. To Gabriel, the Camaro had always reminded him of a bomber-jacketed nightclub bouncer spoiling for a fight with a drunken punter. In comparison, the F-Type was sleek, understated power: an off-duty Guards officer or, he supposed, an ex-SAS member.

He blipped the fob to unlock the Jaguar and slid into the sculpted leather driver's seat. Somewhere else in the airport, his concierge service was attending to his and Eli's luggage and would be shipping it back to the house in Aldeburgh, so the coupe's tiny boot lay empty.

Was that true? Empty? It was how a curious cop would judge it if he asked Gabriel to open the rear hatch. But beneath the carpet, in a specially built concealed compartment, lay a Sig Sauer P226 and a box of jacketed hollow-point ammunition.

Gabriel had never used the pistol on the UK mainland. Never even had it out of its hiding place. But it was a new Department directive and one with which he was happy to comply. Especially for what he felt sure was waiting for him, somewhere out there, beyond the tightly controlled security of the airport.

He checked his phone one last time, left thumb poised over the engine start button, anticipating the long drive home. It was now

5:30 p.m. If he drove fast and the traffic wasn't too bad, he'd be home by nine. As he read the first few words of the latest text to arrive from the network's server, he withdrew his hand.

Presence requested Whitehall soonest. McDonnell.

Change of plan. He texted back that he'd just got into Heathrow and waited. The reply came within minutes. He was to present himself at the MOD as soon as he could get there.

He pushed the start button by his left knee. With a bark from the exhausts, the big V8 spun into life, setting off the alarm on the executive saloons either side of him. Gabriel pulled away and was heading into central London five minutes later.

* * *

Don had always maintained an office at Whitehall. Even more functional than the one he had at Rothford, the spartan space was little more than a bolt-hole where he could retreat between meetings to catch up on paperwork and check and respond to messages from field agents.

Sitting in Margot McDonnell's office, it seemed to Gabriel that The Department's acting head had altogether grander ideas about the role and its trappings. He had taken fifteen steps to reach her desk from the leather-buttoned door where the MOD flunkey had left him with a murmured, 'Miss McDonnell is waiting for you. Go right in'.

The oak-panelled walls were hung with a striking array of contemporary art, mostly abstracts in bright primary colours, that seemed out of character with the nineteenth-century interior of the room itself.

As he arrived at the desk, itself a work of engineering art in cast aluminium struts and tempered glass, his new boss waved him into a chair. More unpolished aluminium and bands of thick, glossy caramel leather.

Margot McDonnell could have been any age between forty

and seventy. Her face was entirely without lines, yet Gabriel didn't think her flawless appearance was the work of a plastic surgeon. The skin itself, pale and unblemished by freckles or moles, had a matte finish and moved quite naturally over the bones beneath as she looked at him. It had none of the unnatural sheen or stretched look that rendered so many celebrities into blank-faced mannequins.

A high, rounded forehead rose in a smooth curve to her hairline. Her hair was pulled back into a bun, so that its surface was a smooth, uninterrupted helmet of shining black.

Further accentuating her oddly blank appearance, she'd applied a pale lipstick that blurred rather than emphasised the outline of her mouth.

Altogether, the effect was unnerving. Waiting for her to speak first, Gabriel wondered whether her voice would sound like one of the artificial intelligences that popped up everywhere these days from call centres to Wi-Fi speakers.

She surprised him. Her voice was warm, and carried a hint of an Irish accent. Somewhere in the South, well beyond the easily recognisable vowel sounds of Dublin.

'Quite an unusual decision, wouldn't you say?'

That was interesting. No greeting. No ice-breaking. Just straight to it, with a cryptic question.

He scratched the tip of his nose.

'Sorry, M— I mean...' He stumbled, hesitating over what to call her before he'd even really begun to frame a response.

'Don was very keen on first names, wasn't he? I'm a little more traditional in that regard. You'll call me Ma'am.'

Gabriel felt a quickening of his pulse as anger kindled in his breast.

'Don *is* very keen on first names, yes. But I'm happy to call you Ma'am, of course.'

She offered a wintry smile. 'Which is, of course, most gratifying. And my apologies for the careless use of the past tense. I'm sure we all hope Don makes a speedy recovery. Although,' she sighed and looked away from him at the view through the huge windows, 'sadly the medical reports from Jerusalem don't inspire a great deal of hope, do they?'

This was bizarre. Just who the hell *was* this woman? He felt she was baiting him, trying to provoke an outburst. Wasn't going to happen. His emotions were locked away, deep in his psyche. It would take someone with a lot more skill in lock-picking to reach them than the stone-faced civil servant facing him across the desk.

'What decision?' A beat. 'Ma'am?'

Her grey eyes flickered, just for a second.

'Leaving for a *holiday*,' she laid special emphasis on the word so it came out sounding dirty, 'when your head of service had just been fatally wounded by a terrorist. What were you thinking?'

His heart was thumping against his ribs. But he simply stared back at her.

'Don was not fatally wounded, as I think we just established. He would have wanted us to go on our honeymoon. And we were both ready to come back at a moment's notice.'

'Of course. And forgive my lapse in manners. I should congratulate you and Eli, is it?'

Of course it was! She was a Department operative just like him. McDonnell would know full well who she was. Gabriel had had enough.

'You summoned me here, Ma'am. I assume for a reason other than to discuss my private life.'

'Oh, but that's just it, isn't it, Gabriel? Department operatives don't have private lives, do they? Not at all,' she said, shaking her head. 'I have to say I was disappointed, on assuming command, to discover that that one of our most experienced operatives, two if you count Eli, had simply abandoned a fallen comrade to enjoy two weeks under the Vietnamese sun. How was Ha Long Bay, by the way? I've never been. Always wanted to visit, though. Those islands.'

Gabriel took two slow breaths before replying. 'What's the plan for tracking the terrorists?'

'It's under control.'

'I'm glad to hear it. But what is it? Where do I fit in?'

'You don't.'

'I beg your pardon? You just said I was one of your most experienced operatives. Of *course* I fit in!'

She cocked her head. The effect was disconcerting, as if this was a behaviour she'd never encountered before 'You seem on edge. Is everything quite all right?'

'Eli was kidnapped while we were in Vietnam. It's connected to Don and the attack on Rothford.'

'I'm sorry to hear that. What did the Vietnamese police say?'

'I didn't tell them.'

'No? Why?'

'No point. Like I said, the person who took her is either the same as the one who shot Don and blew up the admin block or one of their associates.'

'That's quite a leap of logic. Any evidence?'

Gabriel laid it out for her in precise, unemotional language. It felt crazy to be outlining the chain of events that had led to Eli's disappearance as if it were a presentation on a training course.

When he'd finished, she said nothing for a few seconds. She inhaled through her nose so that the wings of her nostrils pinched together a little.

'I've brought in a team to respond to the attack on MOD Rothford, and the attempted murder of Don Webster,' she said on the out breath. 'They are experienced intelligence and field officers. We will find the people behind this outrage and deal with them.'

'Brought in from where?' he asked, though he had a shrewd idea.

'From wherever I need to bring them in, Gabriel.'

'I can help. I *need* to help. They're holding my wife. I need to get her back!'

McDonnell shook her head. 'You're too emotionally involved. It would compromise your operational efficiency. I'll brief my team on Eli's disappearance. I want you to stand down.' She raised a hand as he opened his mouth, forestalling his protest. 'That's an order, Gabriel. An order that I strongly advise you to obey. That will be all. Don't give me cause to bring you back here, will you, there's a good boy.'

Gripping the arms of the chair so that his knuckles cracked, Gabriel lifted himself to his feet. His jaws were clamped; speech was impossible. Instead, he nodded at McDonnell, turned and walked on stiff legs to the door.

27

Eli knew her Torah. And she knew the story of how Abraham was willing to slay his son, Isaac, as a sacrifice to please God.

Now, maybe the Talmudic scholars and the rabbis had their own interpretations about whether either Abraham or God ever really intended that Isaac should die, but the incarnation sitting opposite her clearly saw himself as a sacrificial victim with Don as his father.

He had that effect on his men, she'd noticed. Gabriel himself had said more than once that he viewed Don as a father figure. Now here was one of his 'sons' convinced that he'd been betrayed by that father figure, and had tried to kill him. It wasn't rational. Behind Isaac's calm exterior and patient explanations, she sensed a man for whom reason had become an optional extra in the setup of his life.

She didn't like it.

'What happened after the Taliban captured you? Clearly they didn't kill you.'

He did that graceful thing with his head again.

'Clearly. I woke up in a medical facility. The Taliban medics patched me up. And then, for three years, they attempted to brainwash me, radicalise me. I was to be their secret weapon, roving the world doing to the West what they had been doing to Afghanistan for centuries.

'I let them believe they had been successful. But it was an act. As soon as they released me to go about my new work, I simply disappeared, never to be seen again. Well, until now, of course.'

'Were you planning this all along?'

'Planning? No. Not to begin with. As I waited for them to overrun my position, it was more a dying man's dream. A hopeless vow, if you like, more to give him succour in his final moments than anything concrete,' he said. 'But when I came round in their field hospital or whatever it was, then, yes, I realised I'd been given a second chance by God to settle the account.'

Eli's eyebrows shot up.

'You think *He* authorised this? This *mission* of yours? Detonating truck bombs, killing innocent people?'

'Oh, come on, Eli. Innocent? Really? Webster presided over an organisation whose sole reason for existence is to conduct extra-judicial murders. Everyone who worked for him, from the secretaries up to people like us, knew that.'

'They're still legal. There's proper oversight. Maybe not when you served, but that's changed now.'

He snorted.

'Oversight. OK. And you think that makes it all right, do you?'

'Yes, I do. The people we target are evil. Pure and simple. They—'

'No!' he shouted, making her flinch as his yell bounced off the hard walls. 'There's nothing pure or simple about it, Eli,' he said, back to that weirdly calm tone. 'It's a filthy business. People like us? We clean up the shit of the world. But at least we should be able to expect loyalty from those managing the sewers.'

'We all knew what we were signing up for. If we can't be extracted, we're on our own. It's standard operating procedure.'

He shook his head.

'Wrong. I didn't sign up for that and neither did Alix.

Webster might as well have planted the IED that killed her himself.' He held up a hand as Eli opened her mouth to reply. 'Anyway, as I was saying, God gave me a chance to right a grievous wrong. So I started to plan my revenge. I had a long time. Three years, more or less. All the while having to survive some fairly, I have to say, *primitive* attempts to put my conscious mind through a blender. Plus the time since my release, obviously.'

Feeling that the longer she kept him talking, the better, Eli framed a question that had been on her mind all along.

'If this is about Don, why did you send those messages to Gabriel?'

He smiled.

'Clever girl! Here's the thing, Eli. We used to work together.'

'What? When?'

'It was just after he joined The Department. He'd been a good boy and stopped that idiot Maitland dead, pun intended. Don recruited him onto the permanent company. Badged him in, you might say. He was the point-man when Alix and I went out to Afghanistan.'

As he spoke, a horrible suspicion coalesced in Eli's mind. He'd already mentioned a third member of their team who'd missed the rendezvous. What he said next confirmed it.

'Now, what would you say was the prime duty of a point-man? Let's make it easy for you. We'll do a multiple choice,' he said, an edge of menace sliding into his voice. 'Pay attention, because there are a lot of options. Is it a) feed you real-time intelligence on the enemy's movements and capabilities? Is it b) provide suppressive fire, artillery cover, air support or whatever the fuck you need to complete your mission? Is it c) stand by with fast armoured transport ready to extract you once you've exfiltrated? Is it d) all of the above?' He was shouting now. 'Or, is it e) desert you so your wife gets vaporised by an IED and you get reamed by Taliban bullets?'

She shook her head without thinking, detonating another small grenade behind her eyes.

'Gabriel would never desert anyone. Never! He must have got into trouble himself.'

'Never? Are you sure about that? You know why he left the SAS, right?'

'I—'

'He left a man behind. Deserted him, you might say.'

'You're wrong! Gabriel didn't desert Smudge. The poor man was already dead. It's what caused Gabriel's PTSD. In fact, if you want to talk about betrayal, Gabriel discovered *they* were betrayed. By the fucking prime minister.'

He rose to his feet, seeming to expend just as little effort as he had on the way down.

'You're worried I've got Gabriel in my sights, Eli, I can see that. But you shouldn't be. I could have killed him a dozen times over if I'd wanted to. Now, sit still,' he said. 'I'm going to leave and come back with some food for you. You must be hungry. Shan't be long.'

Eli doubted she could have mounted an attack even if she'd wanted to. Up close to an enemy armed with a pistol, and in full control of her mind and body, she could have disarmed him with a kindergarten set of Krav Maga moves they taught everyone in week one of training.

So she watched him go, committing as many details of his appearance, his behaviour and his story to memory as she could.

Most disturbing was his sudden mood swings, angry and snarling one minute, calm and pleasant the next.

He returned five minutes later with a small plate of rice and vegetables. Not much, which was sensible from his point of view. You didn't want your captive to build their strength up. Starvation rations were an easy and cheap method of control.

'What's your name?' she asked after he'd set the plate down on the floor while keeping her covered with the pistol.

'Why do you care?'

She shrugged. 'You know mine.'

'You think you're building some kind of rapport with me, is

that it? Reverse Stockholm Syndrome?' he sneered. 'You think you can get me to sympathise with you enough to let you go?'

'No, I just thought, if we're going to have any more conversations, it would be nice to know who you are, that's all.'

He glanced at the ceiling, then back at her, those wary eyes scrutinising her as if looking for a tell. He scratched the side of his nose with the pistol's muzzle again, an action she found unaccountably disturbing.

'It's Kevin. Kevin Bakker.'

She smiled. 'Bakker. That's Dutch, right? Meaning baker? I have a friend back home with the same name. Her parents came from Amsterdam in the nineties.'

'My father's Dutch.'

'So do you know what my surname means?'

'Wolfe? It's not difficult.'

'Oh. No, my maiden name. It's—'

'Schochat. Yes, it means a ritual slaughterer. A butcher. All we need's a candlestick maker and we've got the set.'

'You've been researching us, haven't you?'

'Can't run an op without background, can you? Now, eat up or it'll go cold,' he said, toeing the plate of rice towards the bed before leaving and locking the door behind him.

The food had a magical effect on her headache, dispelling it within minutes. She washed it down with some water, then lay back on the bed.

Bakker returned ten minutes later, now dressed in fatigues and a peaked cap. Tactical gear. No longer the slightly soft-edged tourist; here was a fighting man, prepped for action. He still carried the pistol, but in his left hand he held a phone. *Her* phone.

After glancing at the cleaned plate and nodding, he smiled at her.

'Let's make a call, shall we?'

28

ALDEBURGH

After a four-hour drive he'd made largely on autopilot, Gabriel unlocked his front door and went straight to the drinks cabinet.

With a tumbler of brandy in hand, he slumped in an armchair and took a sip of the smooth spirit. Then a gulp. Then he emptied his glass and refilled it.

McDonnell had gone out of her way to antagonise him. All that mysterious bullshit about this 'team' she'd brought in. They were spooks, pure and simple. Probably MI6 but not necessarily. Was that her background? He resolved to find out, the first chance he got.

As he brooded, he checked his phone. He remembered it had buzzed a couple of times as he was eating up the miles on the A12 heading into Suffolk.

Notifications filled the screen. Seven missed calls and a single text from Uri Ziff. He opened the text.

Don passed away last night. He was in no pain. I am so sorry. We have all lost a good friend. Call me whenever you get this. Uri.

Gabriel stared at the screen. The words were simple, the sentences short. So why didn't Uri's message make any sense? How could Don be dead? He was in a hospital. Tubes and monitors and wires hooking him up to a million pounds' worth of high-tech medical equipment. He couldn't have 'passed away'. Uri must be mistaken. He gulped some brandy.

While he'd been en route from Hanoi, the man he'd looked up to since the very first day he'd been introduced had died? Wait! Last night. Margot McDonnell must have known that before their meeting. All that bullshit about the past tense. She knew! She was playing with him.

And then he heard a roaring in his ears and the room darkened until he thought the lights must have failed. Then it lit up brighter than a night raid. Sweat broke out all over his body.

As if galvanised by a force outside his own body, his right arm jerked convulsively and hurled the phone across the room so hard it hit a wooden beam, bounced back and shattered the glass shade of a table lamp.

He stood up and rushed out of the room, threw the front door open wide and raced out of the house, down the short path to the gate, across Slaughden Road and into the car park opposite the house. A stiff breeze was blowing off the sea, filling his nostrils with the smell of salt and ozone.

Stumbling over the cricketball-sized stones where Britta Falskog had lost her life, he rushed down to the water's edge and straight into the waves until he was waist-deep in the freezing water of the North Sea.

He threw his head back and howled up at the crescent moon, a long, agonised cry of grief and despair that wracked him to his soul. He smashed his clenched fists down into the water over and over again, sweeping them left and right, raising great rooster-tails of salt water that entered his stretched-wide mouth and made him retch.

For a split-second, as he looked out into the darkness, and the roiling sea beyond the breakers, he was seized by a sudden, almost irresistible, impulse to walk further out and to keep walking until the black sea closed over his head and everything could be forgotten.

It was only by a supreme effort of will that he turned away, and waded back onto the beach, his clothes sticking to his skin and chilling him to the bone in the cold wind that seemed to be pushing him with the force of a giant hand in the small of his back. He heard its voice, a rough hissing, urging him to *'Keep walking, Wolfe, back to the land, back to your duty'*.

Shuddering with cold and shock, he staggered back to his house and climbed the stairs. He stripped off his sodden clothes and stood under the shower, hissing as the cold jets chilled his already icebound heart until finally the heat came through and he could stand there and let it course over his body.

He only stepped out of the shower when the water began to cool. He'd emptied the hot water tank.

Five minutes later, wrapped in a thick white towelling dressing gown, he called Uri. As he waited for him to answer, he checked the time: 12:21 p.m. So 02:21 a.m. in Jerusalem.

'Shalom, Gabriel.'

'Shalom, Uri. Did I wake you?'

'Ha! A lovely thought, that I should be asleep beside my wife in the middle of the night, and not sitting at my desk, pondering the evil that men do. Listen, I'm sorry for your loss, Gabriel. I know you looked up to Don. Hell, we all did.'

Gabriel found it hard to find any words. His throat seemed to have shut down on him. He opened his mouth. Tried to speak around the lump blocking his windpipe.

'I... what... I mean...' He swallowed, moistened his lips, 'How did it happen? He was doing so well. I thought the doctors said he was stable.'

'Ah, my friend, he *was* doing well. And he *was* stable. But his heart just stopped beating. I spoke to the senior medic looking after Don. They tried defibrillating, CPR, everything. He just died, Gabriel. He took a burst of automatic rifle fire at close range. It was a miracle he wasn't killed outright. It was his time and now we have to mourn him.'

'No!' Gabriel shouted, fearing the tears he could feel welling up would burst forth and swamp his words. 'No, Uri. We have to *avenge* him. Mourning can wait.'

'You have that wrong. We mourn now, and *then* we go back to work. We are repatriating his body at the request of the British police. There's to be a post mortem. They're now treating it as a murder investigation.'

Gabriel coughed out a laugh. 'Oh well, that's all right then. As long as the cops are on it, I'm sure they'll track down his killer. After all, it's not like he's got any special skills at evading capture is it?'

He could hear his sarcasm, could feel the desire to lash out at Uri for exploding a bomb under him. As shame overwhelmed him, he tried to apologise.

'Uri, I'm sorry. I—'

'Stop, Gabriel. There's no need. Listen, get some sleep. Say a prayer, if you like. In the end, life goes on. You have to go on with it. Yes, we who were his friends and comrades will avenge Don. But for now, rest. Oh, and will you tell Eli? I tried to call her, too, but her phone went straight to voicemail. Maybe her network isn't so good in Vietnam.'

Uri's words jolted him back into the present. It was as if he'd forgotten why he was back in the UK. He shook his head. Pushed all thoughts of Don aside. He had to.

'I'm not in Vietnam, Uri. They took Eli. And I need your help to get her back.'

Gabriel explained what had happened, allowing himself more leeway than when he'd had to tell Margot McDonnell. At the end of his story, Uri drew in a deep breath and asked, 'What can I do?'

'First of all, I want to know a bit more about Margot McDonnell,' he said. 'I'm not on the team tracking the terrorists and she ordered me to stand down even in the hunt for Eli. Something's wrong, Uri. Badly. Do you know who she is?'

'Since I last saw you, I've been doing a little unofficial digging on my own account,' Uri said. 'It's why I was still at my desk when you called. When a trusted ally is hit and someone takes their place, I like to know how the chess pieces line up on the board. Official channels aren't always the most profitable route.'

'So?'

'Single. No kids. No living relatives at all, as far as we can tell. According to one of my sources, she was at the Foreign Office until halfway through last year. Long and unexceptional career to date. Then she went on sabbatical. They're doing some more research, but I smell fish, Gabriel. And not the kind you'd eat at a seafood place in Jaffa, either. I'm talking the kind that floats along a poisoned river with half its scales missing and cloudy eyes.'

'You think she's a spook?'

'If she is, it's not the regular kind. My contact inhabits that world and hasn't come across McDonnell before. Says that as far as she has been able to find out, McDonnell has no background in either the armed forces or the intelligence community.'

'What's your best guess?'

'She's been handed The Department to run, and, given its mission and modus operandi, that makes her a very special kind of bureaucrat. So I can think of two possibilities. And, believe me, I have been thinking extremely hard,' he added. 'One, she actually does have a track record in our kind of work and it's been Photoshopped out of existence. Which would make her a very curious beast indeed.'

'Or two?'

'Or two...Well, let me ask you, Gabriel. If you have an organisation with the capability and remit The Department has, and you put a career civil servant with zero relevant experience in charge, why would that be?'

Gabriel ruffled his hair, scratching at his scalp as he pondered Uri's question. He could hear Uri's breathing at the end of the line.

'Because I want things to start going wrong. Either that, or——'

'...or because you wanted evidence digging out that would enable you to close it down.'

'You really think that's it? How could they do away with The Department?'

Uri sighed and Gabriel could picture his shoulders hitching into one of his characteristic shrugs.

'Listen, my friend. I have been in this business a long time. Maybe too long. You and I might feel we are doing good work. But, believe me, there are trends in our community just like everywhere else. Ideas arrive, get debated, blossom into action, then, maybe months, maybe years, maybe decades later, circumstances change and the flowers wither, turn brown and die.'

'But maintaining national security is hardly a trend, is it?' Gabriel protested, unwilling to believe that Uri could see the work they both did as something subject to the whims of fashion.

'Of course not! Protecting national security has been around as long as the nation state. Your Tower of London stands as a monument, literally, to the lengths your monarchs have gone to to protect their kingdom.'

'Then what are you saying?'

'I am saying that somebody, somewhere in your government or one of its agencies, has maybe, and I emphasise that word, Gabriel, *maybe*, decided that resourcing clandestine assassinations has had its day. Maybe they want to focus on quantum cyberwarfare, individually targeted bioweapons, AI agents or cloning super-soldiers.'

'But that's just fantasy! Futurology.'

'Is it? We're working on all of them right now. And if you breathe a word of that you're a dead man, by the way. Not a joke. Look at the way your intelligence resources are structured. You have Five and Six, yes? But also Special Branch, Military Intelligence and The Department. Or look at my country. You know what Aman is, right?'

'The Military Intelligence Directorate.'

Uri grunted his approval of Gabriel's knowledge.

'OK, so how many sub-agencies are there directly beneath Aman? I'll tell you. Eleven. Then you have Mossad, Shabak, the Israeli police intelligence branch and the Centre for Political Research. It's a viper's nest of political ambitions, just like anywhere humans are competing for status and power. And don't get me started on the Americans. They've got anywhere from seventeen to twenty-one separate agencies depending on who you're talking to. I've met these guys, Gabriel. Believe me, sometimes they are praying for somebody to fuck up so they can take over.'

Uri's words were sobering. He was the Deputy Director of Mossad, whereas Gabriel was just a foot soldier, so presumably he knew what he was talking about.

'Uri, I need to find Eli. Will you help me? I've got a feeling McDonnell will shut me down if I try going through Department channels.'

'Of course I will. Just tell me what you need.'

* * *

Despite fearing he'd not be able to sleep at all, Gabriel plunged straight into a deep, dreamless sleep as soon as his head hit the pillow.

Somehow, by the following morning, he'd managed to reach an accommodation with the terrible news of Don's death. He felt the fact of it as a grey cloud louring over him, but he could function. He could think and, more importantly, act. It's what the old man would have wanted, he told himself, and for once, he thought the trite phrase was actually true.

He started calling around everybody he knew who might be able to help him get a lead on Eli's kidnapper. The chances that her disappearance was unconnected to everything else that had been going on was so close to zero he knew he'd be tracking Don's killer, too.

As he ended yet another conversation that was heavy on

promises but light on action, his phone buzzed. As he took in the name on the screen, his mood flashed from despair to joy.

Eli

With a trembling finger, he accepted the call, trying out lines he could use even as the tip of his finger touched the green phone icon.

29

Bakker held the phone to his ear, smiling at Eli. Not some crazy-ass psycho-smile, either. He appeared to be enjoying himself. The muscles around his eyes were relaxed. His skin had a healthy colour to it; beneath the tan she could detect no abnormal blood flow.

He looked her straight in the eye and nodded. Gabriel must be picking up. She could picture her husband on the other end of the line, desperate with worry. She'd thought of calling out, but so had her captor. He'd explained, in vivid, anatomically precise language, why that would be a bad idea.

He inhaled sharply. Gabriel must be talking. Even though she knew it was fruitless to try, she strained to hear his side of the conversation. She imagined Gabriel's responses.

Eli? Oh, thank God.

'No, it's not Eli.'

Who is this?

'It doesn't matter, but you can call me Isaac if you like.'

OK, Isaac, what have you done with her?

'She's perfectly safe.'

Prove it. Let me speak to her.

Eli watched as Bakker stretched out his arm and held the phone in front of her. For the briefest of moments, she considered snatching it from him and smashing it into his face before going for the pistol. Yet again, he seemed to know the contents of her thoughts, and simply shook his head briefly. His knuckles paled fractionally as he gripped the gun tighter.

'Wolfie! I'm fine!' she shouted. 'His name's—'

As calmly as if he was offering her a cup of tea, Bakker levelled the pistol and put a bullet into the wall six inches away from her right hip. She clamped her lips together.

He returned the phone to his ear.

'Say again, Gabriel? I missed that.'

He shook his head.

'That was my pistol. I know how much you like details, so I'll tell you it's a Heckler & Koch USP in .45 ACP. These particular rounds are Hornady jacketed hollow-point. Two-twenty grains. They make quite a mess at close range, as I'm sure you can imagine. I just used it to give Eli a little warning about trying anything rash.' He paused, then looked at Eli. 'No, she's fine.' Another pause. 'No, you can't speak to her again. You'll have to take my word for it.'

As he continued in a bantering tone, Eli refocused, imagining Gabriel's voice again.

What do you want?

'It's probably easier to frame it as what I *don't* want.'

What don't *you want, then?*

'I don't want you to come looking for me. If you do, I'll be forced to adopt an extremely low profile, part of which would, regrettably, involve ditching any extraneous baggage, if you get my drift.'

He winked at Eli and levelled the pistol at her face, puffing out his cheeks and then expelling the air through his pursed lips in a silent mime of a gunshot.

'You see, Gabriel, I had to kill him. His debt fell due. I know that you'll be all fired up to come and find me, deliver the old brass verdict to avenge dear dead Dobbin. But I'm going to be disappearing very soon. I just need a few weeks' grace first. So here's the deal. Stand down. I don't care what the new boss tells you. I don't care what that big old vengeful conscience tells you. I don't care what *God* tells you. You stand down, soldier. At the end of my grace period, I'll release Eli to you in good health and you two lovebirds can resume your live of marital bliss.'

Even if I do what you say, there'll be others looking for you.

'True. But you're the problem for me, Gabriel. Do we have a deal?'

When will you release her? Exactly.

Bakker rolled his eyes. 'Three weeks? Four, tops. Oh, that's funny. Do you remember them? The Four Tops? Alix loved them. Her favourite song was called "Without The One You Love". Which is apt, when you think about it. For both of us.' He cleared his throat. 'So, deal?'

Eli leant back against the wall. Gabriel would say yes. And he wouldn't mean it. Bakker would know that, surely.

Bakker nodded.

'I'm glad to hear it. We'll speak one more time, Gabriel, when I give you instructions for where to find Eli.'

Then he ended the call.

'What did he say?' Eli asked.

'He agreed to my terms, of course.'

'And you believe him?'

'Why, do you think I shouldn't?'

She clamped her lips together. She'd begun to suspect that while he might appear to enjoy their exchanges, he was working according to a pre-arranged plan that was locked down tight in that scrambled brain of his. He might think the Taliban's attempts to brainwash him had failed but even so, three years of psychological torture? Drugs? Beatings? Starvation? Sensory deprivation? You didn't emerge from that kind of hell without being severely compromised.

'Fine,' he said, pocketing the phone. 'On your feet. We're leaving.'

She did as he said, wondering as she did so whether they'd

have had enough time to get a fix on the cell tower transmitting Bakker's message. She doubted it. Bakker would know details like that. He'd have timed the call to perfection.

'Face the wall,' he said.

She turned and then was seized by a wave of dread. He was going to execute her. All that talk about hollow-point rounds. As every muscle tensed involuntarily, he spoke again, dispelling that fear, only to replace it with another.

'How would you like to leave here? On your feet, or in a wheelchair?'

'What?'

'I need to put some restraints on you. But I am acutely aware of your prowess with Krav Maga,' he said, pronouncing the name of the Israeli martial art perfectly. 'If you try anything, which would include altering the position of any of your limbs by so much as a millimetre, I'll have to shoot you through your lumbar spine. I'll make sure I miss all the major blood vessels, but it will leave you paralysed. Far less convenient for me, though I'll manage.'

Something about his calmness was more unnerving than any amount of shouting and bullying. Eli placed her wrists together in the small of her back and waited, immobile, for him to handcuff her.

As he zipped her wrists together with a cable tie, she tensed her arm muscles. It wasn't as obvious as holding the wrists apart, but it would give a little flex once the ties were secure.

'Ever ride horses?' he asked, surprising her with the seeming randomness of the question. 'I did all the time when I was growing up. My favourite horse was called Martha. She was a lovely old thing but she had this trick of taking a deep breath just as you tightened the girth. She caught me out once. I swung myself into the saddle and she let her breath out. The saddle swung round and I ended up on my arse in the stable yard, much to everyone's amusement.' He paused. 'Let's have those wrists nice and relaxed, yes?'

He cinched the cable tie tighter and checked with a finger

between her wrists for good measure. Pronouncing himself satisfied, he led her out.

She blinked as strong sunlight dazzled her. Once her eyes had adjusted, she was able to open them. They were on a beach. In other circumstances she would have called it idyllic.

It was prettier even than the one she'd been staying on so recently. Curving palm trees leaning towards sun-flecked turquoise water. The odd seashell poking out of the fine white sand as if placed there by a stylist for a holiday brochure. And totally deserted.

She thought it was likely they were still in Vietnam. The only other coastline near enough would be Guangxi Province or Hainan Island. She doubted Bakker would want to invite any sort of scrutiny from the Chinese authorities.

She turned. The house where he'd imprisoned her was substantial, with solid wooden walls, pierced at the extreme left end by two high, narrow windows.

'Not bad for an ex-assassin,' she said.

'It belongs to a friend. One last thing.'

He switched her phone off then placed it on a flat stone and hammered it with another until it shattered. He gathered up the pieces and hurled them into the water.

'My truck's out the back. Come on.'

He drove her to a small grass airstrip carved out of the jungle where a light plane stood waiting, its leather-jacketed pilot smoking a small cigar. He seemed even more relaxed than Bakker. Eyelids drooping, full lips curved into a lazy smile around the cheroot. Elvis Presley was crooning from an old transistor radio whose silver paint had worn away to reveal dull blue plastic beneath.

He pushed himself into an upright position and sauntered over.

'*Bonjour*, Kevin. *Ça va?*'

Bakker nodded. '*Je suis* just dandy, thanks, Perec.' He turned to Eli. 'Out.'

Eli climbed out of the Jeep, almost tripping on the sill before righting herself.

'Careful, madame,' the pilot said, looking her up and down. 'You do not want to 'urt that delightful *derrière* of yours.'

His accent was that of a Frenchman who'd spent a long time away from home. She detected a Southeast Asian inflection to some of the words. He must have been approaching seventy. She wondered if he'd been out here since the Vietnam war. His pupils were pinpoints. He was strung-out, but on what? Heroin? Lots of men had got hooked while on active duty.

Eli smiled at him. 'Why don't you come over and give me a hand, then?'

Perec shook his head and raised his shoulders in a loose shrug.

'What, and 'ave my *couilles* kicked up into my throat? Non, *merci*.'

'That's enough!' Bakker snapped, his easy-going persona abruptly replaced with something altogether crisper. 'Is she fuelled up?'

Perec nodded.

'Let's go then.'

'Where are you taking me?' Eli asked as he prodded her forwards with the H&K's muzzle.

'You'll love it.'

The last thing she felt as she clambered into her seat behind the pilot was a sharp sting in the side of her neck. A hornet? A fly? Gabriel turned round from the pilot's seat. 'Sorry, El,' he said in a thick French accent, 'I think he just poured you another Gaza martini.'

30

Gabriel stared at the phone. Something about Isaac's voice had sent the sense of a memory thrumming through him like a bass note on a piano, but he couldn't grasp it or bring it into any kind of focus. None of that mattered right now.

The main thing was, Eli was alive. And she was unharmed. She'd also given him one piece of intelligence and one request.

To anyone listening in, including her captor, those three words: 'Wolfie! I'm fine,' would have been the expected outburst from a desperate captive. But between them, Gabriel and Eli had created a simple code for just such an eventuality.

The name they used would indicate the basics of the enemy's national or racial identity. All the way from Gabriel/Eliyah for white European to Angel/Yah-yah for Chinese. Wolfie/Kitty-cat was reserved for white British.

Then there were the other two words. You could tell a loved one or field commander you were OK in dozens of different ways. And they'd ascribed different instructions to all of them. 'I'm fine' meant *no trade possible, extraction essential*. Whether or not the captive was unharmed now, their assessment was that the enemy had no intention of releasing them.

But that wasn't all. Because he could tell something important from what Eli hadn't said. Tack on the endearment, 'babe' to whichever name you chose and it signalled the captor was part of a radical Islamic group. 'Baby' meant Western terrorists. 'Darling' meant organised crime. Eli had used none of them. Her captor was flying solo.

He ran over Isaac's side of their conversation, analysing every sentence for deeper meanings or revelations about his character, background or motivations.

What had he said? Gabriel closed his eyes.

'You see, Gabriel, I had to kill him. His debt fell due. I know that you'll be all fired up to come and find me, deliver the old brass verdict to avenge dear dead Dobbin.'

It sounded as though Gabriel's earlier supposition was right on the money. Isaac was ex-Department. He'd talked about Don's debt. It was possible to interpret that phrase in various ways, but as someone who'd killed to avenge past wrongs, Gabriel thought he knew exactly what Isaac was talking about. Betrayal.

For a fighting man, that meant a commander leaving for you dead in the field. Gabriel knew all too well what that felt like, had experienced his own murderous rages at those who had betrayed him and his men.

He went upstairs to the room they used as an office and dragged a whiteboard out from a corner and opened out the easel. He popped the cap on a marker and started writing down what he knew about the man he'd fought with in Jerusalem and who was now holding Eli captive.

Enemy = 'Isaac' = probably ex-Department

StrengthsWeaknesses

Pro tactical skillsUnderestimates Eli

Underwater captureMentally unstable?

Restraint/containmentRevenge blinds him?

Evasion/survival

Weapon/sAppearance
H&K USP6'0", athletic build
Others?Piercing blue eyes, heavy beard

Motivation: feels betrayed by Don
Others in firing line?

As Gabriel wrote this last line, the ringing alarm bell that had faded as he worked clanged back into his awareness, demanding attention. Eli, obviously. But Isaac had taken her to keep Gabriel from pursuing him. Fat chance! Even without Eli's coded message he'd resolved immediately to go after the man who'd taken her. This was never going to be ended by negotiation.

Isaac had claimed he needed a grace period before disappearing. He didn't want to be caught before then. But why release Eli afterwards? She'd presumably seen his face, heard his voice, watched him walk. He could get his appearance altered, but however good the plastic surgeon was, there were things nobody could disguise forever. Sooner or later The Department would catch up with him. So he had to kill her. A chill ran through Gabriel. Because, in Isaac's shoes, that's exactly what he would do.

His phone rang.

'Wolfe.'

'Gabriel, it's Sam Flack.'

As well as quartermastering for MI6, Sam fulfilled the same role for The Department when something beyond straightforward firearms was needed. They'd worked together on a couple of operations in the past and he counted her a friend.

'Hi, Sam. What is it?'

'I've been working on the truck bomb for the last couple of

weeks. I thought you could come and take a look at what we've got. I could use a second pair of eyes on something.'

'Sounds mysterious.'

'I'll send you our location.'

* * *

After a ninety-minute fast drive due west under the big skies of eastern England's endlessly flat agricultural landscape, Gabriel reached Milton, a small blue-collar town about three miles north of Cambridge.

The town had a forlorn but tough air about it, like an alcoholic taking a long and rocky road to redemption. If the ex-boozer had thumbed a ride in Gabriel's Jaguar that day, he would have seen an old ash tree that had fallen some time in the night, partially blocking the carriageway, so that Gabriel had to inch past it, offside wheels sinking in the soft earth on the opposite verge before regaining the tarmac.

Once past the obstruction, Gabriel pushed the throttle pedal into the carpet, enjoying a brief blat along the Ely Road before his satnav instructed him to turn right in three hundred yards. With the powerful brakes forcing the tyres into a protesting shudder, Gabriel slowed for the turn and swung in to a short access road ending in spike-tipped metal gates.

Sam's location turned out to be a vast warehouse equidistant from Cambridge and Ely, as if the developers couldn't decide which of the two great cathedral cities they wanted it closer to.

From the outside, clad in smooth, flat panels in graded shades of blue, it might have been an e-commerce fulfilment centre. One of the few dependable sources of regular work outside farming in that part of the world, they'd appeared all over the eastern counties in recent years, sprouting almost overnight out of the soil like enormous cuboid fungi.

But the folk turning up for work to spend their days picking and packing everything from wireless speakers to garden furniture weren't generally required to pass through a security gate including armed guards manning a red-and-white pole barrier. Nor, despite the lurid tales that appeared in the media from time to time concerning personal freedom while at work, were they hemmed in by mile upon mile of razor wire.

After showing his Department ID and waiting until Sam confirmed their appointment, Gabriel drove down a concrete access road before parking in front of an opaque-glass door.

Inside, he walked past a row of glassed-in offices constructed out of aluminium framework and white-painted drywall into the working area. Here was an echoing cathedral of a place, so big he couldn't begin to compute how many football pitches it might comfortably house. He'd taken off from smaller aerodromes. It was cold, too, as if it had its own climate independent of the warmer spring weather outside.

In the distance, he saw a figure in dark overalls, clipboard in hand, standing in the midst of what appeared to be a plane crash. The figure turned, and waved to Gabriel. As he drew closer to Sam, the wreckage resolved itself into a mixture of masonry, burnt and twisted metal, shattered glass, mangled office furniture and thousands of small, blackened chunks of debris.

Sam's overalls were stained and streaked with what looked like grease and ash. In place of her usual brightly-coloured Converse baseball boots, she wore heavy brown leather safety shoes, their bulbous toes concealing steel toecaps. She greeted him with a brief smile and a kiss on both cheeks.

'Hi, Gabriel, thanks for coming. You heard about Don, I suppose?'

'Yes. Have they repatriated his body yet?'

'They have. There has to be an autopsy so there's no date for the funeral yet. It should be a pretty well-attended affair though. You and Eli'll be there?'

'I will. And I hope she will be, too.'

Sam frowned. 'Why? What's the matter?'

'The person who killed Don and did this,' he said, spreading his arm in a half-circle, 'has kidnapped her.'

'Oh, Jesus, Gabriel, I'm so sorry. What's The Department doing about it?'

'They've put a team on it. I'm not involved, although clearly I should be, but the new boss, McDonnell, have you met her, she thinks—'

He realised he was gabbling and clamped his lips.

'But you're working on a rescue, yes?'

'Me? Oh, you can rely on that. The thing is, Sam, I think he's ex-Department.'

She nodded. 'Maybe what I want to show you will help you identify him, then. It's very odd. I've never seen anything like it before. Come with me.'

She led him away from the moraine of bomb-blasted debris and into the nearest of the offices. A long white-topped table dominated the rectangular space, which was otherwise furnished conventionally with a black mesh-backed swivel chair and a functional wooden desk with a PC.

Standing beside Sam, Gabriel looked at the small assemblage of burnt and melted items arrayed before him. He saw a green fragment of printed circuit board, charred along one edge, from which snaked short lengths of blue, white, brown and red wire. A curved triangle of black plastic containing four identical oval holes and two more filled with numbered buttons: a 5 and a 7. And a 10cm strip of thin, twisted metal punctuated with small circular holes.

Sam tapped the metal strip with her index finger.

'What do you make of that?'

'Can I touch it?'

'Go ahead. The heat burnt it clean of any prints or DNA, though we did check,' she added with a quick smile.

He picked it up, turning it in his hands.

'The last time I held a piece of Meccano, I was about ten,' he said. 'My dad bought me a set for my birthday.'

'It's an odd choice for an IED, though,' Sam said. 'A little bit over-engineered, wouldn't you say? You only need a thick rubber band to hold the phone onto the charge. That or some duct tape.

This was built to last.'

Something was nagging at Gabriel's memory. It was connected to Isaac. That voice. Echoes reverberating through time, calling to him. He closed his eyes. Because he was on the cusp of something.

Finally, he recognised him. The beard and moustache had foxed him when he'd been chasing him in the Judaean hills. He brought the Meccano strip close to his nose, inhaled and held it, letting the faint smell of burnt metal permeate his memory.

He was sitting in a flyblown flat on the top floor of a block scarred with craters from fifty-cal machine gun fire on the northern outskirts of Kandahar. The warm air blowing in from outside brought with it the smells of cooking: frying cumin seeds, grilled lamb and freshly baked naan breads, aromatic with garlic, flat-leaf parsley and caramelised onions.

Nine stories down, feral mutts barked in the streets, fighting over food discarded by one of the many street vendors plying everything from chicken *kabob* to the deep-fried pastries resembling Western doughnuts and known locally as *khoujoor*.

Beside him, humming as he soldered wires onto a circuit board was a man. Like Gabriel, he wore *perahan tunban*, the traditional male Afghan dress of tunic-style shirt and loose trousers. His hair was full of dust and tied back from his face. A bushy beard covered the lower half of his fac.

'Hand me that box, would you?' he asked Gabriel, holding out his right hand, palm-upwards, though his gaze never left the mobile phone he was about to wire into a detonator.

Gabriel reached for a small cardboard box. The man slid off the lid to reveal a selection of Meccano strips, oxidised bare metal visible between the scabbed patches of green and blue paint. Gabriel looked at him, eyebrows raised.

The man looked back and smiled. 'Vintage. I buy it on eBay. The new stuff's got no soul.'

Then he selected a piece about 20cm long and, using a pair of pliers, bent it through a series of right-angles until he'd fashioned a bracket that would fit around the mobile phone.

Gabriel nodded in appreciation.

'This is a first for me. An artisanal IED. You're a true craftsman, K—'

Heart racing, he opened his eyes and uttered the man's name aloud.

'Kevin! His name's Kevin Bakker. That's his trademark.'

Sam nodded. 'Why did I know you'd come through?'

'Something's been nagging at me ever since Jerusalem. But I couldn't pin it down. My PTSD has been a little more troublesome than usual recently.'

'I can see how that might have happened,' Sam said dryly.

'Anyway, he called me yesterday. His voice sounded familiar. I think it was starting to come back. I'd already worked out the bomber was a former member of The Department.'

Sam's eyes widened. 'Really?'

'Kevin and I worked an op together in Afghanistan five years ago. The first part went down OK, but the second was a total shit-show. I was ambushed by a Taliban patrol on the way to pick Kevin up. It got pretty kinetic. I ended up fighting the last two hand-to-hand. I killed them with a rock.' Gabriel sighed. 'By the time I got to the extraction point, he'd gone. There was blood everywhere. I recovered a sample and took it back to the UK. It was Kevin's. We all assumed the Taliban had taken him and killed him before dumping the body. It was a total nightmare.'

'So, we have a name. And there'll be a personnel file on him at,' she paused, 'oh, shit.'

'Rothford,' Gabriel said in a flat voice. 'In the admin block. It wasn't just about sending a message. He was covering his tracks.'

'But there are digital files, surely?'

He shook his head. 'Never have been. Too vulnerable.'

'Isn't that a bit, I don't know,' Sam said, waggling her head, 'pre-decimal?'

Gabriel rolled his eyes. 'It's pre-industrial, Sam. But it's how Don wanted it. He told me once. He said, "The only way you can hack that filing cabinet is with an axe, Old Sport".'

He felt tears pricking at his eyes, and swallowed down the lump that had suddenly formed in his throat.

'You miss him, don't you?' Sam asked, laying a hand on his arm.

'Of course I do! We all do.'

Sam pointed at the scattered IED components before them.

'We'll get him, Gabriel. Now we know who he is, it's only a matter of time.'

'Which is the one thing I don't have. He's got Eli, remember? I have to find her.'

'Did he say why he took her? Does he want a ransom?'

'No, and that's what worries me. He said he's holding her as an insurance policy so I won't come after him until he can disappear, but Eli told me to come and get her. That means she doesn't believe him.'

'Then you should go after her. And anything you need, come to me, yes?'

'Thanks, Sam. I will.'

With that, he left Sam to the remains of The Department's Essex headquarters and drove back to Aldeburgh. He needed to plan his next move.

31

He turns, heart fluttering in his chest like a songbird in a cage of twisted wire.

She is walking up the aisle on her father's arm. She looks radiant. Her long white dress sweeps the floor, brushing a path through scattered rose petals. Behind her, the two bridesmaids have serious faces as they hold her train aloft.

As his father-in-law-to-be hands her off, she turns to him and smiles. Beneath the veil studded with pearls, he sees a single tear tracking down her left cheek. It's a beautiful transparent red, like a ruby.

So are the pearls stitched into her veil. They are tear-shaped, and, as he watches, they start to slide across the net and coalesce into larger droplets, then runnels and suddenly they are flowing down her face and dripping onto her bodice, staining it scarlet...

...and there is a roaring in his ears as the church crumbles around them, blocks of white masonry falling from the ceiling and crushing the vicar, the best man, the little bridesmaids, their families, friends, comrades until the air is riven by the screams of the dying...

...and she is screaming too, dissolving before his eyes and then she is just a pink mist hanging in the air in front of him before the hot, dry wind blows across the rocky highway and scatters Alix's atoms into the mountains of Kandahar...

...and he wakes, panting, clutching his chest where the muscles are contracting so hard he believes he is having a heart attack until the realisation hits him, just as it did the previous night, and the night before that, and that, and that and that and that...

Alix is dead.

He wipes a hand over his face, which is slick with sweat. He climbs out of bed, leaving the soaking sheets behind him to cool, and dresses in running gear. Outside it is beginning to get light. He checks his watch. It is 4:26 a.m. Overhead, the Hebridean cloudscape is underlit with sun the glowing pink of pomegranate seeds.

Sighing, he sets off towards the beach, down a track once used by crofters but now only by him and the very occasional guest, such as the Israeli woman currently sleeping in the locked guest bedroom of his cottage.

As he runs, he bats at the sides of his head, trying to silence the voice of his dead wife urging him to run into the sea and keep going.

You'll feel so much better, she says. *You can come and join me.*

'No, Alix, I can't!' he yells into the wind blowing across the banks of seaweed on the beach stranded by the low tide.

It smells of iodine, which makes him think of wound dressings. He shudders and runs on. A new voice speaks. It's the Taliban, who first spoke to him when he woke up. He told Bakker to call him Gibril. Or did he? Isn't that just the Arabic version of Gabriel? It doesn't matter. Nothing much matters anymore.

You should kill her now. You'll have to, sooner or later. And what about those infidels still running The Department? They deserve to feel Allah's wrath, too.

He sprints, arms pumping, trying to outrun the voice.

But Gibril's voice keeps pace with him easily. It's in his own head, after all.

Tell Wolfe to do it. To kill them all. Use her as leverage. He'll do it. He'll do anything you tell him, anything at all, as long as he thinks he's saving her.

He runs on, mile after mile, until his lungs are scorched from the cold air and his legs are burning. He staggers to a halt and collapses onto the sand, grabbing handfuls of the stuff and flinging them high into the air over his head so damp clods rain down over him, getting into his hair, his eyes...and he screams and pleads with Alix to stop but it's not going to work and he grabs more sand and stuffs his ears with it, pushing his palms against them and trying to block out her insistent demands...

After a while, he gets to his feet. Snorting the snot back down his throat, he cleans out his ears as best he can and jogs back to the cottage. He is smiling now, because, despite being only a figment of his imagination, Gibril's suggestion was, actually, strategically A1, tip-top, tippy-top. Yes, that's what he'd do. And he'd demand proof as well.

He runs back to the cottage and, after showering and changing, makes the call.

32

Gabriel hadn't long got back to the house in Aldeburgh when his
phone rang.

'Wolfe.'

'Gibril, I mean Gabriel. This is Isaac. I have a job for you. An
op, if you like. Targets, the whole nine yards.'

'Let me speak to Eli.'

'No. Now listen. Who runs The Department now?'

'A woman called Margot McDonnell. Listen to me. I need to
hear Eli's voice. I need to know she's all right.'

'She's fine. I haven't been mistreating her in any way. I want
McDonnell dead.'

'You're crazy. I can't do that.'

'Then I'll kill your wife, Gabriel, and I'll send her back to you
in pieces. You know I will.'

'Listen,' Gabriel said, steadying his pulse, 'Kevin. I remember
you now. Your name's Kevin Bakker, isn't it? We worked on that
op back in Kandahar in 2017.'

'My name is Isaac. Abraham, he— No! Nonono.' Gabriel
heard a hard percussive sound. Had Bakker just slapped himself?
'Webster sacrificed me. You did, too. You tried to take my place.

But I waited, Gibril, I waited and I suffered and I prayed every night to God to deliver me from evil and forgive us our trespasses so we can, can...get revenge. So I can have my revenge. You have two weeks. And I want proof.'

'Kevin, please. You're—'

The phone went dead in Gabriel's hand. He placed it on the table and poured himself a drink. Bakker was mad. The Taliban hadn't brainwashed him, they'd broken him.

* * *

After showering and changing into fresh clothes, Gabriel left the house. It felt too claustrophobic, and every room reminded him of Eli. He set off up the road on foot, heading for the Martello tower, the old defensive fort that marked the end of any kind of man-made development on that particular stretch of coast.

As he walked, he revolved the central problem in his head: just where was Bakker holding Eli? He'd taken her in Vietnam, so realistically he could be anywhere in the world. But would he be? Or would he want to operate from somewhere he felt safe?

From the sound of his voice, and the way he kept slipping into Biblical phrases and oddly disjointed rants about Don, who he kept calling Abraham, he was coming apart at the seams. Surely that would make him crave some sort of security, even if it was only mental?

Gabriel crunched across the stones and down to the sea where the waves were throwing themselves in over the shingle. He picked up a handful of stones and began hurling them out into the iron-grey water.

'Where are you, Kevin?' he asked Eli's kidnapper as he flung one stone after another into the sea. 'Where do you feel safe?'

The level of vetting they all underwent before joining The Department was extreme. Nothing was kept back from the interviewers and investigators. They didn't so much use a fine-tooth comb on your life as put it under a scanning electron microscope. If there was a clue to Bakker's psychological landscape, times or places that held special significance for him, they'd be in the files.

Gabriel let the last stone in his hand fly and cursed loudly.

Because, as he'd already established with Sam, all the personnel files were in Don's office, now reduced to a pile of rubble by Bakker's IED.

Or were they? Had he actually seen the blast site with his own eyes? No. He had not.

That was the place to start then, wasn't it? At MOD Rothford.

* * *

At the gate, the soldier on duty, whom Gabriel recognised, strolled out from the gatehouse and walked round to the driver's side of Gabriel's car.

'Morning, sir,' he said. 'Oh, it's you, Mr Wolfe. Nice new wheels. What happened to the Camaro?'

'Too big for British roads, John,' he answered. 'She's in storage.'

The soldier grinned. 'If you ever need someone to give her a spin, make sure nothing seizes up, I'd be happy to volunteer my services.'

Gabriel smiled. 'You're first on the list. I need to see the offices, please.'

John wrinkled his nose. 'Not much left to see, I'm afraid. Bastard more or less flattened the place. But you're accredited, so it's your call. Got your MOD 90?'

Gabriel showed his pass and John signalled to the guard inside the gatehouse to raise the pole and admit Gabriel.

As he trundled the Jaguar around the perimeter road, he had to slide over until the nearside wheels were on the grass to allow a flat-bed truck to pass. In his rear-view mirror he saw that its load space was weighed down with huge chunks of masonry and twisted metalwork.

Turning down the access road, he came to the tattered

remains of a police cordon: blue-and-white tape flapping from posts driven into the soft earth to each side of the tarmac.

Beyond the cordon he could see the site of the explosion. It whisked him back to other conflict zones, other times: sun-bleached Middle Eastern towns already ravaged by decades of warfare suddenly plunged into new and terrifying depths of devastation by truck bombs or lone actors in suicide vests.

He parked beside a white transit van marked with the name of a local building firm. He climbed out, stretched and rolled his neck on his shoulders. With the car's engine plinking and ticking as it cooled, he walked over to the edge of the crater left by Bakker's IED.

It was five feet deep at least, and thirty across. The sides revealed the archaeology of the site, from the layers of concrete and hardcore to the tawny earth beneath. Halfway down was a thin black layer before the reddish brown earth reappeared all the way down to the scooped bottom of the crater.

As he stared down into the abyss, a couple of men in hard hats and hi-vis vests came out of the shell of the admin block, carrying a length of twisted steel I-beam between them.

'Hey, you!' one called out. 'You can't be here, mate. Not unless you've got clearance. This is a restricted area.'

He turned to them and waited for them to dump the mangled steel on the ground.

'I *have* got clearance,' he said, showing them his ID. 'I need to get inside.'

The guy who'd spoken glanced at his Department ID then at Gabriel. 'I wouldn't recommend it. There's all kinds of shit could fall on you, trip you up. It's a health and safety nightmare.'

By way of answer, Gabriel pointed at the transit van.

'Have you got a spare hard hat in there?'

The guy shrugged, an elegant *It's your funeral* gesture.

'Door's unlocked. Knock yourself out.'

'Literally,' the other guy said, earning a wry laugh from his gaffer.

From the back of the van, Gabriel took a yellow hard hat and adjusted the inner plastic band until it fitted. He added a hi-vis vest and then picked up a pair of heavy-duty gloves the dark red of veinous blood.

'OK if I borrow these, too?'

'Just put them back when you're done.'

He nodded then made his way inside the shell of the building from which, until recently, Don Webster had run The Department's operations. So far, Gabriel had been doing a reasonable job of ignoring the pull of grief he felt over his old CO's murder. But now, as he inhaled the sickening stench of burnt building materials and took in the shattered interior of the admin block, it assailed him once more.

With tears in his eyes that he knew had nothing to do with the acrid chemical stink pervading the wreckage, he picked his way over the rubble, into the depths of the building, or what remained of it.

He checked over his shoulder that he was out of sight of the two men, then he sank down into the embrace of a sagging sofa, one half blown clean away but the remainder weirdly intact. Covering his eyes with his palms, he wept. Wept for Don Webster. But mostly for himself.

All his adult life, he'd given everything to his country. He'd risked his life, and that of his men, to protect her interests abroad and her citizens at home. He'd taken bullets, been sliced open by knives and bayonets; he'd been beaten into unconsciousness, tortured, and almost turned into a human bomb himself.

He'd never expected much in return, certainly not money. And he'd had his fill of decorations after being awarded the Military Cross in the Bosnian war. That conflict had confronted him with horrors that still woke him in the night, sweating and shaking as he fought to forget the vile images of degradation and abuse visited on innocent people by so-called soldiers.

So why had he done it?

He realised it was mostly because Don Webster had asked him to. Theirs had always been a relationship based on more than the army hierarchy that gave Don a colonel's two pips and a crown, and Gabriel a captain's three pips. Fariyah had put her finger on it during one of their early sessions, when Gabriel's PTSD was threatening to overwhelm him.

'Is it possible you see Don as a replacement for your father?' she'd asked.

He'd denied it that time. And the time after that. But away from Fariyah's consulting room – perhaps out on the boat or halfway across Dartmoor with a tent on his back and nothing but miles of nothingness in every direction – he'd gradually allowed himself to admit to the truth.

Fariyah was right. Zhao Xi had been more like a favourite uncle, with his exciting offering of martial arts and ancient Eastern disciplines for mastering his mind, and those of others. But in Don Webster, Gabriel had found something of his father. A sense of stability, of duty, of a clear and unequivocal sense of right and wrong.

Which was odd, given the shadowy world he'd inherited after leaving the Regiment to run The Department, where black and white were replaced with shades of grey and my enemy's enemy was my friend until they weren't, at which point they'd be wiped out with zero fucks given.

And now the Old Man was dead. Shot at Gabriel's own wedding blessing by an assailant who'd been following his orders and felt himself betrayed when the world had turned maybe just half a degree off true, enough to throw a handful of sand into the fine-running gears of his final operation for The Department.

His final, and Gabriel's third. An early lesson that however black the op, however far off the books it was, however cutting-edge the tech and lethal the firepower, shit still happened to fighting men, just as surely as night followed day.

The Old Man was dead, and Eli was missing, held by the same broken man who'd placed his trust in Don and been let down.

Was this the universe trying to tell him something? Pursue a normal life and see where it gets you? Happiness is for other people? For you, a life of pain and loss, set to repeat for all eternity?

He ground his teeth together, fighting to dispel the dark mood that had engulfed him. It was nothing of the kind. Trying and failing to remember something Zhao Xi might have said on the subject, Gabriel coined his own mantra.

If you don't like the hand life deals you, burn the cards and start over.

He rubbed his eyes and climbed off the canted-over sofa. Somewhere inside this ruined shell of a building lay the clue that would help him locate Kevin Bakker. And when he found it, there would be a great deal of card-burning.

33

Gabriel passed through the shattered remains of a set of double doors, their wire-reinforced circular portholes blown clear across the hallway and embedded in the walls beyond.

It immediately became clear that the internal walls had greatly diminished the force of the explosion. With each yard into the building that the blast wave had penetrated, its power had lessened. Strong enough on first contact with the outer walls to reduce them to brick-dust, here it had knocked out sections of masonry and smashed windows, but left the essential structures unchanged.

He followed the familiar path down the carpeted corridor, past the photos he always stopped to admire. The soldier beneath a frozen rain of tumbling .50 calibre shell casings. The saloon car captured at the point of bursting outwards as a car bomb was detonated. The group of grinning men in desert camo, lounging against a Land Rover bristling with machine guns, their wild beards and headbands giving them the anarchic look of pirates or brigands from some Erroll Flynn movie.

His boots crunched on glass where the glazed door to a boxed-in wooden noticeboard had been shattered. A torn A4 poster still pinned to the green baize inside advised members of staff that the annual barbecue would be taking place on the last Friday of May.

Then he arrived at Don's old office. He stretched out a finger and traced the name on the slide-in aluminium panel between wooden rails.

D. WEBSTER

He slid the thin strip of laser-cut aluminium out of its slot and, after a quick glance left and right, slid it into an inside pocket.

Then he opened the door.

It was as if the catastrophe that had decimated the building and personnel that constituted The Department had somehow been repelled by a forcefield emanating from Don's inner sanctum. Everything was just as Gabriel remembered from his last visit, for a mission debrief. The desk with its ageing PC and pencil pot fashioned from a cut-down 100mm tank-gun shell. The visitor chair, upholstered in well-worn royal-blue fabric, shiny on the front edge. The circular conference table pushed against the wall, currently marked by a couple of coffee-rings.

Actually, not everything. Not quite. Because in the corner behind Don's desk, a rectangle was impressed into the carpet, the fibres mashed down until they lay horizontal. Leading away from the front edge of the rectangle were a pair of inch-wide tracks. The filing cabinet holding The Department's records was gone.

Gabriel cursed himself again. How could he have been so stupid? Of course it was gone! What, did he think that Margot McDonnell or whoever had been first on the scene would have left unattended possibly the most sensitive security records in the UK?

It might have been unhackable, it might have been accessible only to a handful of people with the highest level of clearance, but it was still just a big metal box. They'd just put the whole thing on a trolley and wheeled it out of there. That's what he could see: rubber-wheel tracks. Even now, it was probably locked in some vault in Whitehall while Margot Mc-bloody-Donnell decided what she wanted to do with it.

Gabriel thought he could guess. It would be digitised first, placed inside Byzantine levels of encryption, access restrictions and biometric security, then the papers would be burnt and even the ashes destroyed, dissolved in acid and flushed into the sewers below the Ministry of Defence.

Which, he reflected, was just as well. Would he be happy if every last detail of his own operations were uncovered by WikiLeaks? Like the time he killed one of the very few honest politicians in an African country after being fed a false narrative by the then prime minister of the UK?

Or his own deadly role in terminating the life of a second premier while he was supposedly in an impregnable prison on the UK mainland. The first man had most assuredly not deserved to die; the second signed his own death warrant. But in neither case was there much evidence of the rule of law.

On balance, he thought not.

He ran a hand over his mouth. Christ! With a piercing clarity he'd never faced before, he saw himself, and his colleagues, as the outside world might. No, not 'might'. How it *would* see them. As contract killers. Hitmen…and women. The only difference was, their client was the state, instead of a cartel or an organised crime group. Don's wry remark when he'd hired him echoed down the years. 'The job's pretty simple, Old Sport. You find trouble…and you shoot it.'

The problem was, the media, the armchair generals, the keyboard warriors on Twitter: they loved having the freedom to rail against injustice, to decry over-mighty state security institutions, but they had a child's insight into the cost of that freedom.

They thought democracy was some sort of natural system, as immutable as evolution or the law of gravity. Whereas people like Gabriel and Eli, even Kevin Bakker, knew that there were people for whom those ideas were little more than competing theories jostling for headspace with their own alternative conceptions of reality.

Tyrants, terrorists, twisted personalities of every imaginable flavour: they all fancied a shot at running things their way. And unlike the people venting in 280 characters or marching about perceived injustices or infringements of their rights, they tended to reach for guns and bombs rather than placards and Instagram accounts.

So, The Department. And its counterparts in other countries. In the world he inhabited, the existence of these outfits was accepted with as little shock as one might greet the rising sun on a new morning. It happened. Maybe the levels of oversight, terms of engagement and methods varied, but the concept had proved surprisingly durable.

But what happened when one of the instruments of that durable concept felt he had been betrayed by the very system that employed him?

He went rogue.

And now he had Eli.

Gabriel's only chance of finding him lay in a four-drawer steel filing cabinet, whose location he could only guess at. But there was one person who definitely wouldn't need to guess. And it was she who Gabriel intended to visit next.

* * *

In her office, McDonnell was standing by the window, talking over her shoulder to a middle-aged man with a military bearing who was all but standing to attention in the centre of the carpet. He wore a well-cut pinstripe suit, a Royal Artillery regimental tie – crimson zig-zags over navy – a dark-blue shirt with contrasting white collar and cuffs, and a pair of black Oxfords polished to a mirror shine.

'He says Bakker's got his wife. Is that possible?' McDonnell asked him.

'Anything's possible, Ma'am. He was an outstanding field agent even before he joined The Department.'

'Can we get her back, do you think?'

'Do we know where she is?'

'She was taken in Vietnam.'

'She could be anywhere by now.'

McDonnell turned to face him.

'So, what you're saying is, we don't have sufficient resources to locate and free her.'

The military man opened his mouth. He was about to demur, to tell his new boss that they'd never considered lack of resources when one of their own had been in trouble before. He caught the narrowed eyes and tight lips and performed a mental swerve.

'Eli knew the risks when she signed on.'

McDonnell nodded. 'Exactly. If we find her with Bakker, it's a bonus. But no separate search, yes?'

'Understood.'

He executed a smart about-turn, not quite parade ground standard but still a reasonable echo of his years in uniform, and left her alone.

McDonnell sat behind her desk and spread her hands out on its glass surface, enjoying the cool touch against her palms. She allowed herself a small smile. Bakker had done her a favour. She'd been manoeuvring against Webster for years, gathering little snippets of intelligence on operations that had exceeded their remits, or caused civilian casualties along with the targets.

She sighed and shook her head. All that covert assassination stuff was so twentieth century. The modern world was controlled from cyberspace, a place Don Webster had obviously never visited. You didn't need to kill someone to render them powerless. You could just blacken their name or mess around with their finances.

Want to destroy an Islamic hate preacher? Link his organisation to secret donations from the Israeli state and that was his credibility blown into smaller pieces than any number of IEDs under his car could manage. Need an arms dealer taking out of circulation? Divert funds from a Russian crime gang into his personal account, then leak it and stand back while they did your dirty work for you.

She supposed that there might come a point when she needed some wet work doing. But why assume all that risk and dent one's own career prospects when there were already plenty of arms of the state equipped for that sort of requirement?

For now, the demise of The Department's figurehead at the hands of a former agent had played right into her hands. It had outgrown its usefulness, as had its agents.

Time for a change.

34

Eli stared at the man eating soup and crusty bread opposite her at the small, scrubbed pine table. Most of the time, Bakker appeared perfectly at ease, as if they had hired a cottage on this remote, uninhabited island to get away from it all. He was quite happy to make conversation, and they'd discussed everything from books and films they enjoyed to the relative merits of Israeli versus Dutch cuisine.

But then there would be nights when she'd be woken by his screams, which would continue long into the night, robbing both of them of sleep. The first time it had happened, she'd caught very little. It sounded like gibberish. But then, on subsequent nights, he'd yelled out in Arabic, a language she spoke fluently.

'Spare me, spare your loyal servant. No, take me instead of her. She deserves to live. I am Isaac. You are Abraham. You can take me and leave her be. I beg you, I plead with you, father.'

The woman who deserved to live was obviously Alix, his wife. Was Abraham Don?

She'd asked him about it the following morning, but Bakker had claimed he didn't know what she was talking about. He scraped his spoon around his bowl and sucked the last of the soup into his mouth, before wiping the bowl clean with a piece of bread.

'What are you going to do with me, Kevin?' she asked.

He twitched, so that his whole head jerked around.

'Do?'

'Yes. You haven't asked for a ransom. Why am I here?'

'I told you, to keep Gabriel off my back.'

'But you know that won't work. He's out there somewhere, looking for me.'

Bakker's head did another strange quarter-turn jerk. He pressed his right palm against his cheek as if to stop it moving again by force.

'Yes, well he won't find you. I'll be gone soon anyway. Then he can come and get you.'

'What are you waiting for? Why not just leave now?'

Bakker stuck his fingers into the flesh of his face, an oddly disquieting move, as the tips dug deep pits into his skin. He pulled his cheeks out then squashed them together so his lips pooched out.

'Can't. Not looking like this. They'll find me, you see. Facial recognition's everywhere. Bus stops, town squares, police cars, they all have it now. But soon I'll be a new man. Literally,' he said, grinning. 'Best plastic surgery money can buy. I'll vanish. I could walk right up to a camera and say "cheese" and I wouldn't pop up on their databases no matter how long they searched for me.'

Eli finished her soup. She grimaced and put a hand on her belly.

'I need to go to the bathroom.'

Bakker got to his feet. He unholstered his pistol and pointed it at her face. With his free hand, he tossed her the key to the handcuffs securing her left ankle to the table leg.

Eli unlocked the cuffs and then gave him the key back. Over the time they'd been together, Bakker had told her exactly how he wanted her to behave when she was being cuffed or uncuffed. He been very polite as he explained that she could do it his way or not at all.

'Any funny games and I'll shoot you. First offence through the right kneecap. Second, through the forehead.'

However crazy Bakker seemed, his right hand never wavered by so much as a millimetre whenever he held the gun on her, and she had no doubt he'd follow through on his threats.

She hadn't given up on an escape bid, but she wasn't going to throw her life away until she had something worked out that was better than ninety percent sure of succeeding.

With Bakker behind her, she could picture the muzzle pointed at the small of her back. She thought it was clever of him to always give a precise location for the threatened gunshot injury. 'Right kneecap'. 'Lumbar spine'. It gave the threats added specificity and therefore menace.

The small bathroom was on the ground floor. It had a window, but it was barred on the outside. And in any case, she doubted anyone larger than a child would be able to squeeze through the narrow opening, even without the steelwork.

However, she had, finally, come up with a plan. It had seemed at once so simple and so brilliant that she cursed herself for having taken so long.

Without lowering her trousers, she sat on the toilet. Then she called out, employing a phrase she hoped would momentarily disorientate her captor.

'Kevin, I'm bleeding.'

Bakker paused before shouting back through the door.

'What? How? You're not injured.'

'I've got my period. I need supplies.'

There, let him think about that. Men could be so hopeless faced with such a basic aspect of female biology. She had a shrewd feeling he'd still be humane enough not to want to leave a woman without sanitary protection.

And so it proved.

'What kind of supplies?'

'Tampons.'

She gave him a brand and a type.

'The nearest shop's a three-hour round-trip,' he called through the door.

'Then you'd better get going. I can improvise with loo paper, but if you imagine I'm spending the next three days locked in here, you've got another think coming.'

'Maybe I should just wait it out.'

He sounded sly. Eli had expected this. But she wasn't done yet.

'Kevin, think of Alix. If she'd been in my position, is that what you'd have wanted *her* captors to say? Please. I'm asking you to treat me like a human being, that's all.'

'Fine. But I'm going to lock you in to the cottage. If you try to escape I will find you, Eli, and then I'll have to kill you. There's nobody else on the island, you know that. Nobody to go to for help. And mine's the only boat.'

'Okay, okay. I get it.'

She heard his boots on the hard floor as he moved away from the door. Then the front door opening and slamming closed followed by the scrape of the key in the lock.

He'd brought her over from the mainland on a boat, that much she knew, although at the time she'd still been groggy from the drugs he kept administering. It had an outboard motor and she assumed that's the craft he'd take this time, but she was sure she'd seen a small rowing boat as she'd stumbled up the beach in the fading light of the day.

From the temperature – cool, but not cold – and the low humidity, she'd worked out they were somewhere far from where he'd held her the first time. The grey skies and bleak landscape beyond the windows suggested somewhere Scandinavian, or maybe the far north of the US.

She waited five minutes, then cautiously opened the bathroom door. She closed her eyes and listened. The cottage was silent apart from the ever-present hiss from the wood-burning stove in the corner of the living room.

Bakker had been busy before she'd arrived; each of the windows was barred by a white-painted concertina safety grille, the type that locked with a key. She tried the front door, more for thoroughness than in any expectation that she'd only imagined the sound of Bakker locking it. The back door was also locked. She was a prisoner.

But she also had three hours before he returned. Even if he'd lied, she thought she must have at least half that to figure out an exit strategy.

She went into the kitchen and began opening drawers systematically. Frowning, she scrabbled through the random assortment of kitchen utensils. There were plenty to choose from, but all were made of plastic. Beneath the work surface, she found the cutlery drawer. All plastic, the cheap disposable kind you got at children's parties or barbecues.

A small drawer held a random assortment of crap every kitchen seemed to accumulate, even those owned by deranged killers. Keys, rubber bands, a tube of superglue, an old packet of peppermints, a roll of silver duct tape. She rummaged through it, hoping for a screwdriver or a penknife, but the rest was a mishmash of tiny items of domestic debris, everything from plastic bag closers to the sort of junk that came out of Christmas crackers.

She scanned the work surfaces for a knife block. Nothing. Turning a circle she realised Bakker had removed every single item that she might conceivably use as a tool. Not a point, an edge or a blunt instrument she could use to pry, cut or batter her way out.

'I'll just have to do it old-school then, won't I?' she announced to the empty kitchen.

She eyed up the wood of the back door and picked a spot about halfway up the handle-side. With a battle-cry, she launched herself at it, rearing back at the last moment and delivering a ferocious kick.

She heard a satisfying crack but the wood held. Rubbing her hip, which was tingling electrically from the shock that had travelled all the way up her leg, she backed up and tried again, focusing her breathing and concentrating all her power onto the same spot on the door.

The door protested with another high-pitched creak, but the damn thing held firm. Eli's foot hurt badly; she limped away from the door to sit on a chair and take her sneaker off before massaging her instep.

She shook her head. She had to keep going. What other option did she have? The door was the weak point. All the other exit points were glazed and barred, either on the inside or the outside. No, it was this or nothing.

Standing, she advanced until she was a metre or so from the door. She focused once more on the spot she'd already hit twice. She bounced on the balls of her feet then leant back and screamed as loud as she could, kicking out at the same time.

Something cracked again, but this time it wasn't the door that had given way but a bone in her foot. It felt as though someone had driven a hot needle through the sole, burrowing into the flesh until it hit something hard.

'Fuck!' she yelled, limping away then turning to sit heavily on the chair.

But she mistimed it and tripped, falling awkwardly across the chair and onto the circular rug that covered most of the floor.

She hauled herself into a cross-legged position so she could cradle her injured foot. The pain was coming in waves, throbbing as if a giant hand were alternatively squeezing and releasing her flesh. As she kept up a running stream of invective, she noticed she'd pulled the rug into a series of ripples as she fell.

Distractedly she tried to straighten it, smoothing her palm across its nubbly surface. Her fingers caught on something beneath the pile. A ridge of some kind. She pulled the rug aside to reveal a hatch, set almost flush to the floor. A small steel ring lay in a recess.

Heart pounding, she shuffled aside, got to her knees, all thoughts of her injured foot temporarily forgotten, and heaved up on the ring. The hatch came free at once, releasing a cloud of dust that made her sneeze.

An idea came to her.

* * *

It took Eli almost ten minutes to disguise her descent into the old root cellar. Finally, she managed it by tenting the rug over the hatch and slithering down through the narrowest of gaps before resettling it over her head and descending the rickety wooden staircase.

The smell was of earth and a faint bitter tang, metallic somehow. She stretched out her arms and felt along the walls, which were damp and cold to the touch. No light switch. Cursing silently, she stumbled around, trying to form a mental picture of the cellar. It was nine paces by ten.

She got down on her hands and knees. The floor was compacted dirt, and she scrabbled around, hoping to find something she could use as a weapon. Her questing fingers met something soft and slimy that gave way with a squelch. Her stomach heaved. Hoping it was just a rotting vegetable, she wiped her hand on her thigh and carried on searching.

Despite having been down there for five minutes or more, her eyes weren't registering even the slightest amount of light, a fact brought home to her painfully as she bumped the top of her head into a wall. Swearing, and rubbing the sore spot, she turned and leant with her back to the cold stone. There had to be *something* she could use.

She closed her eyes, not that it made any difference, and pictured the cellar as if it were flooded with light. Whoever had owned the cottage before Bakker had cleared out the vegetable racks, leaving just the musty smell of decay behind. She visualised her route down from the ground floor. And then she smiled. The staircase. Of course.

She felt her way back and located the lowest step with her hands, then got to her feet and stamped down on one end with her good foot. It gave with a loud crack. Dropping to her knees, she worked the fractured piece of wood free. It was just short of three feet long and a couple of inches thick.

After repeatedly hammering it along the edge of the next stair up, she managed to split it lengthways, creating a decently heavy club.

All she had to do now was wait.

35

Although rare, it wasn't unheard of for Department operatives to be seen around the Ministry of Defence's grand corridors and conference rooms. The receptionists, secretaries and civil servants might not always have recognised the men and women who appeared in front of them from time to time, but they carried the correct ID and possessed the necessary clearance, and that was enough.

The six-foot-five security guard who scrutinised Gabriel's credentials betrayed not a shred of emotion on his craggy features as he handed the laminated pass back. In his massive hand it looked like a postage stamp.

'Thank you, sir,' was all he said, before standing aside and depressing a button that admitted Gabriel through the thick glass turnstile.

Now past the first ring of security, Gabriel made his way to the lifts, joining a pair of pinstriped and bowler-hatted gents who looked as though they might have been waiting since 1953. One, his white toothbrush moustached clipped as neatly as a topiary hedge, glanced in his direction and offered the most minuscule of nods.

The lift pinged and all three entered the mahogany-panelled interior. Gabriel had never quite reconciled himself to the contrast between the Victorian appointments of the MOD and its increasingly high-tech remit. It was like finding the nuclear codes inside a velvet-lined duelling-pistol case.

'Floor?' the moustachioed gent asked him.

'Seven, please.'

They passed the short journey in that thick, tangible silence that only lift travel in company can produce. Gabriel stepped out, waiting for the doors to slide shut behind him before turning left towards Margot McDonnell's office down a corridor lined with portraits of sabre-wielding cavalrymen, their faces a match for their scarlet jackets.

His feet made no noise on the thick carpet and he arrived at the outer door in perfect silence.

Don had always forgone the trappings of office and worked in a small room without so much as a typist to accompany him. McDonnell was more traditional in that regard. The first line of defence was an outer office occupied by a secretary. He looked up as Gabriel entered, eyebrows ascending towards his neatly combed blonde hair.

'I'm sorry, do you have an appointment? Only Ms McDonnell is in conference all day.'

Gabriel smiled and pulled out a chair opposite him.

'What I have to say is a matter of national security. I need you to listen extremely carefully to what I'm about to tell you. Do you understand?'

The man frowned, but nodded just the same. How could he not? Especially as Gabriel was already altering his breathing pattern and performing a complex sequence of eye movements that locked the secretary's own eyes onto his.

The message he relayed was a straightforward warning about possible Russian infiltration of the Department's IT systems. But hidden in its syllables, and delivered at a subliminal level, were a series of commands to first relinquish conscious control of his own mind and then enter a trancelike state. Not everyone on whom this *Yinshen fangshi* technique was practised was so amenable to its hypnotic effects, but the young man was a perfect subject. He nodded, eyes glazing, as Gabriel's words burrowed into his brain before slumping, round-shouldered, in his expensive office chair, breath coming in deep sighs.

Gabriel entered McDonnell's office and closed the door behind him. He rounded the metal-and-glass desk and sat in the chair. From this perspective, he could inhabit the mind of the woman who worked here. Where would she keep those hard-copy Department files? He felt sure they'd be somewhere within its four walls.

Normally, he'd have begun his search with the desk itself, but it was so minimal in its construction it had no drawers at all. He scanned the room. No filing cabinets interrupted the book-lined walls. Surely she had to have some kind of filing system? Or was it all in the outer office? Couldn't be. She'd keep them closer to home than that.

He rose from the chair and crossed the expanse of thick Afghan carpet to shelves of bottle green, oxblood and navy leather spines. The books turned out to be bound editions of military journals, each gold-tooled and bearing the title and volume number.

Somehow he couldn't imagine Margot McDonnell reading such outdated material. She was a technocrat, more likely to read the outpourings of the latest cyber-strategists online than anything so outmoded as ink on paper. Especially if put there by men who could remember the era of cavalry charges.

He hooked his fingertip into the top of a richly tooled leather case entitled *Asymmetric Military Strategy* and pulled. It refused to give. He frowned. Tried its neighbour, *Middle East Security Journal*. It, too, refused to budge. A light clicked on in his brain. Of course.

Stretching out both hands Gabriel started to feel his way around the entire bookcase. The switch, when he located it, was hidden beneath a shelf and set flush with the polished mahogany. He pushed up and the whole vertical unit swung outwards.

Here were the files. The recessed cupboard held three steel filing cabinets in battleship grey. Four drawers apiece. But which held Bakker's file? Gabriel started with the leftmost cabinet. He pulled the top drawer but it was locked. Cursing, he tried the other two cabinets. Neither had been left unlocked. It was all he could expect, he supposed, but his frustration got the better of him and he kicked the bottom drawer of the cabinet closest to him.

'Please don't do that, Gabriel, or I'll never get them open.'

He whirled round to see Margot McDonnell standing in the doorway, one hip cocked, her arms crossed over her chest. She stood aside and extended one arm.

'Perhaps you'd better take a seat,' she said, gesturing towards the visitor chair.

He left the storage room and walked past her.

Instead of sitting behind the desk, the obvious power play, she perched on its edge beside him, forcing him to look up if he wanted to look into her eyes. Her legs were encased in opaque black tights; she crossed one over the other at the ankle.

'I need Kevin Bakker's file,' he said, seeing little point in trying to lie his way out of trouble.

'Mmm. Tell me, how did you get past Robin? He seemed a little,' she paused, 'distracted. Did you hypnotise him?'

'It lasts until I release them or someone talks to them. It breaks the spell.'

She raised one immaculately tweezed eyebrow. 'Spell? Are we hiring wizards and warlocks now, then?'

Gabriel wasn't about to fall for such a simple provocation.

'I assume you've read my file. You know my capabilities.'

'Indeed I do,' she said, pushing herself forward off the desk and walking over to the large windows overlooking an inner courtyard. 'I wonder if you know mine, though. I've already given you what I had hoped were fairly unambiguous instructions to stand down. Now,' she held up a hand as he opened his mouth to speak, 'I know you're concerned about Eli, and rightly so. But as I explained earlier, I have a team on that, so there's really nothing to worry about. But what I *cannot* have is rogue operatives breaking in to my private office and treating this organisation as their own private intelligence resource.'

'If you helped me properly, I wouldn't need to,' he said, getting to his feet. 'Don wouldn't have stood me down.'

'Yes, well, Don isn't here, is he? Or had you forgotten?'

Gabriel fought down a sudden urge to take this supercilious civil servant by the lapels of her tailored jacket and yell in her face. She wanted him to, no doubt, but he wouldn't give her the satisfaction. He mastered his breathing and returned to his seat, thinking about Kevin Bakker's demand.

If Margot McDonnell wouldn't help him track Bakker down, maybe it was time to do things Kevin's way after all.

He reached into his jacket.

'Bakker wants me to kill you,' he said, as he showed McDonnell the small black cylinder he'd retrieved from his pocket.

36

With the smell of gunpowder tickling his nose, Gabriel left the MOD through the main doors, nodding to the crag-faced security guard on the way out. He descended the flight of seven stone steps keeping to the exact centre of the space between the classical columns flanking the entrance and hailed a black cab on Horse Guards Avenue.

With the sound turned down, he reviewed the footage he'd just shot on his phone. It would have to do. He glanced up and caught the cabbie's eyes on him in the rear-view mirror.

'YouTube, is it?' he asked.

Gabriel offered a grim nod in return.

'Something like that.'

Back at home, he sent Bakker the video via an end-to-end encrypted messaging service. Nothing secret, just a regular social media platform available to Joe Public.

37

Bakker approached the counter of the little post office and general store on the next island over. Behind it stood a short woman of maybe seventy years, trim in her Fair Isle pullover over a soft cream silk blouse.

'Yes, dear,' she said in the soft lilt the islanders had that made them sound almost Scandinavian.

He rubbed his hands on his jeans then inhaled sharply. He'd faced warlords, terrorists, gangsters, torturers, all manner of threatening countenances during his time in service of his country, but the expressionless face of the diminutive white-haired woman by the till was testing his nerve to the limit.

'My, er, my wife has got her, her...'

'Her what, dear?'

He scrubbed a hand over his face.

'Period,' he hissed out.

She smiled at him, bringing crows' feet to the corners of her eyes.

'And she's sent you out for some tampons, is that it?'

He nodded.

'She wrote down what she needs,' he said, fumbling out the folded piece of paper.

The shopkeeper's expression suggested his lack of knowledge of his wife's intimate needs did not come as a surprise. She smiled again.

'Let's have a look then, shall we?'

Five minutes later, red-faced and sweating, Bakker emerged from the shop clutching a plain brown paper bag. He knew it was stupid, but his emotions were outside his control. Avoiding eye contact with the few people he passed in the narrow little street that constituted the island's only thoroughfare, he made his way back to the rudimentary wooden jetty and clambered aboard the boat.

Halfway across the stretch of dazzling blue water that separated the two islands, his phone rang. He answered without taking his eye off the cliffs looming up from the beach still half a mile distant.

'Yes.'

'How are you doing, Kevin?'

He didn't recognise the voice, but the Russian accent was unmistakable.

'Who is this?'

'Name is not important. I am with Russian Police. A friend of Fyodor Zamyatin.'

Bakker relaxed. Fyodor had brokered his facial reconstruction surgery. This must be one of the cops he paid to keep him out of trouble. At last they were ready for him.

'What do you want? Is it time?'

'Is not time. There is problem. Big problem.'

Bakker's heart sped up and he tightened his grip on the outboard's throttle. They'd better not be trying to shaft him for more cash. The terms had been agreed.

'What kind of problem?'

'Kind of problem where whole operation busted by anti-terror cops. Kind of problem where dentist loses half his teeth during interview. Kind of problem where Fyodor gets himself shot in head *resisting arrest*. And by the way? I watch bodyworn video. First time I see a man resist arrest by kneeling on floor with hands over his head. Pretty piss-poor resistance in my opinion.'

'What about my surgery?!'

'Your surgery? Ha! Surgery is least of worries now.'

'But I paid, Goddammit!'

The man laughed cruelly. 'Sorry, my friend. Operation cancelled.'

'I can't! That was all my funds. I need it doing, you sonofabitch!'

'Hey! This was courtesy call, as favour to Fyodor's memory. But now, you insult me. Fuck your mother!'

The line went dead.

Bakker felt the boat lift off from the surface of the water. It seemed to be floating, then rotating, until he was powering along upside down, head beneath the waves, watching a stream of perfectly spherical green bubbles trailing away from his stretched lips. This wasn't happening, this *couldn't* be happening. He'd planned everything, right down to the smallest detail. Ever since Abraham had betrayed him, he'd been focused on the moment when he'd take his revenge and then emerge from his trials reborn as a new human being, a new man, cleansed of pain, of guilt, able to ascend to the higher level where he could fly among the angels, the archangels, but not Gibril of course, never him because he'd been a part of the plot to have him incarcerated and tortured and brainwashed and *ohgodohgodohgod* he needed to clean his tracks and disappear and get out, get right out before they found him and started on him again.

He hauled the tiller hard over, sending the boat into a crazy circle, white foam washing out from beneath the bow. It was the right way up now – *Ha! It's the only thing that is!* – and he blinked as the spray coated his face, running off his cheeks and down his neck. He licked his lips, tasted the salt, then closed the throttle and put the motor into neutral. The boat came to rest, bobbing on the gentle swell between the islands.

Leaning right over, he scooped up a handful of water and

drank from his cupped hands. They used to make him drink salty water back in the prison. After a while he got used to the vomiting. As it hit his stomach, he retched and brought it back up again, tears welling in his eyes and clinging to the lashes.

Fyodor had betrayed him. Taken his money and then reneged on the deal. No way had he got himself shot. Fyodor always made sure to pay off the right people. This was a deliberate ploy to leave Kevin in the lurch. He'd have to pay Fyodor back for his betrayal, yes, that's what he'd do. Just as soon as he'd got rid of the girl and cleaned up after himself. It was a setback, that was all. Just a silly little setback. He smiled. Then he laughed. As the magnitude of the joke dawned on him, he threw his head back and howled, laughing so hard he started coughing, clutching his stomach and wishing he could stop but it wasn't possible. *It was just not possible.*

He slapped himself, hard across the cheek. *Come on, Isaac, get a grip.* Shaking his head and wiping his eyes with his fingertips, he pushed the control lever to 'F' and opened the throttle, bringing the prow round until it was pointing at his island.

Keeping the tiller straight with his elbow, he pulled the pistol out of his jacket pocket. The old dear in the shop would have had kittens if she'd seen it. The thought made him smile and he had to bite down on his lower lip to stop himself laughing. The time for laughing was over.

As he beached the boat and then dragged it up over the shingle, his phone buzzed.

He smiled. Fyodor had seen the error of his ways. He was calling to tell Kevin the operation was back on.

He glanced at the screen and frowned. Not a call at all. A notification.

He tapped the icon and found himself looking at a screencap of a video. What else to do but hit the little white triangle?

The video was far from steady, but the details of the action were clear enough. It was set in an office of some kind. A man's right arm, outstretched, ending in a small-calibre pistol equipped with a silencer. Filling the rest of the frame, a woman in a dark suit and white shirt, eyes wide, panicked, really; mouth open wide screaming, 'No!', hands held up palms outwards. Then the gun jerking with a muted pop and the woman staggering back into the edge of the desk, clutching her chest before toppling sideways, blood spilling between her fingers and from her stretched-wide lips.

More wobbling camerawork as the man stood over her and fired two more rounds into the mass of dark hair at the back of her head. Then the room swung wildly as the phone was reversed and a man's face loomed into view.

It had been years, but he recognised him all the same. Gibril the betrayer. The man whose inaction and cowardice had caused Alix's death.

Gibril spoke.

'McDonnell's dead. Now release my wife.'

Shaking his head, Bakker pocketed his phone. It was too late. Gibril had killed his new boss for nothing. Nobody got to walk away alive, not now. Eli had to die. Fyodor had seen to that.

38

Gabriel re-read the note in Bakker's personnel file. He'd left McDonnell's office with photos of every document on his phone, along with the evidence he'd sent to Bakker.

Among the details of his military service, operations conducted for The Department and personal life, including the deep vetting, had been a single line recorded under the section headed, 'Property'.

Informed by KB he intends to buy cottage on Isle of Scalpay, Outer Hebrides. Security assessment: low risk.

Had he taken Eli there? It was certainly remote. But so were a million other places on the globe where an experienced agent like Bakker might stash a hostage.

Not knowing what to do was eating away at Gabriel. His appetite was gone and he had barely slept, waking at 3:00 a.m. morning after morning as he tried to figure his way into Bakker's mind. Simultaneously grieving for Don and fearful for Eli's life, his mind was travelling in too many directions at once. The only way he could maintain a semblance of control was to keep working.

The business at the MOD had left him shaken. And he still had no idea whether it had succeeded. Bakker was keeping his phone switched off so Gabriel's efforts to trace him that way had proved fruitless.

His phone buzzed. Speak of the Devil: a text from Bakker.

thank you gibril for purging eden of my enemy now you can come and collect your bride you have to find her first and time is running out

Gabriel stared at the screen. Bakker had lost his mind, that much was clear. Whatever universe he inhabited, it had very little to do with the real one. Without anything more to go on than the single line in the personnel report, he started packing for a trip north.

Flying would be quicker, but flying meant airports, airports meant security and security meant x-rays, scanners and body searches. The items Gabriel intended to take with him would set off every alarm bell and flashing red light going, so it had to be driving.

His Sig Sauer P226 and ammunition were safe in the Jaguar's boot. But there was one final item he needed.

He went upstairs and entered the bathroom. From the medicine cabinet he withdrew a small brown plastic bottle with a white cap and a computer-printed label. Benzedrine: the stimulant of choice for fighting men since the Second World War. He shook two out and swallowed them with a mouthful of cold water from the tap. It was going to be a long session behind the wheel. He didn't intend to stop except for fuel, for the car and himself.

Two minutes later, he was pulling away from the house, and heading through the town to pick up the A12 westwards to Cambridge and then on to the A1 north.

The Benzedrine kicked in as he reached a little village called Church Common. And with it a sense of unreality, married to a razor-sharp alertness that allowed him to perceive every leaf on the trees flicking past the window, every rough spot on the tarmac spooling out in front of him, every yellow-feathered bird flitting around in the white-flowered hedgerows foraging for food or nesting materials.

He put his foot down, taking the F-Type up to eighty, ninety, over a hundred where visibility permitted, guiding its long bonnet around sweeping curves, listening to the engine note rise and fall, rise and fall as he managed the steering as much with the throttle as the leather wheel gripped in his sweatless hands and using every ounce of the Jaguar's power, handling and brakes to weave his way through countless miles of traffic, every driver apart from him apparently hell-bent on driving as slowly as possible, the better to enjoy the scenery, converse with their passengers, listen to the radio or do whatever the fuck people did when their lives hadn't been pulled apart like a fly in the hands of a five-year-old psychopath-in-waiting but none of them mattered and as the car ate up the miles and the second hand of the clock swept round the dial so the traffic bulged out at him during the rush hour and then tailed off as he entered the evening and the roads gradually emptied out enough for him to take the car up to over one hundred miles per hour on average and heaven help the traffic cop who tried to pull him over because that wasn't going to happen so they'd have to keep up with him and then when he outpaced them radio for help – helicopters, more traffic cars, stingers, the whole nine yards – but it would turn into a cross-jurisdictional nightmare as he crossed county borders and sped on north and at some point he'd call for assistance but oh shit that wouldn't be forthcoming now would it, not after the scene inside McDonnell's office and the promises he'd been forced to make so it was eyes on the mirrors and keep watch for trouble and his mouth was dry, his tongue a thick wodge of kapok sucking up every last drop of moisture, and his eyes were unblinking, sand-rimmed, staring ahead, flicking up to the mirrors and it was a long time since he'd had this level of focus, chemical or otherwise – I'm coming, El, I'm coming and if he's hurt you I will visit such retribution on him – the light outside was dimming although somehow this only increased his ability to perceive every minute shift in the road surface, every alteration to the camber, the curve the width of the lane and was that a dip in his attention? better take a couple more Bennies no need to worry about addiction, not at this point in his life so he raises the brown plastic cylinder, unpops the cap and shakes them out and a couple go down his shirt front but he catches two in his mouth and washes them down with a swig from the bottle in the cupholder at his left hip and on he drives, waiting for the new pills to kick in and deliver their lemon-drop-sharp injection of wakefulness and precision laser-guided focus…

…and it's full-dark, well past midnight, nearer to two in the morning, in fact, and some of the urgency has left him; he's driving through northern England on an unlit road, no other cars but him, the only other vehicles long-distance lorry drivers taking loads up to Scotland. A ghostly white shape cruises along the fence-line at the side of the road: a barn owl, hunting on silent wings, its eyes black circles in that pure white face. The moon hangs low in the sky, smiling benevolently down on him, *here, says the fat-faced man in the moon, have another tablet, hey they look just like me don't they?* – he's doing 160 mph, the engine screaming five feet ahead of him, a howl from the exhausts setting the countryside aquiver.

He feels the vibration through every nerve fibre in his body, every muscle, tendon, ligament and bone. His soft tissues are transparent, non-existent, he has taken several more of the little white tablets and although he feels wide awake, there is a surreal air to the inside of the Jaguar now: it pulses around him, one minute shrinking until he feels as though he is piloting a Dinky toy, the next blooming outwards until the steering wheel seems a million miles away from him and how the hell he can reach it is one of life's great mysteries…

His teeth hurt because he's been grinding them for the last hundred miles or so, painful contractions in the sides of his jaw like cramp: he shakes his head. This is not good. He should ease off the throttle – and the Bennies.

Fuck that! Easing off is for when the battle's won and the songs of victory are being sung and the trophies are brought home from the field. He shakes out two more tablets and dry-swallows them – the water went a long time back. One sticks in his throat and burns there. He swallows convulsively, trying to produce a drop of spit to send down his throat after it. Finally it dislodges and descends into his stomach.

Soon, El. I'll be there soon.

39

Waiting for Bakker in the dark of the root cellar, Eli's mind began to wander. She hadn't drunk anything for hours and thirst combined with the adrenaline had dried her mouth and throat, setting off a persistent cough. Her foot was throbbing painfully. But, she reminded herself, she'd suffered worse, not least during her service with Kidon, the Israeli Special Forces' famed 'Tip of the Spear'. She closed her eyes.

The light had that bright-white intensity you only ever got on particular days in the Negev. The sun, directly overhead, burning down like a laser. A bruising wind bullying its way east to west across the desert, bringing with it nothing but lung-searing heat. Even lying prone beneath a grit-encrusted sheet of camouflaged ripstop nylon pegged down with titanium spikes, she could feel stinging grains of sand penetrating her skin like needles heated over a flame.

They'd been following the terrorists for a week and a half. The kill team comprised Eli, Roni, Yael, Dovid, Nir and Lior. The cell they were tracking numbered three, two men and a woman. Of them all, it was the woman who topped the most-wanted list. Martina Bühl, a German national. She was their leader and had planned and participated in the assassination of three Israeli diplomats in Jerusalem the previous year.

Intelligence Section had intercepted a cell-to-cell phone call arranging a weapons buy deep in the uncharted wastes of the Negev. Three captured American FIM-92 Stingers, available to legitimate militaries for $38,000 a pop; considerably more than that on the black market. The man-portable air defence missile system or MANPADS was highly effective against low-flying jet fighters such as the IDF's F-15s, F-16s and F-35s. Against helicopters and slow transport aircraft, it was devastating. The buy must not go ahead.

Nir was the unit's sniper. He would disable the vehicles before turning his attention to the terrorists and the arms dealer. Eli and the rest would then move in to finish the job. They were expecting stiff resistance as soon as Nir fired his first shot.

As the appointed hour grew close, Eli checked her assault rifle once again, even though it was only thirty minutes since she had last run the prescribed series of checks.

A battered truck, its loadspace shrouded in tarpaulins, rumbled along the rutted desert road, its lower half invisible in the wavering heat haze so that it appeared to be floating. Glances were exchanged between the kill team. This was it. The culmination. Eli pulled back the charging lever on her rifle. Her pulse was racing. Her mouth was dry.

Approaching from the opposite direction, the terrorists' 4x4, a once-white Landcruiser, its paint turned tawny by the windborne dust.

Twenty metres to her right, she knew Nir was sighting through the scope on the truck's engine bay, aiming to send a .50 calibre explosive round into it. With the truck out of action, the occupants would jump out, weapons up and start firing.

The two vehicles shimmered to a halt, some ten metres from each other. Nir fired twice. She had time to hear him working the bolt back and forth. The first round blew up the engine. Then he put a second round into the fuel tank. It was a brilliant shot. The truck erupted into a blinding fireball, then the

Stingers' warheads detonated with a triple-boom that rent the air.

And then the world tore in half and Eli lost consciousness.

She awoke in the trunk of a car, being thrown sideways to crash painfully against the insides of the wheel arches as the driver took bends at what felt like reckless speeds.

Captured.

That meant torture and execution. Her body displayed as a warning and a cry of triumph, like a dead crow pinned to a farmer's fence.

She scrabbled around, searching for something she could use as a weapon. The idiots had left a tyre iron beneath the carpet. That one moment of inattention saved her life.

When the car stopped, throwing her forwards against the back of the rear seats, she was ready. The trunk lid opened and a pistol poked inside. She smashed the tyre iron down, breaking the wrist with a loud double-crack. While the wrist's owner screamed, Eli was moving again. She snatched up the pistol and fired twice as she scrambled out of the boot. The car was inside an abandoned warehouse, sun spearing down through ragged holes in its corrugated iron walls, hitting metal stanchions that rose through the gloom to support the roof. In the centre of the echoing space was placed a single, metal-framed chair, a coil of rope beside it, a meat hook dangling from a length of chain overhead.

The terrorist, one of the men, it turned out, toppled backwards, blood fountaining from his skull. Bullets tore through the bodywork behind her and she fired three more shots in answer, scanning for the shooter.

Her left arm jerked backwards as a bullet tore through her triceps. She didn't feel anything except the tug as it hit her. Five shots gone. No possibility of reloading.

The remaining male terrorist lost his cool. Carrying an AK-47 and screaming at the top of his lungs, he advanced on her, his finger locked down on the trigger, spraying bullets wildly. Full auto. Eli crouched and aimed, two-handed, as the last of the thirty 7.62mm rounds left the muzzle and the firing pin hit home on empty space. She put a 9mm round directly over his heart and dropped him where he stood, the Kalashnikov clattering to the concrete floor as he fell.

That just left Bühl.

Eli caught a movement in her peripheral vision, a flash of blonde hair, as Bühl ducked behind a metal storage bin some thirty metres away.

'Give it up, Bühl!' Eli shouted from her vantage point. 'The others are dead.'

The terrorist answered with two shots, fired around the side of the bin. Eli ducked, even though the shots were unsighted and went wide.

'Last chance,' Eli called.

Silence.

Eli levelled her pistol and prepared to charge the storage bin. Then she changed her mind, turned and, on silent feet, crept back to the car's driver's door.

The keys were still in the ignition. With the pistol in her left hand, resting on the steering wheel, she twisted them hard then swung the car around the moment the engine fired, spinning the wheel under the palm of her right hand. Rear tyres screeching on the smooth concrete floor, the car slid around in a circle. Once the nose was pointing at the storage bin, Eli floored the throttle and powered towards Martina Bühl's hiding place.

Eli hit the storage bin at less than thirty miles per hour, but the impact was still immense for Bühl. She was thrown backwards and upwards, smashing against one of the pillars supporting the roof and folding double around it like a piece of soft cloth over a hanger. Inside the car, Eli didn't hear the crackle of Bühl's spine shattering. She didn't need to; the visuals told their own eloquent story.

Eli left the engine running, but put the transmission in neutral and applied the handbrake. She exited the car, crossed to the broken body and slapped Bühl's face. Her eyes, the blue of cornflowers, fluttered open and her lips, blood-crusted from multiple splits, moved.

Eli leant closer.

'*Fick dich, Jude.*' Fuck you, Jew.

Eli shook her head and levelled the pistol.

'*Fick mich? Nicht heute, terrorist.*' Fuck me? Not today, terrorist.

After killing Bühl, she'd driven herself back to Kidon HQ one-handed to be informed that all but her and Roni had perished in the ambush. The fourth terrorist, who'd arrived on a desert-capable off-road motorbike, had used a Soviet RPG; there was barely anything left to bury.

Roni survived by a fluke – she'd been blocked by Nir, who had taken the full force of the blast. Grabbing two assault rifles and firing both one-handed, she'd killed the man who'd decimated the kill team and started firing at Bühl's team in the 4x4, the arms dealer and his people having been vaporised when his payload went up.

Eli sighed and opened her eyes again. In Kidon, they'd considered each other more than just comrades, more than friends: they were family. It had been a painful day and her sorrowing faded only gradually over the following year.

Her right forefinger twitched in the darkness of the cellar. She hefted the wooden stave. It felt good to have a weapon in her hand again, albeit such a rudimentary one. But she had something else, too: the element of surprise. And despite the thousands of years of technological development that separated wooden clubs from the latest assault rifles, surprise was still the foot soldier's greatest weapon.

Bakker would arrive to find her gone. He'd take a while checking the immediate environs of the cottage before realising that she couldn't have escaped without doing obvious damage to the security grilles. Then he'd figure it out: she was still inside.

She assumed he knew about the root cellar. He might even head there first. She had the element of surprise, if you could call it that, but he had all the rest: a firearm, a torch, an unbroken foot. He was rested and well fed, hydrated and fit. She briefly considered making a stand somewhere else. In one of the upstairs rooms, perhaps. But just as quickly, she rejected them. Out in the open, against a superior opponent, the odds were against her. Down here, she could minimise her weaknesses and make the terrain work for her.

She was desperately tired. And the adrenaline had largely dissipated, leaving her yawning so widely her jaw cracked. But she could afford to sleep, she realised. Bakker would make enough noise unlocking the door to wake her and she'd hear his booted feet on the floor above.

Gratefully, she let her eyelids close and was asleep seconds later, the wooden club gripped in her fist.

40

A bang from overhead woke Eli. Heart pounding, she shuffled her bottom against the wall and then pulled herself upright using the underside of the staircase's open framework for support.

Bakker's voice was muffled though she could tell he was shouting.

'Eli? I've got your...things.'

She rolled her eyes. He still couldn't bring himself to say 'tampons'. She shook her head. Here was a trained killer, a former assassin in the service of Her Majesty, who'd have no compunction about killing anyone he was ordered to, struggling to utter the name of an everyday product.

She waited. The silence would get to him pretty quickly. He called out again. More urgently this time. She pictured him, standing on the rug right over her head. He'd have a bag in his hand. He'd put it on the kitchen table and unholster his gun. Any second now, he'd call out her name for the third and final time. And so it proved.

'Eli? Where are you?'

Now he'd figure she was upstairs, lying in wait for him. But then a worrying thought hit her. He could just make himself a coffee and wait. He knew there was nothing upstairs she could use as a weapon. No food either. Or water.

She shook her head. He wouldn't be able to leave it alone. He'd have to know. Because in a hostage situation, there was always a chance, however slim, that your captive had managed to escape. Bars could be dug out of rotten plaster. Boards over windows could be pried free. Ceilings could be breached. Locks, picked.

Bakker's heavy tread thudded overhead. She heard doors opening and closing; at one point, he must have kicked the table. She heard the legs scrape over the floorboards. Then he was climbing the stairs. The sound didn't travel through two floors and she was forced to wait in silence. In the total darkness of the cellar, her eyes started playing tricks, sending green-and-yellow shooting stars flying across her field of vision, spiralling this way and that as if alive.

She started as Bakker's boots thumped directly over her head.

'Eli, I know you're in here. Listen. Gibril sent me a video. He killed Margot McDonnell like I asked. He kept his side of the deal. He's coming to get you. I'm letting you go.'

She said nothing. But her mind was reeling. How could Gabriel have done such a thing? He wouldn't have, would he? Yet, even as she struggled to process what Bakker was telling her, she hoped it was true. To save her, he'd murdered his new boss. He'd killed more important people than her before. Much more important. But they'd been enemies of the state. Targets sanctioned by Don. Would Gabriel really commit murder to save her life?

She had no time to ponder it further. A slithering noise penetrated the deep darkness of the root cellar. She knew what it was immediately. Bakker was pulling the rug aside, revealing the hatch.

This was it. Her heart racing, she braced herself for action.

Bakker threw the hatch open, letting it crash down onto the wooden floor. The light streaming down into the cellar was blinding after so long in the dark and Eli had to squeeze her eyes shut, hoping they'd adjust before Bakker started down the steps.

A thin beam of white light speared down into the darkness as she squinted through half-opened lids. A phone, then, not a purpose-built torch. For the first time, Eli was able to see the layout of the cellar. The walls were bare plaster, discoloured by mould. The floor was beaten-flat earth, dotted here and there with unidentifiable black lumps that might have been rotted turnips or potatoes, left years earlier by a previous owner.

And here came Bakker's boots on the wooden treads above her.

'Eli, if you're down here, I seriously suggest you make yourself known to me,' he said. 'Gibril is coming for you and we can't have you all dirty from the cellar for your husband, can we?'

The angle of the steps meant she couldn't see Bakker, only hear his voice. Though that meant he couldn't see her, either. She waited until she could see the backs of his ankles through the gap in front of her. As he lifted his right foot off one step, she stuck the wooden club through the open back of the stairs in front of his left ankle, then grabbed the other end.

With a cry, he toppled forwards, losing his grip on phone and pistol. The light described an arc that illuminated the ceiling, then the walls, and finally the tumbling pistol before the phone hit the floor, screen upwards. The cellar was plunged back into almost total darkness.

Eli lunged out from her hiding place, oblivious to the pain from her injured foot, and brought the club down where she'd seen Bakker land. It hit something and she heard him grunt. Not his head; the sound was all wrong for that. But he'd been winded by the fall.

She hit him again, then grabbed the phone and shoved it in his face, feeling it vibrate as the facial-recognition software unlocked it.

She desperately wanted the pistol, but there was no way of finding it. If she got into a tussle with Bakker there was every chance he'd come out on top and either beat her to death or shoot her on the spot. Instead, she scrambled her way up the wooden steps.

'Eli!' he screamed. 'You viper! You betrayer!'

Panting, she reached the trapdoor and dragged herself through. She heaved herself to her feet and limped round until she could grab the wooden hatch and haul it up and over, slamming it in place with a crash that released a cloud of dust.

Bakker was still yelling at her from the cellar, screaming out obscenities mixed with Biblical phrases.

She upended the table and pulled it over the hatch, hoping the additional weight would stop Bakker getting out. But it wouldn't be enough. She could tell even as she slid it into position. The fridge, then. She pulled the door open and used the handle to drag it over, shoving the table aside with her right hip at the last moment.

Heart racing, she sat back, and then screamed as a bullet shattered the floor an inch to the left of her knee. Bakker had found the pistol. Four more shots followed, sending splinters of wood flying up into the air. Thankfully, none of Bakker's bullets were as close as the first.

She left through the back door, wishing Bakker had left the key so she could lock him in. She needed to get off the island. She hobbled away from the cottage and made a circuit, trying to keep her weight off her injured foot. It made progress agonisingly slow and twice she stumbled, bringing forth a scream of pain as the ends of the broken bone ground together.

At the front of the house she saw something that lifted her spirits. It was going to be OK. A dirty silver 4x4 was parked on the grass. She hobbled over and pulled the door open. Bakker had taken the keys out of the ignition. It didn't matter. She'd been hotwiring cars since she was a teenaged girl mucking about with the half-ruined Jeeps on the kibbutz. None of them had keys and it was seen as an everyday practical skill to be able to start them without.

She reached underneath the steering column and then swore loudly as her fingertips encountered something hard and grid-like.

It couldn't be. She leant down and looked. It was. Bakker had bolted sturdy steel mesh around the wiring for the ignition. What kind of person did that? The answer presented itself immediately. The kind of paranoid individual who thought he was being betrayed at every turn. The kind who worked for an off-books government agency who exploited any weakness in a target's security setup, from hackable CCTV cameras to unprotected ignition switches.

She looked back at the cottage. Had she just heard more shots? What the hell was Bakker doing? Shooting his way out of the cellar? Or was there another way out? One she'd not seen in the dark?

She couldn't afford to hang around waiting to find out. Sliding out of the driver's seat and placing her good foot on the ground, she looked around. She needed to get clear of the cottage. But which way? A single-track lane led up into the hills. To its right, the ground was flatter grassland, studded with grey boulders ranging in size from footballs to lumps you could hide a small car behind. To its left, the ground sloped down to the sea.

What bothered her was the almost total lack of tree cover in any direction. She'd be exposed whichever way she went. The grassland at least had the advantage of soft going. She turned to go and then, on a whim, turned back and peered in through the rear window. At last, some luck. A golf umbrella lay on the back seat. She reached in and pulled it clear. It wasn't much, but it would help her make better speed.

Using the umbrella as a walking stick, she started off, keeping up a steady if uneven pace across the spongy grass. She was heading for a rise in the ground, reasoning that where there was a rise, there would be a fall, and with it the chance to vanish from the sightlines available to Bakker if he managed to free himself from the cellar.

41

Gabriel arrived in Uig on the northwest coast of the Isle of Skye sixteen hours after setting off from Aldeburgh. The time was 5:51 a.m. He climbed out of the driver's seat and groaned as he straightened out the kinks in his back. The Benzedrine was doing an excellent job of keeping him awake, although his jaw was aching from the tooth-grinding; an unavoidable side-effect.

The sun was just coming up, setting the eastern sky aflame with yellows and oranges so intense the air itself seemed to be burning. Maybe this, too, was a side-effect of the tablets, but it leant an air of unreality to the ferry port. He'd arrived before anyone else, or maybe nobody but him was making the first crossing. He shook his head, trying to focus, but it was hard when every muscle fibre was buzzing.

He walked over to a coffee van with its lights on. The woman inside smiled down at him. Her white hair was cut in a spiky style, feathered at the sides and standing up on the top of her head. It was tinged pink by a string of fairy lights strung across the hatchway.

'Yes, my love,' she said. 'What can I get you?'

He was about to ask for a flat white when the thought of caffeine on top of the Bennies made his stomach flip.

'Cup of tea, please.'

While she dropped a teabag into a cup and added steaming hot water from a hissing spout on her machine, Gabriel turned to survey the ferry terminal. There was enough space for goods vehicles as well as cars, and he'd seen a tall-sided truck filling up at the service station just before he reached the concrete apron that led to the access ramp.

'Here you go,' she said.

He took the cup and, after paying, wandered over to the railing and peered down at the water, almost black at this time of the morning.

If he'd miscalculated, and Bakker wasn't keeping Eli on the island, then he was out of ideas. With the whole world to search, there was no way he'd find her. It would be up to her to get herself clear of Bakker and send Gabriel a message. He knew she had the skills and the experience to make even half a chance into whole cloth. But there was no way of knowing whether Bakker would give her that opportunity.

The ferry sounded its horn, a low, mournful sound that bounced off the buildings behind him. Gabriel climbed back into the car and waited until the hi-vis jacketed official unlocked the gate and waved him forward.

Twenty-five minutes later, he drove off, clanking down from the steel ramp and onto the concrete apron in Tarbert. In his jacket pocket he had a copy of the photo from Bakker's personnel file. It had been taken at least ten years before, but it was the best he had. The plan was simple. Show it around, see if anyone recognised Bakker. Ask if they'd seen him recently. And whether they knew if he had a cottage on Scalpay. Maybe an address. Hell, while he was wishing for the moon, a detailed inventory of his home security measures wouldn't go amiss.

He bit back a laugh. The speed was still flooding his system and messing around with his emotions. Which was the last thing he needed.

He found a quiet spot in which to park and crossed the main street to the first of a handful of shops, a hardware store. As he pushed through the door, the jangling bell made Gabriel jump. *Calm down. We don't want to frighten the locals,* he thought.

Behind the wooden counter, in which a brass rule was set flush with the well-worn wood, a man in his late-fifties stood, a copy of *The Scotsman* open before him. He looked up and smiled, placed gnarled hands with arthritic knuckles flat on the newspaper.

'Morning, sir. How can I help you?'

Gabriel retrieved the photo from his inside pocket.

'I'm looking for this man. His name is Kevin Bakker. Do you recognise him?'

The shopkeeper frowned, drawing deep grooves into the weathered skin of his forehead.

'I'll need my specs,' he said. 'Hold on a tick.'

He drew a pair of greasy-looking glasses from the pocket of his waistcoat and slid them onto his nose, then stretched out a twisted hand for the photo.

After a few seconds, he handed it back, offering an apologetic smile.

'I'm afraid not. Would you be a detective, then?'

Gabriel shook his head and smiled. 'No, nothing like that. Just an old friend, from my army days,' he said. 'I thought I'd look him up.'

The shopkeeper looked sceptical. As if that was the exactly the sort of answer a detective *would* give. He shrugged.

'Good for you, then. It's not many who've the guts to stand up and be counted for Queen and country, now, is it?'

Gabriel shook his head. No, it wasn't. And even fewer who'd take the shilling then turn round and murder their commanding officer.

He entered three more establishments and had variants on the same conversation, each time with the same, negative outcome. By the time he reached the fifth, a general store, the jungle drums had clearly got going, because the lady at the counter seemed prepared for him.

'You'd be the police detective from the mainland, then? How exciting! I don't think we've ever had a detective on the island before and I've lived here an awfully long time.' She winked at him. 'Though I hope that doesn't make me sound too old.'

'Not at all. I was going to ask if your parents were in,' he said with a grin.

Her watery blue eyes widened. 'Och, ye cheeky wee thing! Parents indeed. Now, you've a photo you want me to look at, is it?'

'I do, but I'm really not a detective, police or private. Just a private individual.'

She winked again. 'Whatever you say,' a beat, 'officer. Your secret's safe with me.'

Feeling that the more he protested, the firmer would be her conviction that here indeed was a detective from the mainland, Gabriel showed her the photo. She held it up to her eyes and he felt a profound sense of time wasting as she scrutinised the image.

'Aye. I've seen him. Yesterday, as a matter of fact. Nice chap. Very shy. What's he done? Would it be a murder, now?' she asked in a stage whisper. 'I read all the detective books, you know. I'm an addict. Morag the Murder Hound, that's what they call me in my book group.'

'Why did you say he was shy?' Gabriel asked, deciding to sidestep any further discussions by sticking to asking questions of his own.

'Oh. Well, he had to buy some sanitary protection for his wife. You'd think men would be a bit more with it in this day and age, wouldn't you?'

Gabriel nodded and thanked her, but his mind was whirling with possibilities. Bakker was here. And if he'd been asking for tampons then surely they were for Eli.

'Is that helpful?' she asked.

Gabriel decided that he'd indulge her crime fantasies after all. Impersonating a police officer was a crime, but maybe he could sail close enough to the wind for his purposes without capsizing the boat.

'It's incredibly helpful, Morag. May I call you Morag?'

'She nodded vigorously and smiled. 'Of course, detective…'

A name would add spice to the story she'd no doubt spread around the island as soon as he'd left the shop.

Gabriel smiled.

'Do you happen to know where he lives?'

'I haven't seen him around before, which is odd, because I know pretty well everyone on Harris. And his accent was like yours. English, you know? Maybe London.'

'Could he have come over from one of the other islands?'

'Oh, yes. That's entirely possible. We get walkers, birdwatchers, people here for the whale-watching. It's quite the holiday destination for a certain sort of tourist, you know.'

'Scalpay?'

She nodded. 'Maybe. There's a bridge just up the road. It's a bit of a drive, mind.'

'And if I wanted to get over to Scalpay without using the bridge?'

She frowned, just for a second. Then her brow smoothed out again. 'You mean for a clandestine approach. I see. Well,' she said, touching her fingertip to her chin, 'your best bet would be to have one of the fishermen take you over in their boat. I should think any one of them would be willing. You know, for the police and everything.'

'Not that I'm a policeman, Morag,' Gabriel said.

'Of course. Silly of me!' She winked.

'I don't suppose you'd know of anyone who might have the time to take me over, do you?'

She smiled. 'As a matter of fact, I do. I think Douglas McAlpine is the very chap. Can you wait while I make a quick phone call?'

He nodded and smiled as she picked up a clunky-looking mobile phone.

Five minutes later he was driving back to the harbour, ready to meet a local boat-owner who'd agreed to take him over to Scalpay.

42

Even with the support from the umbrella, Eli was making painfully slow progress away from Bakker's cottage. Each step on her injured foot brought forth a fresh wave of pain and the effort was making her nauseous. She needed to find somewhere to hole up and then get a message to Gabriel.

She checked the phone. No service. Maybe Bakker was making his calls from higher ground. Or the cottage just happened to have signal. It was possible. Gabe's place was just the same, except there you had to go upstairs if you wanted a connection.

Scanning the horizon, she spotted a hill a couple of miles away. It looked high enough, but with her foot in the shape it was in it would take her a while to get there. If Bakker got himself out of the cellar, he'd catch her for sure. He had the 4x4, for a start, and the damn keys.

The hill wasn't an option. She needed to turn things around. He'd be expecting her to run, so she'd do the opposite. She'd hide near the cottage. The place was damn-near impregnable unless you had a tank, so she could lock herself inside and leave him outside. The pistol would be no good against the walls and reinforced windows, so she could wait him out and hopefully get a signal to call for help.

Overhead, gulls wheeled, crying and keening over the grey water. Sea mist was gathering. It seemed to be moving onshore.

Eli looked back at the cottage. No sign yet of Bakker. It looked so desolate, a grey-rendered dwelling all alone in an expanse of low, rolling grassland. Nothing but lichen-scabbed rocks and the odd thornbush bent almost horizontal by the prevailing winds to leaven the barrenness of the landscape.

She headed back, but at an oblique angle, working her way down towards the stony beach, thinking she could work her way around and come up on the rear of the cottage. The going was slow and became worse once she reached the shingle. Unlike the grass, this terrain was unforgiving and as the size of the stones increased from marbles to eggs to cricket balls to grapefruits, her foot kept turning over, and the effort of not screaming cost her dear in bitten lips and ground teeth.

She needed to rest. A chance to recover her breath and give herself a break from the effort of staying one step ahead of Bakker. And then she saw a possible refuge. Half-submerged in the shingle was a derelict clinker-built boat, maybe five metres from stem to stern.

The combined action of sun, wind and waves had taken what must once have been a fine paint-job of red and blue and turned it into the faintest of memories of more buoyant times. Bare wood, silvered where it wasn't scabbed with faded paint, predominated. The ribs of the boat protruded through smashed-out planks of the outer shell like the bones of a long-dead animal propping open its desiccated hide.

She reached it a few seconds later and lifted one side experimentally. It came up easily, pivoting on a boulder that might have been responsible for its demise. Underneath it smelled of salt, seaweed and an old, nose-wrinkling aroma of rotten fish. She slithered under the upturned hull and let the boat down again.

As cover it was perfect. She could see the cottage without having to reveal herself. Out of the wind it was quiet, too, and for the first time in ages she could relax. She checked the phone again. And, miraculously, it was showing a single bar. With a trembling finger, she tapped in Gabriel's number.

It rang and her heart lifted. This was going to be all right. Wherever he was, he could come here and get her. Then she realised, she had no idea where 'here' was.

He picked up and she started talking straight away.

'Oh, thank God. Gabe, I'm OK but I don't—'

'This is Gabriel Wolfe. Please leave a message.'

She started again.

'Gabe, it's me. I'm OK. I'm on an island. From the climate and vegetation, I'd say Northern Europe or maybe Northwestern US. Bakker's got a cottage here and I locked him in the cellar. He's armed with a pistol. I'm on the beach near the cottage under a boat. I broke my foot. I'm going to try to get back into the cottage and lock him out. I'll text you my location. I love you.'

Although the signal was patchy, Eli managed to pull up her GPS coordinates. They confirmed her hunch. But before the app could show her where she was, the screen froze. Cursing, she cut and pasted the strings of digits into a text and sent it to Gabriel.

Two seconds later the phone buzzed. Message not sent.

'Come on, come on,' she muttered as she sent it again.

Again, a two-second wait and again the same error message. She tried again and got the same results.

She swore at the phone and stuffed it into her pocket. She'd have to try again later once she regained the safety of the cottage.

No sooner had she stashed the phone than she heard a thump from the direction of the cottage. Peering through the gap in the boat hull, she saw the back door open. Bakker stood there, pistol in hand, looking this way and that. She scuttled away from the opening, pushing herself back into the darkest corner, a childish move, given that all he had to do was upend it and there she'd be. *Found you!*

He ran a hand through his hair and she could see his mouth working. He seemed distracted, checking the pistol, sticking it in his waistband, then taking it out again. Finally, he sprinted up the track, directly away from her, into the mist, which was now massing over the landscape.

She reckoned it would take her three or four minutes to cross the open ground to the cottage. She had to be sure Bakker wouldn't return. Deciding ten minutes would be long enough, she tried the phone again.

By some fluke of mobile coverage, maybe owing to the changing weather, she now had two bars. She sent the text again and this time it was delivered. Next she called Gabriel.

And this time, when she heard his voice, it was live. Her pulse jacked up as she spoke.

'Gabe, it's me! It's me!'

'Thank God. Where are you, El?'

'I just texted you my GPS. I'm on the beach, under a boat just a few hundred yards from Bakker's cottage.'

'I'm coming, darling. I'm on a boat right now, just crossing to the island. Sit tight.'

'Not much else I can do. Be careful, Gabe. He's out looking for me. He's armed. A pistol.'

'Don't worry, so am I. I'll be with you soon.'

She ended the call, feeling more hopeful than she had ever since Bakker had taken her from the reef. That seemed so long ago: a lifetime. One minute she'd been enjoying her honeymoon with the man she loved, then half-drowned, drugged and imprisoned. Bakker's story was a heart-rending one, but that didn't excuse what he'd done. Though if she felt she'd been betrayed, and lost Gabriel in the process, her own vengeance would be protracted and bloody.

She shook her head. She didn't have time for philosophy. They were up against a madman. He needed to be stopped.

Boots crunched over the shingle. Thank God. She crawled over to the prow of the boat and pushed up against the timbers. Gloved hands curled around the gunwale and helped lift the weight off her.

All pain from her foot forgotten, she straightened up, smiling, as the boat tipped over and crunched down to the shingle.

'Gabe, I—'

'Hello again.'

It was Bakker. Eli staggered back and fell against the boat, ending up on her back with her legs bent over the gunwale.

He pulled the pistol but there was little point in resisting.

'Give me my phone,' he said.

She handed it over and Bakker spun it out into the sea.

'Out.'

She stretched out a hand and he pulled her out of the boat and onto her feet. She winced as she put her weight down and Bakker noticed.

'Hurt yourself?'

She nodded. 'I think I broke a bone in my foot.'

He nodded, pursing his lips.

'We'd better get you back inside, then. Come on.'

He took a couple of steps back and waited for her to start walking back up to the house. She glanced down at the golf umbrella.

'I was using that as a crutch.'

Bakker shrugged and motioned with the pistol for her to start walking. 'Leave it. It's not far. Let's go.'

Had she not busted up her foot she would have considered making a move, but he'd be wise to that and anyway, her foot *was* broken, wasn't it? That was the point.

Inside the house again, he gestured for her to sit on one of the kitchen chairs.

'I need to take a look at your foot,' he said. 'But I need you stay still.'

She smiled up at him and nodded. 'I promise I won't move.'

He shook his head. 'You misunderstand me.'

Then he swung the pistol round in a short, tight arc. Pain exploded in Eli's skull and then all was dark.

43

The boatman gunned the motor and drove his craft in to the shore, killing the outboard at the last minute and shipping it so the hull scraped noisily over the shingle.

'You're sure you'll be all right from here?' he asked, as Gabriel climbed out and onto dry land.

'Completely. Thanks for the lift.'

'How are you going to get back? If your mate's not here, there's nobody else on the island.'

Gabriel wanted no witnesses for what was to come. 'Don't worry about that,' he said. 'I'll make other arrangements.'

The boatman smiled and tapped the side of his nose.

'Backup. Right. I get it. Just give me a hand to turn her round then and I'll leave you to it.'

Gabriel dragged the prow around and then helped the boatman push off and back into the water. He lowered the motor, tugged on the starter cord and as soon as it fired, headed back across the water to Tarbert, waving with his non-tiller hand.

Gabriel turned and walked across the stony beach, checking his phone. According to the mapping app, Eli was half a mile to the north. He set off at a run, touching the pistol tucked into his waistband as he went. As he ran, he scanned the landscape in every direction, looking for Bakker. But this side of the island at least was deserted.

Rounding a green knoll, he spotted the boat. But something was wrong. It appeared to be right way up. He was sure Eli had said she was underneath it. He sprinted the last fifty yards and his heart sank as he reached the boat. Eli had gone, either searching for a new hiding place or under duress, with Bakker. He turned and saw a grey-rendered cottage. Two storeys with barred windows. Bakker's place. Had to be.

Now what? Did he just walk up to the front door and ring the bell?

He didn't have to.

The door opened and Bakker emerged, carrying a rifle. He raised it to his shoulder and fired. The bullet blew a chunk of wood out of the boat's hull, showering Gabriel with splinters.

'That's close enough, Gibril. Throw down your gun.'

Gabriel held his arms out from his sides.

'I'm unarmed, Kevin. I just want Eli back. Let her go and then we're out of your hair.'

'Oh yeah? How's that going to work? You going to swim back to Tarbert?'

'I assume you have a boat of your own somewhere? We could borrow it, leave it for you in the harbour.'

Without taking his eye from the scope, Bakker laughed, a cracked sound in the still air.

'You have a lot of nerve, Gibril, coming here and demanding to borrow my boat.'

'You haven't shot me, though, Kevin. So I think you want to get out of this alive.'

The rifle's muzzle flashed again and a second bullet kicked up a puff of dirt at Gabriel's feet. The report was loud in the open air, a double-crack as the noise bounced back off the house wall.

'Correction. I haven't shot you *yet*,' Bakker shouted through the cloud of gun smoke that drifted up into the still air over his head. It was a darker, bluer grey than the mist swirling low over the grass. 'Now, toss your gun or my next shot will pierce your skull.'

Gabriel slowly brought his left hand down and behind his back.

'Finger and thumb, Gibril,' Bakker called. 'You know the drill.'

As slowly as if the gun were a bomb armed with a tilt-switch, Gabriel pulled it free with his thumb and forefinger, just as Bakker had instructed. He swung it forwards and upwards, so that it described a shallow loop before thumping onto the grass six feet in front of him.

'Now what?'

'Now you come over here. I imagine you'd like to see Eli again, wouldn't you?'

Wondering whether he'd just signed his own death warrant, Gabriel slowly closed the distance between him and Bakker. As he got closer, he recognised the man he'd chased in Jerusalem. Then the man he'd flown to Kandahar with in a military transport. Set up the op with. Left there to be captured by the Taliban after he himself was ambushed.

'You look well, Kevin,' he said, raising his hands overhead as he came to a stop five feet away from Bakker.

Physically, at least, Bakker appeared to be in good shape. He stood erect, yet in a relaxed pose that spoke of confidence in his abilities and many, many years of training and operational action. His face was filled out and his skin was clear, none of the signs you saw in strung-out vets with too much trauma and drugs in their backgrounds to take care of themselves properly.

But there was something behind the eyes that spoke of a mind clinging to the cliff of sanity by its fingernails, just a gust of wind away from a fall, tumbling and screaming into the roiling sea. They flickered left and right, as if activated by a solenoid, unable to hold Gabriel's gaze.

He knew the signs: this was hypervigilance. The ever-alert state that PTSD sufferers could descend into where every rucksack-wearing backpacker was a terrorist with a suicide bomb, every briefcase-toting executive an assassin with a kit-form sniper rifle, a group of laughing partygoers a coordinated squad running interference for the hit team.

You couldn't relax, couldn't let your guard down. Your family might imagine they were walking down their local high street but you knew the truth: you were back in Sniper Alley, the Kill Zone or Ambush Town.

A drunk girl screams as her boyfriend dunks her in a city-centre fountain and that's it. Your fight-or-flight reflex kicks off. Throw yourself down on top of the kids, shove your wife behind a dumpster for safety, then crouch down in a foetal position, whimpering until a kind passer-by leans over and touches you, oh so gently, on the shoulder, and asks if 'everything's all right, love?'

As Bakker regarded him with that oddly electric gaze, Gabriel realised that for him, everything was very far from all right.

This close, the muzzle of the rifle was a yawning black hole, from which a copper-jacketed hunting round could emerge at any moment and take his head clean off his shoulders. He tried to regulate his breathing, keep it slow and steady, not too deep, either, no need for hyperventilating. Bakker was enough of a pro, strung-out or not, to recognise the signs. Gabriel couldn't afford to give away any more of what little edge he possessed.

'Can you lower the rifle?' he asked in a quiet, gentle voice. 'It's a nice one. What is it? A Winchester?'

Bakker let the muzzle fall by a couple of centimetres.

'Browning X-Bolt. Inside.'

He stood to one side and jerked the barrel at the door.

Gabriel went inside, and there was Eli, tied to a chair, a bruise over her left eye and dried blood streaked down over her cheekbone, her jaw and her neck, down into the collar of her T-shirt. She smiled as she saw him.

'Hey,' she croaked. 'What took you so long?'

He went to her and knelt down, cradling her cheeks in his hands. He kissed her, hard.

'Are you OK?' he hissed, hugging her.

'Yeah. I'm fine.'

'Has he hurt you?'

Bakker yanked Gabriel back by his collar.

'No, I haven't hurt her. Though she did a pretty good job of hurting herself. I bandaged her foot. You can check my handiwork if you like; it's a long time since I did any field dressings.'

Gabriel glanced up at Eli. She gave a minute shake of her head. Her meaning was clear. The dressing was fine.

'No, I trust you, Kevin,' he said, turning. 'So, tell me. What do you want?'

Bakker kicked a chair over to Gabriel.

'Sit.'

Gabriel placed the chair beside Eli's. After leaning the rifle against the wall in a corner, Bakker unholstered a pistol and dragged another chair over for himself. He sat facing Gabriel, the pistol lying on his right thigh. If Bakker raised the gun, Gabriel would try to take the bullet.

'OK, I'm sitting. Now what?'

'First of all, none of your Eastern mystic shit. I haven't forgotten. You start using the voice on me and your wife gets a hollow-point in the belly. Are we clear?'

'We're clear,' Gabriel said, glancing at Eli's stomach and thinking that he wouldn't mention its passenger to Bakker.

Bakker nodded, apparently satisfied. He held his hand out.

'Phone.'

Gabriel handed it over and watched Bakker smash it into pieces beneath his boot heel, twisting it down onto the floorboard to ensure the job was thorough. Bakker scratched his head with his free hand.

'I've waited a long time for this, Gibril. A very long time. Since you abandoned me in Kandahar. Do you know how long ago that was?'

Gabriel nodded. As long as Bakker was asking questions, they had a chance. He obviously had something planned beyond a quick kill. There was a chance Gabriel could find a way to either convince him not to kill them both or get close enough to disarm him.

'Five years.'

'Nearly six now.'

'But you've got it wrong, Kevin.'

'Oh, yes? Enlighten me.'

'I didn't abandon you.'

Bakker's eyes flashed and he curled his lip back from his teeth.

'No? What, then? You just decided to take the long way round to extract me? Did a little sightseeing? What?'

'I drove straight into a Taliban ambush. Two pickups, four men apiece. I got my truck turned around, led them into the desert. I was faster than them and I made cover in a rocky gorge about three clicks from the rendezvous point.

'I took out the first bunch with the GPMG but the second crew made it out of the vehicle. I took out two more then the belt jammed. It was small arms after that. When the ammo ran out they came for me with these long, curved knives. I killed them with a rock but it took too long, Kevin. I'm sorry.

'By the time I reached the extraction point, you were gone. It looked like a butcher's shop. There was a lot of blood. Yours, I assumed. I found some tyre tracks and followed them as far as I could but the trail hit this vast rock slab and dried.

'In the end I had to leave. I couldn't afford to miss my own extraction. I took a blood sample back with me. When we got the analysis back it confirmed my worst fears. The eggheads told me it was yours.'

'And you left it at that. You left me to rot, Gibril.'

'No. You're wrong. Don put an intelligence team on it 24/7. He said until we had sight of your body, we were to proceed as if you were MIA.'

'Bullshit!'

'It's not. It's true. But you'd disappeared, Kevin. It was as if you'd vanished from Afghanistan. Normally, we'd have got a sniff of something from one of our local informants but there was nothing. No ransom demand, no video, nothing.'

Bakker rubbed his chin, scratching at the day-old stubble. The whole time Gabriel had been talking, he'd sat, face impassive, listening intently. Gabriel thought he might, just, have a chance of talking his way out of this one. Then Bakker spoke, and everything changed.

'What about Alix, Gibril?'

Gabriel frowned.

'Who's Alex? It was just the two of us, Kevin. There was no third man. Don't you remember? Don said he was wary of committing two men to the op, given it doubled our visibility. No way would he have authorised a third.'

Now it was Bakker's turn to look perplexed. Deep grooves furrowed his brow as his eyebrows drew together.

'I agree with you: there was no third *man*,' he said, jerking forwards and staring into Gabriel's eyes. 'Alix was my wife. Alix, Gibril! With an "i". She died out there. She drove over an IED. All because of Webster. And you, Gibril. You have blood on your hands, too.'

Gabriel realised at that point how far Bakker had become detached from reality. Whatever else the Taliban had done to him during those long years in captivity, they'd stolen his memories and given him new ones.

'Kevin, you weren't married,' Gabriel said. 'I've read your file. I've *got* your file. The Taliban did this to you. They must have needed something to motivate you to kill Don.'

Bakker's head was shaking from side to side with metronomic regularity, once a second. The effect was disconcerting as his eyes never left Gabriel's.

'You're lying. We were married for fifteen years. I remember our wedding day. I remember it all!'

Gabriel calculated the timeline in his head. Saw where the Taliban had made their mistake.

'Wait. How long did you say you were married?'

'Are you deaf? Fifteen years!'

'How old are you now, Kevin?'

'Thirty-four, why?'

'Don't you see? The Taliban fucked up. You said you were captured almost six years ago. That would make you twenty-eight at the time. So if you'd been married for fifteen years you would have needed to be married at thirteen,' Gabriel said. 'They miscalculated. Either they thought you were older than you were or they just assumed we get married as young as they do.'

Bakker's head-shaking came to a stop.

'No. I just got the timings wrong. I mean...' He scraped a palm over his face and then began scratching at a spot between his eyes. 'We were married, but just not for fifteen years. It must have been, it must have been—'

'Ten years? Did you get married at eighteen, Kevin? Remember when we were sitting in that top-floor flat while you put that bomb together?'

'Yes, I remember.'

'With the Meccano strips, yes?'

Bakker nodded, a half-smiled playing across his lips.

'Can't go wrong with Meccano. If you can't have it, build it!'

'You told me you joined the army at eighteen, straight from school. You said it was a great life for a single bloke.'

'No. You're wrong. I couldn't have said that, Gibril, could I? I was married. To Alix. To my wife.'

Gabriel sighed. Despite their reputation for casual brutality, there was nothing casual about the psychological mischief the Taliban had wrought on Bakker's mind. Maybe they had advisers. Plenty of ex-spooks from China, North Korea, Russia or even America who'd be happy to teach their black arts to anyone with deep-enough pockets.

'I said I'd read your file, Kevin. You could read it, too. I brought it with me. It's in my car on Skye. You could come back with me,' he said, seeing a route out of the impasse. 'See for yourself. This isn't you, Kevin. This is the Taliban. They brainwashed you. Implanted false memories.'

Bakker started shaking his head again: left-right-left-right, now at two cycles per second.

'No. No. No. No.'

The single emphatic syllable repeated in time with the head shake.

An image rose from Gabriel's subconscious and sharpened into perfect focus. A playing card. Bordered by a narrow black strip, a colour photograph. A bearded man staring off to one side of the lens. An American marine was holding it up, grinning.

'Number one on Uncle Sam's shit list,' the marine said.

And then the name of the wanted man.

Gabriel held up his right index finger. Bakker's gaze latched onto the upraised digit.

'What?'

Miraculously, his head stilled, eyes front, lips working as if he were chewing the inside of his cheek.

'What was your wife's name again?'

'I told you. Alix.'

'Spell it for me, Kevin?'

'What? Why?'

'Humour me. It's the least you can do given you're pointing a pistol at me.'

Bakker sighed and rolled his eyes.

'A-L-I-X. Happy now?'

'Kevin, they were playing games with you. Taunting you. And us,' Gabriel said, keeping his voice low and soothing, aware that he, too, was playing a dangerous game. 'That's the name of the man we were hunting. Ali X. Nobody knew his last name.'

Something happened to Bakker then. Gabriel saw it. His carefully constructed reality, implanted by the Taliban and then nurtured by Bakker himself, started to fracture. His jaw worked harder as he bit the inside of his cheek, then he winced and a thin stream of blood spilled from between his lips. His face drained of colour, then flushed pink.

'You're lying. You're trying to trick me. Alix died. But we were married, Gibril. We were!'

'What did you drink on your wedding night, Kevin?'

'Pardon?'

'What sort of car did you and Alix drive in after the reception? Eli and I had a white Jaguar Mark V.'

Bakker looked upwards, then back at Gabriel. His eyes were unfocused.

'It doesn't matter.'

'What was your best man's name, Kevin? Where did you go for your stag night?'

'I don't remember. Stop interrogating me! You're the prisoner here, not me.'

Gabriel readied himself. Within seconds, Bakker's concentration would falter and he needed to be ready to move.

But Bakker leapt to his feet, tipping his chair over backwards and pointing the pistol at Gabriel's face. 'You're wrong!' he screamed. 'Anyway, I can't come back. I killed Don, didn't I? That was murder. I'd get life, I can't go back inside a cell, Gabriel, I can't. I'd kill myself before I let that happen.'

Gabriel jerked back as the gun swung wildly, describing an erratic arc that took in Eli as well as him. Had he overdone it? He'd intended to destabilise Bakker. Make him unsure enough of what he believed to start to come apart. But if he lost it now, they'd be dead.

He got ready to move. The distance between him and Bakker was no more than seven feet. He could cover that in under a second. Block Eli with his body, lunge for the gun. Worst-case scenario, Bakker might squeeze off a shot, but he was distracted now and his aim would be wild.

Bakker took a couple of long steps backwards. Not good. Now the gap had increased to nine feet, maybe ten. And the gun arm was level, pointing the pistol directly at Gabriel's head. Bakker's knuckle was white over the trigger.

44

Sweat broke out on Bakker's forehead. Gabriel could see the individual beads forming. The colour leached from his cheeks once more and he was swallowing convulsively as if trying to dislodge a lump of gristle from his throat.

'No. This is wrong. I need to think,' he muttered.

He levelled the pistol, then dropped it by a couple of inches. Up it came again and Bakker straightened his arm jerkily.

'Kevin, I'm not lying to you. I swear it to you on my honour as a soldier. You know I wouldn't use that oath lightly. We can sort this out,' Gabriel said, holding his hands out. 'We can make it all right. You were ill when you killed Don. You need treatment, not prison.'

Bakker shook his head. Wiped his top lip. He was transferring his weight from foot to foot, rocking from side to side, although the pistol stayed fixed on the midpoint between Gabriel's eyes.

'Kneel,' he said.

'Kevin, I can't do that. You can't execute me,' Gabriel said, keeping his tone level, not pleading. His only chance of saving Eli's life and his own was in staying calm and finding a chink of reason in Bakker's disordered thinking. 'They brainwashed you, I told you.'

Bakker reached behind him. When his hand reappeared, it was holding a set of steel handcuffs.

'I said I needed to think. Put these on and lock yourself to Eli's right ankle. I'm going out.'

He tossed the cuffs across the space between them. Gabriel opened his hands but fumbled the catch. The metal cuffs clattered to the floor under the table. He bent down and scrabbled under the table. He heard Bakker tut as he closed his fingers on the cold piece of steel.

As he straightened, he flung the cuffs with all his might at Bakker's head. They whirled round on the short length of chain, catching Bakker full in the face. Bakker yelled in pain as blood spurted from his nose and he staggered backwards, left hand clamped over his bleeding face, gun arm coming up.

Heart-rate accelerating, every muscle firing, Gabriel leapt forwards, like a sprinter coming off his blocks, closing the distance between them, eyes locked onto the pistol, hands outstretched, already angling his body to put his right hand closer to the gun whilst minimising the target area presented by his torso. Eight feet, six, four, one…

The pistol shot was huge in the enclosed space. The round went into the ceiling, bringing down a cloud of plaster dust and paint fragments.

Gabriel closed with Bakker, barrelling into him and knocking him off his feet. He fell on top of him, and scrabbled for the gun, but Bakker's grip was solid and he smashed the pistol into Gabriel's elbow, sending a jolt of electric agony surging up to his shoulder and back down to his fingertips.

Gabriel heard Eli's screams. She sounded a long way away.

He punched Bakker in the side of the head, oblivious to the pain as his knuckles met solid bone. Bakker grunted as he took the blow, then curled his arm, bringing the pistol round until the muzzle was inches from Gabriel's face. Gabriel clamped both hands onto Bakker's right wrist, forcing the weapon away. Bakker's trigger finger spasmed, sending five fast shots into the far wall, deafening Gabriel and releasing a cloud of blazing-hot gases that scorched the skin of his wrists.

Bakker's knee came up, crunching into his groin. The pain was instantaneous and severe, a sick feeling that blossomed in his balls and exploded upwards into his belly. Then Bakker was on his feet, pointing the pistol at Gabriel.

'You fuck, Gibril! I hate you!'

He fired wildly. Every round went wide, hammering into the walls, through the windows, into the ceiling again. Gabriel spun round and fell sideways, cracking his head against the edge of the door. Bakker kept pulling the trigger but the magazine was empty. Wild-eyed, he turned and ran, flinging the kitchen door open and sprinting away from the cottage.

'Gabriel, you're hit!' Eli shouted.

He turned.

'No I'm not. He missed.'

'Your left arm, darling. Look! I think he clipped an artery.'

She jerked her chin at his arm and he looked down.

His jacket was ripped open and blood was soaking into the fabric. Now he felt it. An intense crushing pain as if his flesh was trapped in a sharp-jawed vice.

'Oh, Christ!'

He staggered back until his back hit the wall, then he slid down it until his bottom hit the floor.

'Gabriel!' she yelled. 'You have to untie me. Then I can help you.'

He shook his head to clear it. But the ringing in his ears from the rapid-fire gunshots was disorientating him. The lights kept dimming then brightening, the colours intensifying into a saturated kaleidoscope then washing out like an old, faded photograph. The only thing that stayed constant was the stink of gun smoke, that acrid, chemical smell every soldier got used to from their first day on the firing range, through live-fire exercises and into combat.

The bullet in his arm was hurting. It felt like it was still spinning, rotating around and around, burrowing deeper like a star-nosed mole, pulling at his flesh with sharp little teeth, dislodging gobbets of tissue, sucking them dry of blood then spitting them out. Hollow-point ammunition would do that, which was

funny really, banning them in war but then allowing the police to use them, I mean it's not as if a regular round doesn't shit up your insides pretty effectively, now, is it? All those hand-wringers in their designer armchairs what do they know, writing to their MP saying it's too dangerous for soldiers? Jesus! Have you even been on a battlefield, Son? They're supposed *to be dangerous, they're full of people trying to kill you for a start i hardly think an expanding bullet is the biggest problem we've got to worry about*

once i was facing this guy and wed both run out of ammunition i had a tactical tomahawk id picked up off a dead us marine and he had a machete well we went at each other and by the way i killed him and let me tell you

i think hed have rather been shot with a jhp round than what i had to do to him to get him to lie down i damn-near took his head off

the mess was indescribable and

then i had to

The guy he'd beheaded fell onto him and started shouting right in his ear.

'Gabriel, wake up! Wake up, Goddammit! You have to untie me right now or you're going to die.'

Gabriel opened his eyes. Eli's face was inches from his own. He went for a kiss but his aim was off, clumsy, and his lips smooshed against her chin.

'Get up, soldier, just get the fuck up and get these ropes off me,' Eli barked.

He shook his head. His senses cleared as if someone had thrown a switch. He looked up at Eli, then pushed her off him with his right arm.

She'd shuffled the chair over and then rocked it on top of him. Her wrists were tied behind her and her ankles were lashed to the legs. He got to his knees and leant over, experiencing a sudden swooping dizziness that had him on all fours, head swinging like a stunned beast waiting for the slaughterman's bolt-gun.

Leaning further down he got his mouth around the rope tying Eli's wrists together and started biting and twisting, yanking at the knots and jerking his head from side to side like his old greyhound Seamus used to when they'd play with his favourite blue rubber tug-toy. The brindled dog's face swam into focus, smiling that wide-mouthed grin that seemed to stretch all the way round his head. *'Come on, master, stay focused or you'll be joining me,'* he said.

Gabriel opened his eyes again; they'd drifted shut just as he started thinking about Seamus. He heaved in a breath and gave the loop of rope he was biting down on another yank. It loosened by another couple of inches and now he could get his fingers into it. They felt as fat as sausages and wouldn't obey him but, little by little, he got the knot untied. Eli wriggled her wrists free and seconds later was untying her ankles.

'Here,' she said, grabbing a length of rope off the floor and whipping it around Gabriel's upper arm, 'let's get a tourniquet on you and I can have a look at the damage.'

The pain as she tightened the rope was bad, but it was dwarfed by the sense of relief at finally being with her again.

'I love you, El,' he said as she tied off the tourniquet.

'I love you too, now be quiet and save your strength.'

She crossed to the window and put a chair leg through the bars, giving it a shove to smash the pane. She went outside and returned with a long narrow triangle of glass. Having wrapped it in a towel, she knelt by Gabriel's side and cut the sleeve off his jacket and the shirt beneath it. He watched her working, interested now to see how much damage Bakker had done.

The bullet had gouged a messy trough through the flesh on the outside of his upper arm. But it hadn't hit the bone. He could see the problem though, a deep groove that was still flowing with blood.

'You need to pack that and get a bandage on it, nice and tight.'

'Yes, thanks for that. I have done battlefield surgery courses,' she hissed as she turned the wound in the light. 'Trouble is, I've got nothing to work with.'

'Loosen the tourniquet.'

'What?'

'Loosen it. We need to see how bad the bleeding is. If he did clip an artery I might be in trouble. If he missed then we can improvise something pretty easily.'

'I see someone's feeling better if they're giving orders all of a sudden,' she said, eyeing him with, what, a brief smile?

'Try it, please?'

Eli loosened the rope around his upper arm and they watched together as blood started flowing again. It was a constant stream but it wasn't spurting. Eli tightened the rope again.

'That's the good news,' she said. 'Now the bad. As far as I can see, Bakker didn't have a first-aid kit here, so we'll have to improvise.'

Gabriel jerked his chin at the kitchen counter.

'You can use kitchen towel instead of gauze.'

She nodded, got to her feet and ran into the kitchen where she pulled open a narrow drawer. She returned to Gabriel with the kitchen paper, a tube of superglue and a roll of duct tape.

'Help me close the wound.'

Using Gabriel's right hand and Eli's left, they pinched the ragged sides of the wound together. She dried it with a wad of kitchen paper then ran a bead of glue along the pushed-together skin, blowing on it to dry it faster. After thirty seconds, she nodded at Gabriel.

'Let go.'

They took their fingers away. Breathing steadily, Gabriel waited to see if the wound would burst open again. The glue held.

Next, Eli laid a folded pad of kitchen paper over the stuck-together wound. She ripped off a length of duct tape and wound it around Gabriel's bicep, smoothing down the edges and ensuring there were no air bubbles.

When she was done, he rotated the arm.

'Nice job, doc.'

She bent towards him and kissed him.

'How does it feel?'

'It's not too bad. I've had worse.'

'You're in shock. I'll see if there are any painkillers. Hold on a second.'

While Eli was gone, Gabriel got up off the floor and flopped into a chair, where he looked down at the silver tape encircling his arm. He'd once been stung by a bullet ant in the Brazilian rainforest. That had hurt a lot worse than Bakker's hollow-point, which had produced an intense throbbing sensation like a bad burn.

He'd had friends who'd been hit by all kinds of rounds, from .22s up to machinegun bullets. There seemed to be no rhyme or reason as to how much a gunshot wound would hurt. Some said it depended on the individual's tolerance for pain, others on the exact location of the wound, or whether it did a lot of nerve damage. The consensus, however, was rock-solid. Don't get hit.

Eli came back with a couple of small boxes; one brightly coloured, some kind of over-the-counter pills, the other, a plain white box, with a typed label.

'You're in luck,' she said. 'I've got paracetamol with codeine, and Tramadol. Bakker must have a prescription.'

Gabriel held out a hand. 'Give me three of each.'

'You sure about the Tramadol? I took some once. Hallucinated for hours.'

He grimaced. 'I'll take my chances.'

She popped out four capsules and brought him a plastic beaker of water. After swallowing the pills, he held his arms wide.

'Come here.'

She let him enfold her in his arms, but only briefly, pulling away after a few seconds.

'We have to get Bakker. We can't let him escape. He'll only come back to try to kill you again.'

'I know. I just wish there was another way.'

Her eyes widened.

'After everything he's done, you can say that?'

'He's ill, Eli. They fucked him up. I don't think he really knows what's going on. Did you notice how he called me Gibril? And all that stuff about Isaac and Abraham.'

'Of course I noticed! I've been his prisoner for the last however many days it's been.'

'Sorry. Anyway, I agree. And he left his rifle.'

'I didn't see him reload the pistol, either. You may be able to take him down without killing him, if that's really what you want.'

Gabriel nodded. He got to his feet. Then he looked at her.

'You're limping. My God, how did I not notice? El, what happened?'

She smiled wryly. 'I broke my foot trying to kick the door down.'

'Maybe you should take some painkillers, too,' he said.

'I will. Just get after him, will you? I wish I could help but it hurts like a bastard and I'd be no good on open ground.'

He nodded. 'And you're fine down there?' he asked, nodding towards her belly.

She smiled. 'Totally fine, "down there". Don't worry. I'm not.'

'OK, see you soon, lock up after me.'

With that, he went to the rifle and checked the magazine. It had two rounds remaining. Not ideal, but beggars couldn't be choosers. In any case, Gabriel had a strong feeling this wouldn't be a protracted firefight.

He shouldered it and left the cottage, searching for the man believing himself betrayed by Gabriel and now struggling to process the fact that his wife was an illusion created by his captors all those years ago in Kandahar.

45

A cold wind struck him in the face as he closed the door behind him and listened for the sound of Eli locking it. The weather had changed while they'd been inside. Gone was the bright sunshine and crystalline blue sky. In its place, a flat grey bank of fog that blanketed the island, blown in from the sea on a biting north wind. Visibility was down to maybe fifty feet. How he was supposed to find Bakker in this was beyond him. But he had to try.

He turned through a full circle. There'd been no boat he could see when he landed, so maybe Bakker kept one on the far side of the island. It made no sense. Why wouldn't you keep your only means of leaving the island close to your house?

Gabriel admonished himself. For a man with Bakker's paranoid outlook on life, doing the obvious was probably the very last thing you'd consider sensible.

Bakker had probably erected all kinds of psychological defences to hang onto his sanity, and physical ones, too. He'd have used his tradecraft to protect himself, as he saw it, from his enemies. The rifle at the cottage was a minor part of the overall strategy. Looking back, Gabriel was surprised there hadn't been booby-traps or even a few mines buried in the soft expanse of grass between the beach and the house.

Gabriel tried to think himself into Bakker's mind. What would *he* do in these circumstances? Head for higher ground? A bolt-hole? Another building where he'd feel safe? Maybe he had a cave somewhere up in the hills. Whatever. Higher ground felt like the best bet. Although with the fog closing in, it wouldn't offer Bakker much in the way of tactical advantage. In fact, visibility would be worse the higher he went.

Gabriel set off towards the hills. The temperature was dropping and the damp penetrated his clothing, making him shiver. He increased his pace, holding the rifle's sling to stop it bouncing on his back.

Just another tab into the rough country, he thought, as he ploughed on, the air now moist enough to dampen his skin.

As he climbed, he strained to see as far ahead as possible in the thickening fog. Rocks loomed up out of nowhere, some taller than a man. Bakker could be hiding behind any one of them, ready with a fresh magazine in his pistol. Gabriel unshouldered the Browning and carried it across his body.

The wind picked up, producing an eerie howling from somewhere up ahead. Gabriel knew it was just a rock formation or a stand of trees acting as a giant reed, vibrating as the air rushed through the narrow gap, but the effect was unsettling, as if the island itself was protesting at the weather.

Blinking away the moisture that was beading on his eyelashes, he struggled upwards, realising he was following not a man but a hunch; that Bakker, faced with some unimaginable truth about his own life and what he thought had been driving him on all these years, was searching for a place where he could finally face reality.

Maybe he'd see reason, even now. Gabriel could talk him down. Eli was correct: there was always a risk Bakker would come after them again, but that only applied if Gabriel let him walk. If he could capture him and bring him in, there was a chance the authorities would put him somewhere he could be treated.

It felt odd to Gabriel, after having suffered the death of his commander, and the kidnapping of his wife, to be feeling pity towards the perpetrator, but it really wasn't Bakker's fault. He'd been used by evil people for their own ends. Now it had to stop.

He gained more height, and, in seconds, as he crossed some unseen contour line on the hill, the fog dispersed, changing from a thick, grey blanket to swirling currents of white mist and then just wisps, snaking away from him over the summit.

A hundred feet away, he saw a figure marching away from him, arms wrapped around its torso. Was it Bakker?

'Kevin?' he yelled. 'Kevin, is that you?'

The figure did not turn, but kept walking, taking long strides that gave it a bobbing movement as its head rose and fell with each step.

Gabriel broke into a run, then the figure turned and raised its right arm. It was Bakker.

'Stay back! I don't want to shoot you, Gabriel, but I will if you force me to. Drop the rifle.'

Gabriel halted. He didn't raise the rifle, but he didn't drop it either. He couldn't afford to cede the advantage to Bakker.

'Kevin, it's over. You don't need to do this. Come in. I can help you. *We* can help you.'

Bakker's answer was a burst of fire. Gabriel threw himself to the ground, but every round went wide; Bakker seemed to be shooting randomly.

As he looked up, Bakker emptied a magazine at him for the second time. Bullets whined overhead and he heard one ricochet off a rock behind him, sending sharp fragments spinning through the air and catching him on the back of the head.

Bakker threw the pistol aside and pulled something from his pocket and, as he did so, Gabriel caught something odd about his left arm: it was cradling an object to his chest. He caught a glimpse of a loop of string or flex of some kind.

Bakker's expression was impossible to read. His features were neutral, betraying no emotion. It was as if something had gone from him, whatever made him human, or conscious of what he was doing, blown away on the wind like those serpentine wraiths of fog scurrying over the grass.

Gabriel got to his feet and levelled the rifle at Bakker.

'That's far enough, Kevin. Stop there and put your hands over your head.'

Bakker kept coming, closing the gap between them until he was just twenty feet away. This close, Gabriel could see what he was holding across his chest. His blood froze in his veins, and it had nothing to do with the cold wind scouring the hillside.

The rectangular object Bakker was cradling like a baby was olive-green, with two scissor-like legs, inverted Vs, one at each end. The curved plastic casing was snug to his ribs and he was close enough for Gabriel to read the moulded legend on the side facing him.

BACK
M18A1 APERS MINE

It was a Claymore, the devastating anti-personnel mine developed by the Americans and copied by the Soviets and the Chinese. Without having to see the other side, Gabriel knew full well what the wording was on that side.

FRONT TOWARDS ENEMY

The looped cable he'd seen was the detonator cord. He could see where it disappeared into the simple electrical detonator – what they'd all called the 'clacker' back in the day – clutched in Bakker's right hand. Standard advice in training manuals was to depress the switch three times in rapid succession to ensure the Claymore blew, but, realistically, the first click would be enough.

Gabriel's pulse spiked. Inside the moulded olive-green plastic case were roughly seven hundred steel ball bearings, layered in front of a sheet of C4 plastic explosive. Bakker would be cut in half, but this close the Claymore would take him out as well. Fifty feet was the safe distance for those behind the mine. Fifty. He was less than half that.

He could try shooting Bakker, but there was every chance that in his death throes his hand would close on the clacker and they'd both be history.

'Drop the rifle, Gibril,' Bakker said in a soft voice freighted with sorrow. 'It all ends here.'

Gabriel had no choice but to comply. He bent and laid the Browning on the grass. He straightened and looked Bakker in the eye, willing his breathing to steady.

'You don't have to do this, Kevin.'

Bakker shook his head and raised his right hand.

'I knew you would be a formidable enemy, Gibril. That's why I arranged a backup. I called in a kill team. They should be landing any time now. I'm sorry I won't be there to see it go down, but I realise, now, I have outstayed my welcome here. It's time I joined Alix.'

Gabriel put his hands out, dismayed to see they were shaking.

'There is no Alix, Kevin, there never was. Put the clacker down,' he said. 'We can go back together. You can call off the KT. There's still time.'

'No, there's no more time. I'd leave if I were you.'

Time went sludgy for Gabriel. He watched as Bakker blinked, his eyelids descending in slow-motion, lingering over his eyeballs for seconds before lifting again. His thumb curled over the detonator's pressed-steel trigger. Gabriel urged his muscles to work, but they felt wooden, creaky, unable, or just unwilling to obey the frantic commands his brain was sending. *Run. Run. Run!*

He turned and sprinted away from Bakker, crouching low to the ground and searching for the tall rock he'd passed earlier. Bakker yelled after him, his words carried on the breeze.

'It's not me you should be worrying about, Gibril. I remembered the name of the man who tortured me. You want Abdul Hassan Osmani. He gave me my targets.'

Gabriel reached the rock and threw himself behind it, scrunching himself into a ball, hands clamped over his ears.

Even through his palms, the explosion was deafeningly loud. Fragments of the mine's casing spattered the other side of the rock and black smoke blew all around him, carrying the puttyish, plasticky smell of the C4.

He emerged to a scene he thought he would never see again after leaving the army: a soldier blown to pieces by a mine. Bakker's legs and the lower half of his torso had fallen backwards, his boots pointing skywards. Spread out in a wide semi-circle behind them was a mess of bloody tissue and bone fragments. What was left of his upper body had been blown back for thirty feet before coming to rest on a hummock of now blood-soaked grass.

Shaking, Gabriel fell to his knees and covered his face with his hands.

46

Gabriel searched the ground in a fifty-foot-diameter circle around the blast site. He found Bakker's pistol buried muzzle-first in a hummock of earth. He wiped the grip clean of gore and stuck it into his waistband. He needed his Sig, too. Bakker had stuck it into his waistband. Oh God, was it still there?

He returned to the crater left by the Claymore, and Bakker's ripped-apart body. Reaching down, he rolled the legs over, spilling more viscera from the body cavity onto the grass. Lying beneath the hips was the P226. Gabriel picked it up, wiped it clean and dropped out the magazine. It was still full. That was something. He pushed it down into the front of his jeans. Now it was time to go.

He grabbed the rifle and ran back the way he'd come. Crossing that invisible contour line, he re-entered the fog. It was a soupy, creamy-white, scattering what little sunlight penetrated to ground level so that all shadows disappeared. He was forced to slow down or risk crashing into a boulder and simply veering over a cliff.

Sharp-pointed standing stones loomed out of the white like sentries guarding the way home. He couldn't remember seeing them on the way up: had he come a different way? It was impossible to tell. He stopped for a moment, trying to use sound to get a bearing. To his left he heard the crashing of waves and the rushing sound as they surged up the shingle beach and then drained back to sea again.

If he kept that sound on his left and turned inland by a hair, he should find his way back to the cottage.

Trotting now, he strained to see further ahead than a few feet, anxiously scanning the ground for rabbit holes, rocks, barbed-wire: anything that might catch him out, breaking an ankle or snagging him when he needed to be back with Eli.

Because however delusional Bakker had been at the end, there was one thing he'd said that Gabriel believed absolutely. *I called in a kill team.*

So as he ran on, Gabriel was trying to pick up a second sound over the surf: an outboard motor. Because they'd be coming in by sea, of that he was sure. A chopper would be unnecessarily expensive and, given the current weather, impossible.

How many men? A team could be two: a sniper and a spotter, for example. But somehow, Gabriel was sure Bakker hadn't meant that. If Gabriel were putting together a team, he'd go for a minimum of four men. Bakker knew enough about Gabriel and Eli not to underestimate them. One ex-SAS, the other ex-IDF Special Forces, not to mention their post-military careers.

They'd be heavily armed, too. Pistols, submachine guns, maybe assault rifles. And what did he and Eli have? A Browning hunting rifle with a couple of rounds in the magazine. A clogged Beretta M9 pistol with an empty mag. A Sig Sauer P226 with a full one. After that, it was down to rocks, anything they could improvise inside the cottage, maybe using those window bars, and fuck all else.

Would they head for the cottage? Bakker must have told them he had Eli held there. And with her injured foot he'd not think her likely to make a move to leave. So Gabriel's first priority – his and Eli's – was to get clear of the cottage. Their only hope was to use the element of surprise, maybe construct some sort of ambush.

Hiding wasn't an option. The kill team would just scour the island until they found them.

As he descended towards the cottage, the mist changed character, flattening out into a thick layer that ended a metre above the ground. He raced up to the door and hammered on it with his fist.

'Eli, it's me!' he yelled.

The door opened and he hurried inside.

Eli looked at him. 'Bakker?'

'Blew himself up with a Claymore.'

She nodded, not seeming surprised by the news.

'He said he'd called in a kill team,' Gabriel said. 'I don't think we have much time. We need to leave.'

Eli shook her head.

'Not yet. I found something in the cellar. Come and look.'

He followed her down the staircase.

'Watch yourself, the bottom step's missing,' she said over her shoulder

She'd found a hurricane lamp from somewhere. Its flame gave the dank space a yellow cast and he saw a scrape of earth in the centre of the floor.

'What's that?'

'I think it's an arms cache. I was just excavating it when you banged on the door. Help me, will you?'

He followed Eli's pointing finger. What he saw gave him a flicker of hope. Flat metal, painted olive-green, with yellow stencilled capitals. He couldn't make out the words, but it didn't matter. He recognised military storage when he saw it.

'I was using this,' Eli said, holding up a piece of broken wood. 'Break off another step and help me.'

He stamped on the second-to-last step, breaking it free and creating a sharp edge in the process. It would make a rudimentary entrenching tool.

He knelt beside Eli, who was chopping and hacking at the earth above the storage crate. The soil was coming out in lumps now, and he worked his way in from a different spot. Gradually, then faster and faster, they revealed a metal lid about five feet by one. The stencilling was revealed.

2 RDS 105MM HOW HE

If they'd had a 105 mm howitzer, a couple of high-explosive shells might have been some use. Otherwise, they wouldn't even make decent clubs. He prayed that it was merely something Bakker had picked up to store his gear.

Working frantically, they hacked and scraped away at the sides of the hole until they had enough space to reach down and curl their fingers under the handles.

They lifted the crate out and dumped it down on the floor with a satisfyingly deep clank from whatever was inside. Eli worked the latches free and swung the lid back. Then she looked at Gabriel, a savage grin on her grimy face.

'Kill team, eh? They're going to get more than they bargained for.'

Stacked neatly inside were at least ten canvas Claymore bags, officially designated M7 bandoliers. He lifted out the topmost bag and unsnapped the press studs. Inside lay a pristine Claymore, as fresh as the day it had been manufactured. Boxes of .204 and 9mm ammunition were stacked at one end.

As he stared into the crate, itemising its lethal contents, Gabriel was rethinking his original idea. With Eli's injured foot, they'd make slow going if they left the cottage. And they'd only be able to carry a fraction of the crate's contents.

Eli was ahead of him.

'Let's make a stand here. You can set up a perimeter with the Claymores. We've got the Browning and two pistols plus plenty of ammunition. Hit them hard when they're close then we can pick off any survivors.'

It was a brutally simple plan. Did Gabriel have any qualms about using mines against the men coming for them? None. The clue was in the title.

Bakker, from God knew where, had called in a kill team. Not a punch-up-and-leave team. Not a why-don't-we-all-sit-down-and-work-things-out team. Its members could only be one of two types of men. Radicalised British Muslims, or mercs. Make that three: disaffected domestic terrorists, maybe Irish nationalist, maybe anarchist; in reality, anyone who fancied taking a crack at a couple of members of a secret British security outfit. Whoever they were, they'd be highly trained and sufficiently motivated, by ideology, religious fanaticism or plain old cash, to come in hard.

Gabriel thought back to the man Bakker had named just before killing himself. Abdul Hassan Osmani. A Taliban commander or intelligence officer. If they'd developed the capacity, and the interest, to plan and execute strikes in Britain, that marked a huge strategic shift in the way they operated.

Seizing control of Afghanistan was one thing, and there were endless reports and briefings coming out of the various security thinktanks that discussed in unflinching language the historical inevitability of that happening. But to engage in asymmetric warfare across the globe? Using mercenaries and brainwashed lone-wolf operators like Bakker? That was something else altogether.

It was also something for another day. If Gabriel and Eli were going to deliver that message to the powers-that-be, they had a more pressing, and lethal, message they needed to deliver a little closer to home.

'Get yourself upstairs with the Browning,' Gabriel said. 'If they arrive before we're ready, the Claymores will be useless.'

'Better idea. You go to the top of the steps and I'll throw them up to you. It'll be faster that way.'

He nodded. She was right.

From his position beside the hatch, he could lean down and catch each M7 bandolier as she swung it up to him. There were twelve in all; as he stacked them on the kitchen floor, he was calculating angles and distances. The problem was tactical in nature but geometric in its origins.

Each mine had a factory-defined optimal kill zone out to fifty-metres and a dispersion angle of sixty degrees. The further from the cottage he set them, the earlier he could take out the kill team, but also the further apart he'd have to set the Claymores to still provide 360-degree coverage around the cottage. But as they spread apart, gaps would appear between the kill zones: spaces where a lucky or observant attacker might slip through uninjured.

He could always take a gamble and cluster the mines on one side of the cottage – the one facing the beach would be the obvious choice – and hope the mercs went for a frontal assault. He shook his head. Irritated. Nobody with an ounce of tactical sense would approach a building that way.

No, it had to be a perimeter. There was no more time to ponder the many variables. He had to move. With three bags slung over each shoulder, he left the cottage at a run.

Gabriel took eight long strides away from the front door and set up the first mine, double-checking he had the business-side facing outwards. The Claymores were supposed to be camouflaged by light foliage: standard procedure. But whoever had drawn up the manual clearly had never visited this particular barren island in the Outer Hebrides. There was nothing he could use. If the fog held, he'd be OK. If it cleared, they'd stand out as if signposted in neon.

He mumbled his calculations to himself as he worked.

'Radius is about eight metres. Circumference is two-pi-r, which equals roughly forty-eight metres. Twelve mines spaced equally around circumference means four-metre gaps.'

Having stuck the mine's legs into the soft ground, he moved four paces to his right and set up the second mine. In this way, edging round the cottage in a circle, checking the distance back to the imagined centre of the structure, he set up the perimeter, pausing in his work to fetch the remaining six mines.

After plugging in the detonators, he ran back to the cottage, letting the twelve lengths of electrical wire run through his fingers. Eli was waiting for him in the kitchen.

'All good?' she asked.

'Yeah. Twelve Claymores, four metres apart all the way round the cottage. Help me test the circuits, then we'll wire in the clackers.'

Seating himself, Gabriel took an M40 circuit test set out of the nearest bandolier. The kit, no bigger than a matchbox, would take the electric current from the clacker and light up a little yellow bulb if the signal was good.

Once he'd wired it in to the first clacker, he depressed the hinged metal handle three times in quick succession. Three times he got the reassuring little flash from the test kit. He nodded to himself, satisfied. He removed the test kit and wired in the clacker to the Claymore.

'One down, eleven to go,' he said.

They worked silently, side by side, until twelve wired-in detonators lay in a circle on the kitchen table, each corresponding to the clock-face position of the Claymore it would set off.

'I've been busy, too, by the way,' Eli said.

'Oh yeah? Doing what?'

She pointed at the cellar hatch, which was still folded back on itself.

'Looks tempting, doesn't it?'

'Too tempting?'

'It's an obvious hiding place. Might even house a tunnel opening. You'd have to send a guy down there to check it out.'

Seeing what his wife might have done, Gabriel fed her the line.

'And what might said guy encounter?'

'Nothing until he reached the bottom of the steps. Then, a tripwire.'

He raised his eyebrows.

'Linked to—'

'A fragmentation grenade. UK military spec.'

'Shit! He had L109s?'

'Ten of them. And four smokers. I put an HE over by the window.'

'Where are the rest of them?'

'Upstairs in the bedrooms, half in each.'

Gabriel nodded. Numerically they were down, but in terms of materiel, they weren't doing as badly as he'd feared.

'There's only one problem.'

'You mean, apart from the fact we've got an incoming squad of mercs or whoever spoiling for a fight?'

'Do you think Bakker would've told them about the weapons?'

She paused before answering, worry-lines creasing her forehead.

'No. I'm sure of it. They were buried down there and the earth was tramped absolutely flat. I don't think he'd have suspected we'd find them. Anyway, there's nothing we can do about it,' she said in a tone of finality. 'Put it this way, if they don't get anywhere close to the Claymores, we'll know he told them. Otherwise, I reckon we're in the clear.'

Gabriel nodded. It wasn't much, but it was the best they were going to get in terms of intelligence. He kissed her and she returned his embrace, hugging him tightly before releasing him.

'We'll do more of that when we're out of here, yes?'

'Deal.'

Eli went back upstairs, leaving him with an ironic order not to go back down into the cellar. He heard a muffled smash as she knocked out a window.

47

Gabriel stood by the side of the kitchen window, peering around the frame and striving to catch movement from the bank of fog hanging in the air in the middle distance.

As he waited, he envisaged the enemy. What would they be carrying? Kalashnikovs would be a safe bet. In this part of the world they were easier to come by than American-made weapons. There were hundreds of thousands swilling around the former Soviet Union to this day, some in the hands of legitimate armies, others wielded by everyone from drug gangs to militias and terrorist groups.

They'd be cautious, but overconfident. In his experience, mercs always were. Having survived war zones before going private, they were united by a belief that they were now invulnerable. Unbound by the Law of War, available to the highest bidder, up for a scrap from the Balkans to sub-Saharan Africa and everywhere in between.

What would Bakker have told them? *Be careful, these two aren't some ragtag bunch of AK-toting teenagers high on beer and weed. They're highly trained. Better than you are. You've got the firepower but they've got the smarts.* And he could just imagine the response. Delivered in accents as widely divergent as their owners. English. French. Nigerian. South African. American. *Relax. We can handle ourselves.*

He rubbed his arm without thinking. It set off a sharp burst of pain from the gunshot wound. Swearing under his breath his took his hand away. At that point, Eli appeared by his side.

'Hey,' she said. 'You OK?'

'Yeah, I'm good. How's the foot?'

'How's the arm? I just heard you swearing.'

'I asked first.'

She stared at him. 'What, it's a competition now?'

'The arm's fine. I just knocked it, that's all.'

'So's my foot. I couldn't do the hundred-metre dash, but I can get around on it. I took a couple of those painkillers myself. Excellent-quality stuff. Here.' She handed him the Sig Sauer. 'Full mag.'

He nodded his thanks. 'Did you clear Bakker's Beretta?'

'Yep. Even found a little bottle of gun oil in the crate. As-new condition.'

'Good. How many rounds have we got?'

'Apart from what's in the mags now, a couple of hundred for the pistols and a hundred for the rifle. Grenades, Claymores, all that ammo. Bakker was equipped for a siege.'

'Or another attack somewhere on the mainland.'

'Shit! You think that's what he was planning?'

'It's got to be a possibility, don't you think? After Rothford?'

Eli didn't answer. Not directly. Instead, she pointed into the distance.

'Company.'

Advancing towards the house, still maybe three or four hundred metres distant, were six men. They wore camouflage and were carrying rifles. All had camo greasepaint smearing the outlines of their faces. Only their torsos were visible above the still-swirling mist that hugged the ground, masking the Claymores. Gabriel prayed the wind would hold off.

One man in particular caught his eye. The rifle slung across his shoulder looked more substantial than the assault rifles carried by the other three. A Barrett Light Fifty, possibly, or its British equivalent, the AX50. Both weapons fired .50 calibre rounds, capable of destroying comms installations, thin-skinned vehicles and, given enough ammunition, non-fortified buildings. Such as former crofters' cottages on the Outer Hebrides. Something told him the man was carrying plenty of the five-inch long rounds.

Eli patted Gabriel on the right shoulder then left for her sniper nest.

'I'll hold fire until you detonate the first Claymore,' she said from the stairs.

He returned his gaze to the window. His mouth was dry, and licking his lips then swallowing did little to alleviate it. Beneath his shirt, his heart was jogging along at well above its resting rate, although by keeping his breathing steady he was preventing it bolting like a startled horse.

He looked down at the circle of clackers on the scratched pine table before him. Then back out the window. Five of the mercs were still advancing, now with their assault rifles held diagonally across their bodies or level at their hips. The sniper had dropped back and was setting up his rifle on its bipod on a hump in the grass. His range was only a couple of hundred metres.

At that distance the half-inch diameter rounds would punch holes in the cottage's walls as if they were made of papier-mâché, destroying anything they came into contact with and quite possibly exiting on the far side. Compared to that, the risk of blow-back from the Claymores was so small as to be laughable. The stone walls would easily repel the .22 size projectiles if any did make it that far.

The sniper, wittingly or not, had also positioned himself beneath the likely spread of fire of the Claymores. Gabriel had carefully positioned the convex cases so they were pointing slightly upwards, the better to achieve a kill. There was still a possibility that some of the projectiles would follow a low trajectory, but the bulk would fly well over the sniper's head. He hoped Eli would be sighting on him right now. They needed that heavy-duty rifle putting out of action.

He judged the oncoming mercs were about seventy metres out: twenty more before they entered the kill zone where the ball bearings would tear into their unresisting flesh and inflict horrific injuries.

Gabriel consulted his conscience. Found it clear. This was a kill team. Only one side was going to get off the island when the shooting was done. No negotiated surrender. No cable-ties and a march to a waiting transport. No game of football in No Man's Land. They'd brought assault rifles and that .50 calibre cannon now pointed straight at the cottage. Gabriel and Eli had pistols, a hunting rifle, Claymores and grenades. Fair's fair. You worked with what you had.

The one thing he promised himself was that he wouldn't let any of the mercs suffer a drawn-out death. Anyone not killed outright would meet their Maker with the sound of a double-tap echoing in their ears.

He tried to visualise Eli upstairs. Kneeling below the window with the Browning's muzzle resting on the sill. Funny way to resume the honeymoon. He smiled despite the desperate situation: outnumbered, outgunned, pinned down with no possibility of reinforcements arriving.

The leading merc was looking left and right, signalling to the men on his left and right to spread out. Gabriel couldn't afford to wait any longer. They were almost inside the kill zone. He grabbed the clackers for the two central Claymores. With luck they'd be enough.

He took a quick breath, then squeezed them, hard and fast: click, click, click.

As the muscles in his hands contracted, the Claymores detonated, twin explosions, so closely spaced they sounded like a single blast and its snap-back echo. Smoke and flames billowed upwards and outwards, blowing back towards the cottage. Without waiting to see who was left standing, Gabriel snatched up the next two clackers.

Both hands squeezed down hard. Click, click click.

Two more breathtakingly loud explosions. The kitchen

window shattered, spraying sharp glass fragments into the room. Gabriel flinched as one cut his cheek. Like angry hornets, fragments of the mine – casings? Stray ball bearings? It was impossible to tell – whined and buzzed through the air before smashing a picture on the wall opposite the window and shredding the woven cane lampshade over his head.

Bullets started cutting through the air overhead; Gabriel had sunk to his knees, sweeping the remaining clackers onto the floor. Seizing pairs at random, he fired them as fast as he could. He doubted they'd be doing any good at this point. Any of the mercs not cut down by the first two would have hit the ground immediately. But there was no point holding back, and the explosions themselves would be disorientating, pinning the men down while they waited for the barrage to stop.

As it did, with Gabriel discarding the sixth pair of clackers and moving to the window, pistol in hand. Outside, the pall of thick greyish smoke combined with the fog to obscure the view. Somewhere out there, one or more of the mercs lay dead. But how many had survived, wounded or otherwise?

As his hearing adjusted, he realised some of the shots he'd heard were Eli's. With just the one magazine, she couldn't afford to lay down suppressive fire with the Browning. Once she'd emptied it, she'd have to reload and that would give the remaining mercs precious seconds to advance until they were beneath her angle of fire. Unless Gabriel filled in with the pistol. Far less deadly, far less accurate, but enough of a threat to keep the attackers from closing with the cottage.

'Eli, keep them back!' he yelled. 'I'll cover while you reload.'

Her response was immediate: a one-shot-per-second salvo. The mercs answered back with a sustained bout of automatic fire. The window glass was long gone, but now the rounds tore chunks out of the wooden frame and started destroying the kitchen from the inside. Plaster fragments filled the air, along with a fine dust that entered Gabriel's mouth and nose, forcing him into a coughing fit.

Eli's firing stopped.

'Reloading!' she shouted.

Without exposing himself to the incoming fire, Gabriel stretched his right arm up and fired at the same rate as Eli.

When the Sig's magazine was emptied, he ran to the kitchen counter, picked up the high-explosive grenade, pulled the pin and threw it out of the window. Three seconds later it detonated with a loud bang. He heard a scream. On target.

48

Gabriel retreated up the staircase, which had suffered dozens of direct hits from rifle fire, exposing bright wood beneath the dark stain. Eli was pushing rounds home into the Browning's breech when he reached her.

'OK?' she asked.

'Yep. You?'

'Yep. All good.'

Gabriel dropped out the mag from his pistol and started reloading.

'Here,' Eli said, holding hers out. 'Take mine. It's full.'

He got to his knees and fired a three-round burst out of the window, which had been reduced to a pile of shards on the floor and a few fang-like triangles still puttied into the frame. The wall behind Eli was cratered with bullet holes, the signature of urban warfare from Kabul to Belgrade.

An answering burst of automatic fire gave him the information he needed; they weren't out of the woods yet.

'Loaded,' Eli hissed.

He got out of her way as she rested the Browning's barrel on the window ledge.

'See anything?'

Before she could answer, the rear of the room seemed to collapse in on itself. Lath and plaster exploded out from the back wall leaving a fist-sized hole. A split-second later the whine of a supersonic round reached them, along with the crack from the sniper rifle. OK, so one of them at least was keeping out of the firefight.

Eli squeezed off two rapid shots in response.

'It's hopeless,' she said. 'I can't see a thing. Fog's too thick and the smoke's all mixed in.'

'It works against them, too, though. They know we've got enough ammo for reloads, plus grenades. They'll be figuring out their next move.'

'How many did you get with the Claymores?'

'Honestly? I don't know. From the amount of return-fire I'd say at least two, but I could see even less downstairs than you could.'

As Eli finished her sentence, the wall beneath the window blew out with a bang, sending brick fragments and plaster dust spraying out in all directions. A cut split open her right cheek. Gabriel felt a burning pain on his throat and put a hand up to his neck. It came away red.

'Shit! We really need to take out the sniper,' he said. He lifted his chin. 'How bad is it?'

Eli wrinkled her nose. 'Messy but superficial. You'll live.'

'Your cheek's a mess. Ditto.'

'Cheers.'

'We need to get to the back of the house before he hits us with one of those cannonballs.'

She nodded and they hustled out of the bedroom on their hands and knees, rising to a crouch in the hallway and retreating to the bedroom at the opposite side of the house from the sniper.

'We're not taking any more automatic fire though,' he said. 'We may have killed the other five.'

She shrugged. 'Maybe. Or else they've realised they're just wasting ammunition shooting through the windows.'

Another .50 calibre round smashed into the front of the house, drilling a hole through the connecting wall, spearing over Eli and Gabriel's heads and exiting through the ceiling. As plaster dust rained down on them, they exchanged a look.

'He's pinning us down. Someone else is still alive,' Gabriel said.

'Get the grenades.'

Armed with two L109s apiece, they left the room and headed out to the landing. As they were setting up, the back door crashed open and the air was riven with the insanely loud noise of an assault rifle on full auto sending an entire magazine of rounds into the interior of the house.

Gabriel motioned for her to go back towards the bedroom.

She nodded, getting down onto her belly by the door and sighting at a point just above the top stair. If the merc showed his head above the lip of the staircase, he'd lose it.

Gabriel entered the other bedroom, leaving the door open. Lying prone, he and Eli were safe from the .50 cal rounds, which were systematically ripping the fabric of the house apart, brick by brick. Pale sunlight, filtered into whiteness by the fog, was lancing in at crazy angles through the holes punched out by the sniper.

He craned his neck to peer round the door jamb, caught Eli's eye and mouthed, 'Cellar.'

Would the lure of the open trapdoor be too strong for the merc to ignore? It had to be. You entered a house occupied by heavily armed insurgents, and the first thing you saw was an open hatch leading to a cellar. It could be a trap, of course it could, but it could also be an escape route. Or a hiding place. Either way, you'd have to check it out. If you walked past it, the next thing you might feel would be a knife in your back and a profound sense of regret.

Gabriel heard the unmistakable sound of a fresh magazine being slapped home and a charging lever being worked. So the merc had another thirty rounds ready to go. Heavy boots on the floorboards, amplified by the natural resonance of the cellar and projected upwards by the hatchway. A loud sniff. And, bizarrely, a loud sneeze.

'Fuck!'

The man's voice was deep, guttural. In that one, percussive syllable, Gabriel discerned a French accent. An international team, then. The guy could be ex-Foreign Legion, though just as easily regular French army or Special Forces. Plenty of non-French joined the Legion Etrangere.

Gabriel gripped his pistol tighter. If the merc ignored the temptations of the underworld and headed up the stairs, he'd probably come up firing. Eli might get a shot in but Gabriel needed to be ready, too.

The sniper had ceased fire. An agreement with the merc who'd just busted in through the back door? The last thing he'd want would be to have his arm taken off by a stray shot from his mate. That tilted the scales a little towards Gabriel and Eli.

And then the sound Gabriel realised he'd been praying for. A creak signalling a tentative tread onto the first wooden step leading down into the cellar. Then another. Then nothing.

He counted in his head. Three, four, five, six…

He'd reached eight when he heard a stumble and a French expletive, '*Merde!*' A burst of automatic fire and then the crash of a dropped rifle (somewhere out in the Algerian desert, the merc's old sergeant major would have torn him a new one for dropping it); then the shattering blast as the grenade exploded.

Gabriel felt the vibrations through the floorboards he was lying on. The stink of detonated high-explosive merged with the gun smoke all around him to create the olfactory cocktail recognised by every soldier who'd ever been on a battlefield.

Gabriel re-joined Eli in the hallway, already planning how they could take out the last remaining merc. She was white-faced, lying on her side, clutching her stomach. Gabriel felt a cold blanket of dread drop onto his shoulders as he raced to her.

'What is it, El? Shrapnel?'

She grimaced up at him, her cheeks powdery with plaster dust.

'Think I took a round just before the grenade went off,' she muttered in a shaky voice. 'That last burst.'

She lifted her hand away from her abdomen and Gabriel was horrified to see blood soaking through the front of her sweatshirt, turning the grey fabric a deep plum red.

49

Gabriel felt an eerie calm descend on him then. His wife, his *pregnant* wife, lay before him, badly wounded, a bullet to the belly, yet he felt no emotion at all. The horror vanished. No fear, no panic. In their place, a steely determination that she was not going to die. Not here, not now, not on some Godforsaken, barren, fog-shrouded island in the middle of the North Atlantic.

Watching his hands working, seemingly of their own volition, he heard himself telling Eli to take her palm away from the wound. Gently, he lifted the hem of the sweatshirt and the T-shirt beneath it. The entry wound was about six inches to the left of her navel; an ugly black hole rimmed with scarlet, blood flowing steadily over her skin.

He felt around her back until his fingertips encountered a ragged area of torn, wet flesh. An exit wound. Eli cried out and clutched his other arm with fingers that clawed into him.

'It's a through-and-through,' he said. 'Don't think he hit any major arteries. And it's nowhere near your uterus, either, so the baby's safe. I want you to hold tight. I'm going to dress it then I'll have another look for a first-aid kit. You might have missed it before.'

Gabriel ran downstairs and ripped down one of the thin cotton curtains from an undamaged window in the sitting room. He grabbed the paper tissue and duct tape from the kitchen and raced back upstairs.

After ripping off a square of the curtain and folding it into a thick pad, he pushed it into the exit wound, covered the whole area with kitchen paper and taped the makeshift dressing in place. He repeated the process over the entry wound, using a smaller pad.

Eli was moaning softly as he worked, and she didn't relax her grip on his shoulder. That was a good sign, though; it was when they went unresponsive, limp, even uninterested in what was happening to them that you needed to worry. It was like when medics did triage. The screamers you could leave for a while. Their pain was keeping them alive. It was the silent ones who got treated first. Sliding away second by second, they were too weak to call out.

'I have to go. I'll be right back,' he said.

Downstairs, he scanned the ruined kitchen. Bakker had to have a first-aid kit. Where would he keep it? One of the cupboards. It's where everybody kept them. Even deranged former Department operatives. You didn't bury them beneath the earth floor of your root cellar, or lock them under the stairs. You kept them where you could get to them in an emergency. And by Christ, this was an emergency!

He worked methodically, going clockwise around the room, flinging the cupboard doors wide, wrenching the drawers out so hard he pulled one clear off its runners.

'Come on, come on!' he hissed. 'Where did you put it, Kevin?'

He opened the cupboard under the sink and saw a black Maglite, a box of spare D-cells, and, right at the back, half-hidden by a squat bottle of bleach, a bulky black nylon package. He unzipped it and emptied the contents onto the work surface. This was no mere domestic first-aid kit, plasters for penknife cuts, round-ended scissors and a never-to-be-used triangular bandage. Among the items spilling onto the scuffed-up pine were a pair of red-handled trauma shears, serious field dressings – shit! Why hadn't he thought to check before duct-taping Eli up like a parcel? – a plastic packet containing a QuickClot sponge and several sealed pouches containing pre-filled morphine syringes.

He grabbed one of the syringes and took the stairs two at a time, ripping the pouch open with his teeth as he went. He knelt beside Eli. Her eyes were closed and her breathing was laboured, coming out in rough-edged gasps from her half-open mouth.

He lifted her sweatshirt again and plunged the needle in deep, depressing the plunger and sending the morphine into Eli's side.

He patted her cheek.

'Eli. Eli! Come on, wake up. You're going to be OK.'

After a few seconds, her eyelids fluttered open. She looked up at him and smiled dreamily, her lips lopsided.

'Oh, hey! I was dreaming. We were on the beach in Halong Bay. Did you find a first-aid kit? Did I miss it?'

'Yes. I gave you a morphine shot. Can you feel it yet?'

She frowned.

'Can't feel anything.' She grinned. 'Hey! That's good, right?'

The question came out slurred, '*Tha's goo'ri?*'

'Yeah, it's good. Listen, I have to go. Try to stay awake, yes? Can you still shoot?'

She squinted down at the Browning.

'Not sure. Prob not.'

He handed her Bakker's pistol.

'Take this. You see anyone, you empty it at them, centre-mass, OK?'

'Yes, sir!' She frowned again. 'Hey, what if it's you?' *Whafissyou?* 'I don' wanna kill you.'

'I'll wave a white flag.'

She grinned. 'Cool.'

Leaving her was a wrench, but he had to go. They weren't done yet. He got to his feet, picked up the Browning and turned for the stairs, his own pistol already stuck in his waistband. Reaching the ground floor, he went to check the kitchen window. Zero visibility. Literally. There might have been an entire regiment out there, but if there were, they were enjoying the most complete cover in the history of warfare.

A burst of automatic fire sprayed into the room, tearing more chunks of plaster off the walls behind him. He answered with a volley of shots, firing continuously until the magazine was empty. As he dropped the rifle and went for his Sig, a scuffing sound from the doorway brought him whirling round, just in time to see the barrel of an assault rifle between the shattered wooden uprights of the frame. It had to be the sniper. The last man standing. He'd dumped his rifle and grabbed a more manageable weapon off one of his fallen comrades.

Gabriel launched himself across the six feet separating him from the inbound merc, hands outstretched. He grabbed the barrel and yanked it downwards and inwards, pulling the merc in behind it. The rifle fell to the floor as they scuffled, each man desperate to gain a quick advantage: it was Gabriel's as he headbutted the merc in the face. Blood spurted, and the crack as his nose broke was audible over the merc's cry of surprise.

Gabriel pulled his Sig, intent on finishing off the merc before he could fight back. Instead he found his wrist gripped by steel pincers. Jesus, the guy was strong! He forced Gabriel's arm out wide and then brought it down sharply, twisting it on the way. Gabriel had to let go of the pistol or suffer a broken wrist. Then he was stumbling backwards, as the oncoming merc, teeth bared, reached for his own sidearm.

'You're dead, you cunt! You fucking cunt!' he said, blood dripping across his lips and down his chin. His accent was South African.

Time slowed to a crawl. The merc's arm was coming up. Gabriel had seconds left. He lunged towards the merc and aimed a second blow at the centre of his face. The merc swung left and ducked, his arm still travelling upwards. The knuckles on the index finger curled round the trigger paled as he increased the pressure, then the hammer moved forwards, the insignificant little prong of hardened steel making its short journey towards the primer cap in the base of the cartridge waiting in the breech for its benediction.

Gabriel shifted his weight onto his left foot and hauled the merc round in a half-circle, leaning backwards and sticking out his right foot.

Flame flashed from the pistol's muzzle, a long lemon-yellow spear that burnt Gabriel's ribcage. The report boomed, a thunderous bang, bass frequencies thudding into Gabriel's eardrums, trebles clamouring for attention, screaming and vibrating inside his brain.

Where the bullet went, he knew not. It might have pierced a vital organ or smashed a bone, but the adrenaline flooding his bloodstream was acting as stimulant, painkiller and hallucinogenic all rolled into one: he felt nothing but focus, all non-essential visual data deleted, so that the world was just Gabriel, the merc and the pistol, which was spitting out more rounds, filling the air with gun smoke and the metallic tang of hot brass as the spent cases were ejected into the air, spinning every which way, one catching Gabriel above the right eye and searing the skin there.

The magazine emptied and the merc discarded the weapon, useless now except as a club, and his own massive fists were better suited to the job.

Then the merc was stumbling, his feet tangling as Gabriel tripped him then accelerated his progress with a shove that sent him staggering, weight too far forwards to recover his balance, towards the open hatch. With a scream, he toppled down as his leading foot encountered nothing but air. His forehead smacked against the lip of the hatch on the way down and then he was gone.

Gabriel took the steps down to the cellar at a rush, heels skittering over the worn wooden treads so he almost glided down, holding the bannister for support. The merc was on his hands and knees among the ruined flesh of his French comrade who'd ventured down earlier. Gabriel launched himself off the fourth-to-last step and rugby tackled his man, slamming him into the blood-soaked dirt and drawing forth a howl of agony as his broken nose was mashed into the ground.

The South African wasn't finished yet; it was no coincidence he was the last of them left alive. He bucked Gabriel off his back and was on his feet, arm swinging round in a roundhouse punch that would have put Gabriel's lights out if it had connected. But he was disorientated, half-blind from the pain from his busted nose.

Gabriel moved out of the way then delivered a scything kick to the man's right knee that bent it out to the side, then broke it with a loud crack as bones and ligaments fractured and sheared.

With his man down, Gabriel punched his solar plexus, driving the wind from his lungs with a *whooof*. At that point, the fight went out of him; it's impossible to retaliate when your body is telling you you're going to die from lack of oxygen.

His eyes were stark white against the scarlet mask of blood from his gashed forehead and broken nose, a savage look entirely fitting for someone whose stock in trade was death delivered to order, for anybody prepared to cough up enough pieces of silver.

Gabriel prepared to kill the South African. With all the guns at least one floor above him, he'd have to do it the old-fashioned way. He raised his booted foot above the man's head.

The South African's eyes widened still further and he took his hands away from his belly, holding them up, palms out, begging for his life. Somehow he managed to suck in a breath.

'No, man. Please! I have intel.'

Gabriel lowered his foot.

'You move, you die,' he said, panting for breath himself as the adrenaline started to leach out of his system. 'What intel?'

'Water. I need water, man. Please?'

Gabriel looked down at him. You couldn't deny a prisoner water. Even one who, seconds earlier, had been trying to kill you. But you could delay it.

'Intel first. Thirst won't kill you, but I might.'

'You want to know who sent us to kill you, yes?'

Gabriel shook his head. 'Bakker already told me.'

'Yah, man, I bet he did. He called it in, but he didn't set the whole thing up.'

'Who did?'

'You'll let me walk away?'

'This isn't a negotiation.'

The South African's voice took on a pleading tone.

'Look, man, I need something in return. I get it, OK, we came to kill you and the woman—'

Gabriel kicked him midway up his left thigh.

'She's not "the woman", she's my wife.'

'OK, OK! Sorry, man. But it was a job for us, that's all. No malice in it. You know the drill. Loads of your guys went down the same route.'

'Not this one. You have three seconds, then I kill you. One—'

'No! It was your boss.'

'Don Webster's dead.'

'Nah, man. Your *new* boss. Margot McDonnell hired us.'

50

Gabriel stared down at the mercenary, rocked by what he'd just heard. If the South African had stuck to 'your new boss' – a hopeless last throw of the dice – Gabriel would have killed him. But he'd known her name. He'd known her bloody name.

He'd been betrayed before. By politicians, not line commanders. It was to be expected. To the suits in Westminster, men like Gabriel, women like Eli, even men like the South African and his dead friends, were just resources. Possibly glorified as 'human assets'. But disposable, just the same. Fêted as heroes when it suited the pols, but always blamed for disasters, even when the decisions came from on high.

Don would have faced his own death rather than let down his troops. He strained against the leash that management had looped around his neck, but even when he did have to take the hard decisions, he always acted with at least half his mind on the consequences for his people.

And now Margot McDonnell had helped a deranged former operative procure a team of mercs to take out two of her own people. He felt the anger as a cold metal weight in his gut from which icy rods burrowed upwards through his viscera and into his brain, straining to burst out through the top of his skull.

He stared down at the South African, whose lips had quirked upwards into a lopsided grin.

'Yah, you weren't expecting that, were you, man? Hey, how about that water?'

Gabriel managed to draw in a deep breath.

'You're going to stay there.'

'Sure, boss. Whatever you say.'

'It wasn't a question.'

The kick was fast and pinpoint-accurate. The South African collapsed sideways, his eyes rolling upwards as consciousness left him.

A quick search of the cellar yielded the dead French mercenary's weapons. The pistol had been blown clear across the room and embedded in the wall, barrel first. Gabriel yanked it free: the muzzle was deformed by the impact with the wall. He found the assault rifle, an AK-47, in a corner, bent into a right angle. Both useless. Gabriel took them with him anyway, slamming the hatch shut when he reached the kitchen and dragging the fridge over it.

He went upstairs, and had almost reached the halfway point when he remembered his instruction to Eli and paused. Just in time, as three shots exploded out of the gloom of the hallway, slamming into the wall above and behind his head.

'El, it's me! Don't shoot!'

He realised she was only obeying his previous instruction. He'd said he'd wave a white flag.

He ran back down the stairs and grabbed a tea towel – white with red stripes on each long side into which were woven the words *Pure Irish Linen*. He tied it round the Browning's barrel and returned to the stairs, holding the improvised truce flag above his head and waving it from side to side for good measure.

He took the rest of the stairs in three strides and was by her side seconds later, cradling her head in his lap.

'It's over,' he said. 'I've got one more thing to do then we're out of here.'

Then he squatted beside her and scooped her up, arms beneath her knees and under her arms, and carried her into the back bedroom, where he laid her on the bed. Before leaving, he prised her fingers off the pistol's grip.

Downstairs, he filled a plastic beaker with water and set it down on the table. He retrieved the Maglite from the cupboard then shoved the fridge off the trapdoor. Levelling the pistol, he pulled the metal ring up and let the door fall, raising a cloud of dust as it hit the floor. As he descended the steps, pistol in his right hand, torch in his left, blood spatters and bits of the dead French mercenary glowed crimson in the bright white beam. The South African was still out cold, so Gabriel returned to the kitchen, picked up the beaker of water and took it back down with him.

He waited five minutes, then another five. He used the time turning McDonnell's betrayal over and over in his mind, forming a plan that would mark a definitive break with his professional life to date.

The South African moaned, rolled to his side and vomited. Gabriel passed him the water.

'Here.'

'Thanks, man.'

He drank it off in a single draft and offered the beaker back to Gabriel.

'Do I look like an idiot?'

The man shrugged. 'Worth a try.'

'Not really.' He waggled the pistol where the guy could see it. 'Tell me everything.'

Fifteen minutes later, the South African stopped talking. Gabriel was satisfied he was telling the truth.

'What now, man? You gonna kill me in cold blood? I've seen your file. You're a decorated war hero. You're better than that. Have pity.'

Gabriel stood.

'Like you would have done with me and "the woman"?'

Then he shot the man twice in the head, the noise clanging like cannon fire in the confined space of the cellar.

51

Before leaving the devastated cottage, Gabriel took the rest of the morphine injectors from Bakker's trauma kit. He gave himself a quarter of a dose. Eli didn't need any more.

Back on Harris, he bought a pay-as-you-go-phone from a convenience store, went online and paid for ten pounds of credit. He found a harbour cafe with outside tables, picked one right on the edge of the terrace, with nobody nearby. A young waitress, no more than eighteen, black nose ring and tattoos up the inside of her slender arms, stopped by the table. Gabriel ordered two coffees, and a plate of mixed pastries, 'Whatever you have, I'm sure they're all delicious.'

She smiled. 'That's a lot of food.'

He returned the smile. 'We're hungry.'

Just then, Eli turned pale beneath her holiday tan. Gabriel frowned. She was worried about the video of him assassinating McDonnell, he could tell.

'The video was a fake,' he said. 'I was after Bakker's personnel file in McDonnell's office, but I had a Plan B. A tube of fake blood, low-charge blanks and a lot of dodgy camerawork on my phone. McDonnell turned out to be a surprisingly good actor. I know she was already planning to have us killed by the mercs. I think she was just covering her arse. But her price was my signed resignation. You'll have to resign, too.'

Gabriel checked the phone. The signal was four bars. He made a call to a number the South African had given him. It was answered on the first ring.

'Hello?'

He cleared his throat. Closed his eyes and played back the South African merc's last few words, listening to the vowel sounds, the inflections, the tone and volume of each word. Then he spoke.

'Yah, man. It's done. They're dead.'

'Excellent. Your bonus will be waiting.'

'How much?'

'You can't have forgotten, surely? Fifty thousand each for Wolfe and his wife, like we agreed. Don't start getting greedy now, Pik.'

Gabriel dropped the assumed accent.

'I meant Bakker and the kill team are dead, Margot. Eli and I are very much alive.'

The pause stretched out for ten seconds. Gabriel offered Eli a grim smile.

McDonnell found her voice.

'What do you want?'

'We'll come to that. But for now, you need to send a clean-up team out to the island where you set Bakker up with the cottage. I mean, you could leave them all there for the gulls and the eagles and whatnot, but if the media got hold of the story, well, there'd be the mother of all shitstorms, Margot, now wouldn't there? With you right at its bloody heart.'

'I can place you and Eli there. You'd get hit by the blow-back, too.'

'I doubt that. She was kidnapped by Bakker and I'm not even travelling on my own name. As far as the paper trail goes, we're both still in Vietnam.'

'What are you going to do?'

'Me? I'm going to finish my honeymoon. As you know, it was somewhat rudely interrupted.'

'I meant about me. I have powerful friends, Gabriel, influential friends,' she said, panic injecting a tremor into her voice. 'Tell me your dream job. I can make it happen. Or money? Do you want money? I have a contingency fund over which I have sole control.'

Pulse bumping in his throat as he struggled to master his temper, Gabriel leant forwards and took Eli's hand across the table.

'Listen to me, Margot. You tried to kill me. You tried to kill Eli. From what I learned earlier this afternoon, you had a hand in Don Webster's death, too. I loved that man like a father. And you, for some unfathomably,' he snatched a quick breath as his throat tightened, '*pathetic* reason, took him away from me.'

'Gabriel, please—'

'Kevin called himself Isaac. He saw Don as Abraham. He thought he'd been sacrificed, but he'd missed the whole point of the story. Abraham didn't kill Isaac; according to Eli, that was never the plan. He loved his son. And I loved him in return. So, Eli and I will finish our honeymoon and then, at a time and a place of my choosing, there will be a reckoning. And if you send anyone else after us, I will dump their bodies in Trafalgar Square with full details of your dirty little secret tied round their necks.'

He ended the call, breathing hard.

'We need to get patched up properly,' he said.

Eli nodded.

Gabriel paid the bill, leaving a generous tip. Three hours later, having caught the ferry back to Uig and then driven at a respectful speed south-eastwards across Skye, all the way feeling grateful to whoever had first synthesised opium for medical use, Gabriel pulled into a parking spot at Broadford Hospital and headed for the Accident and Emergency Department.

It was nine in the evening when the final dressing was applied: too late to start the long drive home, so Gabriel booked a hotel room. He ordered steaks and a bottle of red wine from room service before heading for the lifts. After finishing the meal in silence, fatigue finally triumphing over the buzz of the action earlier, Gabriel lay on his back on the wide double bed, with Eli folded inside his arm. After a few seconds, he twisted around, grabbed the remote and turned on the TV.

'I want to see if there's any news about us. We set off enough ordnance to start a small war.'

The BBC news was just coming to an end. As the presenter recapped the main stories, Gabriel relaxed, feeling Eli do the same in his arms. The top story was about a government minister resigning, and none of the others mentioned a firefight on the Isle of Scalpay. He turned it off and closed his eyes.

Something woke Gabriel in the small hours of the morning. A noise from outside the window, a pull from his unconscious mind: he didn't know which, only that he was now wide awake.

Leaving Eli deeply asleep, Gabriel slipped from between the covers and wrapped one of the hotel bathrobes around himself before crossing the room and peering out between the heavy curtains.

The sky was brilliantly clear, filled with innumerable stars, brighter than they appeared from the beach at Aldeburgh. The only time he'd seen so many was on a break in an operation in Mozambique, lying on his back beside Britta Falskog, staring up at the African night sky.

High above the horizon, a faint, wavering curtain of luminous green undulated back and forth. It was completely the wrong time of year for the Northern Lights, yet there they were, changing colour now from lime-green to chartreuse and back through jade, teal and a fresh, grassy hue to lime again.

The pulsing green lights shimmered off a dark shape in the car park across from the window. A lone figure was standing perfectly still, looking up at Gabriel. Something about the stance, the build, the angle of the head was eerily familiar.

Then it raised its right hand and offered a salute.

Gabriel's pulse was racing; he knew who it was.

'Boss?' he whispered.

The figure lowered its right arm and began to fade until Gabriel could see the aurora borealis reflected in a puddle through its torso.

Then the green lights faded, too, until all was black once more and the stars and that huge, glowing moon gilded the scene with silver.

Gabriel remained by the window, willing the figure to appear to him one last time. A dog began barking, snapping him out of his reverie. He went back to bed, careful not to wake Eli. He climbed back in beside her and curled around her sleeping form.

* * *

Finally back in Aldeburgh after what felt like a week-long drive, Gabriel turned to Eli.

'Wait here,' he said as he climbed out of the Jaguar.

He unlocked the front door and returned to the car. He pulled Eli's door open and bent in towards her.

'Let's have you,' he said.

He slid his hands under her thighs and around her back and then he lifted her out of the seat and hoisted her up until she was cradled, surprisingly lightly, in his arms.

He smiled at her.

'I know it's corny, but I want to start our married life off with a last bit of tradition.'

Then he turned and carried her inside, down the hallway and into the sitting room where he left her on the sofa.

'Let's have a glass of wine in the garden,' he called from the kitchen, pulling a bottle of Chablis from the fridge.

* * *

Bev Watchett, the local artist who had once painted Gabriel nude as a fallen Greek warrior, wandered up to the fence enclosing the small front garden that overlooked the sea.

'Hello, Gabriel, I was just passing and I—'

She stopped. He was deep in conversation. On hands-free, clearly, and she'd blundered in without thinking. Just like her!

He turned and smiled.

'Hi, Bev. You know, I met the customer who bought my portrait a few weeks back. Not even slightly embarrassing.'

She nodded, distracted. No earbuds. And no phone.

'Who were you just talking to?'

He frowned.

'Eli, of course. Come and join us, I'll get you a glass.'

Bev stared at him. He was sitting by himself at the table, two glasses and a half-empty bottle of white wine before him.

'Eli?'

'Yes! Meet the new Mrs Wolfe.' He turned away from Bev and addressed a remark to the empty chair opposite him. 'Darling, you remember Bev, don't you?' He laughed, then. 'How could you not?'

Feeling worried for her friend, Bev climbed over the low white picket fence and knelt beside Gabriel.

'Gabriel, darling. There's nobody here. It's just you and me. Where's Eli?'

Gabriel turned to look at her and smiled.

'She's right here, Bev. What's the matter? Can't you see her?'

* * *

Gabriel turns to Eli, ready to share the joke about Bev's lack of perception. But she is not smiling; in fact she is completely expressionless. Not a line, a crease, a flicker of life animates her beautiful face, her luminous grey-green eyes, her generous mouth, until she smiles, sadly, and mouths a single word.

Scalpay.

· · ·

…and he's running up the stairs at the cottage on the island, morphine injector clutched in his fist, tearing at the plastic pouch with his teeth. He reaches the top step and slips in the blood. Such a lot of blood, spread in a lake all the way from Eli's inert form to the lip of the staircase, where it drips down onto the first tread.

'No!' he shouts.

He drops the injector and runs to her side, slithering in the blood before sinking to his knees and lifting her by her shoulders and neck. Her head lolls to the side and a rivulet of blood breaks free of her lips and trickles over her chin.

He digs two fingers into the soft place under her jaw, searching for a pulse. The skin beneath his probing fingertips is inert, and it is cool to the touch. He digs in harder but there is no pulse. He leans closer, bends his head and turns his face away so his right cheek is hovering mere millimetres away from her nostrils. If there is a whisper of breath, he will feel it.

He feels nothing.

'Come on, El, stop playing games,' he says. 'Look, I brought you some morphine.'

He looks down but the injector is not in his hand anymore. Doesn't matter. He starts CPR, hands clasped, thumping down onto her chest wall then pinching her nostrils and blowing air into her lungs. His lips come away stained with her blood, tasting of copper and salt.

Gabriel keeps going for ten more minutes, tears eventually running down his face and dropping onto her blood-soaked T-shirt, before rocking back on his heels, arms limp at his sides.

He looks down at his wife of less than a month. Her eyes are closed. Gently, oh so gently, he lifts an eyelid with the pad of his thumb. The iris is barely visible, rolled all the way up into her skull.

He picks her body up and carries it downstairs and out into the fresh air.

'Let's get you somewhere you can rest,' he says quietly…

. . .

…and his eyes focus once more and it's strange because he's not on Scalpay, stretched out beside a hump of freshly turned earth, arms aching, throat hoarse from howling his grief into the wind.

He's sitting in the garden at Aldeburgh with Bev Watchett, who's giving him a very peculiar look, as if she's an anthropologist and she's just found the last-surviving member of some long-forgotten tribe. Funny. Maybe she has: the Men of Honour, would that be their name?

Bev stretches out a paint-spattered hand and covers his. Her face has changed, mouth pulled down, forehead creased, tears leaking from the corners of her eyes. She puts her arms around him, then struggles to her feet and pulls him upright.

He sees it now, understands why Bev looks so sad. He looks for Eli, but sees only an empty chair. Fool. His mind is up to its old tricks again.

Bev pulls him to his feet and he allows himself to be led inside and placed on the sofa in the sitting room. She perches beside him on the edge of the cushion and pulls her phone out. He hears her talking to someone, a doctor, it sounds like, but he's not listening, not really.

Gabriel closes his eyes and inhales the fading scent of her, the way she always used to smell – of lemon and sandalwood. He is back with her on the register office steps in the centre of a cascade of confetti that swirls around her as she looks up at him and smiles. And then, one by one, the tumbling flakes of rice paper freeze in mid-air and her face stills into immobility, her tanned skin bleaching out like a photograph left in the sun, and he knows that this is the happiest he will ever be.

READ ON FOR AN EXTRACT FROM TRIGGER POINT, THE FIRST BOOK IN THE GABRIEL WOLFE THRILLERS...

CHAPTER ONE

Close protection.

A lucrative business for a man with an SAS background. Especially one fluent in half a dozen languages, and trained by a Chinese master in ancient Oriental disciplines. A man like Gabriel Wolfe.

He shook hands with the businessman who'd just hired him for a trip to Mexico City, then headed out of the discreet office building off Trafalgar Square.

Walking to Waterloo Station, he hooked right into a dim, slime-walled tunnel beneath the pedestrian bridge over the Thames. As he reached the midpoint, the semi-circle of brighter light at the far end darkened: three men with shaved heads and sharp suits were coming towards him.

The man in the centre had a cocky swagger to his walk and was about Gabriel's height. Slim build but fit, jacket straining across his shoulders.

To his right, a giant, well over six feet. Heavy too, with the kind of muscle only steroids can build. To his left, a smaller man, not so keen on the gym, more of a beer and chips guy, soft flesh on his face and pudgy hands poking out of his shirt cuffs.

The leader moved into the centre of the tunnel, making Gabriel's passage a choice between walking over a wino's meagre estate of flattened cardboard and filthy overcoats, or squashing himself against the slimy wall to let him pass.

The other two spread out to left and right. He could smell their aftershave from yards away. Gabriel aimed for a gap on the leader's left but the man mirrored his move, delivering a good bump to his shoulder.

"Oi," the man said. "What do you say when you knock into someone?"

The other two laughed. Confident, smug, self-assured. Clearing his mind, Gabriel remembered the words of Master Zhao. *Do not seek the battle: run like the mouse. But if the battle comes to you, fight like the wolf whose name you bear.*

That suited him fine. He'd seen enough fighting to last him a lifetime. And enough death to last him for all eternity. He wanted to give these idiots a chance. He wanted to get the early train.

"I'm sorry for bumping into you. Now, if you don't mind, I have a train to catch."

The leader hooted with laughter and mimicked Gabriel's voice.

"'Now, if you don't mind, I have a train to catch.' I don't think so, shorty. I want to hear something like a proper apology. Like maybe on your knees."

No. That wasn't going to happen.

"OK, you've made your point, and I've said sorry. I just want to go home."

"And I just want you to say it properly, don't I?"

The others loved that one and cackled. Gabriel noticed they'd adopted a balanced stance, weight on the balls of their feet, fists curling and uncurling, muscles bunching and tightening under their jackets. He tried again.

"Please, let's not do anything we might regret, OK? We can all just walk away from this. I don't want any trouble."

"You pissing coward. Nobody's walking away from this. I tell you what. Why don't you give that old wino all your money then we'll give you a little something to remember us by?"

The old wino turned his booze-reddened face towards Gabriel. Maybe hoping he was about to get a windfall.

This wasn't going to end well, Gabriel thought. They reminded him of the big-boned army brats at one of his schools in Hong Kong. The ones who'd taunted him about his mother, who was half-Chinese, before punching him to the ground and stealing his lunch money.

"If you insist," he said, removing his jacket, "but let me put this down to kneel on."

He folded the jacket with the lining outermost, knowing that everyone was watching, before laying it in a pad to his side. His shirt concealed a hard-muscled frame kept in shape through thrice-weekly visits to a gym run by an ex-sergeant he knew.

The gang almost looked disappointed that the verbals were over and only the beating remained. The leader smirked and clenched his fists, but what happened next took him by surprise. From his crouching position, Gabriel straightened lightning fast, took a step to his left, and punched the giant hard in the throat.

The big man never expects to get hit first: he's relaxed, watching and waiting. So the surprise doubles the effectiveness of the blow.

He toppled, cracking his head against the wall on the way down. Then Gabriel took two quick steps to his right, at the same time pulling the top off the fountain pen he'd palmed with his left hand as he took his jacket off.

The lead thug blinked and focused on the object sending tendrils of fear into his balls. Gabriel let the point of the steel nib hover a couple of millimetres from the man's right eye. The pudgy man hung back; Gabriel barked at him, using his best parade ground tone.

"Stand still!"

He'd mustered out of the SAS as a captain and could bring the tallest, biggest, toughest men into line with that voice. The two thugs stood still. Very still. Behind them, Gabriel could see a young couple, tourists maybe, walk into the tunnel, notice the standoff and about-turn.

He leaned close to the leader's face, then whispered in his ear.

"I used this in the Congo to relieve a warlord of his left eye. We had to practice on dead pigs in training, but men's eyes are easier." The man gulped, his prominent Adam's apple jerking in his throat. He wasn't to know Gabriel was lying. "So be a good boy and be on your way, and I won't use it on you. You can still get out of this in one piece."

He withdrew the pen and stepped away from the shaking thug. *That should do it*, he thought.

"Bastard!" the man screamed before throwing a wild punch at Gabriel's head.

By the time the fist arrived, Gabriel had moved to one side. The heel of his hand connected with the underside of his opponent's chin, clattering his teeth together with such force that two upper incisors shattered on impact. As the man staggered back, clutching his bloody mouth, Gabriel moved again.

No need for overkill, just some summary justice.

One, two, three quick jabs with outstretched fingers to the man's throat, his gut, and, as he collapsed onto the pavement, the back of his neck.

The last blow landed directly above the basal ganglion, a knot of nerve fibres that functions like an on-off switch for consciousness. As the thug passed out, the final thing he saw was Gabriel leaning over him.

"The nearest A&E is St Thomas's," he said.

No need to worry about the pudgy lieutenant. He'd scarpered as soon as his leader's swing failed to connect. Gabriel reached into the leader's jacket and withdrew a brown leather wallet stuffed with twenties and fifties. Three hundred pounds at least.

He returned to the old wino slumped against the tunnel wall and held out the bundle of cash.

"Here, he said with a smile.

Wide-eyed, the wino started counting the money before stuffing it deep into his pocket.'

Thanks, guvnah,' he rasped. 'I saw what you done to those bastards. You're a gent.'

Gabriel shrugged. 'Find yourself a room for the night, and maybe avoid this spot for a few days?'

* * *

As Gabriel approached his front door two hours later, a frenzied barking let him know his burglar alarm was still operational. Half inside, he was almost pushed over by the brindle greyhound snuffing and nuzzling at his trousers.

"Seamus! Did you miss me, boy?" he said, scratching the dog behind the ears. "Has it been too long since Julia let you out?"

Julia was a good friend, one of very few; a fight arranger for the movies who'd burned out in Hollywood and moved back to her childhood home.

He poured himself a glass of white burgundy and looked across to the answering machine he had to rely on owing to the patchy phone signal in his village.

The red light was blinking. One new message. It could wait. Gabriel needed a walk and so did Seamus by the look of his tail, which threatened to come off if it wagged any harder.

* * *

The next morning – after waking from a dreamless sleep with no nightmares, a sign of a good day to come – Gabriel pulled on jeans and a jumper and headed downstairs for breakfast.

He made tea, breathing in the distinctive aroma of what he called "the house blend": one third Kenyan Orange Pekoe, one third Earl Grey and one third English Breakfast. It was a tangy, floral smell that reminded him of his father's morning routine. Always the same, never changing.

His father, a trade commissioner in Hong Kong, always drank tea from a bone china Willow Pattern cup, threads of vapour curling up and catching the morning sunlight slanting in over the bay through the apartment windows. Those moments together were the best time. Before school and its torments.

With the same clockwork regularity that he did everything else, the elder Wolfe would fold his paper, dab his lip with a linen napkin, and stand.

"Well, old boy, duty calls. Queen and country. Mustn't keep the old girl waiting, eh?"

With a ruffle of his son's unruly black hair, his father would leave for his office, whistling a snatch from *HMS Pinafore*, *The Gondoliers*, or *The Mikado*. Gabriel still couldn't hear a Gilbert and Sullivan operetta without being whisked back to those precious mornings. Then he frowned, because, once again, his memory was refusing to replay the darker moments from his childhood.

He'd been expelled from seven or eight schools for fighting, for disrespect, for "lack of discipline." In the end, his parents had entrusted their only child's education to a family friend.

Zhao Xi tutored their much-loved but wayward son for seven years, instilling in him the self-discipline Gabriel's parents hoped he would and the ancient skills that they knew nothing about. Along with karate, meditation, and hypnosis, they'd worked on *Yinshen fangshi*, which Master Zhao, as Gabriel learned to call him, translated into English as "The Way of Stealth."

His father had assumed he would go to university – Cambridge, like he himself had done – and the Diplomatic Service. Gabriel had other ideas and had told Wolfe Sr he intended to join the army. Not just any regiment either – the Parachute Regiment.

From there, he'd applied to and been badged into the SAS, where the emphasis on personal performance rather than strict adherence to arbitrary codes on everything from uniform to the 'correct' gear suited him.

He replayed the phone message from the night before. The caller's voice was warm. Cultured.

"Hello, Mr Wolfe. Sir Toby Maitland here. I need a chap with your sort of skills. Come and see me, would you? Rokeby Manor. It's the big house behind the racecourse. Please call my secretary to fix an appointment."

ACKNOWLEDGMENTS

I want to thank you for buying this book. I hope you enjoyed it. As an author is only part of the team of people who make a book the best it can be, this is my chance to thank the people on my team.

For being my first readers, Sarah Hunt and Jo Maslen.

For their brilliant copy-editing and proofreading Nicola Lovick and Liz Ward.

The members of my Facebook Group, The Wolfe Pack, who are an incredibly supportive and also helpful bunch of people.

My cover designer, Nick Castle.

And for being a daily inspiration and source of love and laughter, and making it all worthwhile, my family: Jo, Rory and Jacob.

The responsibility for any and all mistakes in this book remains mine. I assure you, they were unintentional.

Andy Maslen
    Salisbury, 2022

ABOUT THE AUTHOR

Photo © 2020 Kin Ho

Andy Maslen was born in Nottingham, England. After leaving university with a degree in psychology, he worked in business for thirty years as a copywriter. In his spare time, he plays blues guitar. He lives in Wiltshire.

Made in the USA
Coppell, TX
03 April 2022

75955825R00197